Nigel Cox was born in 1951 in Pahiatua and grew up in Masterton and the Hutt Valley. He worked for many years as a bookseller and freelance writer, and was Senior Writer on the project team which developed the exhibitions for Te Papa. With fellow New Zealander Ken Gorbey he led the project team which created the Jewish Museum Berlin, where he is currently Head of Exhibitions and Education. In 1991 he was the Katherine Mansfield Fellow in Menton. *Tarzan Presley* is Nigel Cox's fourth novel, following *Waiting For Einstein*, *Dirty Work* and *Skylark Lounge*.

Praise for *Skylark Lounge*:

"*Skylark Lounge* is that rare thing – a genuinely ennobling work...Give it a try even the subject matter runs counter to your usual prejudices. It's one of the year's best."
— Iain Sharp, *Sunday Star Times*

"... a book about alien abduction that is art of a high order... Cox's writing is deft and his story-telling sense sure and so from the most unusual material Cox has mined a little gold."
— Ian Richards, *Listener*

"Cox's third novel deserves the widest possible readership – once people would have called it visionary... Cox writes brilliantly."
— Greg Fleming, *Metro*

"*Skylark Lounge* sounds like a science fiction novel, but in fact it's a book about human beings and – most of all – the human heart. It's a small publication, under 200 pages, but for my money it's the biggest book of the year."
— Bill Manhire

"This is a charming novel... consistently endearing. Cox has found a perfect balance between dry Kiwi understatement and an articulate sensibility that's up to the job of conveying mind-bending events."
— Jane Westaway, *Evening Post*

"His writing is sharp and his storytelling sophisticated ... Cox pulls off a fantastic conclusion."
— Sarah Putt, *Xtrasite*

TARZAN PRESLEY

Nigel Cox

VICTORIA UNIVERSITY PRESS

VICTORIA UNIVERSITY PRESS
Victoria University of Wellington
PO Box 600 Wellington

Copyright © Nigel Cox 2004
First published 2004

This book is copyright. Apart from
any fair dealing for the purpose of private study,
research, criticism or review, as permitted under the
Copyright Act, no part may be reproduced by any
process without the permission of
the publishers.

ACKNOWLEDGEMENTS

The names Tarzan, Jane Porter, Kala, Kerchak and Tublat were
originally established in *Tarzan of the Apes*, by Edgar Rice Burroughs,
published in 1914, as were some aspects of their circumstances,
freely adapted for *Tarzan Presley*.

'Over the Rainbow' (Arlen/Harburg)
© Reproduced with the kind permission of J. Albert & Son Pty Ltd.

National Library of New Zealand Cataloguing-in-Publication Data
Cox, Nigel, 1951-
Tarzan Presley / Nigel Cox.
ISBN 0-86473-480-8
I. Title.
NZ823.2—dc 22

Printed in Singapore

To my father,
Jack Cox

CONTENTS

PART ONE
TARZAN OF THE GORILLAS
9

PART TWO
LET'S GET GONE
155

PART THREE
MARSHALL STURT
403

ACKNOWLEDGEMENTS
463

The soul sits looking at its offer.

Les Murray,
"Predawn in Health"

PART ONE

Tarzan of the Gorillas

1

According to the standard calculation, Tarzan was born in 1935. This is the year which is most commonly given and I think we should accept it and move on. Even if they could run a carbon dating on Tarzan's skull they wouldn't come up with, you know, the exact day. So let's forget it, it doesn't matter. 1935. He's human, he's born, so we have to agree that somewhere back in there he had a mother. Tarzan always wanted to have a mother, it was a big thing with him. Somewhere back there he was fed by a mother. Breast-fed. I can see him, and I think the picture is a reasonable one, lying along his mother's arm, with her nipple in his mouth. Now that is a very intimate moment of contact and I think every human likes to think they had it, once, even if no one can remember it. Whenever I've seen babies at the breast they always look extraordinarily contented, gazing up at the elements of colour and light above them, immense shapes, a great statue's face seen from below – but the statue is warm, it breathes. The rising cliff of brow, and the cloud of hair which frames the face, with blue sky behind, and real clouds going past. The face of an angel against the sky. I suspect that

Tarzan's mother may have had black hair. This is not only because his own hair was famously black but because throughout his life he was irresistibly attracted to women with dark hair, pale faces with black hair, and we know that Tarzan was strongly affected in his attractions by promptings from his youth.

So I definitely see him having a period when he felt the satisfaction of being mothered. It may have been short. I suspect it was. Then his bond seems to have been transferred to the she-gorilla he calls Kala, who for his first ten years or so he regarded as his mother. It was only later that he came to understand that she could not have been.

So how did he come to be out in the wilds? Well, it's easy to speculate, and of course so many have. Personally, I hold no definite opinions on the subject. The reality is, there's no truth where Tarzan's earliest origins are concerned, and I don't think there ever will be. You may have read cheap books that claim to know – I've read a number myself, full of stories about how his father was a Lord from England, et cetera, but this is wishful thinking. The truth is, we have information where Tarzan is concerned only from Tarzan himself, he is the sole witness, until he reaches the age of eighteen, which is the first point anyone we know the name of enters the picture. There are however some relevant facts. It is a fact, for example, that there was a cabin in the bush in the area where Tarzan grew up and that Tarzan visited it. That's established. But was the man who built the cabin, and provisioned it, was he Tarzan's father? We don't know. Did this man raise Tarzan for a while? Again, we can't say. We have to face it. We just can't say. So you can tell yourself anything you like about his baby years, and some people have. There are some wild things in those cheap books: pirates, a mutiny and suchlike – really, in 1935?

And there's a grave that may contain a woman's bones,

and that woman may be his mother. But that's not known either. I insist on this. We should be scrupulous. Tarzan was. He never let himself adopt these parents. This piece that was missing was something he carried with him throughout his life.

The only thing that is known for sure is that he arrives on the scene.

For some reason, I see him flying. I can't say why. But I see him in the air. Tumbling through clouds, through the blue. Coming down. Falling. He's just a baby, he's not afraid. Like a cherub or some other mythological being – bemused, the way babies are if you show them a new thing. Of course his name's not Tarzan at this point, it was Kala who called him that, we don't know what his parents called him. Maybe we will one day, there are studies in progress. But until we do I'd rather have him enter the picture as though he fell from the sky – wearing a serious expression. He always had quite a serious face, moody, some would say, plus babies are often serious. So I see him in the air, maybe with a few clouds around – was he thrown out of an airplane? – anyway, he's tumbling against the blue and he's frowning. Naked, of course. Tarzan of the Gorillas was always naked.

And then he lands. Now in any honest picture there's a loud splat at this point, but he lived, so it can't have happened. Did he land in a pile of feathers? Maybe he landed on a slope, and slithered? I asked a physicist once and he laughed at me – a baby could not fall out of a plane and survive. So maybe he didn't drop from a plane, it's too hard to figure the landing, maybe his dad just tossed him up in the air? Tarzan thought about that, too, along with the breast-feeding. Whatever: he arrives. In the bush. In the Wairarapa – in the misty back-hill country of the North Island of New Zealand, in the southern Pacific, in 1935 or thereabouts, and is taken up by one of the tribes of gorillas that live in the area. And, as I said, lives beneath the cloak of the bush. And doesn't see another of his kind until he's well through his teens.

It's hard to believe.

Okay, so that we can get on with it, let's say he just came up out of a hole in the ground, and there he is, lying on a bed of punga fronds, that makes a nice picture – like a restaurant meal. And along comes Kala and says . . . what exactly? It must have been complicated, a gorilla taking a human child for her own.

This is where Tarzan's testimony kicks in. He tells us in his autobiography*, and this was repeated in a thousand interviews, that Kala had lost her own baby and took him as a substitute. Now, that book in particular has been described as "the lurid product of a best-selling imagination" and I consider this a generous judgement, but nevertheless Tarzan stuck to that particular story all his life and so probably it was true. But he won't have been able to remember it happening, he was too young – the big dark gorilla face finding him like a lost golf ball down there amid the pungas, looming over him, she probably bared her teeth, nothing even faintly like a statue this, more of a Halloween mask, something frightful, big round eyes popped, dark squashed nose, and bristling with fur. Great big teeth, bared – he would have screamed.

But she picks him up, takes him in her arms, cradles him, and then presses his head, his pale human face, with its skinny red lips and question-mark ears, presses this screaming thing to her hairy tit and, behold, he sucks. I checked with a zoo scientist, apparently her milk would have been okay for him, once he got used to the taste, and as he sucks she licks the

---

* *Animal Instinct – Tarzan, his own story as told to Truman Capote*, Doubleday, 1959

slime and dirt off his body, glancing round under her brows to see if anyone is going to claim him back.

It's plausible.

Then they're off. It's late afternoon and, having fed, the gorillas are moving to higher ground to find a place for the night. Kala moves three-legged, holding him carefully with one strong arm. Now, an objection I have heard here is that a human infant couldn't hold on to her like a little gorilla, that he would have dropped, but in fact baby gorillas are totally helpless for the first three months of their lives, so Kala was ready to fend for him – she clutches him to her with a strong gorilla hand, and there they go, along the bushland trail. He's tickled by all that hair, and, despite Kala's dedication to shielding him, they are in rough country and so his tender skin is scratched and it bleeds. Kala licks at the blood, a strange taste in her mouth, her nose wrinkles. The pale little thing is sleeping on her arm. She moves carefully, protecting him but making sure also that she keeps up – she doesn't want there to be a reason for the tribe to say she should abandon this baby. Her brother, Tublat, has already growled at her but she glares at him until he looks away.

As I indicated when I used the word earlier, the New Zealanders call the natural growth which covers their land "bush" – you maybe got a sense of it from those movies they made, *The Lord of the Rings*. It's a bit like jungle, with less intense colours, but there's lots of life in it – lizards, rats, opossums, deer. Giant wetas. Some nice green geckos, pigs with tusks, and they have parrots there too, every kind of bird. Tasty pigeons. Lots of undergrowth, and big trees, and a particular treefern called a nikau, similar to a palm tree but with fronds that spread like the spokes of an umbrella, a charming thing. *Punga* I said earlier, and *nikau*, those are Maori words. The Maori are the indigenous people of New Zealand and they have been there for a thousand or for two thousand years, depending on which book you read. They seem mostly to have left Tarzan's tribe of gorillas alone – so much so that you wonder if they actually knew about them. It's surprising, this. There are, for instance, no gorillas in any of the ancient carvings that the old people of that culture made. The carving tradition is extraordinary and depicts everything in the Maori world: whales, mystical birds, bright-eyed ancestors, but no gorillas. I've visited that area, met the local people and talked to them. They say the gorillas were never there in the old days, that they're a modern phenomenon, like the Pakeha. Pakeha are white people, like me, I think this was a kind of joke. But I suspect they're covering up for the fact that they didn't realise.

Because in that bush, in that place, that's where Tarzan was, that's where the gorillas were, I insist on it. Sceptics have said they were imported later for Tarzan tourists to gawp at, but there are pictures of him, photographs, with the gorillas, made by Jane Porter. And so there they go, off through the bush. Kala has baby Tarzan held under her as she moves through the undergrowth, three-legged, one arm reaching and one arm holding, in the broken light, amid the tribe that's spread around her in the foliage like extensions of herself. It's quite warm in New Zealand, especially in summer, and also Tarzan was always close against her body. However, I do feel that he must often have been cold. I have made a study of the climatic records for his early years and it's true that there was a warm patch in the mid-1930s, and a sequence of glorious summers and that even the winters were warm. But he'd been through a trauma, and he was naked – I see him shivering.

Kala holding him close, shielding him with her forearm, twisting her body so that he would be protected. The little guy under there, hanging on – making it somehow.

The gorillas went through the bush on old trails, pushing aside branches they'd pushed aside for years, the way we open a door, moving past familiar plants the way we move among the furniture of our houses. In the evenings they construct a shelter of sorts, gathering branches and leaves and so forth to make a place to be. And so this was where Tarzan would have spent his first night among the gorillas, in a little humpy, that's what the Australians call the sleeping shacks that the Aboriginals of this country used to make, something like that, with branches above him, and leaves all around, and lots of gaps for the night to come in. The call of the morepork, which is a bush owl, and the scratchings and scrabblings of the little mammals, the weasels and stoats and ferrets, the barking cough of the opossums, the running of the little feet of the mouse – these are the sounds you hear in the deeps of the New Zealand bush at night. I have trekked back in there and lain alone in my sleeping bag, listening. Wondering. The shrill of the kiwi bird, which goes about in the dark to stick its long beak into rotten logs. Squeakings, shriekings – then terrible silences. So many new sounds for the ears of the baby Tarzan, there in Kala's arms, snuggling in to get warm. Not that I think he would have heard. I think he would have been in shock.

2

The next few years of Tarzan's life are a blur. He was only a baby and he couldn't remember. But we can see him there, I think, living in the bush with Kala and the gorillas – where he lived at first was a world of sound. The leaves rustling, this was a kind of talk. His head would turn, tuning his ear as a bird came flapping in out of the sky. The flap, flap, flap of it, then the fluster of the landing. The tiny sounds its claws made as they gripped the branch. Scuttling feet – an insect trying to escape. Imagine being able to hear insect feet. And, tock! Then the sound of the bird crunching the insect, juicy, those little insect bones snapping. Flap, flap, flap, flying away – and what did the bird look like? Well, he didn't see it. The bush hides so much from view, it's all those leaves, like a million brushstrokes, and everywhere you glance the light is broken, it's hard to make things out. But your ears rope them in – baby Tarzan was getting sound after sound, which he carefully catalogued. Tiny offerings from all around the circle of his hearing, this was the language he was learning as he lay there along Kala's forearm, playing with the wispy hair that surrounded her nipple. The leaves talked to him, he couldn't understand what they were saying, not at first, but he listened and listened. Sounds, and smells – the smell of the bush, the smell of the weather, the taste of the air, this is what he was swimming in. No TV. No hum of the refrigerator. No suburban house going through its daily cycle. I have a new baby, a son, here with me in my home, and when I look at him he's got such big ears for every sound that's around him. His name is Thelonious, we call him Theo, and he likes to be sure of every single thing he hears. I keep my eye on him, imagining him as Tarzan – what would Tarzan hear? What would he see? Hey, Theo, I call, that's just the kitchen door opening, that's just your mother, hey, hey, don't cry, here she comes, son, listen to the crackle of her feet on the carpet, that's static, you can probably hear it. Me, I'm eighty-one years old now, my hearing is gone. I can remember hearing. I see things happen and I remember the sound that goes with them. Once I could hear, you know, the dew forming on the hills in the distance. Now it's as though it's winter and I'm wearing ear muffs. Now nobody lets me sing. I had a voice like honey but these days I can't hear the noise I'm making – like a parched goat, apparently. When no one's around I sing to the boy. But I see his eyes get big. He frowns. I see his mouth open and I know he must be wailing. Oh-oh, here comes Loretta. But I can talk to him. He knows my voice, talking away there in the night from the first day I put him in her stomach.

No familiar voices for Tarzan.

Last night we had a thunderstorm here, it shook the house. I like big weather but the baby went crazy. His eyes were like marbles, rolling round in his head. And it made me think of baby Tarzan, out there on the hillside, rain lashing down through the leaves, thunder breaking close overhead. Flash! Crackle! – it's different if you're out in it. Then the wind, the leaves being torn from their anchors. Down in the crappy little humpies, the gorillas are crouching, one hand held over their heads. Kala holds him tightly but he's going out of his mind. Branches crack. The rain smacking on his bare skin stings him, thick braids of water are running down his back. Nowhere to hide, and that weird darkness, the air all jumpy, and then right on top of you the mountain-splitting boom! A baby, naked, out in all that – it doesn't bear thinking about.

But Kala, that dedicated mother, nevertheless old Kala somehow got him through. The storms passed, the days and nights simply arrived and then passed – nobody was counting. Nobody even had a watch. Kala and the baby and the tribe, all just following their noses. Imagine for a second the gorilla-songs Kala sang to Tarzan, there on the hillside when the moon was out. Insects flying. Birds after them, looping and diving, there's a warm wind, a clover wind, sweet-smelling, and the fat moon wobbling as though it's full of water, just out of reach – baby Tarzan puts up a pudgy hand. Watching the cloud shapes as they drift across the moon's pockmarked face in the long-shadowed night. You can hear the rustle of everything – no one wants to be the first to move. What's that? Over there . . . But it's nothing, some rodent. Kala and Tarzan listening together, not afraid, there is no reason to be afraid out there in the balmy Wairarapa moonlight. Then Kala sits him on her knee and she begins to sing to him. She goes, Loo loo loo – hey, Tarzan. Loo loo loo, her lips pointy, her big round gorilla eyes shining at him. Tarzan tries to grab the hairs on her chin and she lets him. He twists the hairs – she lets him. Ow, okay, that's enough of that, and she holds him up. She stands and he's held way up there in the air. Slowly she turns him and he can see the clumps of the trees and the scrubby lowlands, the clover meadow, the upslope, the rising dark line that the ridge makes against the sky, and, above, the endless curved splatter of the stars.

This is where he lived.

In the watery light his skin is mottled, dirty brown, thick with dust and grime, crosshatched with scratches, with streakmarks down his legs, there are bugs in his hair, there are scabs and sores on his skin, and on his back something like a leech that Kala has been trying to pick off for days. His grubby little fists rub his eyes, his nose screws up. His mouth is going down. But Kala holds him up there, lets the warm winds play around him. He is alive.

Gradually, as Tarzan began to respond to her, Kala set about teaching him the lore of the bush. Not by talking. The scientific books tell you that in fact gorillas are better than chimpanzees at picking up human speech patterns, but that's, you know, in a lab, these gorillas didn't know any humans, just Tarzan and he didn't have any speech to teach them. But something was communicated. By watching, I presume – Tarzan with his big eyes there in his head, looking everywhere at once, a bit frightened, but then seeing something, a bug, I don't know the names of any New Zealand bugs, but some bug crawled up her arm, he liked the pattern on its back and he closed his paw over it, stuck it in his mouth. That same crunchy sound he heard from the bird. And Kala said, No, Tarzan, we don't eat bugs. He was making a face, the bug tasted nasty, and she said, We eat leaves, gorillas eat leaves. But Tarzan of the Gorillas always ate bugs.

Of course, she didn't actually say, No Tarzan – she didn't actually *say* anything. But she showed him, by twisting him away when they came to the cutty grass, and holding him clear when they passed the stinging nettle, and putting him down into it when they came to the clover. He ate the white clover heads and got the honey. By holding him up when they got to the manuka bushes, which were their favourite. Putting his nose in there so he could smell it. What a nose he developed. Snotty, unwiped, it's true, but he was filthy in every way, what did it matter, he was still in good working order, even dirty he was still a fully-equipped human being. With his nose he could pick up the pattern of the bush around him, punga there, toi-toi up there. The dead fawn on the downslope – ripe! Rain coming from over there, the wet smell of it, the shift of it on his skin. Kerchak there. Kerchak coming over, the silverback, knuckles pressing the earth. Kerchak looking down at him, a big fellow, really big, huge now that he was up close, looming, and wanting to touch. Keeping his eyes on Kala and his hand going towards Tarzan. A wicked expression. Kala twisting Tarzan away. Don't let Kerchak touch, not with that look in his eyes, that is the lore of the bush.

Tarzan tasted everything. He put the whole world in his mouth. Pig's droppings, a brown lizard, there it goes, in, its tail hanging out, flicking on his chin. Bark, leaves, fistfuls of moss. A giant weta's thigh – he stuck his tongue out to taste it. This last item was passed to him by Kerchak. Kala wanted to intercede, but Kerchak was patient – every time Kala reached for the thigh, Kerchak moved it away. He had a point, she knew, and when she was sure that Kerchak didn't mean any harm she allowed it to happen. The big solid thigh, dripping, tipped into the baby's arms. Of course it was too heavy for him and he dropped it. Kerchak picked it up from the dirt and proffered it again. Tarzan leaned forward, stuck out his tongue – and Kerchak snatched it away and held it high above his head, as though to bash out Tarzan's brains. Kerchak screamed. Then he flung the thing from him. It turned, end over end, against the sky and fell into the tree tops.

This is the first story that Tarzan has to tell that is from his memory. He can see the thing against the sky, tumbling, and hear Kerchak's scream.

Tarzan had crawled away from Kala. The gorillas were resting around the edges of a clearing, manuka trunks upright like charcoal strokes with their puffy, leafy tops of green and white swaying up there, out of reach unless the gorillas climbed or bent them down, but providing good shade, and there was just a hint of breeze. Lying back in hollows, dozing, half concealed, there were bits of gorilla poking up wherever you looked, and Tarzan set off to crawl across the clearing – away from Kerchak, Kala noted, away from Tublat her brother who clearly didn't like the boy, but, no, there was no reason why he shouldn't explore a bit, she could see a stick waggling where he was wrestling with it down in the undergrowth, some old flax husk that was light enough for him to manhandle. The cicadas were singing away, a heavy sound that was like white noise, like the sound of the sun. All the gorillas were dozing.

I should explain what a weta is. At one time New Zealand had a number of large mammals, the moa, which was like an emu only bigger, and a giant eagle, called *harpagornis*, but, apart from the gorillas, nothing of any size survived the arrival of humans with sharpened sticks. But there was a large insect. Wetas are spiny, kind of ugly, legs everywhere, long-headed, bulbous, with shiny body parts that are the colour of dark beer – that same translucent amber glow about them. There are lots of species, but the most spectacular were the giant, *heteracantha*, which were cave-dwelling and stood as big as a cow. This variety had T. Rex-type jaws and were really pretty fearsome. Short-sighted, like the rhino, they seemed to blunder a bit, so in any kind of a wide open space they were usually no danger to humans. Their main prey was opossums, this is a kind of marsupial bear, heavily furred, with small claws and sharp teeth but only as big as a cat, there are no shortage of them in New Zealand, down to something like thirty million at last count, they're rampant since the big wetas died out and are stripping the country of vegetation. The last giant weta seen alive was in 1977, when some kids taking drugs got a fright in a cave in the northern part of the country, but you can see specimens in all the museums.

In Tarzan's stories the wetas don't have names. Maybe this is part of what makes them so spooky. They came, over the brow of the hill, antennae waving, dark shiny beasts, and they didn't make any sound. Spiny legs in every direction, large flat eyes. And no names. No voices. As I said, Tarzan was playing at the far edge of the clearing and they closed upon him. They formed a semicircle and then their leader came forward, darker than the others, larger too, made almost humpbacked by his great shoulder muscles. He stood over Tarzan so that the child was in his shadow and some sticky stuff ran from his mouth and slithered across Tarzan's skin. Acidic, it stung Tarzan, making him cry out, and it was this cry that bought Kerchak so rapidly across the clearing, something crabwise in his approach, an urgent four-pawed run, and then upon arrival abruptly stopping to rise to his full height. Kerchak threw back his head, showed his teeth and then slapped his hands on the great drum of his chest. Baby Tarzan heard that sound, unique, and catalogued it – during his musical years he never heard kettle drums without thinking of the day Kerchak saved his life. When he looked up, the weta had risen on its hind legs above him and so the two monsters fell together, like collapsing buildings, and he was kicked aside. There was a terrible roaring coming from Kerchak, his great muscles were working, and then a slow, ghastly sound could be heard, a tearing, as he twisted the weta's head from its thorax. Now the sticky filth ran freely from the open neck and again Tarzan was drenched. The jagged-jawed head was thrown to one side, where the other wetas seized it and carried it off, leaving Kerchak to struggle with the flailing body. He crushed it – his fur was matted with slime – and dismembered it. His roaring was as much a sound of fear and pain as of anger. Throughout no weta made a single noise. When Kerchak finally threw the body from him, they were gone.

 Kala took Tarzan to the stream and dipped him in and patted him and licked him. He had only one actual wound, a long weal on his side where an ankle spine of the weta had caught him – this festered and took a long time to scab. But his skin was burning. Kala licked and licked. If his skin burned then surely so did her tongue but she persisted. The boy would not be comforted. Kala held him close. Now Kerchak came to watch. His fur was giving off a faint smoke, as though the slime was smouldering. He showed his teeth when he saw Tarzan. Kerchak had a large bite wound in his shoulder. He was proud.

Tarzan never lost the desire to clean himself. He spent hours licking and scrubbing. It was almost impossible to get him out from under a waterfall. When, later in his life, he discovered the shower of the modern suburban house he would stay under the water until asked to leave.

3

Tarzan was once interviewed by a more sympathetic writer than Truman Capote. This was Edgar Rice Burroughs, who turned Tarzan's early life into a novel set in Africa – *Tarzan of the Apes*. The book was, predictably, an extraordinary success. Burroughs really knew how to milk a subject and he made the story over into one of his "wild romances", with cannibals and lots of blood. Tarzan liked him. Burroughs also had a tough start in life – he failed at everything, had eighteen jobs, at one point he had to pawn his wife's jewelry to feed his kids. He was flunked out of the army, started small businesses that failed, he couldn't sell snake oil, he failed as a door-to-door salesman of educational lectures. But once he got started as a writer he was a real worker – at one point he wrote eight novels in a twelve-month period. Critics scoff but so far his books have sold twenty-five million copies and are translated into languages like Urdu and Icelandic.

Burroughs' earlier books feature journeys to the centre of the earth and trips to Mars. They're a bit – let's not be coy – trashy. But that last one I do keep returning to. I will read anything that promises to take me back to Tarzan's early life. I want to see him among the tree trunks, moving barefoot along the flattened paths in the dirt, those trails that knot the animals of an area together. I strain to catch the knowledge that was in his feet. Mud-knowledge. Dirt-knowledge. Tarzan knew things that I can never know. But was he conscious? This is what obsesses me. To be human and to be unconscious. To be instinctual. To know what a human knows, without knowing that you know – is that possible? To feel the plants growing around you the same way as you feel the hairs growing out of your head, this would be special. Tarzan, running naked, one skin too thin, the result of his bath in the weta's acids, in shock from mother-loss, soul-lonely for his kind, and yet every filthy pore of him filled with knowledge of the planet at the organic level – wouldn't this be a particular kind of glory?

And then, like an ancient body found in old ice, to thaw to consciousness.

Barefoot Tarzan continued to wander the bushland trails in the company of the gorillas. He was growing – his infant years behind him now, though Kala's breast was still a source of comfort. She never bore another baby. Later, Tarzan wondered if she ever mated with Kerchak again. She seems to have made it her mission to care for the human child. He needed care. The gorillas of his generation were growing fast but even with the extra milk Tarzan was skin-and-bone, eating only leaves and bugs and whatever came his way. Worms, leggy spiders. There's nothing poisonous in New Zealand, there were no snakes in those days, the place was a paradise. But it's not a supermarket.

Moving slowly through the bush, then, there were at that time seven gorillas in the group, and Tarzan. Kala, Kerchak the leader, Tublat, the young gun who would eventually be chased off, an old female called Gincha, a younger female, Enk, and two youngsters, Bo and Jimpi. Kerchak in front, huge, head still, eyes going from side to side, moving steadily on his knuckles, the silver-grey of his broad weightlifter's shoulders making something like an opened book for the others to follow. They'd eaten and were looking for shade. Climbing to the ridge, Kerchak on all fours, pausing bridge-shaped on the skyline, his great tufted head turning slowly as he surveyed the valley. High over the downslope a hawk was flying the infinity sign. Poised there under the welcome sun, Kerchak checked that his family were ready, and began the descent.

The valley where Kerchak's group spent the nights was shaped like the bowl of a long spoon, angled to plunge into the flats where the rushes and swamp-grasses grew. As they started down, peaks and ridges in the green canopy of bush made it look like a tossing oceanscape. Nothing was moving except for the dandelion seeds, which were carried on the updraft as it swept to the ridge behind the gorillas, so that the current in the air was made visible by a stream of frail asterisks. This was something beautiful, but did the gorillas notice? It's hard to know what was in their heads. Only one of the interviews with Tarzan ever touched on this subject. A reporter once asked, "Do the gorillas look at the view?" They look for something nice to eat, Tarzan said. They look out for a good place. At this time Tarzan's English was cautious but there was nothing wrong with his marbles. He asked the reporter, Do you look at the view?

"I am always on the lookout for the work of God."

At this the apeman frowned and scratched his temple. Then slowly he replied, "The gorillas don't know anything about God."

Well, it made a good headline.

At the top end of the valley a tree stood out from the rumpled green of the bush, and from high in it a tui – which is a kind of bird, it makes a noise like the soul of a dredging machine – a tui was singing, as usual, and as they descended the gorillas heard it. They heard other bird noises too, by which they knew that nothing untoward was happening in their valley. They moved like a spread cape behind Kerchak, slowly, pausing in shady spots where the air was sweet, then ambling on. In the afternoons they liked their rest.

But not Tarzan. He was a trouble to the group at siesta-time. The boy would not leave off with his curiosity. He was always finding a new beetle to chase. No one watching him and the beetle making its way along a stick, hanging now from the underside and Tarzan with his eyes just two inches away, following as it went about its insect business, prodding when it went too slow, and then transferring his interest to the hawk which was passing low overhead, he saw the pattern on the underside of its wings, and, scrambling upslope, hurried to find a better opening to the sky. He watched its looping flight, then dropped his eyes to a silver trail of slime left by something making its slow way up the narrow bushland path – and so he explored. When finally the gorillas called for him he had to run, a giddy downhill rush, sure-footed as he slalomed past trunks and hanging creepers. Kerchak would grunt, Kala would scold – hurry! It was so exciting to run downhill. Once, going fast, he met the pigs – suddenly he was amongst them – and had to climb, no hesitation. The tusker rooted round the base of the tall stump he'd scrambled up, opening the ground. Now that was grunting! There was nothing to do but wait. Eventually the boar's attention wandered and the boy climbed down. The gorillas were by then all calling loudly. He was growled at. That night in the humpy, wrapped in Kala's arms, he had a picture of the pigs in his mind – their dark fierceness, the way they always seemed on the edge of anger. The black hairiness of them, that gleaming tusk. So was he thinking about them? Or was this simply seeing a picture? Was he imagining what he would be like as a pig? We don't know. That is, I think, one of the reasons we are fascinated by Tarzan – we think he might be able to tell us what happens inside the heads of animals. He was always watched for animal behaviour. But he said firmly, "I am not an animal."

At afternoon sleepy-time he continued to escape and so by dint of no particular method came to know every inch of the valley. I don't mean that he was familiar with it. That's an inadequate word. He had inside him a parallel universe, a sense-map of the valley, made of crossing strands of odour and temperature patterns and shade patterns and tastes and echo-locations and between-leaf airways which had been gained by sticking his snotty nose right into the dirt of everything. He had that landscape on his skin and in his hair. He ate that landscape and shitted it. Maybe his most sensitive instruments were his feet, which were hard and horny and caked with grime but which usually had a dampness about them – there was a moist layer where subtle information passed through from the earth he trod and read through those feet as though it was a great book.

And in this way he came upon the cabin.

On that particular day the afternoon had stretched and the gorillas were, he knew, not going to travel far to where they would sleep, which was a good thing as he was some distance, perhaps three miles away. He had discovered a nest of the kind of bees which live in the ground and was watching them as they flew in loops and circles all about its mouth – putting his ear to the earth to hear the underworld hum. Something big down in there and yet when it appeared it was made of little buzzing bits. He was listening hard – Kerchak's cough would come soon, and there was also a bird he hadn't heard before, that he was trying to place. Listening, listening . . . And so he became aware of another sound, something with a different quality. At first he thought it was the bees. Does a hive sing? There was a vibration, a shifting level of tones – but where exactly was it coming from? He lifted his head and it was still there. And so now his sound map had in it the hive, and the bird, and a hole where Kerchak's cough would come, and the background silence of the bush which is so loud if you live in it. And something else too. A humming – another humming. Lower in tone, but not in the ground. No, this was in the air. Now Tarzan was standing, turning his ear. That direction.

Following the new sound he scrambled up a north-facing slope. It was a long way, further than he'd thought, but the humming – was it a hum? – drew him on. Moving silently among the treeferns, along a mossy bank, finding a twisty path, and then all at once the bush opened out, there was a clearing, and only luck prevented Tarzan from stepping out into it. Instead of losing his life he peered around the thick trunk of a tree.

What he saw first was the wetas. There were lots of them. At that time Tarzan couldn't count but from his various descriptions of this moment and from studying the site of the cabin I think we might guess that there were thirty or so – great spiny things, all facing the same way, into the sun, which was high in the hole that the clearing made in the sky and pouring warmth down on the whole valley and especially it seemed on this open space, where in the middle of it the wetas were glowing. Was the hum coming from them? There was a tone that shifted. But the wetas had always been silent. However, they were vibrating. It was fascinating to watch. The movement wasn't great. They were tense, their legs and heads held stiff. It was their bodies that were moving – a tightly controlled undulation of the thorax. A current was going through them. There in the sun, shiny-backed, with just a little slime hanging in strings from their jaws, a pulsing mass of giant cave wetas.

His first instinct was to escape. But there was something

fascinating about them, throbbing there in the sun, and also he hadn't yet got to the middle of the sound. At first, shocked by the sight of the wetas, he'd stopped listening and simply gazed, but now his ears were working for him again and inside the hum he heard another sound, something that stayed with him all his life.

Tarzan was a wonderful mimic, this was proved over and over again in the middle years of his career when he could upon demand produce any tune he'd ever heard and make it sound exactly like the original. When asked to reproduce this particular moment he would smile and then a faded look would come over his features, as though he was thinking of an old girlfriend. He would open his mouth and come out with . . .

You, whose sweet brown eyes will hold me,
You, whose little lies don't fool me,
You, with your heart
Right there on your sleeve,
You are the one I believe.

So corny, but Tarzan liked corn, we know this, it was part of his gift to find the essential part of such trite things, that had been worn away by repetition, and to restore it, to sing those old items as though he was writing his autobiography as he sang. There exists a tape of him crooning this old chestnut and while it never made the charts it has quietly sold over a million copies. But at that time he didn't recognise it, he simply heard it, a remarkable new type of sound. It reached him on a shift in the breeze, on a shifting wavelength. Where did it come from? Somewhere in the middle of the wetas, a thing he hadn't attended to because of his horror. The cabin.

Not that he recognised the cabin for what it was either. But over the years he came back to this place and made it his own, exploring every inch of the ground around it, finding tiny objects and insignificant little markings which were of course to him of great significance – all the while listening to that sound, that fascinating sound. What was it? Now, at this first encounter, he tried to make the shapely part of it come clear of the humming – this was like separating out the call of one bird from the mass of the dawn chorus. The humming faded in and out and now he grasped that it wasn't actually being made by the shiny beasts. They were merely shivering to it. The hum was coming from somewhere in the middle of them, something standing there, pointed, with straight lines, taller than him, wooden, something with an utterly different shape and nature than anything he'd seen before.

The sound faded, then came back, changed.
Is there anybody out there?
Or am I here all alone?
Please, if you should happen to hear me
Could you get on the phone?

Into his study of this new amazement came faint from far away down the length of the valley the deep cough of Kerchak, calling. The wetas all heard it and there was a kink in their dance. Tarzan was torn. But he knew that he needed to think – how to go among the wetas, how to get closer to the source of this astonishing new thing. He would come back here. There was of course no need to mark the place, he knew the valley as we know our neighbourhoods and so he padded his way silent back downhill. But at every step his ears sought that sound and, in places in the valley, he could now catch it, faint but clear. From that day his centre of gravity shifted. For him the middle of the valley was now upslope and that is where his mind sat.

4

Tarzan had to wait until it was late fall and the cold had driven the wetas back into their caves before he could safely begin to investigate the source of the sound he had heard at the cabin. In the meantime he found places in the valley where he could pick it up, faintly, natural sound-shells where hollows in the land gathered the humming, and the other sound too, the part that rose and fell in such an intriguingly shapely way. In these spots he would lie, on a mossy bank, eyes half closed, concentrating, while the creeping life of the bush went on around him. He would go into a kind of swoon – in this mood he on one occasion came to suddenly, to realise that a doe was licking his knee. The creature was harmless and bolted as soon as he lifted his hand, its spotted fawn skipping beside, leaving him to drift again on the thin signal. *I'm too blue, to get over you . . .*

   He was probably about six years old at this point, skinny, tall for his age, with a long shaggy mass of black hair that fell over his face. That year he had a sore on his thigh that wouldn't heal, an ugly thing that leaked pus through a thick crust, and many scratches and bites. But he was cleaner. He liked washing. No soap, of course. But the dousing in the king weta's internal fluids had made him feel that on his skin there was always something he should be getting off. Upstream was a waterfall which the gorillas didn't visit, they weren't keen on being splashed, they generally avoid water, gorillas get enough moisture from all the leaves they eat, but Tarzan would stand on a flat stone and let the heavy flow fall upon his shoulders. What a marvellous weight it was, that load which shifted on your back and kept breaking over your head. Tarzan liked to be inside the water, to see the world through its opaque rush. It was cold to the bones, though.

Kala he didn't take to hear the distant sound. The times when he listened were always when she was dozing, plus she would not have followed him such a long way from the group – except, of course, that she would do anything for him. He still slept each night in her arms. This had become a source of dispute. Tublat had on several occasions come and dragged at his body, signalling to Kerchak that this shouldn't be, that this hairless thing was sleeping with the boss's wife, but Kerchak had already received one good bite from Kala over this matter and so he merely put his hands over his head and turned away. Tublat would poke Tarzan with sticks and find spiders to place on his leg, but Tarzan had always been an enthusiastic eater of spiders.

The truth was, since he had discovered the cabin he had grown away from the group. He was always among them for the nights but during the day he was often at the very edge of what could be called contact with them, the limits of connection, busy with his own purposes. They were easy to keep up with, they tended unless threatened by bad weather to move slowly and he had discovered that he could catch up with them in a few moments by swinging from the thick vines, supplejack the New Zealanders call it, a lovely name, which wound like a connecting thread through the densest parts of the bush. He had routes he could travel for half a mile without touching the ground – running down the back of a broad sloping branch, leaping, seizing a vine, swinging – letting go. Ahead was the next vine, his hands would stretch towards it. But in the instant before he caught he was free, in the air . . .

He began to seek wilder and longer flights.

Gorillas are essentially ground-dwelling creatures. Their arms are longer than their legs, which is thought by those who are expert in these matters to be a remnant of a branch-dwelling past, but these days they rarely take to the trees. And so Tarzan's fondness for height became another difference, another source of separateness.

And yet he was part of the group and they would have mourned his death; Kerchak would have fought for him. Tarzan made them laugh. Sometimes it was his skinniness – he was a stringy thing, long, but unable to digest as much greenery as them and needing Kala's milk to sustain him – and sometimes it was his ingenuity. They would see him using a stick to tip a bird's nest out of a tree so that he could lick the egg-goo from the ground, and cackle with delight. And then sometimes he would try and reproduce for them the sounds he had heard at the cabin.

The older gorillas seemed to recognise it. As soon as he started, they broke into a chorus of hoots and yowls. This set the whole group going. Birds flew startled from the trees. The bush lost its silence – it was like the arrival of a gang of kids with a boom-box. The gorillas all grunted his name. "Tarzan!"

Tarzan finding his voice.

Then when the land was cold he followed the bushland trails, slithered up the muddy banks and swung his way along his highway in the trees, following the aural trace until he was once again at the edge of the glade where the cabin stood. No wetas. He could see their droppings scattered thick on the ground and his sensitive nose wrinkled. But there was, he quickly confirmed, nothing to be afraid of. His every sense told him this. What a delicate instrument he was, thinking there at the edge of the clearing, his long dark hair in cowlicks all around his registering head.

Wide-eyed, alert, he picked his way across the open space. Following the manner of the gorillas there was something indirect in his approach to an object, a series of tangential passes, and so it was some time before he was alongside the solid wooden rectangle, where he squatted as though it was a rock he had been used all his life to climbing and from there he gazed around, interested, taking in the clearing and the trees and the drifting clouds.

He was at the source of the sound now and was deeply affected by its vibrations.

Beside him the rectangle was solid, strong. He knew without testing that it would not shift if he touched it. He knew it was wooden, a wood he was familiar with, there were stands that smelled like it everywhere, but this particular wood also had an odour that was part of the thing that was strange and new about this place. Tarzan squatted, letting the histories here come to his senses. Wetas, yes, and the faint feet of smaller creatures, these he filtered out. The usual patina of leaf-litter and mould. Yes, but there was another thing. Tarzan also knew that the wood was hollow and he was afraid of the energy that was humming in there, making this sound. Would it come out?

At the same time he knew that this was no living thing, not a creature. His mind during these years was not given to making pictures, he was a repository of factual knowledge, of the uncontaminated actual, and was used to dealing with the world on the basis of the information that came to him – this was a quality that served him all his life. But then when he lifted his hand so that his finger could touch the wood, his clean brain was entirely in his fingertips. Yes, the sound was in the wood.

It was in the ground too, his feet told him that, but fainter – it was there the same way as it was in the air. Touching the wood made his spine stand erect and his eyes float up in his head.

On a green hill,
On a blue day,
Your brown eyes
Looked my way
And told me
With a smile
That you were gone . . .
What did it mean?

He stayed there touching the wooden walls while the long shadows of the clouds went over him. From that day the weather in Tarzan's head was changed forever.

Finally he straightened, moving his hands up the wall with him like pads, one over the other, so that he would not lose contact. The thing was higher than his head. He found a length of wood that protruded and used it to haul his birdy bones up onto what we would call the roof. Now he could see the whole clearing. No wetas. He crawled along the ridgeline and came to a square turret that smelled of old fire – the chimney. Its hole was covered by a wire mesh. When he put his ear there the sound was thrillingly clear.

Squatting on the ridge pole, listening.

Eventually he dropped down and circled the cabin. The quality of the sound had changed. . . . *and so Allied forces were able to complete the manoeuvre without further loss and take the town. Now here is the voice of Corporal Arthur Stenson, recorded some two hours after the capture was complete . . .*

Tarzan froze. What had he done to cause this change? He

didn't like it, the voice made something in him shrink. Scrambling up one side, he found a place to look through the wall, it was square and he seemed to be able to see into the thing, in to some faint light, but it was like looking out through the waterfall, you couldn't really see clearly. Dropping down again, he found another place to investigate. It was a break in the surface of horizontal wooden lengths and he sensed that this wasn't as strong. He bumped it. His fingernails scratched at it. Now his nose told him that there was a place to sniff, to the side, right at the height of his nose, a strong scent there – phew, strange! His finger touched the small cold thing that stuck out, grasped it. Shook it. Turned it.

A doorhandle – and the door of the cabin swung open.

He jumped back, his foot sliding on a weta dropping. Crouched, he was ready to run. But nothing moved. From the tree top, upslope, the tui continued to sing.

Tarzan entered the cabin in stages – peeping in, then withdrawing to see if anything had changed. The child was in a state of high excitement. Here the humming was quite powerful, it ran a shiver through his teeth. He found it hard to see. The cabin had windows on either side but they were dark with grime and didn't let in much light. But the open doorway revealed all. If he could only bring himself to go all the way in, then he could see what it was that sang. But he wanted part of himself to stay outside, to be on watch and not wholly enclosed.

Then he was squatting on the boards of the floor and his huge eyes were gazing round.

A decade or so later, when the cabin was studied by those who were used on an everyday basis to living among human things, what they found were the meagre practical objects that a reclusive man might take with him if he wished to escape the world and establish a primitive life of survival and thought. There were a couple of oddities, which we shall come to, but in the main the cooking pots, implements, tools and raw materials were entirely commonplace.

However, for Tarzan they were objects of great mystery, especially because every one of them seemed to be alive with that sound which, now that he was inside, appeared to be everywhere in this place. He picked up a pot – apart from the doorhandle, it was the first metal he had touched – and peered into it. Held it at arm's length. Touched it with his tongue, bit it. "It tasted metallic," we say – I guess this is what we mean. Tarzan had no idea of metal and no idea of cooking and no idea of pot – well, he may have understood the purposes of containers, a bird's nest is a container. But gorillas have no possessions and, in the wild, don't use tools. So to Tarzan these objects were just so many random items – art objects, if you like. But even he, squatting there, intuited that these things were of a different order. For example, the spade. Its particular handle, its hard iron shoulders, the sheer flatness of its blade. Its edge. Everything about the spade was as different from say a spade-shaped branch, if such a growth can be imagined, as it is possible for a thing to be. The purposefulness of a spade. Its wroughtness. Even Tarzan, a brain-carrying being, yes, who could figure that if he wanted eggs then he wanted a stick, but who thus far had had little need of that part of our equipment which divines the purpose of an object – even he could grasp that this was something new under his sun.

But not something of great interest, not when there was that sound to investigate.

Inside the cabin the humming lodged itself in his teeth, it was a sensation he could hardly bear. But at the same time the part he liked was more intense too. He moved carefully across the floor – he'd never been on a floor before – to where, low in one corner, the source of the sound resided. As he went close he saw that it appeared to come from an oval thing the size of his hand, black, which was embedded in a panel of wood. This was the place. Tarzan crouched, brought his face close. Looked. Touched, first with a fingernail and then with the hard tips of his fingers. All kinds of information came to him. It was in his arm, it rose up his spine. But his ear was the thing. Without removing his fingers he carefully lowered his head so that it was beside the black oval – the loudspeaker. His lips were drawn back, against the humming, and against something else too – fear, maybe. And so his hearing was filled, his head was filled, with the most wonderful thing, a woman's voice singing, against a velvet curtain of other voices, her voice draped in a lush setting of horns and strings – all arrangement, all shape, all design. The extraordinary phenomenon of human music.

Stranger
In this town you look lonely
Stranger
In this bar you look blue
This place
It's a place full of heartache
But stranger than strange
Stranger
I'm lonely too

Let us leave Tarzan there, listening to the swoony music of that time, and draw back a little.

Expert researchers agree: the cabin seems to have been built some time in the mid-1930s. There are certain indications in the timber and also in the products which were found there which seem to confirm this. Thus, given Tarzan's estimate of his own age, which, looking at photographs from various stages of his career, seems likely to be more or less correct, what we get is a picture of an adult male who in the middle of the depression decade headed for the hills, armed with all he needed to survive. We know he was a man because the print of his skeleton was there in the cabin, full-length on the bed.

This man was perhaps a scientist of some sort, or at least an amateur inventor. He constructed – as Tarzan eventually discovered – a small windmill, some distance away and trailed wires from its site, chosen for its exposure, to the cabin, set in the clearing for shelter, and there connected it to one of the most unique features of the entire setup: a row of glass containers filled with chemical liquids which served, it seems, as a storage battery for the current generated by the windmill. Batteries like this are commonplace now but this one, as suggested by a chemical analysis of what remained of its contents, seems to have been somewhat ahead of its time, as Tarzan found when his investigating fingers touched two wires simultaneously. He was thrown onto his back – that is what he says. Whether he was actually thrown, which would indicate a very powerful current indeed, or merely launched himself away in fright, we will never know.

There was no sign of womanly presence. No flowers in vases – and no documents either, no bones, no signs of a family grouping that might have indicated something of Tarzan's origins – well, there were two toothbrushes, but this might simply have been the man thoroughly equipping himself.

As Tarzan grew older and gradually it dawned on him that the man in the cabin was in all likelihood his father, he began to look for traces of his mother. Alas, there were none. There was a second bed – a sleeping place, he registered it as being. Had this been his, Tarzan's? Or hers? He slept in it sometimes, trying to know if he had slept here before. He dreamed. In his dreams a strange creature sat on his bed and smiled down at him. Such dark hair! That absolute black, a marvellous setting for a pale face, just slightly turned away. When he awoke, sweating, shuddering his way back into the world, his memory would kick and he would strain to recall what he'd seen – he'd dreamed of something! But he had never seen another human being. As the image became clearer he understood that it was of Kala.

In adulthood he became fixated on the idea that the film star Elizabeth Taylor might have been his mother and he researched her past to see if she had at any time visited New Zealand.

His first exploration of the cabin was not thorough. Thoroughness came later. It is a concept that we learn – have you ever seen a thorough animal? He glanced about, wildly, his attention falling first here, then there. Initially all he cared about was the music and he squatted near the speaker, fingers touching, and basked, as you might bask in the warmth of a fire. But then his wandering eyes led him away and he took up the spade, a machete, a crowbar, and weighed these things, and learned what holding them could tell him. The bones on the bed did not interest him, not at first, they were just bones and bones he knew about. The smell of the fire in the fireplace was also a familiar thing. The eggbeater – now this was extraordinary. Quickly he discovered how its small green wooden handle might be turned and the effect that this had on the bulbous tines. What a satisfying *whrrr* he could make with it.

And then there was the cabin itself. Tarzan was not used to being contained. The humpies that the gorillas made were just gestures towards the idea of a roof and walls compared to this solid shell. He stood up in it and felt it around him. So strange to have the world excluded. Then a puff of wind pushed the door closed and he panicked and ran outside. Standing among the weta dung, he looked back and saw the shape of the thing, took in that basic house-shape familiar to us from every child's drawing. The idea of a house, with its sloping roof and vertical walls. In the West we all grow up with this simple little house in our heads, a door and two windows, my boy will be drawing it in a year or two, and it says everything about us as creatures who at the end of the day go inside and close the door. But wild-thing Tarzan, his hair over his face, had no house, and lived in the open bush.

It was the music which drew him back in. *Sweet melody of love, come calling. Stars in the sky, start falling.* Tarzan couldn't understand the words but he got the message. He stared at the black oval speaker and wanted to take it with him. But the electric shock he had received made him cautious. This was lucky (again: luck). He could easily have torn the speaker from its wires and then his story would have travelled in another direction entirely. No music, no Tarzan – not one known to the entire world, anyway. But his fingers continued to explore. There was another black thing, small, not unlike the handle of the eggbeater – when he touched it the music stopped. The tuning knob.

He squatted, startled. He'd moved the radio off the station – now only the humming remained, but louder. His eyes, huge, crawled over the apparatus. What had happened? His imploring fingers caressed the speaker. Come back! He glanced wildly round the cabin, looking for a reason.

His fingers investigated the speaker, the wires, finally the little knob itself. Just the faintest touch and – ah-ha! Music regained – it's a lovely thought. But he had by chance centred the receiver more precisely on the station's frequency. And now the humming was gone.

This coincidental sequence had a long-term effect, as it was the humming, it seems, rather than the music, which attracted the wetas. When, during the summer that followed, the wetas did not return, Tarzan didn't mourn them. In fact he scarcely remembered that they were ever there, so completely did he take possession of the site. Their dung gradually sank into the soil of the clearing and in time there was no trace of them in that place.

5

Tarzan returned to the gorillas bearing the eggbeater.

Upon leaving, he carefully closed the cabin door behind him. Then he opened it again, to make sure that he could. Then he closed it, to make sure no one else could get in. Open. Shut. Open. Slam! All of the birds flew out of all of the trees. He glanced up and realised that he didn't want to call attention to his presence in this place. Carefully he closed the door again. He stared for a long time at the doorhandle. Then he set off down the hillside.

Among the gorillas the eggbeater was no big deal. True, one end of it could spin nicely and it was also shiny in a way that was mildly interesting. It was worth smelling carefully. But no one was going to fight him for it.

Tarzan kept it in the cleft of a branch, and went on with his gorilla existence.

But nothing was the same. His mind saw the house-shape of the cabin, and the objects inside it, and he was deeply engaged by these things. For all his life there had been the gorillas, and the bush including everything that lived in it, and the wetas. Us, the world, and those that can harm us –

three categories. And now there was a new category. Not that his inclination was taxonomic, but over time Tarzan grasped that this cabin contained a different order of life.

The music was clearer now. No louder – he had not yet tangled with the volume knob – but free of the humming. Even when he couldn't hear it it was in his head, falling inside him like rain. See him standing on the ridgeline, catching the wavelengths. Generally the gorillas didn't like to stand and in childhood Tarzan had slavishly copied everything they did. No one remarked on his lack of body-hair – well, no one remarked on anything – but his difference from them was recorded in the communal cortex, the group-think that was the tribe. Tarzan is us, but he's a funny us. A poor copy, a sport of nature.

But standing suited Tarzan's feet. He liked also to walk on two legs, and to climb, and to eat bugs and lizards and eggs, and to wash, and use tools, and swing from vines, and go off by himself when everyone was resting. To stand on the ridge and catch the music and to roll it around in his mind as though it was a marble in a cup. Standing there, he liked to sing, as loudly as he could, his little voice falling onto the downslope and the valleys. He couldn't sing very well. He wasn't used to making complex sounds with his mouth. But he worked at it. What he liked best was singing in the cabin – singing along, with strings and horns to help him, and the singer's voice to follow. He fitted right in. He didn't like to sing too loudly when he was inside, in case the world realised he was there.

The cabin was now his territory. This troubled him. If push came to shove, he wouldn't be able to defend it. He was maybe nine years old, still skinny, lanky, serious blue eyes peering out from under a shaggy dark fringe. His hair bothered him. He would sit on a rock and bite off the ends but that only kept it from becoming a waterfall. It was still over his face all the time. He learned to put it behind his ears, making a question mark with his finger – a girlish gesture. He squatted to pee, too, but all the males did that. He knew he was a male, but also that he was different. Did he ever look ahead and see himself as a brawny silverback? This kind of thinking was not his way at that time – I don't think he could think. When do humans start on that? I know a six-year-old who said to her dad, "How many years have you got left?" But did she really know what she was saying? The whole business of thinking, it's such an area of darkness, everything I've read about it makes me think I haven't read the right book yet. And it's not just about age – could Tarzan think without language? Animals do think. Watch an elephant using a branch to bring down an electric fence. Or is that just figuring? Sometimes I think it's only thinking when it doesn't have a purpose. You look up and now you know something, now and forever more, but you weren't trying to know. But knowing is another thing entirely.

Whatever – Tarzan couldn't think, not at that time – that's my opinion. But he knew. He knew he was different. He knew he couldn't sing very well. He knew he couldn't defend the cabin, and so he was quiet there and always kept the door shut when he was inside, and always opened it with caution. He knew the bush would know of his presence because of the traces he left. The bush is a memory that never forgets. Only you forget. So he was thoughtful. Because he knew, inside, that this was for him, this cabin. This was where he was going. If ever he did look ahead, this cabin was what he saw, and him living in it.

Unsystematically, following his snotty nose, he acquainted himself with everything it contained. Spoons and forks – what could they be for? A lightbulb, like an egg but probably not good to eat. A toothbrush. Two toothbrushes – in time this came to seem significant, but in those early days they were just a pair of stiff little objects that smelled of salt. The books

– such uninteresting things, and of course it's always been hard to concentrate when the radio is on. Singing along, he flicked at a few pages, then looked for something else. More books – such a musty smell. The whiskey bottle, now this was interesting. See how the golden stuff in there plays when you tilt it.

And so it wasn't for some months that he discovered that three of the books had pictures.

Tarzan's place within the Kerchak group shifted a little during a minor incident which occurred around this time. It began with a new taste among the manuka leaves, a taste that seemed to everyone to be sweeter than the rest. Tarzan of course had never found manuka all that tasty, but he followed Tublat, who was leading this initiative, with the rest of the gorillas and so they passed over a long, high ridge to the north and ventured into broken country that none of the younger members of the group had ever visited. Kerchak shouldered his way forward and took the lead, as a silverback must, and, following the new taste, they gradually ate their way down, through the thick bush, to a warm sunny glade ringed by the puffy white tops of the flowering trees. A cloudless sky. Cicadas singing. Tarzan impatient because on this side of the ridge you could no longer hear the music – when from out of the bushes came a huge rushing thing which ran sideways across their path, dark, massive, roaring, now stopping to tear up pieces of greenery. A big silverback, and when they looked nervously round there were strange gorillas everywhere, hidden in the pockets of the clearing. The silverback reared and slapped his chest with his hands, a drumming sound which found echoey hollows inside the head.

There are nine stages of protocol before gorillas come to actual fighting and Kerchak had made the submissive gestures – downward glances, head turned away – long before there was any real danger of combat. The group they had encountered was simply too large to fight. Moving carefully, Kerchak shepherded his little band into retreat. The other silverback was busy tearing up vegetation. Does anyone understand what this gesture means? I will tear your hair out, maybe. He was doing his crabwise running, sideways spurts. Big gorillas can be very frightening. They move so slowly most of the time, clambering on all fours, pausing to take long glances, sitting as though in melancholy thought. Then suddenly the biggest of them is coming fast, pistons pumping – the big ones are square, like trucks. Then they rear up, and all you can think of is . . . King Kong! And if two trucks should crash – wah. But this seemed to have been avoided. Kerchak had got his group moving and they were on the point of escape when without warning a communication sound came from the other silverback.

"Tarzan."

The stranger silverback spoke his name. Now it has been wondered: if the gorillas didn't have words then how was it they had names? Because every time he told his story Tarzan always gave everyone in his group a specific name. When pressed by interviewers on this point he would frown and say in his careful, polite way: "They don't have words. But there are sounds. They sound like grunts. You have to listen carefully. Tarzan is the grunt for white. They called me Tarzan because I had white skin."

Then the silverback came up slowly. "Tarzan." Kerchak circled, on his knuckles, always manoeuvring his big body so that it was between the stranger and his own group. But the silverback was not aggressive. His head was down. He said, "Tarzan," again and again, and, by moving in a submissive manner, was allowed by Kerchak to come close.

Tarzan squatted on his heels, behind his curtain of hair. Through the dark strands Tarzan watched the silverback approach. Inside him was a growing dread. Kerchak stood guard, every muscle in him bunched in case he should need to spring to the defence. But anyone could see this was not going to be a violent occasion.

The silverback settled now before Tarzan and he uttered that grunt again. He was sitting as gorillas do, with his feet out to either side and his big belly rested between. Gorillas have an extra intestine to digest all that greenery, it makes them look like they drink a lot of beer. Their legs are stumpy but they have long arms. Now one of those arms slowly came out. Have you seen that old film called "E.T.", where the wrinkled creature from outer space extends its long bony finger? The silverback's digit was shorter, with a hard stubby piece of nail. This stiff thing reached for the haystack of hair and drew it aside, first to the right, then to the left. The silverback lowered his head. His face came forward and then he was looking deep into Tarzan's eyes.

Kerchak made a warning sound.

But no one actually stopped this happening, not even Kala. And so Tarzan had to meet the silverback's gaze. This was deep, steady and deep. The eyes were dark and there was no movement in them. Tarzan grew uncomfortable and made to rise. But there was a controlling noise from Kerchak and so, suddenly alone, he had to endure the most intense scrutiny.

Deep into Tarzan's head the silverback travelled – Tarzan knew this, and he grasped that in return he was entering the huge head that was before him. And now Tarzan had an idea. It came to him that the silverback was remembering him. Who knows where this idea came from? That the silverback might have seen a tarzan before. Now the silverback's face came to within an inch and he was sniffing. This was contempt. This was impolite – you should sniff from a distance. Tarzan wanted to complain but he did not. A cloud went across the sun and the darkness in the silverback's eyes was misted. Inside

Tarzan a specific piece of feeling was hardening into a permanent shape.

"Huh."

This was the silverback's comment as finally he leaned back and broke the contact.

And from that day – snap! – Tarzan was outside the family.

At first, he spent more time than usual with Kala. When the group settled to take a rest, she would settle near him, staring sorrowfully, giving him affectionate little pats. Tarzan sat with his back to the group, off to one side, and one by one they would come to him. Tublat brought him spiders. They said his name over and over, in tones of affection, and looked in his hair for creepies. Tarzan. Now his name sounded like something you might use to describe a star . . . fascinating . . . distant . . . cold. Nothing could move that lump of feeling that weighed inside him, nothing could shift the image he had of those dark steady eyes putting him under such intense scrutiny. Two dark thoughts. The brow of the gorilla is like a jutting cliff, the eyes are buried. Looking at you, a gorilla seems to give you total attention. It's a serious countenance, as though you are being sternly judged.

Tarzan is a Huh.

And where was the other Huh the silverback had seen? There was no way of asking. Even if he could approach that great dark stranger – which he knew was impossible – what good would come of it? Whatever was in that huge old head would stay there, there was no form of communication among the gorillas which could detail such an experience.

Poor Tarzan.

Dark and darker ran his thoughts. I think we could say he was thinking now – doesn't that always come out of pain? – and that this was the moment that really started it. No longer could he ignore his difference. At the stream he stared sorrowfully at his reflection. His skin, sun-browned, streaked with dirt, was smooth – had he once had body hair, which had fallen out? Why were his eyes so prominent in his face? And what was this water that ran down his cheeks? The gorillas didn't have that.

Kala brought him eggs to suck, lizards to chew, mice, grasshoppers, fat tasty grubs, worms, snails, slugs. Cicadas, crickets, all kinds of bugs. Her milk had dried up years before, ever since he had gradually got skinnier. There were other menu items he had added to compensate, for example the little freshwater crawdads which live under the banks of New Zealand streams, these were sweet to crunch. He spent long hours, crouched beside the clear water, only his eyes moving, the skin of his hand wrinkled and pulpy from spending so long in the wet, where it hung like a pale hook, waiting to grab. Eels, though first you had to bash their heads against a tree. Frogs – spawn, tadpoles, adults, he didn't care. Little birds – bite their little heads off. Pigeons. The New Zealand pigeon is fat and slow, that's why there are so few of them left now, but in the thirties and forties they were thick in the trees. Tarzan would come swinging on a vine out of the sky and crash into the tree where the green-and-white fowl tottered on a branch, catch the meal with one quick fist while the other secured a hand-hold, then drop to the ground and begin spreading feathers.

Yes, but he had to want to do this, and want badly. Dinner rarely presented itself wearing the Eat Me sign. If his will to live was thin then so was his body.

Now it seemed even more that it was the music that sustained him. He lay on the upslope in warm spots, his eyes half closed, and was lifted away to a world of tangled emotion. How those sounds made shapes inside him! Each tune was like an opening in the bush, full of shade and mystery, a place which something would emerge from – you strained to make it out. The thing, when it came, the shape the music made –

this fascinated him. But now there was a new emotion. He was increasingly aware that these sounds meant nothing to Kala. He tried to make her hear what he heard. Patiently she followed his beckoning hand, slowly she settled her bones into the warm spot with the good acoustics. And then? Her dark eyes studied his face. Tarzan, darling. She patted his head, parted his hair, touched his cheek.

So he sang along for her. Such a commotion and she was embarrassed.

All the little lights that softly glow, dear
All the little twinkling stars that rise
They come out so that you can shine, dear
All the little lights are in your eyes – what was she supposed to make of this? Was he in pain? Was he wounded? And the truth is, he was. Something in him was crying out.

6

Edgar Rice Burroughs once remarked, with reference to Tarzan, that a new thought was like rain – you can sense it's on the way.

I've wondered about this. I think I know what he meant. You grasp something, and your whole head lights up, it's like your brain being born again. But then, if you reflect, you see that you had been aware of this possibility, this new arrangement of the facts of the world, and had cleared a space for it in your thinking. Like a mighty space craft, dewy from its long voyage across the dark, it docks slowly – shudders a little as it fits perfectly into the landing site. As you study it you see that it's been a long time coming.

Tarzan continued to visit the cabin but now something was on his mind. He was looking for something. He studied – the radio system with its wires, its battery, its knobs and speaker. Utterly intriguing, but that wasn't it. It was more to do with the sound itself, something inside the sound that had to be separated out. He peered over the edge of the speaker, looked behind it. Nothing.

He held the spade – squatted on the floor with its haft in

his hands, held it, weighed it. The things it was made of, the wood and even the metal, these were strangely wrought, but essentially familiar. No, the spade wasn't it.

It was the shape of the spade.

Now I could pretend at this point that he looked around and saw that someone had designed all this stuff. But I don't think so. If we go down that road, pretty soon we have him thinking, So who designed the frogs? And this didn't happen. No, we are talking about knowledge here, that comes through familiarity. Through handling. From the spark the stranger silverback had struck in his head. Through longing.

Through handling, through time: Tarzan gradually came over many visits to the knowledge that what the cabin contained was quite simply another order of life. And – that there was a connection between this order and himself.

I think this was the most profound knowledge of his life. It's part of what made him so unique, part of his charm and power and eventual success. It's pretty basic stuff – to grasp your own nature, how many of us really achieve that?

Now when he wandered the bushland trails, Tarzan's head was filled with the idea that he was a thing apart. A spade thing, a music thing. What was he? He had no idea – only these associations. The stranger silverback had said "Huh" and Tarzan fixed on this. He was a Huh. It was a Huh cabin filled with Huh things. There had been another Huh once – this thought produced terrible longings.

So he began to spend hours at the cabin and finally a night. It was stuffy with the door shut, but he loved the way that here the world of things enclosed him. With every breath he became more what he really was – a human body.

Kala pined.

In the cabin the whiskey bottle was a favourite. Why was the liquid in there? He would squat on the floor, swaying in time to the music, holding the bottle as though it contained a universe. He could make waves travel up and down its length – while the radio provided a soundtrack, this gave endless fascination. Thus he held it on a number of occasions before noticing that the thing which obscured one side of the bottle was also worthy of investigation. The label. It was like a scab, he could lift its edge with his nail. But that wasn't it.

He'd hefted the spade, studied it, but couldn't recognise it. It was the same with the label on the whiskey bottle. On the label he saw significant squiggles. There were a group of marks and then other marks and then a third group at the bottom. Some years later Tarzan saw this arrangement again, in a bar in Texarkana, and by then he could read the markings: *Cutty Sark*. He saw what the markings in the middle were, a picture of a sailing ship. These recognitions hit him hard. He stood, left his companions and strode from the room, bottle in hand. It is a sign of his fame that the owner not only allowed this to happen but was thrilled by it. For years the fellow dined out on the moment. "Tarzan came to my joint. He liked my whiskey so much he lit out with a bottle. Took it out on the walk. I saw him standin' there, holdin' it up to the light, like it was somethin' he'd never laid eyes on. Rolled it all around. I thought he was gonna, I dunno, pitch it at the moon or somethin' – some kind of a wild animal thing. His buddies went out there and they hustled him away. They had a real big car, a long black thing, Tarzan was a real big guy and they had to kind of squash him down in there. He took that ol' bottle with him, clutchin' it like it made him happy – like it was a baby or somethin', I tell ya."

But I am getting ahead of myself.

The markings on the bottle were a mystery. But, as with the spade, increasingly he could see the quality of intent in them. They were so regular, somehow, not like the objects of the bushworld, which grew twisty and random, according to the pull of the sun. No, the things in the cabin had form.

Tarzan understood now – he was well into understanding things – that his future – his growing sense of a future – lay in the investigations he would make at the cabin. He kept its door shut when he was inside, exited with caution, did not leave objects lying around outside. The eggbeater was returned.

And he took good care to spend quality time with the gorillas. Increasingly he saw that he could lose them, that if he became too estranged they might cast him out, and he would be utterly alone in a landscape where his only connection was a sound that raised great banks of feeling in him. The feelings, he grasped this, were a risk. They were un-gorilla in the extreme. When he closed his eyes it was as though another world lay waiting to swallow him. But that world was shapeless, he had no pictures.

Nevertheless he was not unhappy. Indeed a curiosity had been awakened in him, a boyish eagerness to study and pursue. He was, after all, pure energy.

The thing that had lived in the cabin – presumably these were its bones lying on the platform in the corner – must have moved around and made paths. And so in his mind he had the bones rise from the bed and go outside, wander about. Where had they trod? There was an odour in the cabin, his marvellous nose went down into the layers of smell, parted them as though they were so many hairs on a head, and found the trace, so faint, that was distinctive here. This was difficult work. Many of the scents in that place were unfamiliar. The smell of the glass, for example, this he had already learned, the whiskey bottle held, cold, along the side of his nose. The metallic tang of the spade's iron, the familiar woody smell of its handle. Yes, but on that handle . . . his nostrils widened . . . here was something. Here was a smell that was also on the eggbeater, and the slasher, on the floorboards and on the toothbrushes. So faded, an old pencil line, so faint, but something that could, if you were determined, be followed.

All the time the music was working on him.

Following the intermittent trace he went outside. Those bones moved ahead of him. He didn't see them walking upright, this is too definite, but he had in his mind now the clear idea that that place had been the territory of an ambulatory being, one that made marks and left smells. The trail was cold but all the world was layer upon layer to him, one footprint on top of another, and so he set himself to work.

As he circled wider from the cabin, working, working, he found a path.

A path is a thing of great power for those who live in the bush. On a path you will always have encounters – but can you manage them? Will you eat? Or be eaten? Meanwhile you're going somewhere that everyone else has thought worth going. But this path was old, cold and overgrown. He had to detour, to circle back, through damp, ferny places, through tangled and shadowy growth. Then, glancing up, he saw that he was about to arrive at a second clearing. It was a bald spot, where the sunlight glowed. Standing in the middle of it, wooden, ten metres high, was a windmill.

He squatted near its base, watching up to see its angled vanes turning slowly against the sky.

There was nothing like this in the bushworld, that did exactly the same thing over and over again. Looking at the vanes made his head spin. What kind of creature would it be that had made such a thing? His mind was filled with troubled awe.

It was the quality of intent that he kept finding. The regularness of everything – the cabin, the spade. Not just regular but shaped. Intended. Purpose-built. As he was spun by the vanes a kind of clenched determination formed at the hub of him. To understand this.

He climbed the windmill's wooden frame and was quickly

at the top. Up close, the vanes were fearsome things, swishing relentlessly. The sound they made also reminded him of something, as did the gears, which, through an opening, he could see within the square casing of the windmill's sides – the eggbeater! Yes, this was a large version of that whirring thing. But this had no handle to turn. It seemed to have a power all its own.

Down through the centre of the rectangular pylon a pole ran, the drive shaft, and he put his eye up close to it and saw how it turned. Ceaselessly.

Back in the cabin, he squatted before the speaker and let the sound coming from it take him over. His finger touched the knob which made the sound get bigger. Just held it. There was, to his sensitive touch, the faintest vibration. He could feel through the soles of his feet too. It was in the boards of the cabin.

It was inside his mind. In there something was turning, never ceasing. A driveshaft, spinning. Gears humming. Somehow the very elements of the universe had been coupled together to produce a busy energy, which was so startling to him. The inside of things. The whirling of the stars. He looked down at his chest and wondered for the first time what was inside his skin.

At dusk this confused creature swung slowly from vine to vine, took its pendulum path across the bushscape and rejoined its fellows. It made its own humpy these days, always close beside Kala's, sure, but it had begun sleeping separate – every parent looks forward to this day. Now, thoughtful after the windmill encounter, it drew branches together, carefully laid them on one another, tried things – draped fern fronds and bracken on them, wound them experimentally with vine. The gorillas were long settled but Tarzan, inspired, worked on into the night. The moon rose. Moths flew about, an owl passed low overhead, headlamps burning. Tarzan wrestled with his branches, his fronds. A better humpy – it was a new notion.

Eventually Kerchak made a warning noise, "Desist!" and Tarzan gave a grunt of acknowledgement. He crawled into his structure. It wasn't perfect, but there were clear improvements. The way the branches came to a node at the top, teepee-like, and were wound together with a frond – this was an innovation. It was a design. Tarzan lay curled on his fragrant bed of grasses and studied what he had done. The first branch like *that*, and then another caught in its crotch, and the third goes *there*. And the others. And the fronds, woven like this. The thing he intended, it was clearer to him now. Tomorrow night he would do better.

And so, gradually, he developed a distinctive thing, the Tarzan humpy, with three main poles, and, over time, found that he might as well use the same poles as he had used the night before. Thus he came to have his first personal possessions.

Months passed.

No matter where he was in the valley, his mind was always in that cabin. He wrestled with it. He tried to grasp something – he didn't know what it was. It was in the music. It was in the intent. It was, it was . . . And, at last, having exhausted the possible interest of the enamel plates, and the cups, and the spring traps – smell the old blood on the jaws! – and the bones, and the remains of the bedding and mattress, and the knives, forks and spoons, the rags of clothing on the wooden shelf – all with that faint trace, that faint smell – at last he came to the least interesting items and offhandedly gave them a second glance.

The study of the cabin by qualified researchers, this was years later, produced a carefully detailed catalogue of objects – a list in which there were no picture books. These were among the few things that Tarzan took with him when the time came for him to leave the world of the gorillas. Throughout his life they remained his most treasured personal possessions. At his death they were not found to be among his effects, a fact which contributed to speculation that in fact he was still alive.

I have those books – there were three – that belonged to Tarzan. They are sitting beside me now as I key these words into the machine and when I turn their pages I am effortlessly transported to that place where he first opened one of them, on the board floor of the cabin, with the music coming ceaselessly from the speakers, and the blotchy light of the bushworld at the window. A dreamy, time-lost place.

He had looked at the books before. His first opinion was that they were of no interest. Their smell irritated him, musty.

On that first encounter it's impossible to say if he saw the pictures. Seeing is not a simple matter. As I've said, you have to recognise a thing before you can see it. The label on the whiskey bottle had a picture but not one Tarzan could use. However, on that day when the books revealed themselves to him he had been thinking – wondering, dreaming – for a considerable period, maybe a couple of years, about the origins of the cabin. He'd looked at the books before, more than once. Held them. Hefted them. And it wasn't that one day he saw a picture. But the day came when he looked at one. Stopped and really looked.

That book is called *The Brandon Encyclopaedia of Faces of the World* and is in its way a remarkable object. The Tarzan memorial should have a copy of this, but I am loath to give mine up. I often leaf through it. It has a photograph of the faces, in black-and-white, of every race that walks the planet. The book was published between the world wars and thus reflects the social attitudes of that time. "These savage people hold the primitive belief that part of them vanishes into the lens of the camera and so this photograph is of the only individual available, a poor soul who was forced by his fellows to sacrifice himself, as they saw it, so that his village might receive the handsome reward which the photographer was offering. Thus the look of terror on his face. His compatriots were tall, striking men whose proud features would look splendid in Harris Tweed on Regent Street . . ."

All the photographs are of men. This, over time, caused confusion in Tarzan.

Each page shows a full face and then, opposite, there is a descriptive text, accompanied by a pen-and-ink sketch of the individual in his native dress. Here for instance is a Dane and he has been kitted out, it seems, by that Harris so warmly recommended on an earlier page. The book is arranged, though this is not made explicit, according to a theory of evolution which has the most primitive, the Aborigines of Australia, at the front and gradually works its way through to the Englishman, who stares into the lens with the confidence that only good breeding can give.

Of course all of this was lost on Tarzan. He had no interest in the text, black bugs which even a determined fingernail could not lift from the page. Edgar Rice Burroughs has *his* Tarzan teach himself to read from children's books, but, in the jungles of darkest Africa, where no English was to be heard, no language of any kind – no, this is a nonsense. The real Tarzan learned syntax, I have always thought, from the radio, without being conscious of it and that is why eventually he was able to learn to speak English comparatively quickly. But reading by independently deciphering squiggles on the page, no, this didn't happen.

At first, the pen-and-inks did not interest him. But how he drank up those faces. Everything has a face, increasingly he saw this. Tarzan saw faces in the trees, he saw faces in the mud of the paths he trod with his dirt-thickened soles. The face of the weta, with its oval eyes. The sensitive nose, slender, of the deer. The pig's ringed peepers. But nothing like these. Some of the men were dark-skinned, like Kerchak and Tublat. Look at this wild-eyed chap with a bone through his nose. Tarzan did. He looked and looked.

The inevitable happened. This is from an interview, an account where he seems to have been a little more at ease than usual. The interviews were, for the most part, painful and false things. "So, Tarzan, how many lions did you kill today?" But here he is talking to an unidentified reporter from the *Plains Dealer* in 1959 and for once he talks about something that mattered to him. "I was washing at the stream. A leaf went past on the top of the water. Then I saw something else there and I saw it was my face. I'd seen this thing in the water before but I hadn't looked at it. It looked just like a picture from my book and I sat down and had a good talk to it."

For me this is right up there with the day when man first walked on the moon.

7

I trust that this is now clear: I am proud of Tarzan. He was an autodidact, a natural, completely self-taught, and, when he first appeared on the world stage, somewhat raw. But gradually he became more polished, and his poise and style represent a feat among feats. It makes me think of the Tahitian "savage" Omai who was taken from the Pacific by sailing ship to England in the 1770s, where, despite his strangeness, he impressed all who encountered him with his intelligence and grace. And yet Omai had his fellows to grow up among. Tarzan had to create himself from scratch.

The other two books from the cabin show on one hand the great works of humankind – bridges, dams, zeppelins, skyscrapers, locomotives, highways and gardens – and on the other, pictures of the animals of the world.

Official records show that the cabin also contained a popular medical encyclopaedia, a dictionary, some scientific books, a collected Shakespeare, *The Origin of Species, The Well-Tempered Clavier* (did someone plan to build a piano?) and so forth. No novels, no poetry apart from the Sonnets. But he never gave these strongly-bound objects more than a glance. Books without images held no interest for him.

*

So now the gorilla-boy, his head full of pictures, lies on the gorilla hillside in the early moonlight and looks up at the stars. His humpy is built, the improved model he is so proud of and he is lying outside it, his back on a rather scratchy bed of bracken. The stars are like so many pinholes in a curtain – the light behind it must be very great. The moon is a flying hunk of rock, but he doesn't know that, he sees only a face and he strains to hear what the moon is saying. Around him, gorilla sounds can be heard, small grunts of companionship. He grunts to Kala and she grunts back. A large, red-eyed moth comes, moon-dizzy, and is captured by Jimpi, who knows that Tarzan will eat this and so he brings it to the boy. A hunting owl glides into the clearing, wobbling on its wings, and passes low, perhaps two metres above Tarzan's resting head, and its target-eyes look down and find his, watching back, and in both creatures there is a little jump of surprise and recognition before the bird glides away into the shadows. Later he hears the scream of a mouse.

During the day, when the air is full of thistledown and birds are flying lines across the valley, the gorillas find some shade and snuggle down to take a break from the heavy work of eating leaves. The trees make tall shapes, clouds go past like floe ice, cicadas are drilling. Tarzan watches a hawk covering a hillside, its wings spread on either side of a wire in the sky that it seems to slide along. But there is no wire. The bird loops and turns, passes close. It is a creature of the air, a thing of feathers. Back and forth above the green hillside its feathers take it, rising on the updraft, sliding back down like a skier.
    Tarzan stands, extends his arms, and the warm wind which is coming up the hillside plays on the underside of his skinny extensions, providing just the faintest sense of lift.

He swings through the trees with the greatest of ease.

Yes, swinging from vine to vine, and letting go. Flying. Then coming to rest, exultant, upon a rock: his throat opens, and from him pours a mighty noise, the bushland yell which, years later, gave a thrill of terror and blood to audiences who'd come for rock 'n' roll.

"Aaaaaahahieahieahieaa . . ." The Tarzan call. The call of the hunter, the victor, the one who is master of all he surveys. For a generation it was imitated by boys climbing trees the world over. Up on his rock, Tarzan is only a ten-year-old and his voice nothing to what it later becomes, but he makes the most of what he has and so the sound that comes out of him echoes through the valleys, falling like an avalanche on the bush-covered slopes. Tarzan! Tarzan! Tarzan!

Squatting beside the stream, he floats a leaf and watches it slide away on the water's muscled surface. He knows all the words to *Mule Train*, *Some Enchanted Evening*, and a song with a lyric that goes *Toodle oodle oodle oodle oodle too-too* that I have never been able to track down, but he doesn't know what any of these sounds means. He sings carefully, he always had a good ear, and finds another leaf to float.

Absent-minded, he crunches on a small frog – bites off its head to stop the wriggling.

When he puts the books side by side he can have a picture of a gorilla's face from the animals book and a picture of a white man from *The Faces of the World*. He would like to do this beside the stream so that he could see his reflection and the other two faces together, but he will not take the books from the cabin. The gorilla stares fiercely back at him, a version of Kerchak, all brows and no nose. And then there is this other thing which maybe looks a bit like him. Tarzan slides his gaze from one picture to the other, and he can feel himself changing allegiances. It's a painful sensation, he's losing the gorilla-soul which has his feeling for family in it, his feeling for company and shared lives. But there is another feeling too, one which has been growing. Huh – that is what he calls this. He tries to make the sound come from deep inside his belly, a grunt of a sound, something that is solid enough to have the Empire State Building in it, the Flying Scotsman, the Grand Coulee Dam.

The *Faces* volume has a final picture, a double-page spread taken at maybe a League of Nations gathering, and here you can see many thousands of people, of all races, their faces turned upwards towards something that is behind the camera, a political speaker perhaps. I run my eye over them and a voice starts up in my head: spics, wops, wogs, kikes, honkies, niggers, polacks, slopes, chinks, towel-heads, russkies, they're all people and somehow these are the words I've learned for them – redneck arseholes, queers, fruitcakes, morons, losers, suits, airheads, swanks, spoons, fatties, nerds, junkies, crims, cowboys, dreamers, babes, studs, a pencil-necked geek – the gamut of humanity peering upwards, in every kind of rig-out, hair piled up or greased down, with facial furniture, and headwear, and neckwear, and visible underwear, little dogs clutched like lovers, one guy picking his nose, a cluster of cops on horses, and children held up so they can see and be seen – it's the Milky Way. It's the you-must-be-here-somewhere assortment of humankind, and what is it I've learned? For Tarzan this picture never wore out. He would stare at it while the radio played ten songs. When he looked up he was dizzy. The company of his fellows – and then the silence of the bushworld: this was a painful re-entry.

One morning he was scrutinising the picture of the Aborigine when it occurred to him that beside the dark face there was something that was slim and upright. But then down in the pen-and-ink the slim thing was horizontal to the ground – the Aborigine was throwing it.

It took him a while but the day came when Tarzan took

one of his humpy poles and spent an afternoon throwing it. It could be thrown very well, he found. It went where you threw it.

He became an expert spear-chucker.

He saw that the spear in the pen-and-ink had a sharpened end and so he sharpened the end of his spear too – at first with his fingernails, which was painful, but he was generally used to a bit of pain, and then, another breakthrough, with the edge of the spade. His new, improved spear, made from a specially selected manuka pole, was sharpened with the blade of the slasher. Then he began to think that the slasher itself might be a thing you could wield.

A wonderful period followed, when he took each item in the cabin outside into the light and studied it anew, to see how it might be used. The books could be thrown, but not as satisfyingly as the spear – their wings didn't seem to work very well. The eggbeater could be used to burrow into a rotten log, for grubs, but it wasn't as good as your fingers. The whiskey in the bottle was, as has been established, nice to look at. But for Tarzan what appealed most readily about his new tools were the possibilities they offered the killer.

He killed everything he encountered.

He always sat down at once and ate his kill. Pigeons wriggled fatly on the end of his spear and then were fat in his stomach. Weasels, stoats, rabbits. He tried to spear a worm, just because it was fun to exercise a skill. He ate better, and began to grow. He cut his hair back with the edge of the slasher and was no longer forced to endure lashings when the wind blew. Now he was always looking at himself and his surroundings to see what improvements he might make. He became ambitious – he considered killing Jimpi, just to see if he could, but then looked at Kerchak and decided against it. But ambition is a thing that is always finding a higher peak.

Thus the day came when he went swinging through the

trees, armed with the slasher and his best spear, and went upcountry, into the thicker, higher parts of the bush where no gorillas ever ventured, settled himself into a tree and waited. He was on a solid branch, feet side by side on its back, curved like the claws of a bird, clinging on tight. He was squatting. The slasher was propped up against the trunk. In his right hand was a spear. Below was a path.

The path came down from the ridge and along it, he knew, in time, the pigs would come. He had seen them often while squatting here, as they passed, single file, grunting, squealing, two metres below. They always paused and looked to the left, where there were several piles of Tarzan-dung. The branch was a good place for shitting from and if it meant that the pigs lingered, this was a good reason to produce afresh. Tarzan concentrated.

Then there were sounds on the path.

The sounds were from further away than he'd first thought – they were louder. Loud noises are uncommon in the bush. The creatures have to insist upon their territories, it's true, but to make a fuss of yourself means that eventually someone will come and see if you might be good to eat. But this wasn't just loud noise, it was a commotion. Not pigs. Tarzan's ear told him that it was a gorilla, howling. What would a gorilla be doing up here? But he was not mistaken. Into view came a gorilla, quite large, being dragged, kicking and screaming. Dragged by a weta, which had its jaws sunk deep into her shoulder. The gorilla was Kala.

How calculating are the wild creatures? We like them when they behave as we think humans should. The mother fox fought to her death to protect her cubs – good, we say. But they do figure the odds. Tarzan did look carefully to see how many other wetas there were. He did think twice. Criticise him if you must. Some creatures say, She's gone, I have to live on – do you see the other wildebeest circling back to protect their straggler from the lioness? But it wasn't more than a single thought. I call this intelligence. Then he flung his spear.

He followed it down, bearing his slasher. How effective the spear would have been against the hairy pigs is a moot point – it was only sharpened wood. But he had gravity on his side, and good muscles. His throw plunged it into the thorax of the weta and brought it to its knees. A great spiny leg came up and thrashed at the pole which was sticking from the shiny armour of its side. But its jaws did not release their hold. Kala's eyes burned at Tarzan – now she was silent. He swung the slasher and hacked at the flailing limbs. The jaws still had their hold. Close by, more wetas could be heard. Tarzan slashed Kala free. His skills with the blade were not so finely honed. He cut her. She cried out. But there was no time to worry about that. The weta carcass was falling slowly to its side, the ooze from its organs beginning to fill the air with a fetid cloud. Tarzan choked on his own vomit – seized Kala's arm – dragged her free. Swung them up into the tree.

Now other wetas arrived and were maddened by the smell of that ooze. Their scrabbling below was urgent. Tarzan hoisted his mother onto his back, set off along the branch. But Kala could not hold on, and they made an unbalanced whole. Tarzan's foot slipped – a weta had been forced upwards by its fellows, was treading on the wetas below, and its extended claw, thrashing, caught Tarzan's ankle, leaving a deep gash. Tarzan lurched, began to fall. With a desperate effort he managed to right them, hoisted Kala to his chest where one arm could encircle her, grasped the vine he had snagged close by, and, his feet slithering in blood, launched them.

They didn't swing far. Below, the wetas gave chase. At the first transfer to a new vine Tarzan dropped Kala – she slid to the ground, barely able to slow her fall. Her fur was matted with weta ooze, which was seeping into her wound, where it smoked, but she made no sound. He went down – he no longer had his slasher, and the wetas were coming – gathered her, and set off, staggering, down the path. Her body snagged on bushes and trackside scrub. But the crashing behind them told him he could not hesitate. He could smell the wetas getting closer. He staggered on. But in his mind a cool eye had looked ahead and he had a plan. Ahead there was, thirty paces, a fallen trunk which cantilevered out horizontal from the bank, which he would be able to run along. The wetas would come too, but he would seize the vine he had snagged there, and swing free.

This plan carried them far out into the clear air. But Tarzan had not managed to make his usual run-up and so they didn't have the speed they needed to reach the next vine. They swung back. The wetas were waiting on the trunk.

Tarzan managed to turn himself and arrived with his legs thrust out, so that his feet hit the shoulder of the first weta, which scrabbled like a man on a slippery pole, and fell. But the second weta seized him.

The creature had launched itself forth to make the seizure and this gave them new impetus – together the three swung back out into the air. But the weta's weight was too great and Tarzan's hands began to slip down the vine. Then the weta slipped. It had never managed to get a hold with its jaws and now it began to slither away. Its claws went across Kala's back and down Tarzan's leg, leaving deep weals. Then it fell and they heard it crash into the scrub below.

Slowing them as best he could, Tarzan allowed the vine to pass through his hand and encircling arm. They came to its end and he lowered them as far as possible, then let go. They fell beside the weta, into its ooze, but its head was crushed and it was no longer interested. Together they made their escape.

At the stream Tarzan bathed Kala. She let him. The other gorillas gathered to watch.

The blood and gore washed away easily enough but it was the ooze in her wounds which gave her no peace. Her eyes watched him. He bent over the rend in her flesh and applied his lips to it. The ooze filled his mouth and he began to gag. His tongue was burning and he paused to wash it, then went on. Finally it was all gone and he crawled away to be sick.

The other gorillas closed in, making small noises and patting her. They licked her wound too, dribbled their saliva into it. Kerchak carried her back to the clearing where they had been sleeping that afternoon and settled her there, and they built a shelter over her. She made no sound.

Tarzan bathed his leg. The cuts there were long and savage, he studied them with care. Like a cat he ate grass, and applied handfuls of mud to the wound to keep the flies off. Then he crawled back to join her.

The ooze poisoned Tarzan and for several days he lay, mouth-parts burning, in the clearing beside her. The gorillas brought him water in their mouths and he rinsed as often as he could. His leg was matted, a congealed mass of mud and blood and ooze and pus that he knew would become septic. Nothing a few pills wouldn't fix, of course. And in fact there were pills that might have been helpful in the cabin but he couldn't read their labels. So he brushed away the flies and washed it. He was feverish.

In his fever he saw the people in the crowd photo come swarming towards him. They were making a loud noise – a kind of buzzing, maybe. Like insects. Their mouths were working, he could see inside their mouths, but he couldn't see what was in there. Black holes. Now he was a hawk, floating over the valley, looking down on the gorillas, seeing the tops of the trees, puffy, and when he looked in any direction all he saw were trees and trees and trees.

When Jimpi brought him water, this fever vision held. Even as he leaned over him, Jimpi's face was stretched long, the Jimpi in there was remote. Their mouths touched, the water went from body to body. Jimpi's serious eyes, his shiny black-faced hairiness, the small grunt of sympathy – Tarzan took all this in from far away, from up in the trees.

After four days he made himself get up. He fell, and got up again. He dragged himself down to the stream and washed. His mouth stung, he washed it again and again. His leg couldn't be stood on, it felt like a heavy club attached to his thigh.

He stayed among the gorillas. Their affection was restorative, it was a thing he could feel, inside him, as firm as a muscle. They didn't move so much, fed around that place so that he could be among them. They didn't care that he was a Huh. Even Kerchak came to stand over him, blocking out the sky. His bent finger traced the wound. He sat down heavily, nearby, then lay down on his side and put his hands, sleepy-sign, palm to palm under his head for a pillow, and closed his eyes. He was keeping Tarzan company.

The hawk slid along its wire above the clearing. It had Tarzan's eye in its head. The eye saw everything very clearly, from far, far away.

When the leg began to heal Tarzan limped back up the valley to the tree where he had squatted to watch the path, and looked for his things. There was a foul pool of ooze, covered in dead and dying insects, and weta parts were strewn about. His spear was broken, he found only a part of its shaft. Further up the trail he found the slasher and, even though its haft was pitted with teeth marks, each one like a little poisoned hole, he carried the thing all the way down to the stream and washed it. It was a fearsome object, it had sliced through the weta's plates, cleaved its skull, and he held it knowing that it had the power of death over life in it, a famous thing in his mind like Excalibur the great sword. It was the first weapon ever in that part of the bush and he the first to wield it.

Or so he thought. But some days later, returning again – the battle place drew him back, he kept pacing over what had happened there, seeing how it had played – he was suddenly aware that lying beside the track was an object. It was a long, slim piece of stone, twice the length of his finger, and he squatted over it. There had been rain, a nearby bank had slipped and this thing had rolled down and was just lying there, gleaming. None of the bush creatures would have picked it up, there was no profit to be had from stones, but Tarzan saw that this was no mere stone. Like the slasher and the spade and the eggbeater, it had been shaped. It was pointed at both ends, and swelled smoothly towards its belly, like a slender fish, but hard and green. It was greenstone, what the Maori call pounamu – it's a variety of jade. In one end a hole had been drilled.

He went to the tree where he had placed Kala's body and sat beneath it and twisted grasses until he had made a cord of sorts, and hung the greenstone around his neck. From above he could hear tiny sounds and he knew that the burrowing insects were picking the last flesh from her bones. He could smell her clearly, a sharp tang, decomposing in the sun. He had carried her body here and climbed with it as high as he could, well beyond the reach of the wetas, and placed it securely in a fork so that even when the hawks tore at it it wouldn't fall.

The greenstone hung heavy on his chest. When he looked at it, it seemed possible that he could look into it. Its greens seemed to have depths, like the pool downstream of the waterfall, if you looked for long enough you began to see things moving in there. He sat beneath Kala's tree and in the stone he saw the events of his life which had slowly led to her death. He saw her being dragged by the weta. He saw himself carrying her. He saw her face, dark, slightly turned away from him. Inside the stone he saw the trace of his mother, her pale face framed by dark hair, looking down at him. He sat beneath the tree and saw what he eventually decided was Elizabeth Taylor.

Years later, investigators combed the valley looking for bones in a tree, to see if Tarzan's story could be confirmed. But no such bones were ever found.

Tarzan stayed beside Kala as she lay, struggling to fight the poison of the weta. It had gone deep into her system. The jaws had torn away a hunk of her shoulder, which was insult enough, but the fangs had left their particular trace, deeper, a creeping paralysis that slowly worked its way through you so that the wetas would find you alive but immobile, stranded trackside – they would carry you off to feed to their young. She had lost so much blood. The wound had been washed by the other gorillas, and Tarzan had covered it with mud. The flies buzzed, frustrated. But Kala was not concerned. She knew where she was going. Only her eyes moved. They went slowly over his face.

It came to him that she had been up in the weta's domain because she was looking for him.

He sang to her. The moon came out over the clearing and the moths flew. There were stars. The other gorillas in their humpies grumbled, low, about the noise, but this was no genuine complaint. From time to time one of his fellows would come and study him – Tarzan making this strange noise. He was undeterred, even by the numbness the weta ooze had left in his mouth. He sang around the numbness.

His singing was good now. He had heard the songs so often, so undistractedly, and repeated them, carefully following the ways of each tune. A pause here, a rise to the kiss-off at the climax. A shaping of your throat so that the sound came full and made your chest feel as though the sun was rising inside it. The shapeliness of the thing, the tune, which was as deliberately made as the spade or the eggbeater, this he began to consciously enjoy.

He squatted beside her there in the bracken and leaf-mould, and sang his way back and forth through his repertoire. Dawn gradually eased the dark from the valley, and the shapes of night, looming, suggestive, full of faces, faded to become the dusty old world, so well-known. The sun rose slowly, warming the bones, and then bringing sweat. Tarzan shaded her with branches. The cicadas sang. The gorillas brought him frogs and worms but he wasn't eating. Just a little water, given mouth-to-mouth – first to him, then from him to Kala. He would let no one else touch her. In the last days he became fierce and marked out the place she lay as his territory. Kerchak let him do this. Tarzan became aggressive, bared his teeth. Everyone stayed away. The cicadas sang, then shut down for the night. The cold gathered. Tarzan covered her with branches and leaves.

He sang, his face close beside hers, looking into her eyes. If she could have moved she would have smoothed his brow. His voice just there, at the edge of her, rising and falling, as he worked his way through every tune he knew. Neither one of them understood a single one of the words he sang.

Is there anybody out there?
Am I here all alone?
Please, if you should happen
To hear me,
Could you get on the phone.

8

Kala's death left a hole in Tarzan. He walked the edges of this hole, he looked down into it, he tried to walk away from it. But from this time onwards it was always there.

He was fourteen. By this time he understood that Kala could not have been his mother but this did not diminish his grief. In some way he understood now that someday he was going to unlock the secrets of his past and there would be someone with black hair, someone whose face he could almost glimpse, she would step forward to hold him and he would look into her eyes – but none of this had anything to do with Kala, who had, he knew, given him his life. And so he sat under her tree and sang quietly to himself that he was dreaming of a white Christmas.

He lost weight.

In his hands he held the long, slim stone and tried to understand it. The green had a light in it, and in some way it was as though Kala had gone into this stone – he seemed to see her in there. But at the same time he understood that the stone had been made the way it was, and not by an animal. This was a Huh stone, but not from the cabin – he sensed this. He had found it so far from there, and it had a different quality to it, it wasn't like the things from the cabin which were manufactured, but was of some other order, of things that had been shaped. Of course he could not have explained any of this.

The stone had no smell and so the gorillas were not interested in it. They came to see him and looked up into the branches – Tarzan never looked up – and listened to the insect sounds up there. Then they looked at him sitting, fondling his stone, pale-faced, and off they went to bring him some food. Have a worm, Tarzan.

The stone wasn't the only thing that at this time he was fondling. Despite the weight loss, there was no denying that he had grown, had developed a large frame. He was taller now than Kerchak, taller than all of them – plus of course he walked upright. He was skinny, a sapling, but his shoulders were broad, his arms dangled like appendages and if you'd been there to see you would have said he was going to be a big man some day.

People have speculated about exactly how big Tarzan was, as though this might be the key to his success. It was part of the wildman mythology that he was well-equipped as a donkey and many reporters showed their sophistication by making stylish remarks about "the thigh muscle that bulges out of his pants," and so forth. Well, this is marketing, and the world believes what it gives pleasure to believe. All those film stars who throw the monster punches – fabulous creatures, but shake hands with them and they only come up to your nipple. But a bulge. You can sell a bulge.

Meanwhile teenage Tarzan sits beside the stream, grieving, thoughtfully stroking himself, the length between his legs perfectly adequate for all human requirements but no more than that, rising from its delicate wisps of hair. Hair is sprouting everywhere, a line which runs like a line of ants down his belly, hair starting from his thighs and under his arms, growth spurting everywhere. There are pimples on his chin, mixed with the down – and, ah, here now is something in the stream, milky, clotted, floating away. Tarzan observing this with keen interest through his shiver of pleasure.

He longed for Kala, though. He saw her face in the trees, in shapes that the shadows made. He would turn, expecting her to be there. He knew about death, in the bush it was as familiar as your foot, things died all the time and the bodies lay where they fell until they sank into the earth. Going down the trail, you didn't break stride for dead things.

But what was not common was loss. You had what you wanted – this was the nature of the gorilla's life in the bush. Sometimes your wants shifted, this was only natural. But the feeling that you had had something and now it was gone, that part of what you were made of could go – this was new. This meant you were now made of something else – this new part, which was there in you but was an absence, a hole. So could everything go? Or was it just that the thing that had gone was the thing that mattered most?

There were days when he would not leave the tree.

But there were also restless days, when he pushed his explorations of the gorilla territory to new limits. He returned to that place where he had found the greenstone and, mindful of wetas, searched thoroughly, as he had searched around the cabin, the driveshaft within him spinning, spinning. If one of his kind had been here, up close to the ridgeline, to drop this thing, would he find other signs? Were there Huh creatures hidden in the bushes, watching him? Why didn't they come forward? He climbed, scanned. He threw his head back and gave his loud call and then listened for an answer. He went over the ground closely, looking for any sign. Of course he found nothing. But that was because he didn't know what to look for. No more pounamu has been unearthed, but archeologists have in this area found middens where sea shells had been dumped. Tarzan found these too, sniffed up the faint salty tang. But he had never seen the sea and didn't understand that these things could not have come here on their own.

He returned again to the tree where he had squatted and waited for the pigs. This was where it had started. Now, here he was again, and the tree smelled the same, felt the same beneath his feet. The track was the same. And now here came the pigs. They were dark, bristly, with dark eyes that seemed like fierce little worlds. He could have dropped onto the back of the boar, it was directly below him. Of course there were the tusks to think about, plus there was fierceness in these creatures which reminded him of the driveshaft – that hum of energy. But the pigs were no longer the point. He didn't even have his spear. Tarzan was trying to understand how he could be here, and everything could be here, and Kala could be not here.

Even in grief, he grew. It was his time for growth and while his mind had been stretching, his body had merely been a thing he was in, the shell of him. Now suddenly it had a fascination for him that he had no reason not to enjoy. Part of this, as I have said, was his organ, which he played with the usual teenage virtuosity – but not only this. Every part of him now seemed fascinating. He held his arm out and regarded his swell of muscle. He was taking pride in himself and stood straighter. Upright, he was provocation for Kerchak and had to make sure he didn't find himself suddenly in the silverback's path. Kerchak was not as tall, but there was no doubt about who was the big guy, and Kerchak never shied from a chance to prove it. Tublat had grown too, and often these males could be heard growling and play-fighting. But Tublat's place in the gorillas' scheme of things was clear – he was Kerchak's inferior.

Tarzan was something else. Increasingly it was understood that he was other. Only Jimpi really spent much time with him. Tarzan had taught Jimpi to ride the supplejack highway and together they would swing and chase and explore and test their muscles and beat their chests. But Jimpi was a follower. Tarzan had a design in his head.

And so several years passed.

Nothing seemed to change, it seemed only that there was more of some things. Food, for instance. Tarzan became adept at killing the larger animals, pigs and deer, and thus obtained a better source of protein. His frame began to fill out. The down on his chin became prickly. His voice deepened.

Standing high upon an exposed branch he would survey the treetops and the fall of the valley. His ears would listen and bring him the next tune from the cabin. Ah, he liked this one. And he would sail his voice out into the audience of animals and leaves. He did have the sense that there was an audience, he knew they were all listening to him – the bush listens to everything. Even the cicadas stopped. Sure-footed on his branch, one hand clasping a vine, he was a bell in a high tower. He didn't fling his arms about, or touch his heart when he sang about love, in the manner of singers who need you to know how moved they are. He didn't emote. He just sang. He belted those big songs out – *There Ain't Nothin' Like a Dame* . . .

While he's standing in clear air we might just as well have a bit of a look at him.

He's on his way to being a big guy, six-four, and he's got shoulders and arms and a chest that would be good if you had a door that needed breaking down. A good chest. None of the overstuffed-couch look that you get with the studs on the beach, who pump all day and shave themselves. No, his was all vine-swinging muscle, pig-hefting sinew, spear-chucking, slasher-swinging, tree-climbing, gorilla-wrestling honest bounce. Standing up there, he's naked of course. The personal equipment I have already covered. There's a scar on the outside of his left leg, it runs down to his ankle, an ugly thing, and in fact his whole body has scars great and small all over it. It's not a display surface, not what it became – his skin is dark with dirt. He washes every day but not with soap, not with a flannel or pumice, and the bushworld, well, it's all dirt.

And now the head. Again it's large. A big head on a big body, this is always attractive. Hair everywhere, shaggy, as though he was a proto-hippie. He used the slasher to keep it out of his eyes, but he continued to look like a black haystack caught by the rain. Not that he cared. A strong brow, dark, and blue eyes. Interesting eyes, I think. If we could just move the camera in a bit closer. Yes, *now* we have his face. Full lips, strong nose, large deep blue eyes. Okay, let's say it: the fellow was good-looking. You don't get your picture on the cover of every magazine on the planet because you look like a hedgehog. He was pretty, even – disturbing in a big guy. When the scars healed, and his hair was cut, when he was dolled up for the stage, this pretty quality became disturbing. When we start to really study the face, there's strength in it, but also a devoted quality. The more you look at this the stranger it becomes. Big good-looking guys get what they want. Such faces shouldn't yearn. This is the face of someone who is searching. His eyes actually look at you. This is somehow tragic. He is supposed to be so far away, so unattainable. What is he yearning for? What could such a face possibly want? This is, I think, what gave him his special quality. His yearning for something beyond himself. And he had no clue what.

Let him sing.

Let him swing through the branches with Jimpi, let the rains fall on him, let the spear be steady in his hand at the moment he launches it. Give him a year or two here, just to enjoy himself, to expand. He was a powerful being in the bushworld now. He didn't hide himself. When he was happy on the trail, he sang. If he felt like it he would let forth the long yell that, in time, became so famous that audiences wouldn't let him leave the stage without hearing it. Aaaaaahahieahieahieaa . . . Give him time to study the books in his cabin – he thought now of that place as his. Give him room. If the bushworld has anything it has room. Let him grow.

And give him his privacy. We don't need to be there when the urge takes him and he strokes himself a length.

Give him a thousand evenings, with the dusk falling, the fat moon rising, the stars, the looming shapes of night. What's a thousand – three years? That's about right. Let the winds play on his skin, and the rain run down his back, and the sound of the bush fill his ears – the big circle that he's listening at the centre of. Let him lie on his back in his humpy with the soft fresh grasses beneath him. Give him owls, and hawks, and fantails, and pigeons, every kind of bird, New Zealand is full of them, to fly his thoughts around. The taste of rabbit on his lips – a little blood there, too. The shape of the valley, like a great spoon, a cupped hand containing a myriad of worlds, and they're all his. Every pathway here, every wriggle made by a worm in the dust is known to him. He hears a weta scratch its forehead high up in the valley. He hears the passage of the owl's wings. He stretches and turns on his side and pulls the blanket which he has borrowed from the cabin up to his shoulder so that his skin doesn't shiver in the night, and closes his eyes.

Now he's finished his last song and he drops from the branch and sets off through the highway among the leaves to find some gorilla company, something for dinner. Let him go.

9

Jane Porter when she steps up to the camera is an entirely different proposition. Equally complicated, of course.

For a start she's not a natural blonde. The world in those postwar years was in love with blondes – Anita Eckberg, Jayne Mansfield, and, *the blonde goddess*, Marilyn Monroe – if you wanted to be a player you had to be blonde. Furthermore, lovely Marilyn was all woman. Compared with the stick-figures sold to us as sex objects these days, she was fat. And Jane was built on the Monroe model and had curves you had to steer around or come off the road. But we don't see her that way. I've talked to modern kids about how they see Jane Porter and they have her looking pretty much like them, slim and shallow-chested. They put her in their clothes, they have her navel showing – as did Marilyn, of course. Marilyn however is trapped in the millions of pictures taken of her at that time and so we see her on video and wonder what the big deal was. A big lump of country girl, sure, and storytelling eyes. Ah, don't get me started – Marilyn looked as every woman should and I won't hear another word on the subject.

But she is fixed in time. Jane Porter on the other hand is reinvented for every generation. They see Jane with Tarzan and he's this beautiful hunk and she's a babe, and that's the way everyone wants to see it.

Plus Jane had brains.

She was American, a California girl, an entomologist, and her journey towards Tarzan started in San Francisco, where she boarded an ocean liner, the *Stella Maris*, bound for Sydney and due to pass through Vancouver, Hawaii, Fiji, and Auckland on its way. She was twenty-three years old and intended to study the world's largest insect, the giant cave weta, *Deinacrida heteracantha*, which lived at that time in three separate colonies on the northern island of New Zealand. It was 1953.

In the years that followed, Jane was shrewd in the manner in which she managed her place in the market. She was careful not to overexpose herself. She knew that what she had was in essence a bit part in a mythology. This was, I think, a good place to be. It set her above her fellows, it gave her a certain cachet, and we all like to have that on our side. However, it also gave her a life. Tarzan himself was the centre of the mythology and you could say that he gained the most from it. But he also had to live inside it. In the end he was of the opinion that he was its victim. This never happened to Jane Porter. She was no one's victim.

Eventually she wrote an autobiography, *My Wild Heart**, in which, as I say, she presented herself shrewdly, and in that book she described the *Stella*'s voyage as uneventful – the great ship "plunging through the waves". Her language is throughout the language of passion – clever, I think. She knew her claim to fame was that she found this wild thing in the back of beyond, this animal hunk, and went with him to his

---

* *My Wild Heart – how it led me to Tarzan and other astonishing discoveries*, by Jane Porter, Anchor Books, N.Y., 1965

lair and did it with him. The world likes to imagine them lying there together on their bed of grasses, unable to speak to one another, but fucking wildly. She knows that. The truth? The world is not interested in the truth.

And so she was able to have her life and eat it too?

She disembarked at Auckland, caught the slow train down the northern island to Wellington, found a cheap hotel, and set up a visit to the entomology department of the national museum – this is the forerunner of the now world-famous Te Papa, in those days it was called the Dominion Museum. Here she encountered Dr Stimpson Utley who had catalogued and carded more beetles than was wise and whose knowledge of the insect world had been gained, as all such knowledge must be, on his knees with a magnifying glass and a specimen bottle. He could tell her everything, he said, so why would a creature in her shape wish to go alone out into the scary bush – here he exhibited his left forearm, which had a hunk missing, a friendly nip from a weta exercising its jaws before the camphor did its job. Wouldn't she rather just come round for dinner?

His maps however were detailed and she was on her way out of his office within three hours, a record, promising to return the next day for tactical advice and a canteen lunch. This she postponed, indefinitely as it turned out. Instead she bought a supply of dried food and three new Penguin paperbacks – orange-and-white covers, with formal black lettering. Nineteen-fifties Wellington struck her as a canteen-lunch town, grey-faced people with their heads down, pressing along the sidewalks into a chill wind – while waiting for her railcar she took a taxi round the bays and saw however that the harbour was "grand enough to welcome Odysseus . . . The little houses falling down the hillsides, the pockets of shadow and light, the suddenness of everything. The gulls crying made me think that the little settlement had lost its mother."

A railcar on a branch line took her north again to a frontier town called Masterton, where she saw no earthly reason to linger. In fact her desire was to hurry. It was as though this journey of hers had at every moment to be pushed ahead with, in case she faltered, and became a mere sightseer. The local bus carried her to the coast. She spent a night in something called the Marine Hotel, near Castlepoint, visited the Castle Rock, climbed to the lighthouse. Drank sweet cold beer in the garden bar. The hotel bed was rock-hard and had biting things, she was tempted to go for her collection bottle.

She was careful not to tell inquirers what she was doing. The local people found her exotic, though there had been Americans in the country during the war, and wished to protect her from what they understood to be a nature, both human and animal, that was too vigorous, too rude for a pretty little thing like her. So she took to saying she was an artist here to make sketches of the coast and finally managed to get a ride, twenty miles of gravel road, up the coast with the mailman, who, at the end of the gravel, had to be firmly instructed not to wait for her at this time the next day. And no search parties, please.

Then finally she was leaving the world behind.

She trudged north above the high water mark, cross-referencing Dr Utley's maps with the Lands and Survey one-inch-to-the-mile, pausing on huge bleached driftwood logs to rest her legs. In fact, each map made the other seem wrong. Utley had hand-drawn his and she was confused about which pencil line related to which trig point on the survey sheet. In the end she walked for three days, was confronted by a heaving piece of sea that need swimming or skirting, and turned inland. Anyway, the gulls were driving her nuts.

Not a soul for miles.

With her watch she took readings from the sun and told

herself that she knew what she was doing. At nightfall her camp was made within the sound of the sea – she could hear breakers in the distance when she woke to add another stick to the fire. Of course there were no wolves in this country, a scientist like her knew this, that howling was just the wind blowing through the holes in her soul.

Up at first light, and inland.

The bush was tough to move through if you didn't find a trail, Utley had warned her of this and so she searched diligently, parting thick handfuls of leaves and peering. No trail. It was tiring to have to keep pressing all the time, and she had always hated climbing. The bush plucked at her clothes. Up, down, through valleys, tramp, tramp, through streams, looking always for sign, for scratchings – wetas like to leave territorial markings on tree trunks. She wasn't afraid, no, her heart was tough and she revelled in the challenge. Pity about the rain, though.

On the third morning she finally found a decent trail and made better progress. The coastal ranges were well behind her now and she could see, when she paused on a ridge, the shoulders of the land, poking up through the tailings of mist, heaving, green. It was sweet country, "so fresh-made," she wrote, "it was still dripping. I licked the droplets from a broad leaf, and rambled on. Every now and then I would remember why I was here and search for weta sign. But this was an earthly Paradise and I was the first white woman to have trod it."

It was in this mood, her eyes somewhat heavy with dew, that at the end of the fourth day she stepped into what looked like a friendly clearing and found she was surrounded by gorillas.

"There was a terrible rustling in the undergrowth. Something immensely solid and dark came at me, turned aside, tore at the vegetation, then disappeared. I was frankly terrified, and ran. I saw a huge, apelike shape – black eyes burning. Its hands beat upon its chest. I saw its large white teeth. I ran back down the path, saw a likely tree, and climbed it."

Silence.

There she stayed, thinking carefully. She had always known that the first encounter with the wetas was going to be risky. After the first encounter, well, you knew they were there and took precautions – as long as you were still alive. But this had been part of her plan, to survive and come back with photographs – "the first lady! Alone and beautiful she faced them!" – that would make her reputation. So she was prepared for challenge. But not great apes.

The chest-beating, she realised when her heart settled, and the vegetation-tearing – these things she recognised from Zoo II as gorilla behaviour, and knew she had stumbled upon a real scientific discovery. If only she could survive.

Meanwhile she stayed in the tree.

Tarzan was brooding over an image of the Grand Coulee Dam, a smooth arc that curved away into the photographic distance, so moulded and full of intent, when Jimpi burst through the doorway of the cabin and clutched his arm.

Jimpi didn't like the cabin and had rarely disturbed him there. The gorilla was so serious. He took Tarzan's arm and held it and looked into his eyes. Who knows what passed between them? But Tarzan put down his book and went with him.

What was that long smooth thing that curved across the page? As they swung their way down the supplejack highway, Jimpi turning back to make sure he was coming, Tarzan had that image with him, that knowledge of the world of intent and design. He was also accompanied by some words which had been in the air while he was reading – he sang them as he travelled.

You are
My star
The one that I see first
I feel that I might burst
In the night
Like fireworks
In the night . . .

It was dusk and the bush was smothered in a warm, late autumn light. Jane Porter had come in autumn, knowing that wetas were less active then, fat from summer, getting ready to settle deep into their caves. But wetas were no longer uppermost in her thoughts. Now she was putting her brain on the rack, trying to recall what she knew about gorillas. Shy, retiring creatures – this phrase had been repeated in all the literature. They don't attack. The dominant male, the *silverback* – finding this word gave her comfort – makes a mock charge, and . . . ah, now she had it! There were nine stages of aggressive display before anything actually happened. Just like the stages of alert that the President works through with the A-bomb, and the point was the same, to avoid an explosion. Then, while you were cowering in shock, the silverback silently led the group away to safety. So. With any luck she might now be alone.

She waited half an hour. Silence. Cautiously, she descended.

Nothing could be seen or heard. There was her backpack, where she'd slung it at the foot of the tree. Down she went – the crackling of a few sticks was unavoidable. But she couldn't hear anything moving. Retrieving the pack, settling it on her back, she gradually became aware that she was not alone.

She crouched, assumed a submissive posture, and turned as slowly as she could manage. There, in the shadow of a low branch, was a gorilla. Not the silverback, this one was smaller. Then she noticed there was a pair of feet beside it. Human feet, she recognised them instantly, deep brown and rather dirty. Ah-ha. She had been on the lookout for this – the native people of this land. A Maori warrior. "Hello," she said clearly. "I'm Jane Porter. I'm an American."

Well, this was the 1950s and Americans believed that they held a special place under the sun.

Her impression was that the gorilla had been showing her to this Maori – his mission complete, the gorilla backed away. Then, from the shadows, a creature stepped. He was not a Maori. He was a man, one glance told her that. A good-looking man. "Tall, dark and handsome – there's no denying that I instantly said this to myself." He stood upright, his spear at his side, a piece of greenstone hanging in the middle of his well-formed chest, and seemed to study her.

Tarzan's gaze was, yes, studious. Quite simply, he had never seen anything like it. Slowly, the recognition formed in him that this thing belonged to the world depicted in his books. The coverings on its body, the thing on its back, these were from the world of design. But there was something different, something he couldn't figure. For one thing, it spoke. It moved its mouth and shaped sounds came out – sounds that belonged to the world that his songs came from. It was alive. It was covered. But that wasn't it.

Boldly, he crossed the distance between them and took hold of the creature by its arm.

Jane Porter was cursing herself for being so slow. Now she was in the grip – quite a fierce grip – of this man and was being scrutinised by him. Such burning eyes. Looking at everything, everything. No, he was not a Maori, she was sure of that, his skin and features bore no resemblance to the pictures in the books she had studied before she left – for one thing, he had no facial tattoo. She'd spoken to him, but he hadn't responded – her impression was that he didn't understand English. But English was the language in New Zealand. Now his attention was focused on her boots and while he peered down at them his grip relaxed – she wrenched herself free and began to run.

Effortlessly he ran beside her.

She stopped – she wanted to get into her pack, there was a bowie knife in there. But she didn't think it was his intention to harm her. The most powerful sense she had was of his curiosity. His plain, frank astonishment.

Tarzan was overwhelmed by a confusing mixture of emotions. This was one of his own kind! That fact he grasped, and he was overwhelmed by it. It was nothing short of a miracle. It was the biggest event ever. And yet there was something strange, an emotion he hadn't anticipated. Well, everything was strange. It had different colouring than he had expected – blue eyes, blonde hair, pale skin. It was not hairy. In fact it was very smooth. But that wasn't it.

Jane was somewhat curious herself. She squatted on the track, trying to undo the buckles of the backpack, and the man squatted before her. Man? He was about eighteen, she judged, but he was a man – this was no boy. Covered in scars and dirt, and with wild, dust-streaked hair. He had made no sound with his lips. It was his eyes that were doing all the talking. He was squatting there, their eyes met each other and, from twenty centimetres, he gazed into her face. Only a lover ever looks into us from this distance, or someone who means us harm, it was shockingly intimate, but again he had hold of her arm and she was unable to move. The intensity of his study was frightening – the astonishment of it, and also another quality. A hunger, perhaps, though that is a mere appetite. A yearning.

Jane Porter was no shrinking violet. And she began to grasp what was happening. "This thing that was holding me had never seen another of its species. It was finding itself in me. It held me and I could sense the recognition that was taking place. I smiled at it. Slowly, like a sunrise, a warmth began to spread across its face."

Jane's first smile was forced but then came a real smile. And without warning a connection was made between them. Looking into each other's eyes – he still held her arm, but less tightly – from an intimate distance, they explored this connection. Seeing you affects me. Pleases me. I like looking at you – a powerful thing.

Now Tarzan became curious about details and he began plucking at the stuff that was covering her.

Jane was wearing a khaki bush shirt with the sleeves rolled up and he slid his finger inside her sleeve and lifted the material – he bent his head, trying to see up in there. She let him do this. His cheek was close to her arm and she realised he was smelling her. Not sniffing, but drinking her up. It was an intrusive sensation, completely intimate, and she was embarrassed. Amazingly, he seemed to sense this, and drew back.

How alert he was, listening, registering – here in his world in the wilds.

But his curiosity was not reduced and she saw now that he was staring at her throat – at the opening of her shirt. His hand reached out. "Quite delicately, he touched me. His finger lifted my shirt, he fumbled at the button. I pushed his hand away – no one likes a fumbler. Then I undid the button myself."

It was dusk. She unbuttoned her shirt, opened it, lifted it away from herself, then sat down to work on her boots. He peered, closely attentive to the workings of the laces. She was aware of his face, down there in the action, but didn't allow herself to be put off. Her boots were removed, her socks. He gazed at her feet – her toenails still had pink varnish, somewhat chipped. His fingernail picked at it. Then he looked up at her again and his gaze said clearly: more. She stood and unbuttoned her trousers. Down they slid. Off came the white underthings. Then she stood there, as naked as he was, in the dusky light, at the base of the tree she had climbed, at the edge of a small clearing, while the little birds looped and dived in the evening sky.

Taking her clothes off for him, what was she thinking? She hardly knew the guy.

Many have asked this, and then without pausing to let her get a word in, pronounced her loose or worse. Her own words on the subject are, naturally, arranged to promote the highest of motives – "I thought this creature's circumstances to be of such a unique order that special conditions applied. Besides, what harm was done?" By this logic the bank is always robbed by philanthropists. But she did not strip for him. This is what the lurid books suggest and they are simply wrong. She took her clothes off and stood there in the interests of science. Of humanity. Though, knowing Jane Porter, she would most likely have made the best of herself.

If so, it would have been lost on Tarzan. He was studying her, head to one side, trying to see. What was this? He walked around her in circles, "and he made a noise – 'Huh.' At first I took it as a comment and was offended. But it was as though he was trying to say something. Then he came closer and he put his hand on me."

Yes, but exactly where did he put his hand? She doesn't say.

"He touched me. From his fingers I felt a spark jump across a gap. It reminded me of the Michelangelo on the ceiling of the Sistine Chapel, where God's finger reaches out and everything that is holy is transmitted. Knowledge of yourself, of what you are – this is what Tarzan's fingers were bringing to him, and in that quiet clearing, a miracle of sorts was taking place. I allowed him to stroke my skin."

Tarzan kneeled. His fingers were touching, yes, but his other senses were working harder. His nose drew her into him. Inside him, a fundamental piece of knowledge about human beings – that men like women – was registering, and this knowledge was making him dizzy. He laid his cheek against her thigh. His nostrils widened and his head swam.

"Then I saw that he was becoming aroused and everything changed."

It did for Tarzan, too. He felt her fingers in his hair, she was pulling him upwards, and he rose without resistance and stood beside her. She found that having his face close to hers was not any easier than having it at her thigh. His expression was alarming – nostrils flared, eyes gazing upon her completely without reserve. She needed to control the situation. And so she took him in hand.

"His mouth opened in surprise. He leaned back. I supported him. A groan escaped from his lips. I had been in the back seat of a few automobiles and I knew how this went. The normal thing happened and he was relieved, so that we could concentrate on other matters." Such a sensible account of such commonsense behaviour.

And perhaps that's how it really was. But Tarzan has quite another memory. He was already overloaded in the new-sensations department – then, while he is standing beside her, the most astonishing creature he has ever seen administers a lightning bolt, which flashes up his spine and explodes inside his head. For Tarzan the bush he had lived in all his life suddenly became the backdrop to a moment. Caught in his memory: the way the light was, slanted and soft; the way the rough bark of the tree left a print upon her skin. He can hear the birds, see them flying loops in the dusky air, and the rich smell of the leaf-mould, the smell of the manuka flowers. Ah, the smell of everything, the smell of her in particular, it washes over him and his eyes glaze. And Jane Porter standing there close beside him without her clothes, faintly pink and, in his mind, simply swollen with feeling, with the knowledge of the glory of her body, and with what lay within it. Glowing. Years later, when he understands how humans keep themselves hidden inside their garments, how careful they are about where they put their hands, he replays this moment and he is simply astonished at what took place.

Quickly she dressed, put her pack back on and started up the trail. She had no clue where she was going but she knew from the automobiles that she had to keep control and so she led them away from that dangerous moment, left it behind. Tarzan followed, like a dog forced to walk after too much dog-dinner, staggering a little, but determined not to lose her. In this fashion they walked into the middle of the clearing where the gorillas had established themselves for the night.

Some of their humpies were better now. Jimpi in particular had done his best to imitate Tarzan's improved methods of construction and his structures were often still more or less standing a week after he had built them. So what Jane saw was a ragged collection of leafy teepees, a shanty town, arranged loosely in a circle. From the shanties the gorillas came forth to greet her.

She was afraid. For one thing, they did not approach her directly as Tarzan had done. There was an encircling, an angular approach, that meant she didn't know where to look if she was to keep them all in her eye. In a few moments she was surrounded. They were large creatures. Carefully she shifted her pack until it was in front of her, it felt more protective there and, reaching inside, drew the long bowie knife from its sheath. Now the silverback came and he was immense – slow moving, then coming fast. Heavy shoulders supporting the ridged, tufted head, that rose so alarmingly at the back – as though he'd had a head injury. Dark eyes so buried in the dark face, obviously seeing – but seeing what? Nervously, she glanced around – where was the man?

Tarzan was close, but somewhat behind her – well, it was she who had led them here. Then suddenly he was a gorilla again. Without knowing how he knew, he understood that Kerchak was going to be angry. The smells! And so it proved – Kerchak reared up, he roared, he bared his teeth and slapped his palms upon the drums of his chest. He was not interested in Jane. It was Tarzan, another male, with the smell of sex on him, that was causing the trouble and so it seemed to Jane that Tarzan hid behind her. In fact he knew that Kerchak was not interested in Jane and was using her to dodge behind, but she felt betrayed. Then, seeing that everyone was distracted, she took her chance, and ran.

Tarzan ran too. Kerchak chased them – a bouncing, four-legged run that was surprisingly fast. He was gaining. Tarzan grasped Jane Porter, swept her off her feet, carried her as he had carried Kala, in his arms. She was nothing to him, a feather. Along the back of his launch-branch he ran – Kerchak close behind – seized the vine that he kept anchored there and, without hesitation, simply launched them into space.

Jane, looking down and seeing the treetops passing beneath her, hearing the roaring of Kerchak, rampant but stranded on the fallen trunk behind them, feeling herself held firmly by those muscular arms, had no choice but to hope that this was all some astonishing adventure, a sequence from a childhood book, which would all come out right in the end.

They were flying through the air.

He swung her from vine to vine and quite quickly they put several kilometres between themselves and the gorillas. "What red-blooded woman could fail to be moved by this? You have seen the photos of him yourself – he is handsome. He is dark.

He is immensely strong. He carried me as though I was a child. My hand inside my backpack still clutched my knife, but that was only a reflex, an irrelevant detail. Beneath us the tree tops passed, a blur, and the air rushed over my cheeks and tugged at my hair. I was completely safe – and I was flying. This man, this creature of the wild, was flying me away to his lair. It was positively mythological."

Finally, Tarzan judged that they had come far enough, and he slid down a thick vine and set her upon the ground. They were in thick bush and the dusk was on the point of turning to night. When she listened, there were rustlings, small disturbances in the undergrowth. And in the distance, larger sounds. Jane was afraid. She knew there were wetas hereabouts, and now gorillas – what else? She looked for her protector, the man who had swung her so effortlessly and thrillingly through the trees and found him squatted, not far away, beside the track, peacefully taking a crap.

He inspected the results, straightened himself, then reached a hand out towards her. So that he wouldn't take hold of just any part of her, she offered a hand in return and so, joined by their fingers, they moved off. He was leading and she had no choice, she felt, but to follow.

After a stiff climb they emerged from the bush cover and came out into an open space. It was now almost completely dark, no moon, but the stars were casting their cold light. Tarzan stopped and crouched, so Jane crouched too. He was silent. She saw him turn and knew he was looking at her – his serious face was close to hers, but in the darkness she couldn't be sure of what he was thinking. He seemed to be listening, so she listened too. And, faintly, she heard a tune and words she knew. *In the cool cool cool of the evening, tell 'em I'll be there* . . .

Civilisation.

"I was divided clean in half. On the one hand, here was a

sound that told me I was about to find shelter, safety among my own kind. But on the other . . . My heart had already been torn from its sleepy hollow by this astounding creature who lived in his wild world like a noble ancestor of our race. He seemed to be all instinct, all body-knowledge, an animal and yet more manly than any man I had met. To be flown through the trees in his arms – there are not many times in life we can say the word 'thrilling' and mean it. But he had induced a shiver in me, a trembling excitement. Now, to know that civilisation was going to reclaim me was, to at least half of my heart, a large disappointment."

Nevertheless she followed him towards the source of the sound.

Tarzan had a notion in his head. If he could bring her together with the cabin, these two elements would fuse and make a new thing – suddenly all the bits of him would fit together. He had to restrain himself from dragging her. But gorilla society, despite boisterous moments, is essentially gentle and considerate. He knew how to treat a lady. So, hand in hand, they crossed the open space and he presented her with the wooden structure.

That simple house-shape from a child's drawing stood before Jane and she wept to see it. Tarzan was puzzled. Was she unhappy? He patted her – his serious face peering from behind its fringe of hair. Jane smiled, a big brave one, to show that he shouldn't concern himself. She wiped her eyes and pointed to the cabin.

Have you ever tried to teach a child to understand the meaning of your pointing finger? A dog? Our established gestures of communication, they are all learned, and slowly. Tarzan was eighteen and had never been offered so much as a thumbs-up. He looked at her extended finger as though it was offered for his inspection.

So she led the way. Tarzan accompanied her closely, their

shoulders bumped. He wasn't used to how you walked next to a woman. She let him reach for the doorhandle.

Now the song was *Tennessee Waltz*.

It was dark inside and, frankly, it stank. Feral. She didn't want to go in. But Tarzan had and, alone outside in the dark, she felt she had to follow. He was squatting on the floor and she came close beside him and lowered herself. The stink wasn't so bad once you became hardened to it. "So this is where the wild man had his lair. A disappointment – I had wanted to sleep under the stars, in his arms, if possible. But instinctively I knew that this place was not his creation, that he had only borrowed it. So where was the owner?"

She figured, if there was a radio there must be power, and so she patted the walls for a light switch. Nothing. Then she remembered being in old cabins like this one and felt around in the air. Aha, a string to pull. And, voila!

Tarzan was, she saw, startled. Terrified, even – he gazed up at the bulb and, if she was honest with herself, she would have to say he cowered. So she switched the light off – which made him jump. In the sudden darkness, neither of them could see, it seemed dangerous, so she switched it on again. This was too much for Tarzan and he bolted for the door. She saw him out there, looking back. A look of determination came upon his features and he made himself return. Slowly – it was clearly an act of will. Then, with his feet firmly planted on the earth outside, he peered round the jamb, and watched as she inspected the place.

"Now here was a mystery. Though it was in wild disorder, this was a cute little cottage. It had a basin mounted on a stand for washing, with a pipe to lead the waste away. A ewer. A bookshelf with a small library. Crockery, cutlery, Manchester – the place was a regular department store. Well, a five-and-dime, maybe. Beds even. But one of the beds was occupied – by a skeleton."

To Jane the place contained a mystery, but nothing in it was in itself mysterious. Toothbrushes, she knew about those. But then she saw that Tarzan was watching her with a fierce curiosity. She grasped what was needed. So, like a home demonstrator, she began to make familiar use of the things around her. Taking water from the canteen in her pack, she cleaned her teeth over the basin. Ugh, the toothbrush was old and stiff, and tasted of salt. She took the folding chair from where it was propped in a corner, unfolded it and sat down. She reached for a book and pretended to read. She unlatched the window and opened it so that the air in the fusty cabin might be refreshed.

Tarzan entered, crossed to the window, started down at the latch. He lifted the slim brass bar from its little nipple and immediately the window fell shut upon his fingers. "Agh," he said, and sucked them. Where had that hand been? So dirty! The blow clearly hurt him, but he was too fascinated to really care. She came to stand beside him and showed him how the latch and bar worked. Carefully, he opened and shut the window until he had it mastered. "Huh," he said.

Then she taught him how to use the light switch.

Tarzan stood on the folding chair, his nose an inch from the brightly burning bulb. How could he stand so close? But he could not tear himself away. Never had anything been so intense – not even the sun. Inside the glass there was a kind of life. Nothing that moved. Tiny, angry life. Tarzan felt the driveshaft humming within him. The world was doing press-ups, atoms were spinning. His face was moist with sweat, the bulb threw off a fair heat when you were eyeball to eyeball with it. When he came down he was dazzled, utterly blinded.

Jane took his arm, helped him. Was his weakness physical? His eyes told her that inside his head equations were being tackled. Worlds being assembled. They sat on the stoop, their shadows one shadow inside the oblong of light which folded out from the doorway. Moths, attracted, flew in from every corner of the bush and the night air was filled with aerobatic displays. An opossum screamed. Gradually Tarzan's eyesight returned. He had no comprehension whatsoever of how the thin piece of string, the bulb, and the light it gave might be connected. It was the same with the radio, now playing *Shrimp Boats* – how the wires and knobs produced the sound was simply not a thing to be understood. To not understand, this produced a painful longing. But what he did grasp, increasingly, was the vast promise of his species. Somewhere, in the place where Jane Porter had come from, all the pictures in his books came alive and were lived among. She would go back there, he would go with her, and he would see everything and understand. This was such a happy thought. She was leaning her head against his shoulder, stroking his back, every now and then glancing into his face to see how he was faring. The companionability of this was very pleasing to him – like being with Jimpi, but better. When the radio gave him the cue, he began to sing.

On a green hill
On a blue day . . .

The moths flew loops, made spirals. An owl slid across the long box of light in the clearing and was gone. Looking up, seeing the tall dark shapes of the encircling trees, and then the stars, Jane Porter was astonished by what she was feeling – a giddy, wild-headed sensation of falling and being held at the same time. Tarzan sang like a dream. There is of course something sappy about singing. Musical movies, where the star suddenly breaks into song, and, by a fountain, begins in broad daylight to throw his arms and voice about, this is an insult to our higher powers. Every musical that Hollywood eventually pasted him into was a joke to Tarzan – the memory of them is painful, they show them on cable and everybody gets a laugh. But music is nevertheless a primal force. The scientists say that our earliest ancestors, guys who literally didn't have a pot to piss in, made music – I read this recently. And to hear music being made live, up close, it's a powerful thing. No CD can capture it. Have you ever sat near a piano and heard someone actually play Schubert? Beside Jane on the stoop the big fellow had music, he had music within him, he had no artifice, only the style that came with the songs he had learned, pure, from the radio. His innocence could restore those corny old songs to their original meaning. And he had a voice. When he threw his head back in the night and let those love songs come out of him, Jane Porter fell. She fell down, down, and just kept on falling.

Your brown eyes
Looked my way
And told me
With a smile
That you were gone.

Yes, out there in the wild, miles from home, Jane Porter was gone.

There were many pages in the Tarzan songbook and that night Jane Porter was offered a connoisseur's selection. Her head was settled upon his shoulder. Her arm went inside his and held his bicep. The stars rained down out of the sky, everything was falling. These two young people, both in their own way under the influence of the strongest forces on the planet, and so far from anything that might say, resist – what could go wrong?

Well, nearly everything. For a start, there was a skeleton on the one bed, and an unnerving sense that somehow a skeleton was missing from the other. The wetas, in their caves, were woken by the singing, suddenly coming now from the place where they had once gathered to dance to the hum – the memory caused restlessness, and a young weta was trampled, and eaten. The great silverback Kerchak, rolling in his humpy two kilometres to the north, was restless and uttered groaning sounds which were of ill omen.

But it was autumn, the liquids in the pipes inside the wetas were already beginning to slow, to thicken. After a brief frenzy, they sank back to sleep. The silverback simply couldn't be bothered. Sleep, sleep, that's what the dark is meant to bring.

And so there remained only the problem of the skeleton.

This was no problem, to Tarzan. He collected the set of poles he kept, with his slasher, in the crotch of a branch at the edge of the clearing, and set about gathering grasses.

Jane watched through a haze. She didn't think. Instead, cloudy images, great shapes wheeled in her mind. Her skin shivered.

But she was a practical girl. She had seen this man take a trackside defecation, had smelled his cabin. She knew that up close he was not any fragrant advertisement for Old Spice. She fetched down the whiskey bottle and, keeping her eyes on him, administered herself several slugs of cowpoke measure. Phew! Her eyes watered, her throat burned. She felt like a forty-niner preparing to have a tooth pulled.

Was she a virgin? Her book is coy upon this point. "I was familiar with men. But in fact they were only boys – older than him, but skilled mainly in bragging and rushing about. Tarzan had the same thing they had, but in them it was tiny, lost inside. With him it was all he was. Pure nature. I had a place in me where I wanted that. I knew that my soul, once touched by it, would be changed forever."

Of course most who pronounced upon the book quoted that passage, but took care to omit the last sentence. They said Jane was determined to sell her body, then tried to get her to pose nude. But Jane, one of life's winners, courted the tabloid crowd and rode their leering all the way to the bank – with her clothes on.

Meanwhile Tarzan had pulled all the grass he needed and was wondering what to do next. He looked, perhaps puzzled, at Jane.

Then what happened?

His interviews refuse all details on this night in particular, and his "autobiography" is all details that its author enjoyed providing. "I seized her, carried her to my lair and threw her down." But Tarzan never said that, and he didn't do it. At that time Tarzan had no concept of lovemaking. Within the gorilla group Kerchak handled the duties which ensured the continuance of the Kerchak line – this was only natural, like eating leaves. There was an issue here, Tarzan did understand that, which lay at the heart of gorilla society and made rings of power, of dominance around the big guy. There were fights, and times when you could not go near the females. Tarzan knew the rules. And he was dimly aware: the younger male gorillas had something on their minds. But he wasn't part of that.

He had simply made her a bed.

And so it was she who turned out the light. She took him by the hand. She hadn't cleaned her teeth, the whiskey was thick on her tongue. She was carrying her pack but not because she wanted her nightie. The bowie knife – for misunderstandings – it was there if needed. Her heart was beating so hard she was afraid she would pass out. His hand was perfectly happy to be in hers, he came with her quite easily.

They were at the edge of the clearing and Tarzan's leafy structure could be made out, just a little way in, standing in the shadows of the bush. She knelt at its entrance and put her hand out to see what he had placed on the ground. Grasses, bracken – it smelled fresh, herby.

10

Tarzan of the Gorillas and Jane Porter of California, USA, swung through the jungle. They sailed through the air at the end of every vine there was. They had many a mile to go before they rested that night.

The grasses, when Jane put her hand on them, were slightly damp. The night was, if anything, cool rather than hot. She wished for a covering and thought of her blanket, tightly rolled at the bottom of her pack. But that was, she knew, more a desire for modesty, to be covered from the world, than a need for warmth. That's the point, Jane, she told herself – there is no world. And, for the second time that day, she began to unbutton her shirt.

    Tarzan kneeled close before her to watch. Her clothes were complicated, you could study the fastenings and layers – his curiosity was sticking out a mile. The shapes of her, the warm, womanly smell, these items he collected and stored away, and went on staring. Then his hand came out and he touched her skin.

    Jane took him in her arms, drew him close and pressed her lips to his. What was she doing? What did she want? Tarzan didn't understand. But she showed him. She wanted to put a part of her body into his – her tongue came into his mouth. It was an astonishing sensation, to have someone inside you where you couldn't see, where you could only feel. To concentrate on the feelings. To feel the aliveness, the intent of another person as they moved sensitive parts, the lips, the inside of the mouth, the tongue, against yours, and all the time their face was so close, the sides of your noses were rubbing, and you were breathing and they were breathing – yes, this was a fascinating and pleasing thing. To pause and look at each other, and then to start again, and, at such proximity, to manage the tilt of your face, such complicated manoeuvrings, the docking of a space station, and the way your mouth was, and to think all the time of what the other might be wanting, this was new. It was, he thought, the thing that was at the centre of all the pictures in his books. There was such sweetness in it, a tenderness that he had never known.

Also something fierce.

Jane had him lie down on the bed of grasses, which smelled like everything that could never be put in a jar – like a great dewy morning hillside that has been stirred up by your bare feet – and she brought their bodies together.

It was difficult, in the morning, to concentrate on anything else. There was no reason not to touch each other, no timetable, no train to catch. And no one watching.

Between times, they began upon the complicated endeavour called communication.

It began with water. Jane Porter had some in the canteen in her pack but not much. She drank a little, then offered it to him. He sniffed the metal of it, sniffed the bunghole at its top, looked down in there with one eye. Listened to the splashing sound. Then he tried to do what she had done. But, when he swigged, the metal hole of the canteen banged against his teeth, the liquid ran too fast and flooded his mouth and came pouring out his nose. When his coughing fit was over, she helped him to try again. He drank. Then she pointed to what was left in the canteen – not much after he'd spilled most of it – and made her eyes wide, made the looking-for face. Mugging for him there in the morning sunlight of the clearing – Tarzan frowning. "Water," she said, then said it again, louder this time. She pointed to the canteen, splashed its contents, said, "Water?" with a question mark and searched the landscape. Did it again and again. Smiled at him, encouragingly. Big Tarzan working away at her meaning. She made water-noises with her mouth – he thought she wanted to kiss again and so there was a delay. Then she went back to it. She made a panting face that said she was thirsty. She tried to imagine how a gorilla might drink – she got it wrong, but bringing a cupped hand to your lips was in fact how *he* drank – and she saw a look of recognition spreading slowly across his features. Possible recognition. That word with *cognition* in it, it means successfully to think. But the *re* part means to find again something you had before. This was bigger than recognition – Tarzan had never had a thought of this order. He was unsure, yet very excited. Staring into her face, checking, he took her hand and began to lead her. She was saying, "Yes, yes," and "Water?" and "Where water?" and then saying "Yes! Yes!" Off they went, running. She wasn't used to running naked, it was difficult, and their progress was marked by him pausing to search her face for confirmation – just like a dog. It's easy to think of him at this time as a dog – fetch the paper – good boy! People treated him like that all his life. Reporters especially. "While I watched he expertly popped the top from a Coke, poured a glass and drank – and never spilled a drop." To think of this still gives me pains from the anger.

And then they came to the stream. *Voilà!* from Tarzan this time, and more "Yes! Yes!" from Jane. She kissed him and clapped her hands. Tarzan knew about clapping, he clapped too, and then he slapped his chest. He was so proud! Also he was modest – she saw this, there was a kind of restraint in him, it was the first time she'd noticed it. He closed his pride down a little. So serious, in some ways – it made her think.

Side by side they knelt by the stream and lifted the water to their mouths. Surprisingly, he drank with some delicacy. She was deeply moved by this – had noticed it during the night, how careful he was with her. This didn't mean she wasn't sore, but that was, she acknowledged, her fault, for encouraging him so hard. But he had a great command of his body. It took only one face-full from the canteen for him to learn. Anything physical, this he was quickly the master of.

Then she had him stand in the water and she washed him. If she had only thought to bring some soap, she had a small bar in her pack, and there had also been a yellowed, cracked piece drying on the washstand at the cabin. She would have liked, too, to have her clothes, and to have brought the canteen to fill. But the wild rush down the path, of them learning to do something together – to transfer a thought from one to the other, this had been too headlong for clothes.

He washed her in return, somewhat wide-eyed, then watched as she squatted nearby to pee. His scrutiny of bodily matters was embarrassing, but she understood that he had to learn everything she did.

A dragonfly, moving above the water's surface like a length of shivering ink, came and went and came again, and they watched it together. *Uropetala carovei*, she thought, and recalled, distantly, that in fact she was here to study the wetas. Later, Jane, she told herself, and she tried to ask him what his word for this slim flying thing was but he had no word. He seemed to have capture of everything by looking at it, and to know what was behind him just as well as what was in front. His body was a sensory organ, he read the world with it.

Every time she looked, his curiosity was rigid.

She led him back up the path. She was hungry. The sun was up, there were birds flying, a local breeze gave a slight chill to the skin. She wished he would hold her companionably, drape his arm across her shoulders, but he didn't seem to know this kind of behaviour. Inwardly, she began to fight a small frown – a small voice which said, What can it ever be with this guy? The thought was, she discovered, painful to her. Then, as they walked, he spoke. Quite clearly he said, "Water."

She turned and threw her arms around him. She made a number of what she thought of as do-it-again gestures but he would not. He simply smiled back into her face, obviously pleased with his achievement.

"Water" – this set her thinking.

At the humpy she dressed. Tarzan, having no clothes to put on, sat close by and watched. And this was companionable. He was utterly fascinated by her – never had she thought that buckling her belt could be the finale to a performance. Okay: sexed, washed, dressed, what she needed now was breakfast. She set off for the cabin, Tarzan following. On a shelf she had seen two cans, and there was a can opener – before his eyes, she screwed the butterfly shape in a circle around their tops and lifted their lids.

Tarzan had his face in close. These metal things, he had investigated them, but they had had no door. The butterfly shape had turned in his hand but suggested no purpose. Now he saw that everything in the cabin was good for something, that sometimes you put one thing with another thing and then a surprise happened. He stared round at the cabin – so what went with what?

She used a fork, and held a slice of tinned peach, dripping with syrup, near his mouth.

So sweet! He chewed a bit, took it out of his mouth to look at it, put it back in. Kept chewing and sucking at his teeth until every vestige of the taste was gone. Noisily, he licked his lips. Then he looked so steadily at the can that she had to laugh. He looked at her face and got it: she liked his desire! They both laughed at him – though she could see that laughing was something he was also learning how to do. She forked him out another piece. On a thought, she fetched down an enamel cup, poured an inch of syrup and passed it to him. He held it, looking down into it. Then, remembering how you had had to manage the canteen, he lifted the cup and drank. This was a major piece of thinking and Jane's little voice said, He's a quick learner. And she was happy all over her body.

. . . walking down the aisle with six feet of barefoot muscle by your side . . .

Tarzan was astonished by the syrup. As sweet as . . . And his memory gave him an image of Kala – her milk as sweet as this. He gazed at Jane with Kala on his mind and was happy and sad and wanted to suckle from her all at the same time. He took the can and fork from her, speared a curved smile of gold and fed her in return.

After breakfast he showed her his books.

They sat side by side on the stoop and while he watched she turned the pages. As she looked at the pictures, her idea of him became more complicated. She saw how he had sat here, with the radio for company and sung over these images and gone deep into them, deeper perhaps, she realised, than she would ever go. She wondered, what was it like to see a picture of an airplane and never see the real thing? The Empire State, what was a skyscraper to him? She had the idea that he had made a religion of these images, that he worshipped something in them.

He held her head between his hands and looked into her eyes. She was happy about this. She wanted him to study all he could. She felt he was going into her head, like a miner, and bringing something back. She let him.

He presented her with the eggbeater and the slasher and the spade. She did her best to demonstrate the use of these things – the eggbeater, without eggs, was a challenge. She beat some water for him, but he couldn't see a point to this activity and she couldn't tell him. This caused confusion. To see him thinking, and not getting anywhere, it pained Jane. Quickly they moved on to the spade, where, under instruction, he dug a successful hole, seeming not to mind that his feet were bare, and then squatted to study it. Again, she could see him thinking, So now you have a hole in the ground – and? How could she explain gardening? But, as she watched his gaze went over the objects in the cabin, appraising each thing anew, trying to imagine the world in which it was used.

He led her up the path and showed her his windmill. She had known that something like this would be around somewhere, otherwise the radio and light would not have worked, but to see it here, on its own, its vanes turning slowly against the blue Pacific sky, was a shock. Who had built the cabin, lugged all this stuff up here? The skeleton, presumably. But why? And what was he to the gorilla-man?

Who was this guy anyway?

She sat him on the stoop and, using a pair of scissors from the implement drawer, cut his hair. There was no question about it, he was handsome. He shook his head, clearly pleased with its new lightness. The scissors were a source of wonder. He picked up tufts of hair from the dirt and snipped. So satisfying. She saw that he kept the scissors, didn't want to relinquish them. He needed a belt, pockets. However, it was altogether pleasing to look at him there without any clothing. Bodies were not available for scrutiny in 1953, especially male ones. Especially naked male ones. What a piece of work is a man. Isn't the human skin, for example, something special. The smoothness of it, the suppleness, the callused horniness. The way it repairs holes you make in it, the ways the repairs keep a trace of your carelessness, little lines that tell such stories. Especially the skin of the face. The stories round the eyes, the stories in the creases. He had, she noticed, a frown line.

And so their first morning passed. In the afternoon the sky became clouded and sleepy heat filled the clearing. Tired, they went to the humpy. She knelt before him and began upon what was at only its third occurrence already a ritual – the unbuttoning of her shirt. He watched from so short a distance that he seemed actually to be involved. Indeed his hand came out to help and she allowed him to fumble with a button.

She successfully conveyed that they should be more gentle with each other.

They lay entwined in the bed of grasses and dozed. A rabbit came into the clearing, came up close to sniff at them – Jane Porter woke up and so did Tarzan. She saw him deciding whether he should catch it, and she thought he might too – rabbit dinner was a shared idea. But instead they sank back and let the long shadows of the trees turn across the afternoon.

She kneeled in front of him and looked into his eyes. He didn't mind this at all, though he was distracted by her breasts. So fine – but she made him look at her. She touched her chest with her finger and said, "Jane."

The wait was so long. Watching his face, she had the impression of his mind flying like an arrow, low across desert sands, featureless mile after mile, nothing but sand, and then, finally, there was the exact thing he was looking for. "Jane," he said back.

Oh, she loved him for that. But did she pause to think where this was headed? Did it occur to her not to civilise him? Where does language lead us but knowledge, and where does knowledge lead us? I was going to say, to sorrow, but that would be glib, I think. He was that most happy of things, an innocent mind, and we always think of innocence as being happy, but is it? In my book it's knowledge that pleases us. The toddler who figures that the fridge door swings shut by itself spends all day opening it – not because he can, but because he enjoys knowing what will happen next. We think that knowledge destroys us by letting us know we are going to die, but Tarzan knew he was going to die. In his world things died on a daily basis. It's the idea that it might be possible not to die which is the most corrupting – stops you from getting on with things.

But was she thinking ahead? Imagining an improved Tarzan, the Mark II with Special Features? Her book comments that she "saw wonderful possibilities in him, that he might bring together the physical mastery of its body that an animal has with the power of a mind undistracted by the false promises of the material world." Perhaps – but this sentence contains, I think, some rote thinking left in her from her pinko period. Like lots of liberal people of that time, Jane liked to say she was a Communist. It was good for shock value. But when the time came, Communist or no, she showed a fine command of how to make a commodity of herself.

And what did Tarzan think he was doing, just saying "Jane" like that? What were words to him? Wasn't he just a throbbing hunk of meat? The gorillas made sounds, had sounds for a few important things, but the idea of talk, of a conversation? They did converse, but by way of glances, by subtly altering the physical distance they were from each other, the angle they were at. A group of gorillas is a web of power lines – but is that talk?

He made the sound, "Jane," flat, uninflected, and frowned. What did it mean? The thing in front of him pointed to itself again, its finger touched between the bumps that he liked and made that particular noise again. And looked at him. So he made the noise back, "Jane," because he could see that she liked it.

Over and over.

Then she pointed her finger at him and gave him the question face.

He looked at where her finger was pointing – he had learned this – and there was his length of greenstone. He gave it to her, but she laid it aside. Then she pointed again.

Over and over and over. "Jane." Point. "Jane." Again. And the question face. This must be what it's like, she thought, to mother a baby. It wasn't something that appealed. Jane Porter never gave birth to a child.

A small lizard appeared at the edge of her vision, moving among the leaf-mould. She saw now that he had been aware of it for some time, that he wanted to catch it. Is that what he thought about all day? She held his face between her hands, held his attention. He stared back into her eyes so fiercely that she had to steel herself to hold his gaze. Then his mouth opened and he said, "Huh."

Jane's turn to stare. "Huh." She pointed to herself and said, "Jane," and then to him and said, "Huh?"

Tarzan felt the driveshaft spinning inside him. He felt full of power. He knew what she wanted! Pulling himself up a little he pointed his hand to his chest, said, "Huh," then pointed to her and said, "Huh" again. And sat back, hugely pleased with himself.

"No, no – I'm Jane. Jane." She stabbed him in the chest and said, "Huh?"

This seemed to pain him. Yes, the big face was filled with a huge sadness. It was as though she'd disappointed him. He frowned so deeply, she let him go – let him catch the lizard, refused it when he offered it to her, watched him eat it. Raw lizard, it wasn't on the menu at Antoine's.

First catch your rabbit – he speared one and presented it to her. So how do you dress the thing? She knew what he would do, she didn't want to see the raw meat go in and so, in a sequence that astonished him, she skinned it, gutted it, thrust a stick up it, lit a fire with matches from her pack, and sat to turn it over the flames. Tarzan's face in everything she did. Frowning. Astonished. He recognised that quality he had identified, of intent, of design. She'd had a plan and followed it. Then his first taste of cooked meat – he spat it out. But she ate her portion calmly and so he tried again.

They sat by the fire and watched the flames. Tarzan not getting too close, she noticed. Long shafts of sun slanting across the clearing began to signal that night would come – she started thinking ahead. Maybe the cabin would be good to sleep in? Though she loved the bed of grasses. Now she caught his eye and saw that he was waiting. She looked at him. His finger went to his chest. "Tarzan," he said.

Then they were kneeling beside the fire, knees touching, face to face, and she said, pointing, "You Tarzan, me Jane."

The tape recorder in Tarzan's head was always a good one and so, pointing first to himself and then to her he was able to say, "You Tarzan, me Jane."

"Yes, darling," she said, "you clever thing," and she held his large, warm head in her hands and kissed him.

And so they spent several happy days wandering the valley, naming things. "Tree," she would say, slapping its trunk, and then hear him back as he recited. At first this was enough. He had a good ear and a good memory, and was also somehow a blank page for her to write her language on. Plus maybe he had a sense of syntax from the songs. He had never understood their words, but do babies get it when we say to our loved one across the breakfast table, "Of course, language is just a set of sounds that we have common understandings about." Of course they get it – the babies, I mean. They learn and learn, they eat language and become masters of grammar. Go to a foreign country and listen to the locals on the underground. They're all doing it, conjugating verbs like crazy, never a fault, and did they study? Well, a little maybe, but nothing like you with your phrase books and your Teach Yourselfs. You have to eat a language, drink it, have it reconfigure your cells. Jane realised this and she began to talk to him, whole sentences, about what she saw in his world, things he could relate to. But she also gave him long monologues about the pictures in his books. Here they are then on the stoop of the cabin, heads close together, and as her finger traces the outline of the Empire State Building in the silvery black-and-white photograph she is saying, ". . . and these little guys here are windows, they let in the light, for the worker-bees, all heads down in there, tails up, chasing the big moolah."

"Moolah," he said.

In fact, Jane realised, she had not the slightest clue what took place inside the Empire State.

And the big guy? What was happening inside him? Who can say. His head was being flooded, new sensations, new ideas came pouring in and they slopped around inside him like a gumbo. What was she trying to tell him? He had images of the driveshaft, turning, turning, and repeatedly he took her back up to the windmill, made her climb it, look inside. He would stare at the long shaft and then turn to her face, as though asking for comment. Well, she explained, as best she could, it carries the turning of the vanes down into, what was the thing called? – the alternator, and then inside there . . . Oh, electricity, it was hard. But as she struggled to remember her high school physics she grasped that this was not what he was asking her. What then? Tarzan couldn't tell her. The picture of the Empire State, for some reason he always stopped at it, and so she worked to divine what he was seeing. He sensed a driveshaft there too, down through its length, something spinning.

And then there was the language of his body. He had always worn it without noticing, maybe a little disappointed that it didn't have the hairy covering of the gorillas. But it was just there, like the air you were swimming in. And now it was something to be looked at comparatively – his and hers. And its parts. His actual foot, for example, she was stroking it, feeling its shape and so it was as though he for the first time grasped its form. It's a primal thing, the human foot – as Rodin pointed out, nothing else has exactly that shape. So well-designed, when you think of it. Jane was thinking that way. She had by now become a little deranged – she acknowledged this. I don't think there's harm in recording the fact, it would happen to the best of us, to be so suddenly liberated from your clothes, your customs, your fellow judges. To have so many big questions thrown in your face. To be so caressed. To have yourself so unreservedly worshipped: all of this is likely to unhinge, and Jane saw that it was happening, recognised it – went with it. So down at the end of his body she was crooning, "Foot, foot, beautiful thing, look at it, lovely bones inside their skin. Everywhere you've trod is written here, all the paths you've trod are remembered in here so that you can run so fast – your foot is so clever, darling." Tarzan looked along the length of himself and tried to understand. This creature that had come into his world. Her body. Her talking. What she knew. What she made him. He was never going to let go of her.

His feelings too were working within him. He'd had feelings before, been aware of them – at Kala's death, for instance. But these sudden waterfalls, this water moving underground – huge things were shifting inside him. And so he made his traditional response, and sang.

He didn't sing to her, that wasn't an idea he understood. He sang as though he was making something – he had the shape of the tune in his head and he designed his throat so that it came out right. Here he is then, up on a rock, his hands still, no need to emote, his face still, letting his voice fall on the valley. Listening to the shape that was in him come out right. I guess he was aware that she heard him. I think we could admit that. But he didn't understand that his voice was good. He was just singing. His big head thrown back, the dark forelock down over one eye. Big shoulders, big chest, big biceps – how many singers really are big guys? Sinatra was a little rat, John Lennon had the chest of a teaspoon, how many rounds would Michael Jackson go with anyone you care to name? It's not manly to sing, that's what we think, you need to be paid millions to compensate for that. For millions, okay. But for pleasure? For self-expression? I once knew a fisherman, this was in Greece, named Thanasis, he would take me out in his boat, he laid two miles of nets and out in the middle of a bay in the Med he would turn the engine off, go up to the bow, brace his feet, and for a couple of hours would pull the boat through the water, retrieving his catch. Fifteen years of that – the guy had a chest like a building. He was this wide. Then one day I saw him walking down a backstreet, fisherman's cap on his head, dirt road, chickens in the trees – Greece is such a sweet old place – and he was singing. Not too loud, but no self-conscious little warble either. Some Greek song, incomprehensible. He saw me there, sitting on a stone fence, and he waved. He walked towards me. But he didn't stop singing. Singing and smiling at the same time, it's a clever feat. He went right on past. I sat there and cried. This was in the early 1980s, I'd been dead maybe five years. Memories, I guess.

So here, just like the fisherman Thanasis, is Tarzan, and he's up on his rock and behind his head big puffy clouds are sailing past. Hawks are making slow circles in the air, fantails are tumbling, and there's warm sunlight on the cascade of leaves, a chorus of cicadas. Jane Porter at his feet. As I said, he throws his body open. He has a lot to let out. He's got no reason to hold back – holding back is not a concept he's familiar with. A statue of a man, then, a statue with finer feelings, a big figure, who has everything he needs and yet is still yearning for something but he can't imagine what. Listen to him sing, it's naked emotion.

It's *Somewhere Over the Rainbow.*

Go on, you know the words.

11

In this fashion an extended sequence of happy days followed. Tarzan on a crash course, Jane letting herself go just a little off the rails.

But not too far. Jane Porter always knew where the main highway was and she was always precisely as far on it or off it as she chose. I hope that we all understand by now that I admire the woman. She went after what she wanted in life and got it. Presented by chance with an extraordinary circumstance, she opened herself to it without reserve. Kicked in the teeth, she picked herself up, regrouped, then set about exploiting her assets with consummate skill. She died pretty and wealthy and famous. My kind of girl.

And so, there in the bushworld, the time came when she took a page from her notebook, sat down beside him and began to draw. Tarzan had seen paper before, but he asked to see the pencil, and examined it. It had a strong smell, very pleasing. And then there seemed to be something inside it – Jane was making something come out the pointed tip of it onto the paper. He found he could do this too but his markings didn't have the shape of hers. She was making something.

A weta.

"Yes," he said.

She had her clothes on and was wearing the pack, though most of its contents were now stored in the cabin. As they swung through the trees, the pack often snagged, she wished she'd left it behind. But she needed her camera, binoculars, notebooks – and the bowie knife. She wished she could have left her heart behind too, it was beating so hard it was difficult to think. It wasn't just the thrill of being held by strong arms as you sailed through the air – she felt so secure she found she could even look down in wonder at the bush passing below – but the knowledge that at every moment he was bringing her closer to the monstrous creatures which for so long had crawled in her imagination.

There are people who love insects. In entomology departments you can find guys who have stick insects perched on their shoulders like parrots, guys who chase flies round their kitchens so as to offer them as love-tokens to something that rears up on some of its legs. Jane Porter was not one of these. The creepy-crawlies made her skin creep, always had. But she had been driven by her mother, a towering force, to stop shrinking away from the scuttling thing in the corner, to get down there and eyeball it. "Know thine enemy, kiddo." So Jane had been presented each birthday with books which detailed the doings and beings of everything from the katydid to the stag beetle. She sat in bed, covers up to her chin, and shuddered as she read. Her interest grew – well, how can you fail to be gripped by, say, the habits of the male *xylocoris*? These guys, which are part of the bedbug family, will sometimes rape another of their species – another male. The rapist's sperm will finish up in the vas deferens of the victim so that, the next time the victim jumps a female, the rapist's sperm goes in with the victim's, and then who knows who the daddy is? Fascinating! The mites which lived on her skin – young Jane would explain at pyjama parties how she had studied them under the microscope her mother had given her. She would describe the roach as the most likely survivor of an A-bomb blast – "Imagine a planet crawling with roaches!" This gave her a certain cachet, and cachet was a quality that Jane always sought to have. Call it an instinct for the spotlight.

But gradually she became fascinated – obsessed! – by the Komodo dragon of the insect world, its T-Rex. She first saw a giant cave weta in a book called *Astonishing Creatures and Amazing Facts,* and would not rest from pestering her mother until they had driven down to Kalted's Insect Kingdom in Fresno, a drive of some 500 miles, where they studied an example mounted on a plinth and murkily lit in the best Chamber of Horrors tradition. Norman Kalted had worked in the theatre and he knew that no one would come to see specimens in jars or read insect textbooks. They wanted to be threatened, filled with loathing – and for loathing Norman was their man. He had a tape of slobbering and crunching sounds which he played while you looked at the big weta and then a somewhat unscientific roar which suddenly boomed forth at the end of each walk-through, along with a large set of legs which descended, twitching, from a dark spot in the ceiling the moment he thought anyone susceptible might not be watching. The screams kept him in business. But Jane, on her visit, was strangely calm. She knew that this thing, rearing on its plinth, meant nothing, dead – she just wanted to have an impression of it to hold in her head while she read. She told Norman that the roar was bogus. He agreed, soothingly, that this was not the actual roar of the giant cave weta which was actually still living now, you know, down there in little New Zealand, but rather was an orchestral piece designed to indicate the majesty and power of these awesome creatures –

and was a knowledgeable girl like herself looking for work during the summer vacation?

Thus she entered what one of her colleagues in the department called "the bug business" – though it was no business, there were no jobs in the field, well, none that a sane person would want, but she had her obsession to play out, and so now here she was, in the arms of this fearless jungle man, hurtling towards a date with loathing and threat.

Being in the air was one thing. But when Tarzan descended to the floor of the bushland and indicated that they would be walking from now on, her dread increased. To be down at their level . . .

Tarzan retrieved his slasher and spears from the tree where, earlier, he'd cached them and – cautiously, she noticed – began to lead them down a well-established track. What came through here, that made such an open way? Something big. Now he crouched and indicated that she should study the pattern in the dirt. There, as clear as a leaf, was a large spiky-edged print. Were those claw-marks on the tree trunk? She got out her camera and tried to take a photograph but her hands were shaking.

Tarzan, she could see, was utterly concentrated. The frown line stood out on his forehead. Now she realised that he was receiving messages – collecting the signals of the bush. Then swiftly he turned, lifted her off her feet and began to retreat along the track. She twisted in his arms, trying to look back, but could see nothing. How serious was this? He paused, had her clamber onto his shoulders, then climbed.

He stationed her on a thick branch, thirty feet above the ground. She had a hand-hold. She saw him studying her to see if she was okay. Not her so much as her position. "I'm okay," she whispered.

Squatting there beside her on the branch, he put his hand over her mouth and said, "No." There was such tender concern in his face when he looked at her. Right then, with her heart in such a mess, she touched his cheek, stroked it. But he was all business. He had her turn and see where the vine would carry them, to a lone tree across on the far side of a ravine.

"Yes," she whispered.

Then he climbed down again.

On the ground he went back up the trail, pausing often to glance at her. She waved that she was okay. But that wasn't his concern. He wanted to be sure she could see him. Then he urinated carefully in the middle of the track. He stabbed a spear into the ground at an angle so that any passing creature would bump into it. He whacked the slasher against the trunk of a tree – it made a loud "thock." The piece of bark that fell he rubbed on his thigh, then held under his armpit. He laid it carefully on the track. His head had a design in it – this knowledge made him dizzy. But he stuck to his plan. When everything was ready he threw his head back and gave his yell. The challenging, triumphant Tarzan call. "Aaaaaahahieahieahieaa . . ."

Up on the branch, Jane gave a shiver. How did she come to be here, perched in a New Zealand tree, with this creature that did its business like that while she was watching, that could utter a sound like that – waiting for a weta?

Now he was beside her again, squatting on the branch, feet side by side, balancing like a bird. He had planned this encounter with such forethought. Carefully she took her hand from her supporting handhold and instead gripped his shoulder. She liked the intent feel of him. He inclined his head so that his cheek touched her fingers. Then he went back to watching.

Here they came.

At first all she heard was a rustling – but such a rustling. The bushes twitched, then a weta, the size of an Afghan hound, came into view, antennae dancing. Jane was disappointed – this was less than half as big as the specimen she'd seen at Kalted's. But what a thing it was, all shiny plates and jagged legs. A bulbous, spiny, half-blind thing, fumbling its way. It came to the spear – touched it with an antenna – jumped back. Its head began to go from side to side. She saw that its jaws were working. It lowered its muzzle to the trail, suddenly reared back and held its head aloft. Slime came sliding from its mouth-parts. Then its thorax began to pulse, causing the plates on its sides to emit a loud click.

Again, Tarzan's hand came to cover her mouth.

Now the noises from up the trail grew more intense and from the bushes emerged a huge bull weta, darker than the small one, bigger than Kalted's, and frighteningly alive. Jane's fingers dug into Tarzan's shoulder. Down in her stomach she was fighting to control her revulsion at this thing. "It's only a natural emanation of the planet" – this was her mother, but Jane was a long way from home now. Beside her, Tarzan was immobile. She realised that, like the target shooter who stops his heart before he squeezes the trigger, Tarzan had stilled something within himself, was sending out no signals. Whereas she – she was broadcasting to the nation. She tried to be cool, and watch like a scientist.

Now there were many wetas and they were wrestling with the spear, shaking it angrily, fighting for it, crunching it in their jaws. They scrabbled at the blaze he had made in the tree trunk – a weta tried, clumsily, to climb, then fell back. The track where Tarzan had made his moisture they tore up, frenzied.

The smaller dog-weta had gone on down the line and now it came back and apparently reported that there was nothing to be found. This seemed to increase the frenzy and within moments all that heaving, spiny mass had fallen on it. Its legs came off, its body parts were dismembered. This was a soundless process. Slime flowed from working jaws and made the track slippery, the great bodies slithered and clawed. A distinctive odour arose – weta slime smells like rotting pears – and Jane couldn't take it. Her stomach heaved and from her mouth vomit flowed and fell to the ground. The nearest weta raised its head.

Then they were far away. She found she was lying on a mossy bank and he was bringing her water in his cupped hands.

Kneeling at her feet, Tarzan studied her. With her covering of clothes it wasn't so easy to read her signals, but he tried. He sensed the shame in her, the distress at the loss of control, though he could not have named these things. He came close and settled his head on her stomach, his ear. He could hear gurgling in there, and feel a flutter. Through the opening of her shirt he could smell her clearly. There was fear.

And it was true. As though it was a book she had to keep reading until she had learned, Jane was recognising all over again that she was out in the wild, that this was no zoo with fences. There were gorillas here, pigs with tusks, wetas, and who knew what else. The darkness beneath the trees, for the first time she was really afraid of what it might contain.

The wildness within him also.

She became watchful and thoughtful, and less adventurous. So now the initiative in their pairing swung back to Tarzan. He looked at her and wondered what she might want, and tried to provide it for her.

Her first need, he decided, was more water, and he led her to the waterfall. Tarzan always washed after a weta encounter and so he undressed her and drew her under the falling curtain. She had left her cake of soap here and now they soaped each other thoroughly then stood beneath the plunging weight. It slapped their skins, tugged at their hair. She made a rushing cave of her mouth. She worked on her feet and hands, wishing she had a stiff brush.

Tarzan wasn't keen on soap, for him it removed a layer of information. But he allowed himself to be washed, because she wished it, and because it did feel pleasant – on his skin and also her washing of him. He felt she was shaping him, somehow. He felt different. He wasn't sure he liked it. But it was as though through this strangeness he was finding a way to go through the mirror. There was someone inside him, he sensed that. Who was it?

After the waterfall he took her downstream and had her sit quietly while he fished for crawdads. He offered her one and she held it, curling in her fingers and wondered: could she manage this on an empty stomach? He was crunching into his. No – and she indicated that she wished to gather and keep her share. She took off her shirt and had him deposit the catch there. Then she said, "Cabin."

Behind her on the trail Tarzan studied the workings of her brassiere.

Under his attentive gaze she used a precious match to kindle a fire – wasn't he supposed to know how to rub a stick between his hands? – and set a pot to boil. She was determined he would learn to like cooked food. There was no way they could sit at a public table anywhere in America if he was going to insist on raw lizard. Tarzan thought that cooking food spoiled it. It seemed to him like a variation upon rotting it, its flavour twisted in a manner that was perverse. But he was doing what she wanted. Not out of obedience. He was after that thing which might live in him.

Their next observation of the wetas was more successful. She knew what to expect. This time, up on the branch above the track, she had her camera out. Of course this was no pocket-sized digital window – rather a book-sized black flat thing with unfolding bellows. But she got her back against the tree trunk, steadied herself. The loud clicks alerted the wetas to the fact that their souls were being stolen, they rose in protest and Tarzan had to swing Jane away to safety. But not before she had obtained what is now considered a classic picture of a rampant *heteracantha* in the wild, a full-grown male clawing its way up the trunk towards her. She held her nerve, eyeballed him through the viewfinder. The film wasn't fast enough to capture the drool, there's a blur descending from the jaws, but that only makes the picture seem more lifelike and vivid.

Then they were away and the bush had hidden them again. The successful weta study had at least in part reawoken in Jane her civilised self. She was more purposeful than she had been in the first days – her studies, which would be used in the outside world, seemed to bring that world here. She began to wear her clothes more often. She tried to think what he would do for clothes. Obviously, any small-town charity store would provide him with an outfit. But until then it was a matter of getting his parts covered. If he arrived in the world in a fringe of leaves, how would that go?

For Tarzan the weta trips were a mystery. Jane had explained to him at length why she wanted to bother the loathsome monsters but his grasp of the language, particularly when it included words like *university* and *science*, simply wasn't good enough for him to follow. He tried to picture her in her world. The photograph in his book with the mass of people worried him, he would look for her in it and everyone in the crowd would stare back at him. He studied every face – obviously this was all the people in the world – and couldn't find her.

He had asked her – successfully indicated to her – that he wanted to know what the place she lived in was like. She drew him pictures of her sorority hall and talked to them. "So this is Alice's bed and this is my bed. Bed, you know, like in the cabin. You know bed, Tarzan, in the cabin there. Bed, come on, I'll show you – and she gets in under the blankets, like this."

Tarzan didn't like the sound of Alice, Jane had to draw him a picture of Alice all alone and Tarzan and Jane together before he stopped growling.

But Jane also made sure that they didn't spend all the non-weta time in the teach-Tarzan mode. She had recognised that when she took him from this place they would never come back. Well, obviously, they could return, as though on holiday, but Tarzan would be changed. He might take his city clothes off. But he would never again be a creature, and she would never again be as alone with him as she was now. So she made sure there were long periods when he led them, when she merely followed, and saw his world as only he was able to show it. She signalled the start of such times by getting undressed. This sometimes sent a mixed message, but the results of that were nothing to complain about, quite the opposite, and then they could always go back to the Discovery Channel, time was not a problem in the big valley. So they would ramble, sometimes holding hands, Adam and Eve in the wild garden. Except that Eve packed a camera.

Tarzan singing quietly. *No one can take away from me, this feeling, that I was lost, and now am found . . .*

Thus it was that Jane was able to take good pictures of the gorillas in their natural habitat and it was from these, along with the weta snaps, that she made her first money. Her pictures of Tarzan were, of course, what made the real dough, but that was later. The gorillas had the same reaction to the camera as the wetas – they didn't like the click.

Tarzan's approach to the group was cautious. He'd been completely out of contact with them for maybe ten days and in that time he had become a man. His movements were different, his smell was changed forever. And he had her with him. The pale thing.

He chose the afternoon rest-time to introduce her – everyone was more likely to be easy-going on a full stomach. He had warned her, "Go gorilla. Go gorillas," and looked to see if she understood. Yes, please. And so they proceeded slowly, Jane just behind, her hand on his bare back, somewhat crouched, along a skin-scratching path that worked its way round the side of a low hill. As the bush began to thin out Tarzan paused to carefully snap a twig. Then, in a low voice, he began to sing *How Much is that Doggie in the Window?*

Jane giggled, it was just so cute to hear that particular song sung so tenderly, but Tarzan put his hand over her mouth. Stinky hand, where had it been? But she had firmly put such thoughts from her mind, at the same time as her sense of smell, all of her senses, had been opening. Her instincts seemed these days like a source of hard knowledge that she could draw on. So, instincts, what was going to happen here with the gorillas?

To the accompaniment now of *Some Enchanted Evening* they emerged into the fringe of the clearing, and immediately he had them sink into the tall grasses. There they stayed, Tarzan crooning, she could sense a definite come-hither tone in his voice, and staying most of her movements with his hand. No, don't unfold the camera. No, don't cuddle me. She felt embarrassed, she was going to meet her boyfriend's family and she was naked. Cautiously, he raised his head, and then indicated that she could look too. He was rustling the grass with one hand. At first there wasn't much to see, just a hairy black leg poking up out of the grasses like a periscope, its toes twitching. She imagined some lolling creature, on its back, belly full of sun. Rather jolly. Then something began to approach. Tarzan she saw was watching out sharply.

Tarzan was watching out for Kerchak. Kerchak would think that if Tarzan had taken a mate, that was a good reason for him to go off and be on his own with her. So no problem.

But if Kerchak decided that he wanted her for himself . . . Or merely that Tarzan shouldn't have her . . . Tarzan did have his slasher. But to strike Kerchak with it – this made a horrible picture.

In fact the first visitor was Jimpi. He was huge. Jane couldn't believe how big he was, up close, two-thirds the size of a man. If that doesn't sound big, remember that he was in her face. The wild is smaller on TV. Jimpi came straight up to them, and sat down five feet away – just out of arm's length. His back was somewhat turned towards them. Casually he gazed skyward as though he might be keeping track of an interesting cloud. Then, rotating slowly on his shoulders, his great head came round and the dark eyes were looking at them. Jane was behind Tarzan. Her heart was pounding so hard that it hurt. Tarzan seemed absolutely relaxed. He continued to sing. Jimpi rocked, moved as though he was going to just wander away, then without notice of any kind simply reversed his movement and came on to invade their space. He took hold of Tarzan, his shoulder, then rubbed his head on Tarzan's chest, so that Tarzan was singing right into his ear. Jimpi patted Tarzan, slap, slap on his back with the dark hairy hands. His head came up and he was looking over Tarzan's shoulder, right into Jane's eyes.

Such judgement.

Jane worked to control herself. The gorilla seemed to have taken possession of Tarzan and so she felt she couldn't touch him, she was scared this might be provocative. So she squatted, naked, alone, just behind him and tried to gaze back calmly. But Jimpi knew. His eyes, so steady, so impenetrably dark, were incurious about her, because he was already in complete cognisance of the facts where she was concerned. Tarzan leaned back and this drew Jimpi more or less on top of him, and closer – Jimpi extended a hand. So Jane mirrored the gesture and then she and the gorilla were touching. He needed moisturiser, his skin was dry, dusty. His hard nails pressed into the flesh of her palm, relaxed, pressed again – checking she was real. He scrambled over Tarzan as though he was so much dirty laundry and settled beside Jane, and there he stayed. Just seeing what she was like to be beside.

And so the encounter progressed. Jane felt, as they moved slowly out into the middle of the group, that her heart was a bad motor, whacking away in there, sending out shudders which disturbed everyone, but they all seemed nonchalant to the point of rudeness. One by one they came over, cosied up to her, got a sense of her. The pink thing. Weren't too excited. She came in for a certain amount of fondling, of pawing – all of this done with a surprising delicacy.

Then Kerchak. This was different. Perhaps because Jimpi came first, Kerchak made a point of taking absolutely no notice. Tarzan didn't want to force the issue. He wasn't going up to the big boss and saying, Get a load of my girl. No. But he wanted to make sure that Kerchak had any reaction he was going to have now, on a full belly, at his ease, in the sunshine.

Every time Tarzan managed to flick a glance his way, Kerchak's back was turned.

Now Jane was taking photos. There were gorillas all around her and she proceeded in the most random manner to snap them as they disported themselves about the clearing – her eye somewhere over the viewfinder, her finger pressing any time it happened to find the shutter. It was hell sitting naked in the grass, she was always shifting, twitching, she wished she had a hairy hide – and a hat, the sun was fair beating down. But this was unique, she thought – to be here among them, in the pod, in the pride. She made sure she got several shots of Tarzan being gorilla-intimate – these were going to be important, she felt. His story was slowly forming in her head. She clicked and clicked, it gave her something to do. Then, in one moment, Kerchak turned, came swiftly as though he was going to pass by, turned a little more, reached and without hesitation took the camera from her.

Rocking on his knuckles, he was immense.

The brave girl in Jane rose up and she had the impulse to take the camera back. This she suppressed – she could sense Tarzan, coiled, beside her. She let her head loll, studied the little world down between her toes. A small grasshopper was on her left foot. Kerchak was looking into the thing as though he knew what it had taken. His finger she saw was not on the shutter – this would have been fun – but on the catch which opened the back of the thing. Her film was about to be spoiled. Her hand began to move up – she had to stop him. Then he lost interest and placed the thing on the ground. Closer to him than to her – it was still his. Turning his back, he rose on to his stubby legs. He was bow-legged, potbellied. But there was nothing comical in this, he cast too big a shadow for that. The back was broad, like the back of a wave, silvery-grey across the heavy shoulders. The head was elongated towards the rear, it made you think of ancestral skulls, of a rock-headed, crew-cut GI. What was in the head? He looked over his swell of shoulder, his rolling eye caught her – took in Tarzan – and that gaze was fierce. Then he was giving them his back again and, flexing himself, he began to beat his chest. Large flat hands, slapping rhythmically, sending a unique signal. Pattering out.

That was all. He sank to his haunches, gave a sigh, then ambled away into the shade.

Jane was impressed by his dignity, and by his skill in asserting himself without provoking a confrontation. She saw who Tarzan's role model had been.

But in the days that followed, they stayed apart from the gorillas. Tarzan chose this. Jane would have joined them, she understood a unique opportunity when she saw one, but she also saw that, if he was to leave the bush with her, they had work to do.

She made a point of documenting Tarzan. So here he stands beside a wild pig he has just speared, one bloody foot on its bloody neck. Jane's shadow is there in the foreground of the photograph – probably this was no accident. Here he is on a rock, singing. Here he swings from a vine – she had to make him do this for her, he found her purpose hard to understand. Again, the image is blurred. Now he has his head back, giving his call. She didn't bother to censor these photographs, the newspapers themselves could do that – a blur that might have been a frond. She photographed the cabin and the windmill, tried to take pictures of the bush, but she didn't really have the camera for that. Black-and-white film, it takes a master to penetrate the shadows. But, blurred or overexposed, these photographs are the cornerstone of the Tarzan Archive today and have been reproduced many millions of times. As she foresaw.

Night in the cabin. The rain had begun falling in the early afternoon and was now making a steady beat on the roof.

Once she had photographed it she moved the skeleton outside and set about making the cabin a place of refuge. The nights in the humpy were the stuff of dreams but one night of being dripped on was enough for her – so stiff in the morning. Now she had Tarzan bring the grasses in from the humpy, because they were drier than anything they were going to find at this stage of the day. She unrolled her sleeping bag on the bed frame and spread it as a cover. She pushed things into corners, hung her damp shirt over the back of a chair.

A handful of wild flowers standing in the empty peach tin.

Tarzan sat in the doorway, watching closely. Though he didn't speak, he was troubled by what she was doing –

changing things. He didn't know what a museum was, nevertheless for him that's what the cabin had been, an historic site, where you could never move anything because then it could no longer be read true. But then her every movement was teaching him something. Also, he saw how much nicer she'd made the place. A woman's touch was not an idea he was familiar with either, but something inside him, an ache, was diminished, and he looked on Jane as she busied herself as though she was a fabulous treasure.

So was Tarzan in love with Jane? Well, since it was the subject of pretty well every song he knew, the word was a thousand times familiar to him, but not its meaning. Of course he had looked so deep into her eyes – surely that counted for something? Yes, but. And their bodies ... Yes, yes, but. The feeling that she was his and his alone? The sense that he would go with her, because he knew inside himself now that he had to go somewhere, and where was there but where she would take him? The sense that now when he looked, part of what he saw was what she was teaching him to see? Teacher, saviour, angel – you might wash the feet of such a person. Have you ever actually got down there on the floor with a basin and made sure the water is warm enough? The human foot is a lovely thing when held, not as accommodating as a hand, nevertheless up close it seems extremely personal, unique, and washing and drying a foot, done with care, takes time – there's all those toes to get between. Loretta washed my feet one day and this was how I knew that it would be acceptable for a man of my age to touch her. But it was returning the favour that really meant something to me. That told me what I was feeling. Of course there's the religious echo too but I never give any thought to that. What I'm interested in is the way the knee bones press your skin into the carpet – you lift your trouser leg and the weave has been imprinted. You see other things down at that level, all the baby dirt and the dust where the mites live, you've given up your lofty perspective, but in fact the main item is the foot, hovering there in the air and your face up so close that you can see how the practical side of things, the sole, is hardened from its everyday contact with reality and how this hard part is fitted to the uppermost side, which, comparatively, is more or less ornament and often has the texture of milk, the pale, soft cool of it, with the lines spreading from the instep, like a river delta, out to the promontories of the toes. I have dried between Loretta's toes. Our little Theo bites my ankles. She will most probably be wherever it is I am, for the next times, anyway. She definitely appears in my will and she is I am sure hanging out for the freedom and opportunity she will inherit on the day that I finally can no longer move my chemicals around. She would be a fool if she wasn't. But does that mean she loves me? Does any of it mean I love her? Love was a hole that Tarzan had to try and fill with his voice – Eve Kersting told him this when he was being trained to move an audience. But was there a hole in him where the love muscle should be? Jane came to think so.

However, that was later. Now, with the rain sounding on the roof and with that big hunk in the doorway, getting his feet rained on but not caring, and why should he, she was making a little home, and so there was a happiness in her. Women and homemaking, this is not a generalisation we're encouraged to make, nevertheless I suggest there's some truth in it – go on, think the less of me. Also, after the alarms and strangeness of her recent days, for Jane the prospect of a real bed, of walls, these things gave her comfort. Now it was her turn to sing. *Shrimp boats is acomin', their sails are in sight . . .*

They ate rice, which was strange to him, flavoured with manuka, and drank manuka tea. The use of the leaves of this tree, which the New Zealanders also call *tea-tree*, she had learned of in her preparatory reading and, for Tarzan, who for so many years lived hungry among gorillas while they complacently munched it, this was a strange kind of triumphant homecoming: This is what *we* do with manuka! Going to the fireplace, he put his nose over the pot and inhaled, as she had done. His cheeks clammy with steam, he smelled something good. He took the sensation deep into his chest. It was remarkable the way human beings – he had learned this term – did things to their food. But this was a quality he was beginning to understand more and more, that human beings changed everything they came into contact with. They made things into other things. They had a design, a shape in mind – manuka, pot, fireplace, chimney. Far away in the back of his head it may be that he wondered what shape Jane had in mind for him. But this thought was as deep buried as any question about what he might make of her, especially when here she was, all homework now done, and drawing him to her. And one more time with the buttons.

The rain beat steady on the roof, then began to beat harder. On the bed frame, on the mattress of grasses, Jane and Tarzan paused to listen. Outside in the dark, rain pelted down on the ten million leaves, burst into little streams that ran headstrong down the hillsides. Far away, the gorillas huddled, miserable, and waited for morning. Ants were flooded from their nests. In the cabin, Jane wanted to shut the door but Tarzan wouldn't have it. Being shut in made his heart pound. This worried Jane, who knew that ship's cabins were small places. Perhaps they could sleep on deck? But he would have to learn – *have to*. Meanwhile she didn't fight it. Instead she drew him to his feet and insisted that they went outside.

The rain wasn't quite what she'd imagined – colder, and the twisting ropes of it made patterns in the dark which were suggestive, scary. But she pulled him to her and kissed him hard. It was like being in the waterfall, except that the fall of the water there had the quality that you could never outlast it. This was for now. This was once only. "I understood I would never be here again," she wrote in her book. "We would be leaving all this behind." And she dragged him down and had them fuck in the mud.

Of course the humpy had its own magic and two nights later, when the ground had dried, they slept there again.

But the seasons were changing. It was appreciably cooler. The wetas, she noted in her notebook, were quieter, slower to respond to Tarzan's provocations, less aggressive – soon they would be sealing themselves in their caves, shoulder to shoulder like cows in a herd, and waiting out the winter. She imagined them packed in there – it seemed like too much energy in a confined space. Of course, woe betide the wetas who were last to wake.

She had at least two publications planned now – a paper on the wetas, and a broader, more popular study on Tarzan in his valley. To this end she had him explore further than he had ever done, to push outwards. Together, they climbed the ridgelines, went deep into the dark, tangled places of the hinterland. Everywhere she sketched, took photographs, collected specimens.

Her body was browner. Not the dark, ancient tan that lay leather upon Tarzan's skin, but she was through the worst of the sunburn and would look, she thought, upon her return as though she had been in a tropical paradise. Good.

Tarzan was in shorts. She had done a final, thorough inventory of the cabin and found an old pair of trousers, gone in the knee, which had been used for rags. She cut them down, patched a hole, and buttoned him into them. One problem solved.

Tarzan wore the shorts as though they were something he was forced to carry.

*

Jane's face, when Tarzan tried to see it, was composed of curves. The rising arc of the brow, the arch of the eyebrows, the concave, out-sloping line of her nose – retroussé, this is called. These were so unlike the shapes of his own face, or of the gorillas. On the underside of her left forearm were three moles, widely spaced, like the marks he'd seen on the pale tops of mushrooms. Tarzan saw that these marks made a triangle – he saw that pattern. This had a connection to the three poles he used to construct his humpy. He knew of three stars that stood in this arrangement in the night.

There were so many parts of her to see – so many ways of trying to see the astonishing thing that she was.

At night they studied the books, Jane talking carefully about each picture, picking out details to explain. Tarzan frowning. Jane was careful not to stroke him at these times, he was very responsive to touch. She loved to listen to him learning. It happened so fast – in sudden leaps. He had her accent, she noted.

She did not, as his "autobiography" claims, teach him to read and write. That he did himself and it took years. This book is its culmination. Nor did she eat raw meat or "encounter the noble Maori tribe who rules that land," or need to be rescued from being raped by Kerchak. This is pure fantasy, but for the rest of his life Tarzan had to live among people who took such stuff for gospel. Only a liar would say he had no benefit from such mythologising. But it hindered his struggle to find the thing inside him.

Jane discovered that the radio could be tuned and she tried new stations. Tarzan growled when she touched the knobs, but she made soothing noises and soon they were listening to talk – nasal male voices discussing the dipping of sheep, an egg-free recipe for pikelets – and assorted symphonies. Tarzan stared at the little speaker – how could so much be in there?

Then, late one night, when she had switched to long wave, "Listen to this," she said, "this is from the States!" And through the hiss and whistle they caught American voices which were full of a brash energy. So slick, she thought – it was some cornpone southern station, with jumped-up southern music. She didn't care for it, but she could see that Tarzan was fascinated and so she let the dial be. The deejay's voice came through, like jive from outer space: ". . . now do like the Dewster says and make like a bunny rabbit. Well, not exactly like a bunny rabbit, it ain't gracious to run so fast, ever'body see how white yo' tail is. Whoa, not sure where this is headed, betta get me outa here – try this, it's from the Big Boy, Arthur Crudup, this is *That's All Right* – and it is! So get yo' tail unnailed – and tell 'em Phillips sent ya! Dee-gaw!" (Looks *terrible* written down, but that really is how Dewey Phillips sounded!) Tarzan's face close by the speaker, his expression moving around as each new turn in the music came through. Jane tried to imagine what was passing behind his eyes. Clouds, a train of clouds.

He liked to have her remove every item she had on her person. The cheap ring she wore on her pinky, the shiny bangle, the necklace with the little locket, containing a tiny picture of her dad, now dead, these things he collected and placed in a neat pile. There was an order to the way he liked her to remove them – first the ring.

    He struggled to do buttons up – what exactly was the point? But quickly he was an expert at undoing them.

How can it be autumn, she wondered, and the leaves not fall? But it was definitely cooler.

12

Then they were packing and preparing to leave the valley.

They had made a last trip to the wetas, now hibernating, and, moving cautiously, crept right up to the rock wall where Tarzan had said their cave would be. Jane photographed the dung field, the bones, the marks on the bark of the trees. She put her ear to the bung of hardened slime at the cave's entrance and imagined them behind it, a mass of spines and bulbs, pulsing slowly. The smell of them in there – phew! She took a final photograph, of an antenna, like a devil's whip, lying abandoned on the ground, and then they left that place – as far as Tarzan was concerned, forever.

There were keys on a nail and Jane locked the cabin, and took them with her – this led, four years later, to the breaking of the lock and was probably responsible for the early deterioration of that place. His books she had in her backpack, along with her camera, which had captured every aspect of the valley.

She had prepared for their departure for several days – getting them to each of what she guessed were his favourite places and having him say the word *Goodbye*. Goodbye waterfall – did he understand? She also took him to the bones of the man she was now sure must be his father and had him bury them, and make a cross. Carefully, at her instruction, he tied the two sticks together. She had him select a small bone, from a finger, as it turned out, and this was carried in the backpack too.

Together they worded a note, which Jane wrote and then pinned to the door of the cabin. It's now in the Archive – faded and curling: *This cabin was built by the man whose grave may be found near the windmill. In all likelihood he is the father of Tarzan, who was raised in this valley by the gorillas. Until it is proved otherwise, the cabin and all its possessions are the property of Tarzan. You may use them but please respect them. If you have any information which may correct these facts, please mail it to Tarzan, c/- Porter, 383 Fairway, Petaluma, California, USA.*

The invitation to use the cabin was, Jane knew, at cross-purposes with locking it. She tried leaving the door unlocked. She tried leaving the note inside. In the end she left the two things to contradict themselves.

Tarzan looked at the note on the door, fluttering in the wind. So this was how those black bugs in the books worked – he had never really understood before. It was like the territory marks that the wetas made – you could say something and it kept on being said, even though you weren't there. He decided that he would learn to write.

The burying of his father's bones had an unexpected consequence. After he had lashed the two sticks together for a marker, Tarzan led them high to an isolated piece of ground, a thickly covered spur that ran down from the main ridge to come to a hillside point which hung in the air, then dropped away. It was an exposed spot, lonely, covered in low spiky thorn. There was an edge to the wind – a hawk floated slowly past. It was a hawk-wind place, tossed by updrafts – Jane shivered. But from here the whole circle of the valley could be seen. Then, down in the thorns, Tarzan showed her a small opening, elongated, and at its head there was another pair of sticks, this time held together by two screws.

Why had he never shown her this before? They squatted. Jane said, "Your mother?"

Tarzan's face didn't change. "Maybe."

"Your father carried her up here and dug a hole for her."

"Maybe."

Jane scraped at the yellow lichen that hung from the crosspiece. Her fingernail worked at the old wood. "Usually there is the person's name," she said, "and the dates." But there were no clues.

"D'you want to dig her up?"

But they left her there with the hawks and the view.

Tarzan never agreed at any time in his life that this was definitely his mother. Perhaps he hoped that somewhere she was still alive. Perhaps he wanted to keep seeing the face framed by black hair, rather than old bones. Perhaps he didn't want to interfere with his feelings for Kala. But maybe he missed something? Maybe there was something buried in there with her that might have made a connection for him? He brooded on these things for many years.

Then, when the time came, Jane Porter glanced back at the cabin in its clearing and said the goodbye words but Tarzan didn't speak. She tried to make him, she thought it was her responsibility. "There it is. Have a long look. Darling, I have photographs."

Suddenly she was not feeling quite so sure of herself, as her book explains. "I had told him what I had in mind and he had agreed. But this was like those treaties signed by the Indians – how much did they understand of phrases like, 'the lawful pursuance of civilisation's destiny'? Did Tarzan make a real choice? Not if this means he knew what he was going into. But who among us knows that, really? He was physically stronger than me, much, and could easily have resisted. In fact, if he had required me to stay I would have found it hard not to do so! My bowie knife against his hand and eye – a toothpick against Tyrannosaurus Rex. But he shouldered his slasher, put on his marching shoes, so to speak. And we hit the road."

Tarzan led them towards the gorillas and she thought that they would farewell them too. His approach again was cautious. This time they were wearing their clothes – Tarzan looked terrific in shorts, she thought. But then, when he was sure of the position of the group, he climbed a tree. She looked up and saw he was retrieving something. He put it in his pocket – the first time she had seen him do this. Then he settled himself on a high branch and seemed to gaze out over the valley.

She looked up into the branches and saw him there, then considered the way he had ascended – without a sign to her. And so she stayed where she was. Sat down and waited, amid the small sounds of the bush. He was at least an hour.

What Tarzan had collected, up there alone, was a bone of Kala's body, from the small number that had snagged and remained. He was aware now of this bone in his pocket. It was new to him, this feeling for things. The way that things could be given names, and the way that the names had muscles in them, and the way that those muscles pulled at you. It was new to sit on a branch with clothes on, too new, and so he took the shorts off, a difficult manoeuvre when you're up a tree, and dropped them down through the branches. He saw the woman down there pick them up. He saw the top of her hair, he hadn't seen this before, the way her sun-coloured hair was divided down the middle of her head, the way it seemed to grow outwards from a point towards the back. She didn't look up. He watched as she folded the shorts, placed them neatly beside her, sat down again. He could feel muscles working in his head as he looked at her. He didn't have words for what he was feeling. She'd said so many words to him and he'd done his best to collect them. He felt he now had a great many things inside him and this was a strange feeling – it made him feel as the shorts did, that he had to carry these things, and that they were hard to understand, the precise benefit of them, plus they seemed to be awkward, to get in the way. To catch and to snag. To be a trouble. He knew this word and up there in the tree, with the valley around him, he said it out loud, quite clearly: "Trouble." He heard the sound of his own voice, sensed the pocket of air in front of him, where the sound was, and the way the sound was out in the valley now. For so many years he had been dedicated to not making any sounds – to treading carefully and making his blood slide silently through his pipes. Now he had put something of himself out into the air, that seemed to be it, something from all the things inside. He wasn't sure it felt good to do this. But he was going to have to, he thought, if he was to become the thing he sensed inside himself.

His eyes went slowly over the valley and he didn't know what he was trying to see. Always when he'd looked he was looking for something. There were the trees, and the trees were arranged into the shapes he knew – leaves, branches, trunks. Among the leaves were shadows and inside the shadows, if he looked for a long time, he could see in there too – into the dark. His senses would go into the shadows and draw out the hidden world. His nose went everywhere, in the valley there were no places that were hidden from him, and everywhere he could simply look and know.

Whereas in her backpack, the things there, these things were impossible to know.

He looked down and saw her still down there and he had a strong rush of feelings which made him want to say a word out into the air. He wanted to say her name. But he resisted.

He kept looking down and that made the feelings come more strongly. It was frightening, it made him giddy – he was *never* giddy. But he kept doing it. He felt his heart flexing its muscle. Gripping the branch, he tried to understand what was happening. He felt her calling to him, calling him down out of the tree. He could see the shorts there beside her, with the bone from Kala's body inside them and the bone and the woman were close together in a way that muddled him. He wanted her to look up. There she sat, still, and he knew she was listening. She was calling to him but she wouldn't look. He felt his feelings swelling, rising – suddenly they went click, and solidified inside him, and then he felt calm, and content that he was going to go with her.

He looked up again with the knowledge inside him and looked at the valley as though it was far away. Just some trees.

He could sense that he was close to balancing everything now. He was aware of Kala's bones beside him, and of the occasional movement within the upright strength of the tree as it continued to take his weight, and of the small places down in the hidden roots of the bushworld, where the mice and the lizards and the creeping, fumbling bugs were crawling away from being eaten, and towards eating, their tiny mouths chewing, and the bendy ferns growing and the shadows of the clouds going slowly across everything. The cicadas, working on their wall of sound – the wind stirring the leaves. Hawks flying. The sun. He breathed it in and breathed it out. It would be false to say that he remembered it all – remembered everything he had done here. To consciously remember, for the purposes of making yourself feel something, for no practical purpose, this he had not yet learned. But it might be said that, for Tarzan up in the tree, seeing was a kind of remembering – that everything he saw had his memories in it. Is that true for all of us? Can we see without remembering?

Maybe an artist, who can see colours only. Tones and shapes, seen from a distance.

The gorillas were there, bending branches down, eating. It was mid-morning. He couldn't see them but he knew what they looked like. He heard their faint sounds. These sounds made another kind of feeling inside him, and again he began to feel dizzy. Again this feeling became a solid thing, a knot, and this was a painful knot.

Far away, faintly, from the cabin, there was a tiny signal and he concentrated on this and heard a song he knew. So faint! He didn't feel like singing. He let the song from the radio be in the same valley of feelings as the gorilla knot and also the swelling of certainty that was so strong for the woman who was down there calling to him.

Then he stood and balanced on a branch and leaned back, let out his Tarzan yell and frightened everything in the valley. Over and over it echoed. Everything in the valley heard it and brought him to mind – even the wetas in their slow-pulsing cave. Even the dead stones. But there was no sound in reply. No one had ever replied to this call, and so he climbed down the tree and put his shorts on.

13

Jane knew the direction to the coast, Tarzan knew how to travel quickly through this landscape and so once they got started they made good progress. In shorts, with his slasher at his shoulder, he looked sporty, she thought, marching ahead confidently through country he had never crossed before, to a destination he had no grasp of.

Tarzan had no such grandstand thoughts. Now that the decision was made, he simply liked being near her – well, perhaps he did sense he was on his way to another world. He sang.

Miles and miles and miles and miles of water
And every one is wet and can't be crossed
And you are there, standing on the shoreline
Looking like a dream that has been lost – and what could this be about? Increasingly he understood that the songs had words that had meanings. This was a realisation which thrilled him. It was as though his familiar possessions were growing, it was as though they were caves that he had wormed his way into and was now realising were huge, full of echoes. The songs themselves, their tunes, this was simply a magic he could not grasp, how the tunes could have such strong shapes –

what were they made of? But it was the words he chased. Suddenly they had come alive, they swam in him, flitted like bright tropical fish against a reef. "A dreams," he asked her, "what are it?"

Meanwhile they clambered, slithered, ducked under branches, splashed through creeks. It rained – Jane felt a trickle going down her back. It would be nice to have a hot shower, to sleep in fresh linen. But inside her something was being stretched – it was as though a great rubber band was attached to the cabin in the bush and that every step away from it took greater and greater effort. Never to be here again, where the greens, the smells, the moisture rose like pure oxygen to fill your head with a pungent clarity – was she really longing for traffic lights and neon? Inside Tarzan, she knew, the snapping of that band was going to be painful.

Then, late afternoon, a faint mist became observable in the air. Tarzan noticed it first, she saw him pause and gaze about. His tongue appeared.

They climbed a steep bank and thus were able to see, in a vee between two hills, a wedge of blue. "It's the ocean," she said, "I told you, remember."

Tarzan stared at it, plainly puzzled. "It is very height." The frown line stood out on his brow. "We would go around the side."

"Yes, darling, we would go around the side."

But shortly after they came up onto a ridge from where a decent stretch of horizon could be seen. Tarzan insisted on climbing a tree. He called down, "It is everywhere." Was that panic in his voice? It was endearing, in such a big fellow. Standing beside her again, he studied her face and, seeing that she wasn't worried, broke into a smile. She hugged him, reached up to tousle his hair. He was in for such an adventure.

At the shoreline he ran up and down, like a dog barking at the waves. Well, they were exhilarating. Up close, the water heaved and fell, the colour of a dirty sky. Leaving her clothes in a pile, she went in and splashed. Tarzan followed, a look of utter astonishment on his face. He recognised what he was in as water, but there was so much of it! And what made it go? He stood, great thighs taut against the pull of the backwash, and roared. His voice sank into the sound of the waves, it was as though here you could make all the noise you wanted without disturbing anything. Horrible taste, though.

They sat, dripping, on a bleached log, Tarzan taking in lungfuls of old seaweed, pungent wrack. The sound that the shingle made as the waves ran back was fascinating to him, it was like something talking. You couldn't quite catch it, a gravelly voice, an under-sound. Then the long running line of white foam on the dark of the shingle. The waves racing towards you, thick, and then getting thin, and then dying at your feet. The way, looking out, you could see light through the waves. And how the waves never stopped coming — for all of this she gave him time.

The coast was deserted.

They slept in humpies within the sound of the sea. On the fourth day she saw a fishing smack, away to the south – when she pointed it out to him she saw he had been frowning at it for some time. "A ship is going on the water," he said. She saw that he had figured this sentence out, a good sign, she thought.

Increasingly there were orange dots among the whitecaps – floats. Then they were coming round a headland and, in the wide circle of a bay, boats were riding at anchor. In the sand-hills, cabins and a vehicle. Instantly Jane saw what a strange couple they were going to make – her looking like a mad lady scientist, which of course she was, and him with his shorts, the greenstone, the slasher and nothing else but a great tan.

His hair suddenly looked utterly wild – well, it wasn't so much the hair itself but the look in his eye that made it seem as though some big energy was close to being out of control. She felt something rise in her, a defiance, and she got ready to be challenged.

She didn't have to wait long.

There wasn't really a road, just a line of puddles and some tyre tracks in the sand, which they followed. A local wind was at their backs, it seemed to be pushing them on into something. Jane leading the way. Clouds going fast. Then ahead, among the landward sandhills, a dwelling with, at the roadside, a tractor. Tarzan was staring at the vehicle. Cabins he had seen but what was this? "A machine," he said. "A wheels." How we do like to put a word to a thing. The door of a cabin opened, and a grizzled old fellow, in oversized gumboots and woolly hat, ambled down between the jumble of floats and fishing gear to stand at his gate, watching.

As they came up he said to shirtless Tarzan, "Don't you feel the ruddy cold?"

Tarzan gazing at him as though he was the prophet Ezekiel. Jane counting under her breath. The fisherman frankly studying them. Tarzan said carefully, "You are a guy."

"Well, it's Stan, actually," the guy said, and held out his hand. Tarzan looked at it hanging there in the air until Stan withdrew it. Jane had told him not to touch anyone. Now the guy slid his gaze over to Jane. "Bring one back alive, didya, dear?" Measuring Tarzan. "Big fella, in't he."

"He only eats human flesh," said Jane, unflustered, "and he hasn't killed for three days."

"Yanks," said Stan, equally unflustered. Measuring them closely now. Tarzan studying Stan's gumboots, the frayed rope which held up his trousers. The mailbox, the fence, the metal lobster pots, the floats, the big-wheeled tractor with a rusty can on top of its exhaust pipe – these items received from him the kind of wide-eyed scrutiny we might give to, say, an authentic flying carpet. There was no getting around it – Tarzan was bug-eyed.

"We're from a circus," she said.

"Pull the other one."

Jane, unfamiliar with this expression, nevertheless understood that her credibility was being challenged. She knew enough not to attempt further explanation. "We've gotta hit the road," she said, and tugged at Tarzan's arm.

The guy called after them, "Better not let the hories see him wearing that greenstone, they'll have his guts for garters."

His words blew past them, they had a tail wind, and Jane was urging them on – within five minutes they were half a kilometre away. She risked a glance back. Now there were two men, the one they'd spoken to was pointing. She hurried them. Tarzan was utterly silent. He'd done well, she thought – hadn't gone and smelled the man – hadn't done anything at all. Of course, she'd coached him. Now, as they walked she set about explaining the etiquette of the handshake.

They kept to the shoreline and made good progress. She found Tarzan hard to keep up with, he was so eager. The sea delighted him – not just its restlessness, its vigour, but the scale of it, which he was constantly climbing dunes and beached logs to contemplate. "Is it the biggest thing?" he asked her.

"Yes, I think it must be."

But it wasn't the only biggest thing, not for him. For example, soon there were the fields which, divided by their fences, ran, bright green, away towards the hills. There were the sheep, so much easy eating just standing there, and then, later, the boxes, which was where, Jane said, all the people lived. But the biggest, biggest thing for him was the road, which started suddenly up out of the gravel at his feet and stretched away, black, undulating, into the distance. At first it was patchy, broken by stretches of gravel, and then it took on a rounder and more even shape, and acquired a broken white line which ran down the middle of it. It was hard, jagged even to his toughened feet. And it smelled strongly, reeked, just like the sea, only this was different. This, he knew, had been made. It wasn't everywhere, like the sea, it was just in this long narrow place, but in that place there wasn't any end to it. He kept looking ahead and there was always more road. He got inside a bus – that's what Jane called it – and she paid with some clink-metal called money and there was a brown-faced human-being with a hat on his head, he was inside the bus, and the bus was making a noise. There were windows that opened, you could put your head out, and the land kept going past the windows. There were boxes with tidy grass around them and creatures – human beings – everywhere, all of them wearing clothes. People, Jane said. People getting on, people getting off. Jane and Tarzan sitting right down the back, Jane not explaining anything, there was too much to explain, she just let him look, plus she didn't want to call attention. Bicycles, motorbikes, cars, trucks, a swaying double truck full of baa-ing, pissing sheep – the powerful smell of that. It was all completely astonishing. But nothing was as big as the road. Those things came and went. The road didn't stop. The bus kept on being on top of it, everywhere the bus went there was more road. Even when they got off, Tarzan kept looking ahead but the road just wouldn't end.

PART TWO

Let's Get Gone

14

A few years ago I learned on a visit I made to the Science Museum in London that the sun sings. They have there an old IMAX presentation about our local star. Like IMAXs everywhere, the volume was up near the pain level, people around me complained as wave after wave of sound pressed them back into the seats. But since my ears are now all but dead I was right at home. And so practically every fact offered by that great wall of images seems to have stayed with me – for example, the age of the sun, which is four and a half billion years. Well, this isn't a did-you-know session, if you want sun facts you can check any website, but did you know that the sun sings? Because it does. It hums. It sends out a vibration that even the scientists call singing – Tarzan would have enjoyed knowing this. He would have stood outside and listened. He liked to think of the whales singing deep in their watery highways, and of the crickets in Africa which sit inside little bowls they have dug in the dust, sound-shells, so that their songs can be heard, on a good night, up to seven miles away. Jane told him that one, of course, and so he was always listening out for faraway crickets – for whales, for the language of the leaves, for a radio faint in the distance. Tarzan was fascinated by physical curiosities. "Hey, guys, d'you know that scientists have discovered a lake at the North Pole? The ice cap's meltin'!" He could become tedious in this mode, but he was Tarzan and so everyone had to listen. Towards the end he became especially trying, as he often repeated himself. But at the beginning of his career every new factoid of this sort made him glow with happiness – it was as though he was getting closer to something. And so when I heard that about the sun singing I immediately thought of him, new to civilisation, standing out in the garden at Jane's house, body held still, face radiant with new knowledge, listening for a sound that was so everywhere that no one could hear it.

In fact the house with the garden wasn't Jane's, it was her mother's – for some years now Jane had been away at college.

Jane's mother is Carole Porter. How to introduce her? How to introduce the whole Western world that was so impossible for Tarzan to see, even though he was right inside it?

Here we go . . .

In Petaluma, the flower of Sonoma County, lived a woman who wore her hair in a flip and when she stood at her kitchen window with a glass of water and looked, what she saw was not the long driveway, lined with shade trees which ran down to the Fairway, nor the lawn with sprinklers, nor the tumbling flight of the jays that disputed possession of the prime spot in her garden, atop the tall plum tree that needed pruning, though she did wish that they would just stop.

Sometimes she saw her husband, Mike, standing there, hands on his hips, leaning back a little, somewhat side on, regarding her. But he'd been dead at least a dozen years.

Occasionally she saw her face reflected in the window – well, pooh to you!

Usually at least half her thoughts were drifting towards *The Rand McNally Atlas of American Highways and Major*

Contributing Roads, open before her on the bench top, each page patterned with spurting red lines which would carry her to someplace new, out there where the map turned into a road you could run your tyres on. Some place she hadn't been to yet.

But on this particular occasion what she had her eye on was her daughter, Jane. Jane in a hammock, with a book, reading aloud to a young man who was sitting cross-legged on the lawn at her feet with an expression of listening intently. Well, there'd been booky young men before, but this one had no shoes, no shirt, and, even by California standards, a remarkable tan. Good-looking – handsome, even. Plus he was large. He took up a lot of space. Character? She couldn't tell. The guy's face had only the one line, on his brow, and there was nothing so much to be garnered from a frown line – if his story was as Jane told it, he had plenty to frown about. What was missing, she thought, was a sense of his being bewildered. She had seen him at a loss – confronted, for example, by a mix-master rather than a faucet. But he'd simply waited to be shown. Shouldn't he be gob-smacked by the twentieth century? But his gaze was steady, keen – surely this was a good sign? A lusty creature, she supposed. Carole Porter had no illusions about her daughter, or any other human creature, in this regard – and at least for once he was worth lusting after. But, as she'd said to Jane, "When you've had the sex, what are you going to do with him? Keep him as a pet?"

Yes, where was this going?

And so it was Carole who, a few days later, made the first move in the direction that eventually saw the bronzed man from the bush picked up and lifted away into the spotlight.

Jane, for her part, also had a plan. Her idea was to have Tarzan come back to the Riverside campus with her, where she would reorient her dissertation so that it included him as a field of study – using him, yes, but what was wrong with that? – while she taught him how to win a meal ticket in the urban food chain. Probably they would get married quite soon – in her mind they were already engaged, though when she mentioned this to her mother, Carole said, "Would he know engaged if he met it in the dark?" He might, in time, become something like a zoologist – or maybe just working in a zoo, Jane thought. A gardener, perhaps, something where he could work outside. A sportsman.

Jane was away, at the supermarket, when Carole set the Tarzan ball rolling. Carole could see him out there in the garden, just sitting, and thought she might give him a little push. She rang her friend Eve Kersting. This was something Carole did almost every day, they'd been friends for years, Eve had been her maid of honour. Carole told Eve, come on over, I have something to show you. Well, nothing wrong with that, except that Eve was a reporter.

The story which resulted from this visit appeared first in the Petaluma *Clarion-Herald* and was in fact a very nice piece. Jane had come home to find her personal discovery being questioned in the presence of a notebook and pencil. Jane knew Eve, had done for years – "Hi, Eve." Eve hadn't been in Jane's Tarzan Plan, not an interview at this stage, but then maybe it would help – maybe it would mean that she didn't always have to explain him. Jane knew that Eve could be trusted to make the story a good one and so she sat down beside Tarzan and stroked his forearm while she listened. Neither of the older women missed this little touch. Jane threw in the odd answer of her own, and helped Tarzan to clarify his.

Local Girl Brings Home a Wild One!

Well, Eve couldn't help that, it was the editor who wrote the headlines, but the story itself was nicely managed: . . . *and so here in a California garden he sits, all instinct, all* muscle, soaking up the sun, and yet you can tell he's got a brain. When asked, What do you hope to do here? he says, carefully, "I have to learn." In fact, he seems to have learned rather a lot in a short time. But his grasp of geography is, as yet, a little hazy – for instance, he placed the city of Wellington, capital of New Zealand, in America – "on the other side of the America ocean". But an airplane ride with a good globe in hand will fix that. Meanwhile his discoverer and patron, pretty Jane Porter of Fairway Drive here in Petaluma, plans to write a study on Tarzan in his environment for her PhD. Could be one dissertation worth reading.

"Thanks for the 'pretty', " said Jane, staring at her picture, page three, above the fold – her head not quite on his shoulder, but inclined that way. Probably not a good idea to let her prof get the wrong impression, and she told herself to think when she was in public with him. Except that why shouldn't they, they were in love.

And then the phone rang.

The *Clarion-Herald* story was a good one and had been picked up, Eve said, by several of the big city majors, and Tarzan would maybe be getting a call. "Oh, exciting." That was Carole. But no great drama.

Then the phone rang again. This time it was another of Carole's acquaintances, a man named Fred Goodson, a real estate developer with big teeth and an extensive collection of dazzlingly white shirts. Unfortunately the teeth were yellow. But never mind, the guy had money – in fact it was Fred Goodson the Third and he always appeared beside a late-model sports, in whatever was the brightest shade of red available that year. His hand resting on its fender. Not a friend, exactly, but Carole had partnered him at doubles, on the broad, well-watered courts of his club, and had, once, had one too many Manhattans with him, deliberately, to see what might happen. But behind his back people called him The

Third and this struck her as something he should have dealt with, either got rid of the ancestral caboose or else had the nous to make a joke of it himself, first. Plus there was a foul miasma associated with the teeth, when he leaned in you had to clench your stomach. So, nothing special doing in that direction, but there was no reason not to play tennis with the guy, and now here he was, saying that he had a bowling alley to open, in the Martinas Valley, and maybe the jungle man could, you know, make an appearance.

The names of these good folk carefully collected and kept, by the biographies, by the Tarzan Archive.

It was Carole who had picked up the phone. "Make an appearance – what would he do? No, I don't think they *have* lions in New Zealand, Freddie. Obviously. A loin cloth – where exactly do you buy those? No, I agree. Well, there's a yell he does, it cleared the birds from the trees. Oh, I don't know what kind of a yell – a jungle yell. Yes, wouldn't it. So how much were you offering? Oh, come on, Fred. No, you wouldn't be *giving* him anything, Fred, you'd be *paying* him for doing a job. Yes, all right, we can find a spear I think. No, fifty's not enough. No. A hundred – good. All right. At two o'clock – it's on the Boulevard isn't it? We'll be there. Oh – make sure you spell his name right, do you have it? Okay. Okay, ciao, Freddie. Ciao."

When two o'clock Saturday arrived there was no spear. Carole had come up with a loin cloth made from an old builder's apron of her husband's – it was decent, just – and he had his greenstone pendant, and a knife, and Carole had had the idea of applying just a little lipstick, rubbed in, to the old scar on the calf of his left leg, to make it look more livid. Various spear-like sticks had been tried but they all looked too fake. Well, the loin cloth looked fake too, but that was okay, they could just say that usually he had been naked – which was a selling point, Eve thought. Eve had decided to come along, to follow the story, and so she was sitting in the front seat, beside Carole, who was driving, and Tarzan and Jane were in back. The knife was Jane's bowie, which, under the dark suit Jane had had cut for him back in Wellington, New Zealand, was inserted into the strap of the loin cloth – was in danger of slicing it, in fact.

Jane, close beside him, was full of misgivings. Wasn't this exactly the kind of carny stunt that she should be keeping him away from? But then, he did have to earn a living, eventually – it would be good for him to earn some money so he could understand what it did. You never understood until you'd worked to earn it. And he didn't seem troubled, sitting there, huge inside the car. He was in his best clothes. The idea was, he would come out on stage as a civilised man and then strip – there was no other word for it – to the loin cloth. And then he would do his yell, gather up his clothes and walk off. They had rehearsed this. Tarzan had been completely relaxed, had shown a pleasing mastery of the buttons, though it was clear he was concentrating. The stylish suit from New Zealand wasn't, unfortunately, quite so stylish here in California, in fact it looked rather dowdy. But Eve had said it made him look English, and so they got him a furled umbrella, a nice touch. And he had his little speech off perfectly. "Hello. I am Tarzan. I am from New Zealand. I was raised in the wild by gorillas, and never met another human being until this year. Now I have come across the ocean to California to learn the ways of the world." He tended to stumble over California, and after three sessions with the globe no one was really sure he got it that the blue bits were water. Eve had suggested he might take the globe on stage with him, American grasp of geography being what it was, but this had been vetoed as too risky – if someone asked him where Africa was he might come off looking retarded. The speech, the strip, then: "Now here is the way I let everyone in the jungle know I had made a kill." The yell. A wave, pick up the clothes, and off, remembering to twirl the umbrella.

Did he really understand?

The carpark was nearly full but the promise of free bowling and root beer was, Carole suggested, probably what everyone had come for. A few people stared at him as the four of them walked in a phalanx towards the big low building where the event was to take place – well, it was sweltering, not suit weather, he was probably the only man wearing one for miles. Overhead was the big curved sign, Rainbow Bowling Alley, and then near the entrance a billboard with a cartoonist's vision of an enraged gorilla carried the words, *Tarzan the Ape-Man! His first personal appearance! See the Wild Man from the Jungle!*

"Are gorillas apes?" asked Eve. No one was sure.

Inside, it was chaos. People were milling, waiting for something to happen, they stared around, looking for the thing that might justify their having bothered to turn up. Tarzan stood out as taller than everyone else – well, not just tall. He was plain different. His eye seemed wild, but this may have been fright, at the people, and at the noise of the machine that reset the bowling pins. It was malfunctioning and pins were dropping and spilling everywhere. The alley was, Jane saw, a peculiar place, wide, low-ceilinged, like a slot, with the lanes making lines of perspective that ran parallel to the grain of the wood of the floor. There was something maddening in this. Jane was worried. She had brought Tarzan out here the day before, to get him used to the ambience, but the machine hadn't been going then, and there were no people. He'd never been in a crowd.

Fred the Third spotted them and came over, flashing his teeth. "Hi, Tarzan. I'm Fred – remember? Look, Carole, get him out of here, you can't have him being seen until the big moment. In there." They were ushered into the octagonal fishbowl from where the management would monitor the action – no privacy there. Tarzan was instructed to sit on the floor, out of sight. Then Fred was gone, but could still be heard, shouting instructions.

"What makes Fred Goodson angry?" Tarzan asked.

Jane, holding his hand, said, "He's not angry, darling, just a bit excited." She was interested to note that he'd remembered Fred's surname. The hand didn't seem sweaty at all. They looked at each other. This was civilisation – the home of the brave.

Eve knew a little about how to give a performance. "What you do is," she said, squatting to speak into his ear, "you just think about what you're doing, not about them, okay?" Tarzan nodded calmly. Okay, so he wasn't nervous. But that was because he didn't know what he was going into.

There was a crackling noise, followed by, "Testing, testing, one-two." Jane exchanged glances with Eve, then quickly set about trying to explain to Tarzan what a microphone was. Fred's amplified voice, metallic at the best of times, now bounced off the low ceiling, the flat surfaces of the polished wood. The machine had mercifully been turned off. ". . . and of course, to Delaney's For Delite for the root beer, they're just down the Boulevard, after you've had your free bowl, why don't you drop in there and try their Rainbow Ripple, it's delicious. Okay, now it's time for a special guest, I know you've been waiting to see him, all the way from the darkest jungles of New Zealand, way down there in the tropics, raised by wild gorillas, he's the original wild man – he's just barely used to sleeping in a bed, but if you had the lovely Jane Porter to be your teacher you'd be a fast learner too, let's give him a big hand, Rainbow Bowling's own . . . Tarzan the Ape-Man! Come on out, Tarzan!"

Carole gave him a pat on the back, or was it a push? – anyway, suddenly he was out the door of the fishbowl and walking, they all watched, with a steady gait, across the polished floor, his shoes squeaking, this could be heard clearly in the silence that had now begun to fall over the crowd which until then had been murmuring – a low sound like the pattering of rain, fading away. Tarzan saw Fred standing there, up on a higher place, a stage they had called it, went to him – stood next to him. Fred's red face looking up at him, the smelly hole in Fred's face saying in a low voice, "Okay, Tarzan-boy, do your thing."

Tarzan watching Fred walk off the stage. Then he turned to face them.

Silent humans gathered under the low roof.

He looked among them. Smelled them. They smelled so strongly, his nostrils wrinkled. There was a kind of shiver coming off them, he could feel it in his stomach, there was something alive inside them.

In the crowd a girl's voice said, "Mommy, make him say hello to me."

Tarzan found her eye. "Hello," he said.

Everyone cheered.

The cheering was the strangest sensation, it came from that thing that was inside them. It was a sound that went all around you, it had a strange force in it – he stood there frowning, trying to catch the feeling.

Now they were all watching him closely.

The microphone on its stick was standing there but after giving it a serious looking-over he ignored it. He said, in his firm, careful voice, the first word of his speech: "Hello."

"You said that," shouted a guy from the back. Hush, went the crowd.

"I am Tarzan. I am from New Zealand. I was raised in the wild by the gorillas." He paused and looked around, and then, like Kerchak, so far away in the leafy shadows of the bush, he lifted his hands and beat them on his tightly waistcoated chest. The crowd roared. It was the most wonderful sound, it made his head feel as though the back of it was lifting away. He felt as though he was full of bees, as though there was a great humming inside him. "And I never have met another human being until this year." Looking down at them. They were looking into him, into the feelings inside him. They were reaching – they wanted what he was feeling. "I have come to Cala Fornia to learn the ways of the world."

Then, as though to show them what their world was like, he began to take off his clothes. This took some concentration, he had to look what he was doing. But in between buttons he looked back at them. Face after face after face, just like the photograph taken at the League of Nations gathering in his book. As he finished with each article he folded it and draped it on the chair which had been set upon the stage for that purpose. He knelt to get his shoes off. The drop to his knee was so gracefully done that there were small noises of appreciation. He placed the shoes neatly, side by side. Carole had told him to take off his shirt last, if he ended with the trousers the crowd might shout for the jackpot and he might oblige. He straightened up, unbuttoned his shirt, then, finally stood there, in his loin cloth and his skin.

"Wow," said a male voice, quietly.

Someone clapped, there was a whistle, then scattered applause. But no one was quite sure what to do. He stood, looking down into their eyes. The faces in the front row were close, he could have extended a finger. Unconsciously, his hand came up to touch the greenstone pendant and all eyes followed the movement, expectant.

There was hissing from the fishbowl, backstage: "The yell, Tarzan." That was Fred.

Alone on the stage, Tarzan said the words, as instructed. "Now here is the way I let everyone in the jungle know that I have made a kill." But when he drew his breath in for the shout, it didn't seem right. The yell was for when you were outside, when you had to let everything that was far away know you were there and how you were feeling. The people here were so close to him, they knew what he was feeling, the yell wasn't the right thing.

More hissing from backstage.

So he stood up straight, looked just above their heads, and opened his mouth.

Somewhere over the rainbow
Skies are blue,
And the dreams that you dare to dream
Really do come true.

In the car there was silence. The wheels on the smooth blacktop road made only a small sound, a murmur. For once Carole seemed to be driving slowly. They had the windows down, the warm afternoon air, smelling faintly of oranges, flowed over them, filled them with the wellbeing that California tries to bottle and sell. As advertised, the skies were utterly blue.

It was Eve who said it. "Nobody said he could sing."

"Don't talk about him as though he isn't here," said Jane.

Carole asked, via the rear-vision mirror, "Tarzan, why did you choose that song?"

Fred had been so impressed. The Rainbow Bowling Alley on Rainbow Boulevard and he sings . . . *Over the Rainbow*! The guy was a natural. Briefly, Freddie saw himself as Tarzan, impressively tall, in great shape, noble, and at the wheel of a late-model red sports, driving them wild – the world at your feet . . . He'd offered to sign up Tarzan, for special duties, right then. "A bit of gardening out at the club, plus appearances – the guy could do a spot on stage each night – heck, maybe he could, you know, take groups of youngsters up into the hills, show them how to track a bear." The possibilities were endless.

Carole said that she would get back to him. Seeing that Tarzan would need managing.

Eve was thinking that, written up right, this could make *Life*.

And on the bench seat in back, Tarzan and Jane were holding hands. Jane was so in love. When you first grasp what is inside the one you love, when you see the warmth and distance of the country back in there, this is a good day. When you see the qualities with which they will love you. She saw now that he was so full of feeling, and that he was going to survive – to thrive – in this world. He was such a *rara avis*, such a diamond found in the dirt.

Tarzan was thinking too, but not necessarily about Jane. He felt the fingers of her hand in his, the skin of her arm. The hip-to-hip warmth of her. Also he liked the smell of the air, the blue sky untroubled by clouds. But these were so many sensations.

When he'd stood there barefoot on those smooth, polished boards, with Jane and Carole and Eve, whose names he knew, back over there, and the roof up there, and the machines out in front of him, then everything had been arranged, he felt, so that they – *they* – would be before him, and he before them. A setting. A shape. There was hole in them that needed and he had something in him that had to come out. When everything fitted, he saw, then that was the driveshaft. Suddenly he was grasping it: this was how the world worked. You made it go around you.

He had known what to do.

When he sang all of the people were pleased. He had felt that. He had just made what was inside him come out into the air and it had made everyone happy. And then they'd clapped and this was like when you came down the track and frightened the little birds out of the grass – up they went like a connected, twisting thing, dots of birds making a single dark shape that flowed around in the air as it moved off. It was as though you had talked about yourself to each one of those people, as though suddenly they knew you.

Now, in the car, he said to Jane, "What is that song about?"

Carole had, after several calls from Freddie, agreed to another performance, at the club, at night this time. Same routine, quick on, quick off – two hundred.

Except that this time everyone was sitting down, they were much further away. It was dark, Tarzan had to use his night eyes to see them through the cigarette smoke which made his throat burn. This time when he stripped it was a strip – getting naked in front of people who had been drinking. Did he notice? He tried to reach them but they were further away, this time the yearning in his singing was so strong it broke your heart.

"Encore means they want you to sing another song – do you know another song?" hissed Carole. "Okay – only one more then come back. Tarzan?" The big fellow nodded, and turned and went back out there, dressed in his skin and a loin cloth.

On a green hill
On a blue day
Your brown eyes
Looked my way . . .

There was a great shuffling of chairs as they stood up to clap, it wasn't as nice somehow as the bowling alley. No children this time. But definitely they liked him.

. . . and so you see that rare thing, a naked emotion on stage, writes Special Correspondent Eve Kersting. *At a time*

when the American mood has encouraged its performers to offer routines, to charm, to be casually pleasing, like a cigarette after a meal, no more – here is the human thing itself, telling you what it is, how it feels to be in the world. And what he is telling you is not either that he is in love with himself. He's not off in some tree house – Tarzan looks you in the eye, he talks directly to the private person inside. Plus he's got the voice to do it, a voice that might come out of a tree, warm with life, a voice from a river. I was lucky to be there.

When they went for pizza, everyone stared. This was just Tarzan and Jane, on a warm evening. Jane in slacks, the big guy in cutoffs and a white tee. It was, Jane thought, like dating the quarterback. Except that the quarterback was always an arsehole.

Mind you, Petaluma in the mid-fifties, this was a small town, there wasn't a lot to stare at. Plus Tarzan was interesting. He didn't pretend no one was staring. He stared back. He smiled. When they waved, he waved too. It was disturbing – the quarterback never smiles.

Okay, this is how you behave at the drugstore. This is how you answer the telephone. Don't cut yourself when you shave. This is the toilet, this is toilet paper – this is how you wipe yourself. That's Mom's room, don't go in there unless she invites you. I think you'll need to bring a sweater, darling. This is how we order at the drive-in – don't look at the people in the other cars. Just ignore him, the guy's a retard.

Now what he had there was a switchblade, it's a kind of knife. If you meet guys like that you should walk away. Don't run – you're bigger and stronger than they are. But don't fight them unless you have to. If you fight them, don't kill them, okay.

After the drive-in they would go to a place that Jane knew about, where there was a view of the town and, with luck, no other cars. They would look down on the lights and she would explain the movie. "See, his name is James Dean and he was trying to tell everyone . . ." What, exactly, Jane? What was James trying to tell us? "That he was full of feeling."

Then they would drive slowly home, the big car seeming to find its own way between the letterboxes, under the trees, among the houses. They had done drives where he had to tell her which direction to take at every intersection. She was afraid he would get lost, but then you always get lost, some day, it's what you do when you do that matters – so should she be trying to get him lost?

But he seemed always to know where he was going. It was uncanny, he never once seemed bewildered. He would stand patiently, waiting to be shown, waiting to understand. But there was no doubt in him.

When he was on his own she would see him looking ahead – he was looking ahead when he was just sitting on the lawn and studying the clouds. Where would he take them? Jane had the feeling that her life wasn't her own any more. But that was because now it was *they*, wasn't it? Yes. No need for the question mark. The two of them, going somewhere new together. It was exciting.

Soon he would be wanting to get behind the wheel.

15

"I've been thinking I might take a drive," said Carole, over the breakfast coffee. She had out her *Rand McNally*, once it was open it was only a matter of time. "I've been thinking Memphis."

Later, on the lawn, they were gathered beneath the plum tree, on a tartan blanket, shaded from the sun that burned in the endlessly blue California sky. Drinking Kool-Aid – normally it would have been wine, Carole often drove across to Napa, came back with a trunkful of clinking bottles, but somehow everyone thought, without discussing it, that they shouldn't offer Tarzan alcohol.

It was as though he was a child – don't let him see that gory picture in the magazine. But he wasn't a child, you could see him thinking all the time. Thinking about you. It was rather like being in an intergalactic beauty contest, as though someone from outer space had come to report on your lifestyle. How ordinary you suddenly seemed, and how fabulous.

His ability to make everyone feel they were fabulous served him well for years.

He'd fitted in amazingly easily – but there a few hiccups.

Given time and a bit of leg-room he had managed to somewhat blot his copybook. Old Mrs Petrescu from over the fence, for example, had complained that she'd seen him using the garden as his bathroom. Jane made him find the turds and bury them, and Carole gave the lecture. On several occasions he had been found with the telephone receiver in his hand, saying nothing – it was obvious that someone had called and he'd picked up but not spoken. This everyone found extremely disturbing. To have missed a call, this was a big deal. Who did they expect, the president? Plus he had once, only once, touched Jane when they were in public. They were at the druggist, a Coppertone promo had reminded him how nice it was to reach under and feel her hidden skin. Jane was cool, didn't make a scene. Later she explained. Laid down the lore. Oh but at these moments it was such a different world from the bush, where they had run naked down the slippery track to stand under the waterfall. Each morning Jane rose early – Tarzan was always up – and worked on typing out her notebooks. He would be sitting on the lawn in the dawn hush. He liked chairs, to him they were one of civilisation's most useful products, and so he usually carried an armchair out there with him, and sat, and listened, and thought. Jane, when she looked up from her work, would study the back of his head. She wanted to teach him to read, it was so obvious that he had an inclination towards that kind of armchair exploration. But not too soon. She didn't want him to fail, not at anything. This was the most remarkable thing, that he kept being successful. She had to think, she had to see how his experiencing of the world should be ordered. To make rulings, to explain, that was her task. She could shape him as she wanted – a thrilling prospect. And she was recording his every development, as a scientist. Yes, she was in the middle of a unique experiment. It troubled her only mildly that perhaps he was her specimen. Aren't we all specimens, to each other, to be studied and learned from?

But then she would return to her field notes and remember how he had carried her to the bed of grasses, remember standing naked in the rain. Maybe they could go back some day?

Meanwhile he kept his pants on in public.

Keeping his clothes on was work. Everything in America was work. It was like being round Kerchak all the time, you had always to be careful of what you were doing. Tarzan could feel how the gorillas were far away from him now, on the other side of the ocean the liner had crossed, yes, but also on the other side of all the rooms he had been in, the things he had done and seen. It was as though there was a continuum of rooms, the hotel in Wellington, the barbers, the tailors, the immigration office. The cabin on the ship – it was as though when he looked back he could see the walls of each of these places around him, and somehow they were all joined up, making a kind of tunnel, which he could look back through to where he used to live. What he used to be.

When he was putting on his clothes he had to get the order right, see him now, dressing button by careful button in the morning light of Jane's bedroom, if he wasn't watching he pulled the boxers on after the trousers, which was not correct. So he paid frowning attention to sequence – first the socks then the shoes. First Jane met him then he put on the shorts. The bus, then the hotel in Wellington, then the ship. Then America. He had the sense that if he lost any part of this sequence then he would never understand.

He felt he was always inside something now, not just rooms but clothes. Not just clothes but a description: We are having dinner. We are going to bed. And, hanging over all that, like the hawk hanging over the valley, a bigger description: I am learning to be a man. That is what has stayed with me. To look back along everything and get the sequence right, that is still my project. I am getting ancient now and now everything is work to me: first the underpants, old man, and then the strides. And I have never stopped having to learn: how do you be a man?

What would it be like, I still wonder this, to be a man and not to have to be careful about it?

On the tartan rug a kind of pattern had been made by the plastic plates, they lay, bright disks of primary colour, before each person. The Kool-Aid wobbled in the cups, full of light. Carole was running a finger over a page of the *Atlas*, tracing the route they would take – if they left early and drove hard, two and a half days, she thought.

Tarzan sitting as a gorilla sits, upright on his backside. Jane, luxuriant, lying full-length, her tumbling head of hair in his lap. Eve, who had taken a sudden vacation, Eve who knew a oncer when she saw one and was thus going to be around for the next three weeks, was sitting on her calves, never far from her tote-bag with the spiral-bound notebook and pencil. And Carole, who had commandeered the armchair, from where she was presently announcing that they should go down through Albuquerque, Amarillo, and Oklahoma City, so that they would arrive in Memphis around, oh, some time after noon Thursday.

"Why Memphis?" asked Jane, sleepy in the sun.

"You'll like the South, honey." Jane's eyes opened. "We're all going."

Jane sat up, looked from face to face.

"Eve rang her Uncle Sam," Carole said. Everyone looked at Eve.

"He's the brother of my baby sister's husband," said Eve, blushing. She was a small, intense person who wore dark lenses more often than was strictly necessary, it gave you something to hide behind. "His name is Sam Phillips. He's an unusual man – a bit crazed. He has an interest in music. He owns a recording studio and makes records. He records Negroes. In Memphis."

"We thought," said Carole, "that he should hear Tarzan."

Jane got up quickly, pulled Tarzan up. They left – they got out of there. Later Jane and Carole had an exchange. Carole was making decisions, like always. Just don't, okay. It's my life, I found him, we'll figure it out – thank you.

But Carole knew best and calmly went to make sure the car had plenty of gas.

Eve wasn't sure where the middle of this story was. Our lives through his eyes? Civilisation And Its Contents? Jane-and-Tarzan, a love story with a difference? Angles on the thing kept floating through her head, large bodies, like ice floes, no, more vague – like banks of cloud. She was never in the way, had never at any time in her life been in the way, and Carole had made it clear that she was welcome to come, indeed, might be invaluable. Who knew how to play this thing? Maybe that was another angle, Eve thought – What We Did With Him? So would she be in the story? Eve thought no. But it was she who had thought of Sam Phillips, who'd made the call. She'd only met him once, but Mr Phillips was a person you remembered. He'd remembered her back. "Sure, bring him on down, I'll talk with him." Deep Southern to Eve's California ears, not exactly a drawl, but considered, serious. Mr Phillips was a serious man, she thought. Formidable, somehow. It was her instinct that he might know what to do.

No blood relation but both of them in their own way intense.

Because they did have to do something. You had to follow your star, that was the American way. Or your fate. Things had to play – this is what Eve and Carole said to each other. Because he was an American. Well, he was now.

*

Jane announced at dinner that they weren't going. She'd thought about it, as she'd told Carole: don't you be interfering. That's that, okay? But then Tarzan spoke up.

This was a comparatively rare occurrence. He always answered a question, and occasionally he asked one. He had to compose his sentence before he would speak it and so conversation could be slow. But it was rare that he proffered something unbidden.

"I would like to go to Memphis," he said. He was looking at Jane.

Oh.

Jane saw at once that she had been selfish, this wasn't about her and her mother, she needed to think again. Okay. But there was no need to be a walkover. "Okay," she said, "it's a good idea. Thank you. Okay, we'll go, me and Tarzan. We'll fly, he's never been in an airplane. Eve, could you please write a letter of introduction to Sam Phillips."

But they couldn't afford to fly.

Carole Porter at the wheel of a vehicle was something to be reckoned with. The woman was born to drive. She never accelerated, never slowed. But, as though it was a natural thing, they simply went faster than everything else on the road, and so there was a fair deal of overtaking. Big rigs, family saloons with dogs hanging their barking heads out, delivery vans – they all fell behind as the long green Chevy, a broad vehicle by today's standards, moved smoothly among them. Both hands on the wheel, cigarette trailing a plume, Carole knew how to cover the miles.

They had the windows down. Eve in front, following as politely as she could the conversation in back. Tarzan, she heard, was astonished by the roadside billboards. Well, they *were* huge, like great cinema screens and Eve realised that she had stopped seeing them. That they were beautiful. Jane was explaining each one to him, devoted, intoxicated, as they all were, by the chance to see the world anew through his eyes.

They passed through cactus country, through the white-caked desert, through small enclaves of off-road stalls, smoke rising. Through wheatlands where a single texture flowed to the horizon on every side. All of this had to be seen as though in a movie, unspooling – Carole paused only for gas. Hungry? Eat the radio, we never stop.

Between songs, Eve punched the tuning buttons. Tarzan sang along – they let him sing alone. He seemed to know the words to all the oldies, *A Bushel And A Peck*, and all the sentimental stuff you couldn't stand unless it was him singing it – how he did give the life back to a tired emotion. But the hillbilly dances, the black men moaning out their blues on the race stations – she could tell from his expression in the oblong mirror: this was new to him. It was such a listening face, it visibly took in things and squirreled them.

Jane, at his side, was alternately bored and excited. She had been victim of so many drives with her Mom, the necessary passenger, especially after her pop died. Hours of nothing but blacktop and candy. Her Mom with her lip stuck out. But this trip was different. *Eve seemed to be tuning us in on Tarzan's future*, she wrote in her book. *It was as though she, at the controls of the radio, was controlling him. She would find an old ballad, something like* Stars Fell Over Alabama, *and he would sing along so sweetly that maybe even Mom was affected. The car appeared to slow. Out the window, birds kept pace with us, skimming low over the roadside shoulder, up and down on the currents. Tarzan singing with his eyes open. Seeing the American movie as something we were living in. Then Eve would find a gospel station, as we went East and South they took up more room on the dial, and he would cock his head, his lips forming an interested smile. It could almost make a believer of you, that gospel. The country and western no one could abide, but Eve forced it on us. It was so painful, the stuff those truck drivers weep to, it rots the mind. Eve seemed not to care and persevered even when Mom spoke to her. The hillbilly bands were better, full of jump and whiskey. But it was the Negro music that was the strangest. I guess I'd never listened to it too much before. Eve seemed to like it, she kept bringing it up on the dial. It really made Tarzan sit straight, not that he was ever a slumper, but he had his frowning, thinking face on. I must admit, at that time, I couldn't hear what there was to be so interested in. There was a thump, I guess these days I'd call that the beat, and some words which then seemed to me so strange, so forced through a twisted aperture, that I couldn't help but hear them as belonging to other people who led other lives. Devil et mah heart now – what did that mean to me? And Tarzan? He'd seen very few Negroes. At that time California was pretty much entirely a white state, not because of prejudice so much as distance – the Negroes just hadn't come that far west. We had one family at my high school, the Hosclaws, Glen Hosclaw was in my home room, he was too fat, but he beat me out for the dean's prize. It wasn't until I got out in the world that I really encountered America's other culture. Tarzan had asked, after his performance at the bowling hall, why did the one man have a black face, and we had gone back to the books we had brought with us from the cabin in New Zealand. I had to explain again about all the tribes of the world.*

But none of that came up during the drive. Tarzan didn't know that that music was made by Negroes, for Negroes to listen to. He just listened. Drank it up. Eve, at the controls, played him as though he was an instrument.

All the while, Mom was pointing us across the continent. Gallup. Albuquerque. Santa Rosa. Tucumcari. Amarillo.

Oklahoma City. Muskogee. Towns, cities – names from legend and song. Keeping company with the Arkansas River. Little Rock – Tarzan knew the Little Rock song. Twice we stopped, to sleep – only because we complained – Mom would have driven through the dark. But sleep was impossible. All through the night, all you could dream of was road and the sound of wheels . . .

Then finally the great green highway signs began to have the magic word on it, spelled out in large white letters: Memphis. They showed this to Tarzan, watched him mouth the sound while he stared at the word. He was a long way from reading. But words, he already knew that you had to find the deep shapes which lay inside words.

At that time Memphis was a city of some four hundred thousand, already calling itself "the birthplace of the blues," the place where Martin Luther King was bound to die. When the wind was blowing out of the west the reek of the river would stink up the streets as though they were awash in Mississippi mud. Otherwise it smelled of cigar smoke, and honest perspiration. On Beale Street the long cars cruised, wide and low like metal smiles. Neon fizzed, the sidewalks were packed with drifting bodies, men in shirtsleeves and suspenders or sweating in seersucker – overhead a swinging sign announced the Miss. River Cafe, which is where they retreated, the three women and Tarzan, road-weary, but all of them stimulated by the constricted vigour of the South. Tarzan especially was keenly interested in everything. From the radio high in the corner something with a jump beat could be heard as they sipped their Cokes. Tarzan tapped his toe. Up and down the street music fell from every doorway.

Their waitress, a slim, calm Negro woman in a checked apron, said, kindly, "Visitin' Memphis, are you?" and gave them directions.

*

Now, at this point I think we should pause to make some acknowledgements.

It is often claimed by the uninformed that Tarzan and Sam Phillips were the inventors of rock 'n' roll. But it ain't so. If you look back along the years, there were signposts everywhere pointing to the new thing that came together at Sun in 1954. With the benefit of hindsight, you can make a big deal out of *Rocket 88*, cut by Jackie Brenston and His Delta Cats as early as 1951. A year later Lloyd Price made it to number one on the R&B charts with *Lawdy Miss Clawdy*. Big Joe Turner had a hit with *Shake, Rattle and Roll* and it was still only 1953. That same year, *Mystery Train* by Little Junior Parker. Wynonie Harris, Louis Jordan, Joe Liggins and The Honeydrippers, et cetera and et al, all through that period there were guys of every musical persuasion out there feeling for something – any website will give you a hit parade of rockin' performers from those pre-Tarzan years. But at that time no one thought this was a movement, something that, hey, hey, my, my, would never die. Mud was being thrown at walls. Speaking of mud, I guess at this point we should be kind and namecheck fatso Haley and *Rock Around The Clock*. Fine, I admit it, this lunker found a big audience, but face it, Bill Haley wasn't beautiful. That kisscurl never really rocked. But he gets his nod.

Also there were the times – I will grant you the times. Jimmy Dean had already come through with the image of the soulful outsider. And, in *The Wild One,* Brando added leather to that. Fine. But these guys were only moody. It was only a style. Look at Jimmy standing there in the road – all he wants is a fair shake at joining the country club.

Added to the mix: there was a beat. Drummed up by the black man and with an ancestry that goes all the way back to Africa. Great rhythm, the best, and warming feet near any radio that it came out of. But was it going anywhere?

Now hear me on this. Tarzan came in from the bush and, guided by Sam, he picked up the moment and carried the century away. He gave fighting room to the voice of the underside – he took what was hidden in the deeps of America and gave it a place in the sun. You can chant your Lenin and Marx at me, talk about the impact of television, fling your academic volumes until your pitching arm gets tired. The postwar boom, the invention of the teenager, all of that is egghead discussion designed to obscure the facts. The truth is simple: Tarzan made low culture important, and the rest is history.

Of course he didn't understand what he was doing. The guy was only six months out of the trees.

And it started in the Sun studio.

On that first day Sam wasn't even there. He met Tarzan, as agreed, shook his hand, but this was in Miss Taylor's restaurant next door to the studio. He ran his eyes over him. Some eyes. Every account written of Sam Phillips always mentions them. They're set below heavy brows and in a face that has maybe a hint of Abraham Lincoln about it, rounded cheekbones and a square jaw. Probably Abe didn't use as much pomade. Sam's hair was wavy and magnificently sculpted – one interview records Sam as being "terrible about his hair." A slim nose, a high brow. But it was the eyes that counted. Deep blue. Some writers have said they glittered. Some say he had a hard look that reminded them of a gunfighter – but did any of those hacks ever stare down the barrel of a gunfighter's eyes? Sam's eyes weren't so special. I looked into them. It was what was behind in there that counted. Ten thousand miles.

No one ever mentions his ears.

Sam was interested, polite. And Sam always had fellow-feeling. He looked at Tarzan and saw him – saw his predicament. But anyone could tell he thought if Tarzan had a place anywhere it was a circus. He asked Tarzan what kind of singer he was and Tarzan said, "I sing the songs on the radio." Well, fine – why not? Except that what Sam wanted was a sound that no one had heard yet. *If I could find a white boy who sings like a black man, I'd make a million dollars* – those are the words attributed to him. They're so mythologised, no one will know if he ever really said them. Nevertheless they serve. They put white and black together and come up with the money. But all that money is in fact a distraction. Sam also wanted to give voice to something.

After the talk, he sent them to the studio, saying he had a date at the bank – Sam was hard-pressed around this time – and that his assistant would see to it. He would come by shortly.

And so it was Marion Keisker who first put Tarzan's voice on tape.

A recording studio is basically an empty box that reverberates right and at that time Sun was just another box on a backstreet – a former retail store. Marion was just another woman in love with Sam. No, that is disrespectful. Marion played her part in the discovery of Tarzan. She was a lovely woman, full of spirited grace, recently divorced, with a nine-year-old son, who had her own show on WREC, *Meet Kitty Kelly*, and knew how to run the recording equipment at Sun almost as well as Sam himself. She took in this strange group – Carole, red-haired and somewhat imperious, the shadowy Eve, and the younger woman, blonde Jane, golden almost, hanging on the arm of this big rangy fellow with the full dark head of hair and the sombre suit – and did her best to make them at home. Sun wasn't large. The women all squeezed into the control booth and looked out through the glass at Tarzan alone in the studio gloom. "Does he have a guitar or something?"

Marion had been briefed by Sam – this was, she knew, the guy from the jungle. Well, he was big enough, and there was something about the way he carried himself, as though it was he who was the civilised one. But why did he belong in a recording studio? "All right, Tarzan – is it Tarzan? All right, are you going to sing us something?"

He looked at them and began to sing towards them. *Over the Rainbow* – a song sun by a kid in a movie, why choose that? He wasn't singing into the microphone, he seemed unaware of its significance, but Marion was getting a sound, the red needles were swinging, she decided to ignore it. He was in tune okay. But he sounded pale, strangled – she had expected somehow more. She could tell by the mood in the booth that something was wrong. The women – were they *all* his women? – were agitated. She had to restrain the blonde one from opening the studio door and going in to speak to him.

The song ended and she stopped the tape. "All right, thank you, I have that." And she rewound it and played it back. Well, she'd heard worse. In fact it almost had a quality to it. What quality, exactly? Marion tried to think where Sam might go from here with this. But she had already decided what she would tell him: Nothing doing.

Now the pretty blonde one had gone in and was speaking up to him. As Marion watched he dropped to one knee and so Jane Porter crouched too. It was touching to see them together. There was definitely something in the way he moved – he might make a dancer.

Marion too went out into the open studio space and addressed him. "Could you sing into the microphone? This thing." Her eyes went to Jane's, two people on the management level checking to see if a subordinate has got the message. Apparently – Jane was nodding. "All right, well, Tarzan – do you have another song for us?"

Marion has said in interviews that she was later ashamed of how she spoke to him that day. *He was hard to read. He didn't give anything away. I had it in my head I guess that he was a wild creature and might paw at the curtains – sorry, but it's true.* But she was in her own way as instinctive as Sam and so she managed to put him at his ease.

Then, to her surprise, he spoke to her. He said, "Can I hear the sound of it?"

It was, she said, like a creature being offered a mirror for the first time. *When he said that I understood that he was a thinking being behind the brown face and I felt as though I'd been cruel. Suddenly I had to make a point of having a really good look at him.*

Crouched now in the middle of the studio floor, Tarzan and Jane listened to the playback. They were both frowning. Then Jane stood up and announced, "He's going to sing it again." Then she returned to the control booth.

Doesn't he know anything else, Marion wanted to ask. But she had become hesitant and had decided to let this go its own way.

Tarzan stood out in the open space of the big room. There were no windows and the air smelled of all the people who had ever been in it. It was the human smell, but there was something different about it. He had been noticing this smell ever since he'd been in Memphis, it was the different smell of the black people they called Negroes. The ones they were all careful with. Negroes had been here. There'd once been a dog. Someone had been sick in here, too, over in the corner, and there was the room smell that he always noticed, the smell of the colour, he thought, that was used to cover the walls. The walls were pale green. The air was hot.

Tarzan trying to think what a man would do.

From the other side of the glass the women were watching him. Eve was watching the most carefully. He knew that Eve saw him best. Jane's eyes were big. Carole was smoking a cigarette and you couldn't see her face clearly. And there was this new woman, from the studio, Marion – their faces in the rectangular frame of the glass. The woman called Marion spoke to him, her voice came down from a machine in the ceiling: "All right, Tarzan, we're ready."

He took off his clothes. There was no chair to put them on so he laid them on the floor. As he undid the buttons on the waistcoat he felt his chest come free. He was still hot but at last his skin could breathe. He got his shoes and socks off, but, as Jane had told him, kept his trousers on. The microphone thing was standing there – he walked up to it, took hold of it. He was going to have to sing to this piece of metal. The bit at the top was long, like a banana, and it had holes in it that made a pattern. There were patterns everywhere in America. This was the thing he had to understand, why they made patterns, and who made them. The microphone was cold, hard when he touched it. But there was, he knew, life inside it.

In the pale green light of the room, he looked the pattern in the eye. Then he sang his song again.

Ah, but this was different.

These two tapes can be heard today, one after another, on the CD called *Sunrise – Tarzan's Early Masters*. The first version, so thin and pale, is nothing you would ever return to, a curiosity. But the second hints at everything Tarzan was to achieve. The unaccompanied voice puts a dream inside each word, the words stand in the air as though carved from stone – in places the emotion is too much for him. And yet that song is such a chestnut, it's hard to get much out of. Plus if you saw him do it. That's what Marion said, later, to Sam: that his voice was good, really good – this is from another interview – *and he had the sense you know of there being a shape to the sound, to the song, that he has to bring through.*

You could hear how he didn't really understand, at that time, the meaning of all the words – just in the way he said some things. But that worked for him. The song is full of him trying to get to something, to an understanding. I told him: Sam, you have to see Tarzan. Then it's different. When you see him you understand that this is extraordinary, and then you start to listen all over again. He doesn't move, he doesn't even tap his toe. He just stands there and gives you, you know, his feeling. I could hardly control myself. I had a desire. I don't mean like I wanted to go to him or anything. But as though I had to tell him something, something of what he had made me understand, about myself.

Not that she said any of this at the time.

She simply told them that that was better, much better, and now she could see why they thought he might make a singer. Yes, it was a voice of recording quality. She busied herself with making the acetate, and typed on its label, *Tarzan, Over the Rainbow, Take Two*. Then she had them pay the $3.98 plus tax that it cost to make a recording.

This irritated Carole, to have to pay. She thought they had come down to do a test with this Sam Phillips, to see if he wanted to sign up Tarzan – and he wasn't even here. And now to pay – hell, they were just another gaggle of dreamers cutting a disk so they could say they'd made a record. She went outside and stood on the walk, smoked a fast cigarette.

Tarzan was dressing.

Eve and Jane were watching Marion's face. She was a nice person, anyone could see that, and she'd said he had a good voice – but what did she really think?

Then it was over. Sam Phillips had never turned up. Tarzan had his clothes on now and was standing at the door of the control booth, waiting. Marion handed him the acetate. Her first instinct had been to give it to Jane, but she stopped herself.

Tarzan took it carefully, didn't look at it, held it down by his side. Did he understand what it was?

Then they were walking down the Memphis sidewalk and it was two-thirty in the afternoon. "Well," said Carole, "where's the car from here?" If you looked for it you could see the smoke coming out her ears.

"I'm going to stick around," said Eve. Carole turned and looked at her and now it was clear whose fault this all was. This fiasco. Behind her dark lenses, Eve coloured up. But she stood firm. "I'm going to talk to Sam Phillips."

"Me too," said Jane.

"No," said Eve. "This is family."

Carole let out a breath. "Okay, Evie. Okay, you do that. Me, I think I'm going to make a run down to Jackson, I've never been there. Anyone like a ride?"

No, they all chose to stay in Memphis, they took rooms at the Peabody Hotel. Carole drove off. Eve called Sam Phillips and later on that day she met with him and spoke to him, about family and what it might mean in the modern world. How far they'd driven. What good manners amounted to – oh, yes, by the time Eve met with Sam she was ready to deliver a broadside. Meanwhile Jane and Tarzan took themselves off to the hotel and made a test of its fixtures and fittings.

That night they all went out and enjoyed the sounds of Beale Street. They sniffed at doorways, they laughed at the jump that the sounds put inside them. In a noisy club where the great pianist Earl "Fatha" Hines was in command they found a table at the back, kept a low profile and listened. That is, Jane and Eve watched Tarzan listen. Had anyone ever listened like that? He seemed to gather the music – not swaying and moaning, no, he was upright and still. If computers had been invented then you might have said he digitalised it. He was making a memory. But more than that

– he was trying to understand it. Music, when you go in between the notes, down in there you will find all the mystery that has ever been present on the planet. There have been archeological finds which suggest that the cave men made music. What it sounded like we'll never know. But undoubtedly they found the place that music takes you. Music has an inside and when you go down into it, when you stand in that place, you don't need to think any more about your bank balance or your poor old body or the torment of that commenting voice which just won't shut up inside your ear. This is our earthly reward, seek no other.

I guess I am the living proof that given their earthly reward what can men do but seek further.

The session at Sun the next day was different. Marion was there again, and Eve and Jane. Carole, away on her drive, was replaced by Sam, who was now at the controls.

Sam wasn't in any apparent hurry to start recording – plenty of time for that. He'd played Tarzan's tapes. He'd listened to Marion on the subject. Now he wanted to find out who this guy was. He took the big fellow – Tarzan was probably aged eighteen at this point – out into the middle of the studio floor, found him a folding chair, had him sit. Sam had a chair too, together with the nearby microphone they made a strange trio in the gloomy green of that large, pale, windowless space. Jane decided to join them but Sam, with a glance from his blue eyes, kept her in the confines of the control booth. Will you always be where he is? This is what his eyes seemed to ask her. Can you ever be? It stung Jane. Suddenly Tarzan seemed to be having a life that she wasn't part of. *I saw the two of them together and all at once I knew that they would make a male communion which I would serve only as a waitress; as a servant or camp follower. But I loved him! How can it be that the one you love has a sphere of life in which you play no part? Now I saw, there in the control booth at Sun Records, that, though I had brought Tarzan into the world, I might not keep him. The world might take him. Of course, I was born a fighter, I would not sit by the fire crying bitter tears into my knitting. But I have also cared passionately about the natural order of things. The way the world should be. That is why I brought him out of the bush – which had been a right action. But now I saw, with a clarity that brought a twist of pain to my insides, that perhaps the natural order where Tarzan was concerned might not include me . . .*

So she stayed with the other women in the booth, watching from behind the glass. This was a recording studio, the mike was open – they would hear anything that was said. But they couldn't speak.

Sam was used to these little meetings out in the barren landscape of the sound stage. He had made a point, since Sun began, of recording Negro artists, was passionate about their music, and some of those artists, before they gave of themselves, had needed more than just a slap on the back and a dotted line to sign on. Difficult men like Ike Turner or Chester Burnett who called himself Howlin' Wolf and could be as cussed as the dark, painful world he sang about. But Sam had talked them all round and so he felt no doubt within himself as he settled face to face with the big fellow from the wild. Not so big – the Wolf after all was six foot three, a great height for that time, a heavy-shouldered, glowering man, who looked hard through a scowl to see where you were cheating him. Who spoke in a terrible voice that sounded like the actual Devil. Who tried to intimidate. Tarzan was none of those things. Compared, he seemed mild, calm. But watchful. Sam sensed a flywheel spinning, somewhere deep inside. He started in by asking, "So you like singing that song about somewhere over the rainbow?"

"Yes, sir." Tarzan already picking up the Southern manner of working an honorific into a sentence.

"Well maybe you can tell me why you like it so much."

... *lahk* it ...

Tarzan frowned over this. He felt the keen gaze of the slim man opposite him, the pressure that Sam could put on a point. Sam's eyes were going over his head, looking for a way in. Tarzan felt as he had out on the stage in Freddie's nightclub, as though the spotlight might burn. He saw that he was going to have to come up with some words. "I do not know the right way to say it," he said.

Sam wasn't going to let him off. "That's okay, son. You just say it any old way you can."

There was a long pause, during which Tarzan did not look away. That is what the black men did and Sam had let them do it – people have to be given thinking room. But this Tarzan looked right back at you with his eyes open and so afterwards it was in Sam's mind that he had gone in there and given the boy the words he needed – was that true? It was true that somehow they had between them come up with his answer. Tarzan said carefully, as though the words were a thing he was assembling, "It says the skies will be blue. But they are blue. So it must be another blue."

"Very good," said Sam – slim, all wrists and cheekbones, tense in the chair, with the long slim line of his tie dark like an opening to his insides. "Another blue, I like that. And so what's it like, this other blue?"

Tarzan and Sam sweating on this problem together. Finally Tarzan said, "It must be better."

"Heck, I think that about says it," said Sam. "A better blue. I'll have to think about that. Okay. Okay, Tarzan, good. All right, now: another question." Sam had no nervous gestures. He could focus his nerves, put everything he had into his gaze. Again, putting that heat on Tarzan, he asked, "What is it you want?"

Had Tarzan ever wanted anything? Well, yes – in the bush he had wanted his mother. He had wanted Kala not to be dead. To go with Jane. But these were not the answers. He knew that. He felt the eyes of Mr Sam Phillips working him over. They were bringing him to something. He felt a shape forming inside him – something familiar, something far away. He said, "I want to go to the Empire State Building."

Sam laughed. "The old Empire State, huh. Ain't she a beauty. Okay. And what do you want to do when you get to the Empire State Building?"

"To go to the top."

"And when you get to the top?"

Oh, there was definitely a right answer to this, Tarzan could tell. Sam Phillips was frowning down hard, Tarzan could smell the burn of him. "I want to sing."

"On top of the Empire State?"

"Yes."

"Sing somewhere over the rainbow skies are a better blue up on top of the ol' Empire State Building?"

"Yes, sir."

Sam leaned back and regarded him from a distance. "Well, I believe that might just be worth listenin' to."

It was interesting, everyone thought, how Sam Phillips didn't want to see Tarzan sing. *Seeing him* had been the pitch they had all given Sam, especially Marion, and they had all been sure that if only he could see the man from the jungle digging his way into the unsuspected depths of that bluebird song, why, then – but no. Sam had taken their word for that. He had played the tape, and that was enough. Sure, the voice would sound smoother if he had some backing, if he had been miked more carefully. But that was only smoother. Sam didn't need a smoother ballad singer. He needed . . . Well, he couldn't put a word to that. All he knew was, he needed something new. There was a thing that could be arrived at, a further direction in music. But where did it lie? It was not a lost highway. No, this was yet to be found. It was a road that had not yet been surveyed, across a territory that no one else even thought existed. But it did! Sam was sure of it. So how do you get to an unknown land? Maybe this oncer from way out on the edge of things could go there.

In the studio, Sam had stood, rested with his hand on the back of his chair and stroked his chin a while. Everyone waited respectfully. Then finally he strode to the control booth and confronted the women. "Okay," he said, "I'm interested." His eyes went round them all, no one was sure who he should be addressing. Who owned Tarzan? "Marion, make out a standard contract. One year – to record exclusively for Sun, plus another two years on my decision. Have him sign it." Now, looking at these people from his own social order, Sam seemed to falter. The communion he'd made with Tarzan was broken. Now the whole thing seemed cockamamie. But Sam refused to be daunted. "That's right. Have him sign it. Then everybody go home. I have to think what to do next."

"How much does he get for signing?"

This was Carole.

Sam rounded on her. "He ain't done anythin' yet. When he does somethin', and it earns, he'll get his share."

"But if he signs, he can't record for anyone else," said Carole stubbornly, "he should be compensated for that."

"Compensated? I'll give you compensated. When will I be compensated for all the brain fever I am going to have from thinking how to make something out of that jungle boy? Get outa here!"

Tarzan, sitting alone in the middle of the studio, had watched their movements through the glass. In the bush he'd seen Kerchak and Kala and Tublat in communication of this sort. Deciding. He knew they were deciding about him. Should he go and see? But he stayed where he was, on the chair, and tried to know what could be known of this room that was called a studio. The world in America was full of rooms – this was a singing room, apparently. A music room. There was a piano in the corner – he went over and touched it. His finger fell on a white key and the instrument rang. He remembered the black man, sweating on the stage the night before, Mr Hines, and the place that the music had made. How that one note reverberated. But it was, he understood, the way that many notes stood side by side with each other that made the thing that he liked. He tapped two keys but it didn't happen. What made it work, was it the instrument or the man? Sam Phillips asked him what he wanted and he knew. He wanted to go inside the music – to somewhere that was a place but had no walls. But he didn't know how to say that.

16

Jane was down in Riverside, talking to her professor, whatever that was, arranging their lives, and so she wasn't available to explain for him. Tarzan sat around the house, or out in the garden. Carole brought him sandwiches, which he ate dutifully, and then she went inside again. Only Eve stayed with him. He liked Eve. She sat near him the way the gorillas had sat near him, completely watchful but not bothered. Sometimes he would ask her something and she would try to explain. But she seemed more puzzled by his questions than Jane, and wanted to think about them instead of always giving him an answer. He watched her writing in her notebook, and tried to figure what was taking place. They could all read and write. He felt as lonely because of this one thing as anything else.

Before she left, Jane had explained it that Sam Phillips had liked him and was going to do something for him, but nobody knew what – "so we just have to wait." Tarzan didn't understand waiting. What was waiting? His whole life had been waiting, hadn't it? This was just more of it.

Then a package arrived, delivered by a van that Eve said was from the Post Office. Special Delivery – Tarzan had to sign. Make a mark, said Eve, like you did on the contract. He held the pencil, pushed it across the piece of paper on the man's clipboard. The man was excited, Tarzan couldn't understand why. Make another mark, said Eve. So he made two marks and the man gave him the parcel and then he went away. Eve said he was excited because Tarzan had been in the newspaper.

She called Carole and together in the shade of the plum tree they talked him through opening the paper-wrapped thing. A knife for the string – ah, look! Music, Tarzan. Because the parcel was from Sam Phillips, a complete set of the Sun back catalogue – worth a fortune today. The thick slices of vinyl were heavy, it was as though each one of them was loaded with feeling. At the centre of each vinyl disk, around the hole in the middle, stood the Sun logo, yellow and chocolate, in broad rays, with black musical notes dancing – the whole arrangement was very optimistic. Plus there were some recordings on the Chess and Modern labels, R&B, and various selections of other music, country, gospel, mountain folk – along with a note, typed on Sun letterhead. *Dear Tarzan, Sam says for you to play these every day. Sincerely, Marion. P.S. – someone might find you some better radio stations.*

And so Tarzan's musical education took a lurch to the dark side. On these disks there were no strings to be heard tidily sweeping up the emotions. No words about *my sweet heart and yours*. No, here the heart was a thing that went boom, the man's actual organ inside his aching chest. You heard the bang of his knees as he fell to prayer, to sobbing, the spring as he jumped up at you to tell how good he feel. Splayed black fingers slapping the piano keys, dusty black shoes beating out a cakewalk on the slapboard. Down between the notes, Tarzan found the gaps that so pleased him, the reverberating intervals that echoed across the distance between his ears. There were hoofbeats in there, heart-thumpings, fists pounded on closed doors. The sound of shotguns, the sound of trains, the crack of a mean whip. Exultation and despair – that was what was on those records. And over the banging came the throats. The earth opened and a voice came out. The moan of a boulder, the endless imprisoned sigh of a cliff-face. Such primal voices. *Broke ma back for you baby, an' you split ma heart jest fo' fun!* Tarzan had had Jane show him where his heart was, and now he sat with his fingers feeling the throb of it while he listened. He learned off the names: Howlin' Wolf I have mentioned, plus Jackie Brenston And His Delta Cats, Little Junior Parker, The Prisonaires, B.B. King, Rufus Thomas, Little Walter, Billy Riley, Rosco Gordon, Sonny Boy Williamson, Joe Hill Lewis – who were these people? What did they look like, to sing like that? Tarzan for the first time had the sense that there were individual human beings behind the sounds he was listening to. He tried to visualise them singing. To know what state they were in.

To know how they lived that made them sound like that.

Lately he had taken to going for walks around the neighbourhood. He was looking for these music-making people – all he saw were letterboxes. Miles of tree-lined and shady drives, with tended lawns and on each lawn a collection of rooms that was called a house. Jane, who had returned now, would sometimes accompany him. But he didn't ask her questions any more, not about this. He sensed, correctly, that she didn't know about this, about the place inside the music and the human beings who went in there to make it. Well, this was just not where they lived, it seemed. This was California, where only blue skies were permitted, and tanned, smiling faces. Still, it was nice to have her there, beside you – there was also a music in that.

Then when they paused, she would hold his head between

her hands and look in, as Sam had done, to see what he was thinking. She allowed herself to do this, and he permitted it. She wanted to stay with him, to hear what he heard – those deep rhythms! Yeah, funky. But he was six foot four and had a stride that really covered the ground, it was hard to keep up with him.

Touching his body, her fingers found that the flesh near his armpit was going soft, the skin on his neck was loose. He felt this himself. It began to drive him crazy to sit around all the time. Every day he saw a new thing – the Wastemaster, for example, that lived down inside the black hole in the sink – and he made careful note. But his limbs were waiting, waiting, he could feel a shuddering energy building up in him, he felt reminded of how the air in the bush had got all jumpy before a thunderstorm. Unless there was music playing he couldn't sit still, and he took to hunting the squirrels and chipmunks that scampered through the trees behind the house. The first time he killed he was watchful to see if this was a transgression – apparently not, though Jane, when she saw the remains of the squirrel, took him on a special wildlife tour of the district. That's a cat, that's a dog – not them, okay? That's a gopher, you can kill all of those that you like, that's just a gopher snake, but if you hear one make a rattle you be careful.

She found him under the house, looking to see where the pipe from the Wastemaster went. And in the bathroom he would stare down into the water of the toilet. So many pipes went into the ground – then where did they go? And where did all the water come from? She drove with him up to the reservoir, together they looked down on the subdivided landscape, the houses and farms that it served spread out below.

Patterns, America was covered in patterns.

She took him every place she could think of. This is a Little

League game, that guy is the catcher, there's the batter, these are the rooting parents. They're staring at us because our picture was in the paper, just act normal – you can wave if you want to. This is a fire engine. This is the fire house. This is the courthouse. This is a funeral parlour. This is a beauty parlour. This is a beehive hairdo. This is a pageboy. That's a cockroach, there, going under the fridge, get it! Good boy! Oooh, don't eat it.

The oceans don't fall off because of gravity.

Fish get oxygen out of the water.

Plants do so breathe.

Everything inside you is made of chemicals. Your feelings are chemicals – and electricity. When you have a smile feeling, this is some chemicals going from one place to another inside your brain. By electricity, I guess. I'll have to look that up, electricity is hard – d'you want ketchup on your dog?

Meanwhile he kept listening out for the source of that sound. Nights he sat in the front room with the volume on the hi-fi turned down so that Carole could follow the Jackie Gleason show – a fat man pulling faces. His ear down beside the speaker, his eyes on the weave of the carpet. One after another he played the records that Mr Phillips had sent, going inside them and trying to find out what they were made of. The sound was so big that he could not imagine a horizon large enough to contain it. It went all around you. And then, later, outside in California, he simply could not find this. No, that wasn't it. He could, too, if he really concentrated – for example, Jane had it in her. He would walk beside her when she was explaining and he could sense it in there, way beneath the words she was saying, within her body, lying deep in there like the sound that was inside the waterfall. It was in her walk, it was in his walk, it was inside the cars going past, their throbbing engines. He felt it in the trunks of the trees, he felt it coming up through the soles of his feet. Yes, but it was so faint. He wanted to be where it was all that you could hear.

Jane and Tarzan took a Greyhound down to Riverside, to Jane's campus, where she had arranged rooms – just to have a look around. Alice, her former roommate, came for coffee and said she would babysit, anytime.

Prof Hingle, a serious man, shook hands. But then they just stood side by side, the two males, while Jane tried desperately to whip up a conversation. Hingle never chatted and Tarzan could let an hour go past, no sweat, between sentences.

Hingle later remarked that this was going to be science she was producing, wasn't it, as opposed to, say, babies?

There was no hi-fi in Riverside – well, Hingle had one, Jane said, and when Tarzan asked, they had gone to hear it. In his room Hingle played them Schönberg, which Tarzan listened to in silence. Hingle served them green tea, which reminded Tarzan of the manuka tea that Jane had once brewed. He liked it. But he never asked to go back.

There was no beat in Riverside.

Tarzan caught a Greyhound back to Petaluma.

Jane racked her brains.

At weekends she too caught the Greyhound, six hours of sitting so they could be in bed together. Also it was useful for her studies. For them to be together and then apart, she found that when she was with him all the time she couldn't see him so scientifically. But shouldn't love be part of science? She thought about discussing this with Hingle but decided against it – it would make him doubt her. There was, of course she agreed, no place in science for magic or God, "or even patriotism," as he had once remarked. There should only be facts. But love was a fact, wasn't it? It felt like a fact, the aching lump of it inside her.

Tarzan, meanwhile, was doing time. She saw that. He was waiting. He had learned all the simple procedures – unbutton your shirt, place it in the basket, carry the basket to the laundry. He chewed his steak methodically. And he understood things, for example, he knew when Carole wanted to talk to Eve, just Eve, and he would take himself off – Carole told Jane this, both of them in faint awe of his ability to know the unspoken. But, like a man in prison, he was doing time. He was just plain waiting. What the hell was Sam Phillips playing at?

Every morning Tarzan would become very still around eleven o'clock, Carole told Jane, become even more watchful. In fact, she realised, he was listening, for the mailman. Carole listened too but heard nothing.

There never was another parcel from Sam Phillips.

But an envelope turned up, with a stamp bearing the words *Atoms For Peace*, and Tarzan's name. This was from someone called Edgar Rice Burroughs, who, according to the letter it enclosed – Carole read it out – was a famous author. Eve had heard of him. She turned up her nose. His books had made him a millionaire, he said, though at seventy-nine he was more or less retired. But Tarzan's story, "as retailed by the press," had intrigued him and he wondered, very politely, Carole thought, if he might be granted an interview?

Carole was somehow charmed by the idea of a seventy-nine-year-old whose curiosity was still so energetic and she told Tarzan he should say yes.

The first interview took place on Carole's lawn, with Tarzan and Mr Burroughs in armchairs and Carole and Eve a carefully measured distance away on the tartan rug. No notes were taken. Eve was tempted to record the occasion, but she thought she had no business hitching a ride on someone else's train, and Burroughs said he could no longer read his own shorthand, but would remember everything that mattered. This statement alarmed the two women.

But Burroughs, sitting there, was rather a sweet old guy, with lovely manners and a definite twinkle in his eye. From the first he did all the talking. His large, brown bald head glowed in the sun as he sketched in for them his early life. His father, George Tyler Burroughs, had been a Civil War veteran and the family was prosperous – Edgar attended a number of private schools, including a military academy and later served, he said, in the Seventh Cavalry. Carole at this point wondered if anyone might like something liquid to wash this down with, whereupon the old man produced a box of tea from his briefcase and asked if she could brew them all some – Carole had thought wine. But they sat under the plum tree and drank the hot tea, it was very pleasant, while Burroughs entertained them.

He did in fact ride with the Seventh Cavalry. He was a millionaire. He had also had a number of years, over a decade, of extraordinary failure, and he had never forgotten this. His voice was warm and his cloudy green eyes glowed pale as he painted scenes in the air which had them all hanging on his next word. Short, and rather stooped now, jowly, with a nicely rounded little belly, he gave the impression of being able to remember having once possessed an immense vigour – something like a fortune which had been thoroughly and enjoyably spent. At sixty-six he had been a war correspondent in the South Pacific, he said, "floating around in the sun while the boys were looking for someone to fight."

Afterwards, Tarzan always held an image of this man in his mind, where he stood alongside Sam Phillips as a model for what the human being should be.

When three hours had passed a large silver car came

creeping slowly down the driveway – "A Rolls Royce!" Carole exclaimed – and from it a uniformed driver unfolded. "Please wait, Andrew," said Burroughs, quite kindly, and the driver got back into the vehicle.

Then finally the old man fell silent. His legs were crossed, his hands were rested on the top of his belly. The cloudy gaze fell on Tarzan. "So, tell me, young Mr Tarzan," he said, "what are you planning to do here in America?"

The "interview" continued on and off over a period of six weeks and during that time Burroughs only ever asked Tarzan the very odd question, and none of the questions were about his past life.

Nevertheless the old man's eyes had been open. When, eighteen months later, the interviews turned into a novel – Burroughs' final publication – it bore only skeletal resemblance to Tarzan's life. For one thing, it was set entirely in Africa and, over time, this did as much as anything to confuse Americans about his origins – forever after he was "the man from the jungle" and people asked him, how exactly do you kill a lion? But *Tarzan of the Apes* contains the essence of the young Tarzan, his determination, his spirit, his bewilderment, and conveys something of the raw power, constrained by intelligence, which was the impression he gave in those early years. Also, it turned Tarzan's life into a classic story, which has repeatedly been filmed and retold. So now, across the years, I salute the book and give my thanks to its magnificent, undaunted author.

That was later – by the time the novel was published, the question of what Tarzan would do in America had long been settled. But between the Burroughs interviews and the start of his career there lay a shapeless time of waiting, a time of restlessness and confusion, which had to be endured.

He knew all the words to all the records now, and could sing them to himself as he strode through Carole's neighbourhood. However, when he appeared, on two further occasions, at Freddie's club, he stuck to *Over the Rainbow*.

Waiting, while ideas mixed inside him: this he thinks was the reason for the thing that happened.

After what proved to be his final nightclub appearance, Freddie dropped him home in the red sports car, for which he had Tarzan get dressed again – "I can't be driving around with you in a loincloth." Then the house was empty, Carole was out somewhere, as soon as he stepped inside it Tarzan felt how the walls had nothing to contain. Except him. In Jane's bedroom he threw off the suit from Wellington, which lay on the bed as though exhausted. He kept taking off clothes until all he had on him was the pendant round his neck – even this was annoying. He should, he knew, put on at least some boxers. But ever since he'd met Jane, he saw this now, he'd been inside something, first the shorts, then the sequence of events.

This is how Tarzan constructed it later, lying in the dark, putting one action after another. I can feel that Tarzan in my head even today, a frown, a determination to understand everything that has ever happened.

He left the house and went to stand out in the garden, letting the night air go close about his skin. There were houses around, he was still inside the neighbourhood, but in the shadow of the plum tree the light from their windows was blotchy and dim. He looked up. Up in the vast American darkness he could see the stars. Jane said these were different stars but he didn't want to see that. They looked the same. He wanted to yell – to yell so loud the gorillas in the valley would hear him.

Jane had had him pull on the shorts. That was her idea, to put him into something. But Sam Phillips seemed to have another idea for him. Sam could show him somewhere in America that was open.

Nevertheless he was warm towards Jane. She was miles away but the thought of her was a thing he liked. There was something he wanted with Jane.

These thoughts pulling at his muscles.

Carole's car swept up the drive and the headlights caught him. They went dim like the life fading out of something. No, like something drawing the life back into itself. Carole came across the grass, which, dry, crackled beneath her feet. "Hi, Tarzan," she said. Her gaze went up, swept the stars. "It's a great night for it." He was expecting her to be angry because he wasn't wearing any clothes but instead she said, "Would you mind fetching my cigarettes, they're on my bedside table."

Tarzan wasn't used to being in Carole's room. Her smell was everywhere – the smells she put on herself. The rooms for sleeping in were always the strongest. There was something here he was confused by: the way the smell had Jane in it too. Quickly he picked up the little packet with the sharp corners and carried it outside.

Carole was studying the stars. But she hadn't always been. When he'd walked away he had felt her eyes on his back – he had the idea that she had wanted to see him walk. Yes, there was an idea inside her, something that was making her heart pound.

She stood next to him in the shadows and smoked a cigarette. They didn't talk. Something was going to happen and he waited to see what it would be. Then Carole said to him, "D'you think it might snow, Tarzan?" The question hung in the air. Was this what was going to happen: snow? Tarzan gazed around, he wasn't confident about where snow might come from. "Do they even have snow in New Zealand?" He wasn't sure. Snow was white, he knew that, and this was somehow connected to him – after all, his name was also a word for white.

Then he felt her touch him.

She'd done something with her hands and now he realised she'd been switching the cigarette from right to left so that the fingers of her right hand could touch his back, low, where his butt began to swell. The tips of her fingers were going up and down, slowly, as though they were trying to cause something.

Was she still thinking about snow? She had moved and now her hand came round too. Well, he knew how this went, he remembered, once again he was under a tree, he closed his eyes and his head went back. At this time Tarzan formed the impression that women would come to him and try to please him, which was an idea that stayed with him all his life – and was as it turned out more or less true. But Carole's other hand was also busy, she was working on her buttons and after opening her clothes she reached up, pulled his head down and kissed him hard on the mouth.

Now she moved away, but not very far, squatted and urinated. Complicity wasn't a word that Tarzan had heard at this time, but it was on her face when in the middle of her act she turned and looked into his eyes.

Kissing again, her mouth was hot and she tasted of smoke – she still had the cigarette in one hand, he saw, held away to the side so that no one got burned. Tarzan didn't much care for the kiss. Inside his head the thought formed clearly: Jane wouldn't think this was right. It was Jane who told him what was right. But Carole's hand was stronger than her kiss and somehow it was strange, it was Carole who told Jane what was right, the authority went upwards, and so that somehow made this okay – didn't it? Then they were down on the ground.

Tarzan felt that she wanted to see what he would do. Well,

he knew what to do, no problem. But ideas were coming into his head, it was like being in her bedroom, somehow Jane and Carole were in this together, it was an unstable mix, it was nice, but strange, and then there came the moment when Tarzan said, "Where will the snow come from?"

"Later," Carole said, and she turned them over so that she was looking down now into his face. She wanted to know what he was feeling – she wanted, she wanted . . . Then her head lifted away so that Tarzan saw the taut line of her neck which was a lovely thing he just had to run his finger up.

Young Tarzan having sex with the older woman and old me too, thank you fortune, with sweet thing Loretta: this juxtaposition gives pleasure somehow to the angels, who shower gifts down for their own amusement.

At Christmas it rained for a week, solid, and in winterless California this was a pleasing diversion. But mainly the sky was an unchanging, endless blue.

Tarzan paced the neighbourhood, waited for the postman. No snow.

17

When finally the skies opened and a call did come for Tarzan it wasn't so much a summons as a faint suggestion. Sam Phillips was not one do anything fainthearted but it seemed in this instance that perhaps he didn't want to be held responsible – anyways, if the boy would like to get himself down to Tennessee, for a week or two maybe, Marion had found somewhere he might stay, and Sam himself was developing a notion of how he could go about the unearthing of anything that might lie within Tarzan.

This call was taken by Carole and she welcomed it without reserve. Of course he could come, what else did he have to do but hang around the house? Of course he would like to stay with this family Marion recommended – they understood his background, didn't they? We'll wire you to say when he's arriving. For two weeks. Ciao, Sam. Ciao.

For Carole it was completely clear: he had to go. Eve, the face in the background, seemed to agree. Tarzan of course was keen. Which left Jane.

Jane had done some thinking. She was tied to Riverside, but they didn't have to live on campus. She'd found them a house, a nice old place, with a garden and with the privacy they needed. It was expensive, she would need to waitress at night, and he would have to find something – she knew of a vacancy at a local grade school that needed a janitor. It would be a start. Also she needed him for her studies – she had decided that. She had to have him. Eve might be writing about his career, whatever that was, and Burroughs might have interviewed him, but she, she was the one who had seen him in his natural state. She was going to publish on him. He was her subject, and she needed him at hand, so that she could chart his progress scientifically. Plus it was cold nights.

They were in the kitchen when the return to Memphis was debated – standing in the kitchen near the window with the view of the driveway. Jane felt the united front against her. She felt her feelings, just chemicals, as she had explained to Tarzan, her chemicals moving around inside her body. It was late evening, the windows were dark, but in Carole's house no one pulled the curtains, especially since Tarzan's arrival – he hated being shut in. Looking out, she saw the gorillas on the hillside, dark eyes in dark faces, watching to see what would become of him – if he would find what he'd left them for.

She drove him to the airport herself. She explained to the hostess who he was, how to speak to him. She checked his bag. She had explained how an airplane worked, about how the vacuum above the wing provided the lift, taken him out to the little airfield at Petaluma to watch the planes take off and land. She'd told him about the way he must sit quietly and look out the window.

Everyone must find what will become of them.

Then she kissed him goodbye.

She stood on the tarmac and listened to the sound of the propellers as their whine rose to a loud hum. She had gone on board and settled him in his seat. Last row at the back, where no one would see him if he acted strange, and now she looked at his face in the lozenge of the little airplane window and waved. She was wearing a scarf, it flapped wildly in the prop wash.

Then finally he was alone in America.

As had been arranged, Marion Keisker was standing at the foot of the wooden steps in Memphis that led down from the plane. She kissed his cheek, and had a look at him, into his eyes, to see how he was – okay, apparently. The kiss gave him a surprise – Tarzan could feel the print of her lips there, faintly moist, and she'd been wearing lipstick, which he could smell, along with the other smells of her, and of the big room, the lounge, through which they were walking, as they made their way to the place where she said his bag would come. "So how was the flight," she said, "have you been up in an airplane before, Tarzan?"

In his mind's eye he saw the land laid out below so that you felt you could understand it. "I saw all the roads," he said, "but I could not see where they started."

She was easy to talk to, this woman, easier than anyone he'd met. Well, Marion ran an interview show on the local radio station, she knew how to put people at their ease. As they drove towards the city – he'd been inside the plane, then inside the building, now he was inside the car – she asked him questions, and he said what he saw. He could sense her trying to get the shape of him, to get a fix on how much he understood. It was a question he had asked himself. He could use a light switch but where did the light come from and where did it go? Where did automobiles come from? Now he was worried, here in this new part of America, with its unknown arrangement of streets, and without Jane to be the thing he was going back to, that he would get lost. He said this to Marion. "Ma'am, I am worried that I will become lost in this new city."

"Call me Marion. Well, I thought about that too," she said, and she pulled the big car over to the curb. "Now, Tarzan, I have arranged for you to stay with a family who live right here in Memphis." Tarzan looked out the window – they were alongside a vacant lot, there were piles of garbage, gopher mounds, he wondered if she intended him to stay here. Marion caught his expression and said, laughing, "No, we wouldn't do that to you." Then she grasped that he might well have been able to cope with this proposition and was slightly taken aback. "No, we are going to have you stay in a house. Now the thing is, this house is quite close to the studio, I am sure you'll be able to track us down. But this is what I wanted to tell you: the family you are staying with, they lost their boy. He died." She looked to see if he understood what this meant. "His name was Elvis, Elvis Presley, he was eighteen years old, and he died not a couple of miles from here, his truck got crushed by an oil tanker. He was a truck driver, for Crown Electric, that's an electrical contracting company, it was just awful, this was only a year ago, they are just completely torn up – that's his parents, Tarzan, where you'll be staying. I'm sorry, listen to me, I shouldn't say torn up, I should say they are sad. Do you know sad, Tarzan?"

"Yes, I know sad, Marion," he said.

She looked at him there across the long bench seat, big, serious-faced, California bronzed, in his chinos and his white shirt and tie. In those days people still dressed for airplane flights, he had worn a jacket, but in the car the air was hot and she had told him to take it off. He was holding it across his knees, awkwardly, she thought. She had never seen anyone who was so dressed by his clothes.

"So Gladys, that's Mrs Presley, she might cry over you a little bit. Mr Presley doesn't say too much. Elvis was a nice boy, maybe shy, but he had lovely manners." Not unlike you, she was thinking. Tarzan's manners were impeccable, but was that simply because he didn't know how to express his desires? It's easy to be polite if you always stand back and do what you are told.

Tarzan was thinking about the kiss – was this woman a Jane or was she a Carole? The smell of her said Carole. The memory troubled Tarzan. So who was this Mrs Presley going to be?

As they proceeded on into town, Marion continued to explain. It had been her idea, she said, that Tarzan might stay with this family. They weren't wealthy, like the Carole Porters, their house would be smaller and simpler, for example, the Presleys didn't have a telephone, so Jane, she was his friend, wasn't she, Jane would have to ring the Fruchters who lived upstairs and Mrs Fruchter would come down and get him. Gladys Presley had come to Sun Studios hoping to get a new acetate of the recording her son had made, he'd had the original in the truck with him when he died, and so it was destroyed – Elvis had come to Sun maybe a year earlier and paid to cut a disk, "just like you, Tarzan," but no tape had been made of Elvis Presley, just that one acetate, and so now his voice was gone forever. This visit from the tear-stained woman had stayed in Marion's mind and when she and Sam were thinking of where Tarzan might go she had made the connection. But, as she said, the Presleys were poor – he did have the money they had asked him to bring, didn't he.

Tarzan produced an envelope from a jacket pocket and proffered it. "No, no, you give it to Mrs Presley."

These days when you pull up at 462 Alabama you will find, set in the sidewalk, a large bronze plaque with these words on it: *This was the site of the house where Tarzan stayed during the turbulent year of 1954, when he cut the first disks which would so dramatically propel him into worldwide stardom. From these humble origins, rock 'n' roll was born.*

Number five in the Tarzan Presley Heritage Trail of Memphis. The old house is gone now, these days you have a condominium with a view of the new city, and it's hard to get an impression of what the neighbourhood must have been like, what is it? sixty-some years ago. But at that time there was a sense of air and light, especially for the Presleys, who had just graduated from living in the Lauderdale Courts over on Winchester. On weekends, Elvis and Vernon would, according to an interview with Mrs Fruchter, stand out front and polish their old Lincoln as though it was a Cadillac. To finally have their own place, to have both Vernon and Elvis in work, and Elvis had already cut a record – it was only a you-pay acetate, but anyone who had seen him toting his guitar knew that the boy had dreams – it must have seemed as though the Presleys had finally managed to find a place in the sun.

And then he was struck down.

America at that time – this is also hard to recall. The famous songwriter Bob Dylan, describing this period of Tarzan's life, has written that he walked "the path between heaven and nature in an America that was wide open, when anything was possible." It's hard to recall that time, now, when America has become the symbol for everything blind and all-consuming and aggressive and shallow, a comic-book nation, it's so hard to recall how, during the 1950s, American style, American know-how and can-do was such a blessed and attractive thing. Please remember: the idea of America, this then was the great and happy idea of the world. The nation was going somewhere, and the whole planet was just itching to follow.

Yes, in the little towns, in the ordinary houses on the quiet streets, the future was being made – all you had to do was figure a way to get on board.

It was into the fever of that dream-pumped, heart-weary world that Marion Keisker carried Tarzan, and deposited him. She was parking outside a tall house, a solid Victorian thing, set on a low rise, solid, with at that particular moment the sun behind it, so that it glowed like the Sun Records logo, full of promise and hope.

On the porch Mrs Presley was standing with a hand on the rail, waiting.

At seven Marion returned and carried him over to Belz Street where he was to try out with a musician, a guitar player that Sam had found, who was maybe looking for a singer. Now this guitar player was of course the one-and-only, the incomparable Scotty Moore – except that at that time he was not the one-and-only anything. He was just another guy, an ex-Navy deckhand trying to make a go of it down in the food chain. True, he had a band, a country band, the Starlite Wranglers, and they had played a few places. They had even cut a record, and it had sold – but only three hundred copies. The truth was, the music was no more than a cloud of hope. In reality Scotty was working shifts at Firestone, making tyres, and so were the rest of the Wranglers. They were struggling. Scotty's house on Belz was no slice of heaven. Visiting 462 Alabama and then the house of this tyre-maker, Tarzan was seeing the real America, the level at which most folks lived. This was not California. But no one was down in the mouth. As I said, this was a time of optimism, everyone who had an instinct sensed that a change was going to come. Sam knew it, Scotty believed it, if you listened to Dewey Phillips on WHBQ you could hear it being prophesied. Well, no one took Dewey for more than a crazy guy with too many beans in his head. But these were men, like so many in the nation at that time, who had their heads up, who had an idea, a notion – except that no one knew exactly what the notion was.

As they drove, Marion asked, "How did you find Mrs Presley?"

"Good."

Well, he would say that, wouldn't he. Marion tried to think of the right angle. Tarzan was watching her. He watched all the time, it was disturbing, usually men of his size behaved as though the world was beneath their notice and everyone better get out of the way. "Did she cry?"

"I think she did."

"Poor woman."

"I am going to sleep in the bed that Elvis sleeped in."

"Slept," said Marion automatically, as she would with her son. Tarzan didn't seem to mind. "She's still got his room just as it was, I imagine. You'll be there with all his little things." Now a thought occurred to her and she asked, "What kind of a boyhood did you have, Tarzan?"

"Boyhood." He looked at you while he was thinking, you could see right into his eyes. "I grew up with the gorillas. We played fighting. We learned all the smells and all the places. I followed my mother. She showed me how to do all the things. We were outside all the day."

It was the most anyone had heard him say. Marion said, "And you learned to sing off the radio?"

"Yes, ma'am."

He was watching her driving, how she did it – it made it harder to do. She wanted to give him a memory drug, make him talk for her interview show. It was as though he had a paradise inside himself but didn't know it. And here he was trying to join the human struggle. But he had no friends, had never had a friend. He'd never played ball with his dad or had his mom read a bedtime story or had a birthday. Could you become human without these things? And yet he'd had paradise.

"Now Scotty will have you sing some of those radio songs. You sing your best for him, okay. You're a good singer, Tarzan."

"I know," he said.

"Do you?"

"Yes."

"How do you know?"

"I can feel what everyone thinks."

That about sums it up, Marion thought. You can feel what we're thinking – just like how a dog knows when you're blue. It was the knowledge that humans longed to have about each other and yet he couldn't use it because he didn't know what it was good for. All of this rolling around her head while she was trying to drive – she overshot her turn and had to make a left to get back to Belz. Meanwhile he was relaxed, she could feel that about him. It's not that we have no idea, she thought. It's that we'd like to know without doubt.

"You are completely unique, Tarzan," she said. "You don't know what I mean, do you?"

"No, ma'am."

"Don't worry about it." She was parking. "Now, you go in there," she pointed, "and you do what Scotty tells you. No, I better come in." She escorted him to the door and knocked – did he know to knock? – and waited. It was a narrow house, squeezed by its neighbours, pinched into place. When Bobbie who was Scotty's wife appeared Marion did an introduction and then got out of there. Bobbie was as wide-eyed as a raccoon, she wasn't the raccoon type, but meeting this big wild animal, Marion could see that's what she thought, had made her come over all bug-eyed. Marion wanted to go with him, to smooth his path. There would be no one in there that he knew. But she made herself go back to the car and drive away.

Tarzan stared after her. The man called Scotty said, "Hi, Tarzan, come in, sit," and pointed to a chair.

Scotty had Bobbie call Bill Black, Bill was a Wrangler too, he kept his bass fiddle at Scotty's house, with two kids Bill and his wife didn't have room, and then they sat in the front parlour while Bobbie served them Cokes. It was a hot night,

Tarzan was sweating. He found it hard to understand – he thought he had come to sing, but there was no microphone, no stage. After California, everything here was old, tired, everything was small – or else it was new and too bright, not solid enough to contain the world, for example, the plastic cups, bought cheap, were transparent and, when Bobbie poured, seemed barely able to hold the dark, fizzing Coca-Cola. Scotty Moore was a skinny man who held his head back, his gaze went off to the side. Tarzan tried to answer his questions – yes, he had sung in public, yes, they liked him, no, he couldn't play an instrument – but he could tell that the man was feeling awkward. The woman Bobbie sat on the arm of Scotty's chair, she seemed to want to be close to him – Tarzan realised that she was afraid. The shades weren't drawn, people going past on the pavement could see in.

Then Bill Black arrived and everything that followed suddenly began. All at once it was easier – people seemed to know what to say. Bill was a happy man, he made everyone laugh. Tarzan could feel a big smile inside himself, he heard himself laughing too, it gave him a surprise, but he was pleased. Then when Bill said, "I guess we'll play something you know," and began to thump out an intro to *Over the Rainbow*, Tarzan was ready.

The other men sat on the couch and so Tarzan sat too. It was hard, singing while you were sitting down, he couldn't make his voice go out, plus they didn't really know the tune. Bill made a mistake, used a cuss-word, then said, "Let's have another try." When he looked at Tarzan, Tarzan knew he had made the mistake on purpose – to help him. Tarzan took a big breath, then stood up. Standing, he was big in the small room, they all leaned away from him. Overhead, the lightbulb was too close, he could feel its heat. But he knew this was what he had to do. He had to sing out all the things he had inside him when he sang this song.

Why oh why can't I? . . .

"Well, that was all right," announced Bill cheerfully. Bobbie clapped. Scotty had his head down, was busy with his guitar, but he seemed pleased enough. "C'mon, Scotty, let's do that again!" Grinning Bill, an easy man, and hunched, pinched Scotty – they both had jobs to do, it was Bill's job to say any words that were needed. But Scotty was the one who had the inside muscles. Tarzan could see a pattern between the two men, they were both part of it, and the woman too, she was in a different pattern, with Scotty, and there was a pattern in which she was also with the both of them. So where did he fit? Tarzan could feel that Scotty was trying to answer that. Tarzan had liked to hear him play the guitar, when the men played with him it was like they were two and were trying to make it be three. It was hard – but pleasing – not to be the whole thing all on your own. He sang the song again, and they liked him.

But there was something they didn't like.

"Well, fine, Tarzan," said Bill, "just fine. So what else do you know?"

Tarzan wasn't sure what he meant.

"Do you know any other songs?"

Oh. So many. Tarzan didn't know their names. He didn't even know he should know. He just started to sing and they would try to follow him. *Goodnight Irene, Hi-Lili Hi-Lo, How Much is that Doggie in the Window?* Tarzan sang as though he was standing on a rock in the middle of the bush. If he looked at the men, if he thought about them, he got the feeling, strongly – it was like sexing with Carole, it wasn't right. But he didn't know what else to do. *Cool Water. In the Cool, Cool, Cool of the Evening*. Sometimes they didn't know how to play the song, he was the one who knew, he just had to keep going – he always sang each one right through to the end. They didn't know *The White Cliffs of Dover*. He particularly liked singing that one, it made you feel as though you were going up into the skies.

They played together and he sang, and there were those two parts. Sometimes there was one part and those were the times that Tarzan liked, when they were all one part together. Sometimes they came with him, and then sometimes he felt he was going with them, this was such a strange feeling, he could feel the music pulling around inside him, then for moments suddenly it felt wonderful. He had a sense of a huge possibility, something big and open, if only he could find it.

But there was something they really didn't like. He didn't know how to find out what it was. They broke for another Coke, Bill's wife arrived, Evelyn, with Bill's sister, Mary Ann, and they looked at Tarzan – when they were drinking Cokes everyone just sat there and looked at him. Then they were talking, about something that had happened at Firestone. Bill was explaining things to Tarzan, trying to be nice, but it was clear that they all wanted to look at him. He wondered if he should do the act he had done at the nightclub, take off his clothes, maybe give them a yell. It was as though they wanted something. But the feeling wasn't right for that.

Bobbie liked him now, he could tell.

Scotty had put his guitar down and was talking to Evelyn. Bill came over and sat by Tarzan and asked him where was he hanging out – where was he living? "An' you learned all those songs right off the radio down there in Noo Zealan'?"

"Yes, Bill."

Then there was a knock at the door and it was Marion come to get him.

18

That night, all the biographies include this sequence, Sam rang Scotty. This conversation is part of the legend. "The guy can sing okay," Scotty reported.

"But?"

"I dunno, Sam. Who wants to hear that old crud? *Somewhere Over the stinkin' Rainbow* – I mean, if we went out playin' that we'd have every grandma in town thinkin' we were such real nice boys. *Doggie in the Window* – man, I can just about figure out the chords."

Even on the phone Sam was keen, his voice went hard to the point. "Well, did you try him on anything else?"

"Sam, he's green – he's like precisely straight out of the trees. The guy needs a keeper. Bill talked to him, you know Bill, but he can't even say what the songs are called, he just starts singing them. And such grandma's favourites."

"You said."

Nevertheless Sam Phillips was encouraged. Who knows why? This is the genius of the man, that he saw possibilities where there was apparently nothing – here he saw an opening for invention. And maybe he heard something in Scotty's voice, something that Scotty couldn't say. He told Scotty – again, this is legend – that he would hold the studio free the next night and that they should come by at seven.

Scotty only grunted.

Marion asked Tarzan, on the drive home, how it had gone, but he seemed confused. "They said I could sing good," he said. "But they didn't like it."

"They didn't like it?"

"No, ma'am."

"What didn't they like?"

"Nobody did know." He was frowning. It was as though you were with someone who was retarded, she thought, you had to think what they might understand. But he wasn't retarded.

She felt for him, would have talked more. But there was her boy at home – when they arrived at the Presleys, Mrs Presley was waiting on the porch, and so Marion drove away.

The Presleys' house standing there like a little box you had to wear on your back all the time.

Mrs Presley had buttermilk for him, she said, and she took him into the kitchen. She sat him at the table and talked to him. She was a dumpy person, pale, and with his instinct for hidden workings he could tell that she wasn't whole, that inside her the eggs were broken and the milk was spilt. But her pale face was set in an intensely black frame of hair and, with her large dark eyes, which were alive with the knowledge of life and death, she made you notice her and care about her, and listen hard to everything she said. Now she asked him, "Do you pray, Tarzan?"

Tarzan received the news that the Lord was the reason he was living with great interest. He readily got down on his knees. Mrs Presley said the words, which he repeated, *Our Father, which art in heaven*, and he had his hands together, eyes shut tight, when there was a knock at the door – Mrs

Fruchter from upstairs come, panting, to say it was long distance from California, a Miss Jane Porter, "for your guest."

"He can't come, he's eating," said Mrs Presley, "tell her to call back tomorrow," and Mrs Fruchter went away. *Caint.* "California people can be a nuisance with the telephone," she told him, had him get back in his chair. In the small room, hunched over the small table, Tarzan listened. Mrs Presley cooked, brought him things, he had never seen a human being move so quickly. Then she would stand off to the side to look at him. Sometimes she put her arms around his neck and put her cheek up against his. Tarzan allowed this. The tablecloth was brightly coloured, a flower pattern, Tarzan wished that there weren't any plates on it, he wanted to figure how the pattern worked. Mr Presley came in from the porch, stood diagonal in the doorway, all elbows and skinny neck. The buttermilk tasted strange, but all the food he'd eaten since the bush had been strange.

"You're just like any other boy," she told him.

At night she came into his bedroom and knelt at the end of his bed. He allowed this too. It was dark, he couldn't see her face. She was speaking, he knew it, but he couldn't hear anything. Her hands were clasped so tightly, he could sense the great pressure there. He could smell the tears on her cheeks.

The day was a long day, spent waiting. Tarzan, up at first light, sat out and watched the cars go past. He ate what he was given, went where he was told. Vernon showed him how many times the big hand of the clock would go round on the way to seven p.m. Tarzan knew about clocks. He watched the hand, it was hard to catch it moving.

He sat in Elvis Presley's room and looked at the records that Sam Phillips had sent him. There was no record player, so he just looked. He couldn't read the titles but he held each vinyl slab and tried to remember what might be contained on it.

Mr Presley fetched him and had him come and sing for Mrs Presley while she was doing the ironing – Mr Presley led him through, holding his elbow. Tarzan had to sit on the sofa, it was hard to sing sitting, but the room felt too small when he stood. When he sang *Cool Water* she cried and said Elvis had sang that one.

In all the rooms Tarzan could smell a person that he couldn't see. He could smell him in the bedroom. In the pillow.

From the porch, the old black Lincoln could be seen, parked squarely across the gateway, as though you might want to run down the path, jump in the car and escape. But no one ran. Except for Mrs Presley, everything moved slowly. There was no lawn here, only tufts of dry grass, and dust. Vernon, standing beside him, said, "My boy wanted to be a singer." *Mah*. "It's like you're havin' the life my boy should've had." Vernon always seemed to be looking away, or looking down. Sometimes he seemed angry inside. But then he stood beside Tarzan for long periods, as Jimpi had done, stood next to him, as though he liked being in his company.

All day Tarzan waited. The house was too small to pace about in and he didn't know the neighbourhood, so he sat in chairs – in the front room, on the porch, watching the shadows crawl. Then he went to Elvis Presley's bedroom and sat on the bed. Then finally Vernon led him in and together they looked at the clock. Soon after Marion Keisker arrived and drove him away.

'So, Tarzan,' she said.

Tarzan listened, but there wasn't any more. He looked at her, driving, and for the first time a weight of doubt came into him. Everything was hard to understand here, he didn't have Jane to explain. Things were wrong – Mr Presley was wrong, and Mrs Presley had a big lump of feeling inside, and the singing with Scotty Moore and Bill Black had not been right. He wanted to ask Marion what she meant.

But Jane had told him that if he didn't ask, didn't say anything, people would be satisfied with him. Because you're so big, she said. So he watched and listened, and waited to see if he would feel better. But he was carrying a weight.

In the studio at Sun Records he sang *Over the Rainbow* for Sam and *Goodnight Irene*. He sang all the songs he had sung at Scotty Moore's house, all over again. *Walkin' My Baby Back Home*. Scotty played along again, and Bill talked and laughed and slapped away at his big, thumping instrument. There was a microphone this time, Tarzan liked that because it meant that there was an upright thing next to him when he was standing, for company. For a home base. Scotty's son was there, too, Floyd, from his first marriage, who had come to stay for a few days, and Floyd had his little guitar, almost a toy, but he could play it quite nice, Scotty said. Sam Phillips said, "What the hell – long's he's stayin' out of the way," and let him sit in, though Tarzan could see Sam's eyes bright on the boy, as though he was the reason the feeling wasn't right.

Because it wasn't.

Tarzan sang, he sang as he'd sung in the bush, he did what Jane and Eve had told him and imagined he was high on his rock there, singing along with the radio. He broke his heart open. Sam came out and adjusted the microphone, talked to him like an uncle. "You have a good voice. You are really singing for us now. Keep at it there, Tarzan." For the first time he sang with his eyes closed, he didn't know where he was – he went right inside the song and at the end came out, blinking, to find himself in America, in the pale green looming space of the studio. He listened hard to the musicians – Bill's thumping sound down at the bottom and Floyd's little plunk,

plunk there in the middle and Scotty chopping and filling in up top, dime-store Chet Atkins, with just a little Les Paul. It was Scotty in particular, Tarzan realised, that the bad feeling was coming from. Scotty was playing, Tarzan thought, like he was eating food he didn't care for – as though something had gone rotten. Tarzan wanted to ask: What is bad? But he didn't think it would be right. They played a song that Tarzan liked, *I Love You Because*, and he thought it sounded good. But Scotty faded out halfway through and when Tarzan got to the end of the words he turned and asked Scotty, "What should I do?"

Scotty was embarrassed. Tarzan, when he spoke to you, was clear and strong. A direct question from such a big guy, who just one minute ago had been laying himself wide open, spreading out his heart through a slow weeper – *I love you because* – well, it had a force.

Sam came bustling out of the booth. "I was just thinkin' on that. Tarzan, son, you're singin' up a regular storm there. Now, now, believe me – it's comin'. I do believe that. Just take it easy. Rome wasn't built in one day." There he paused and looked to see if Tarzan understood what Rome was. No sign from the big man, who was listening carefully. Tarzan, in a white shirt, open at the collar, dark slacks, hands by his hips, ready – but for what? Sam said, "I was just thinkin' – how about we try one of those sides I sent you. How about . . . *I Got a Woman*. Let's try that."

Well, Tarzan knew the words. He had sung them, up in Jane's bedroom. He tried to make them come out of him. But he couldn't find the song. The musicians seemed not to have real parts to play, they just seemed to play little bits, Tarzan couldn't hear how it all fitted together. And where should his voice go? He looked at them for help. Scotty kept his head down, talking to his son about the fingering. Bill was always looking back, saying, "Good, Tarzan – go, man!" and trying to give him something. But Tarzan couldn't find the direction.

They tried *I Can't Quit You* and *Rocket 88* and *Devil Man Got My Baby*. Tarzan was so lost. Far away, somewhere small, he could remember the horizon he'd once heard inside these songs – how they had seemed to be the only way to the open. He had pictures too of the streets in Jane's California, where he'd strode out, finding the sound he had heard. But that was somewhere now that was far away – he didn't know how to bring it here. And the music the other guys were playing made it harder. They weren't with him, he wasn't with them. Sam appeared again, like a genie, appearing to make little adjustments, to encourage – and he spoke thoughtfully to Tarzan. "Do you get what the song's about? See, the guy had a woman, you know, like that girl Jane you came here with, just like you and Jane, and he's lost her. Jane's far away right now, isn't she. And she might always be far away, from now on, mightn't she." Sam looking to see if this was bad news to Tarzan. "And this guy, he can't tell why that might be, so he thinks that the Devil might have taken her – well, he knows it's his friend, but he doesn't want to think of his friend in that way, see, so he says, the Devil got in him, and he got in his baby too. Like the Devil might get your girl Jane." Sam looking hard at him. "Are you familiar with the Devil, Tarzan?" Tarzan didn't think that he was. Sam laughed – a twisted, frustrated sound. "No. Well. I'm not sure I'm exactly familiar with the Devil either." *Ahm. Ahm not showah*. Everyone laughed. Sam, eyes full of an idea, trying to give it to Tarzan. "Well, the Devil, now, he's someone bad, someone utterly bad. Ah, like a spirit. Like a demon."

Surely the wild man from the jungle knew what a demon was.

They all got in on it – relieved to have something to do. "Like something just evil," said Bill, screwing up his face.

Little Floyd chimed in. "Just something that burns and pains up your soul." Scotty gave the kid a look, but Floyd stood behind his statement.

"Like all your ugly thoughts turned into a person," said Bill. "Like a man made of fire, just burning you right up."

"Okay," said Sam. "I think that close to covers it – Tarzan? So that's what I want to hear in that song – a bit of Devil! Okay? Okay, ever'one? So let's just play it now!"

But they couldn't just play it now.

They worked over every song that Tarzan could think of. In his head was a man made of fire, he could see that – but he didn't know how to sing it. He didn't know what that might sound like when it came out of your throat. Finally Scotty broke a string and they settled for a break. Scotty was a pro, he never broke a string, maybe he was trying to say something. Whatever – Sam bristled out with Cokes, they kept it going, Sam and Bill cracking away at each other and everyone enjoying them. But there was a lost feeling, a feeling that this wasn't the day. Well, it was late, no point in losing sleep, there would be other days – that was the feeling.

Tarzan aching.

Is through desperation the only way?

Sam had decided to fix a new tape in the machine and he went back to the booth. Bill was squatting with Scotty, making talk. In the pale green room a faded old atmosphere began to settle, as though the action was over for the night.

Now: what occurred next has become the centre of the legend, its beautiful moment. This event has been so often written about, so worked over – everyone wants to go inside it, to ask again: Exactly what started it? What were the things that came together – please tell me.

Because this is the moment when a new America was born. I do believe that. Nowadays, there are new Americas every six weeks or so, every time the share market gets a fever, with every new logo on CNN. And there's always been different Americas, the mountain places, the one-horse backwaters, the street Americas. Fine. But I am talking about something else.

One morning, eating flapjacks at the kitchen table, Tarzan asked Mrs Presley, "Can you tell me please – what is the Devil?"

She turned at the stove, her mouth open. "Why, Tarzan! Wherever did you learn that word?" And she set right down at that table and fixed her dark-worried eyes on him.

Maybe it was Floyd started it, maybe it was Tarzan. Certainly it was those two first, and no Devil in either of them.

In some recountings Floyd comes up with the song, sometimes it's Tarzan. This latter is less likely, I think. Well, he had heard the song, he often said that, on the radio in the cabin. Which he might have. Not on the National Programme of the New Zealand Broadcasting Service – no, sir. But Jane had sometimes managed to drag in a station that was skipping off the clouds. She wrote in her book, *We heard disk jockeys raving from across the Gulf, we heard swamp music and the sounds of the city. Tarzan didn't understand, but he always listened. And he remembered everything he ever heard.* So maybe they picked up Dewey Phillips – I do realise that earlier in this account I mentioned his name, and this was no accident. Hail, Dewey, I hereby salute you. Dewey said they caught him for sure, Tarzan and ol' Jane, when he played that song he always felt it was reachin' out, special – well, he would, wouldn't he. But it is possible. And, because of the way things went from there for Tarzan, it's been my belief that it *was* he who came up with the song, it was Tarzan who was the desperate one, and so I want to explain how this might have been possible. But I am not going to die for this. It was Tarzan and the boy and if Floyd should get a major credit here, well, he definitely was half of it.

Maybe there was a thunderstorm, lightning forking down. Maybe there was an angel passing, heard the Devil's name.

The sound of the boy's guitar was later described as "somebody plunkin' on a bucket lid," and that just about gets it. On his little bitty guitar he was plunking and Tarzan was hollering, Bill came in, slap slap boom, and Scotty must have fixed that string because he was in there too, this was just fooling, it was just ever'one lettin' go cause the whole damn night had just been a total wipeout. It was nothing, it was just a letting-it-all-go dumb noise, this is how it's always been described – when Sam's voice came over the speakers: "Hey, what's that you're doin?"

Scotty: "Nothin'. Nobody knows. We're just foolin'."

Sam: "Well, back up, find a place to start and do it again. That's what we're lookin' for!"

Those words have been carved in stone: because that was Tarzan Presley's first glimpse of his future – and the birth of rock 'n' roll.

Please note that in fact it was Sam Phillips who recognised what he was hearing. If another man had been at the desk ... who knows? Sam had a notion, he had a vision. He sensed something in the America of that day – its motor was running. Sam had been listening out for some years now, his ears were to the ground. This old phrase, it describes people listening for the far-off pounding of horses' hooves – war coming. Have you ever actually pressed your ear to the ground? Me, I don't hear any hooves. What I hear is groaning, heaving, as the tired old planet hefts its load.

The song itself was a blues thing, *That's All Right (Mama)*, a minor hit for a black singer-songwriter named Arthur Crudup in 1946. Yes, I always have heard that "crud" in there too, maybe that's why he went by "Big Boy"? Arthur "Big Boy" Crudup, it's a serious name. I never met the guy, who knows what was big about him? On the original Arthur has just the laziest voice, as he tells his baby that everything is sweet. *It's all right*, he sings this phrase with such easygoing charm.

But he just walks the tune.

In Sam's studio down in Memphis, Tarzan and the guys worked the song over. Sometimes they played it draggy. Sometimes they raced it up. Suddenly Scotty came into his own, Scotty and Bill, that little bit of experience they had – they threw the tune around, they tossed it back and forth. But Sam has said that the key factor was that they were all amateurs. "We was all such damned amateurs. That's what I'm so proud of." And then stir in the other magic of Tarzan and Floyd. The boy getting his first taste of juju – he'd never hit such a primal beat before – and the wound-up singer, the lonesome oncer come in from the edge of the planet. On that first record Tarzan's voice is so young. It's trying to find itself. But at the same time it gives out that beautiful confidence, the absolute belief that at the heart of nature everything is all right. And yet there's also such yearning there. It's not in *need your lovin'*. No, this line is muted, it's held in. What the singer is holding back for is the chance to throw everything into the assertion – *that's all right, now, mama!* It's such a strange line to hang your hat on. Because there's so much suggestion, isn't there, that everything might in fact not *be* all right. Isn't it that his mama – his baby – has been bad? Oh, this terrible confusion between mother and lover, between baby and child – you can hear how Tarzan is struggling with that. But out of this mess of emotion comes something that is just so downright appealing. Isn't he saying here, I can take it, all of it – and it's *still* all right. I'm still all right, we're still all right, after what you did, everything is *still all right*. Because – listen to this –

when all the words are done, then he goes into *La dah da dee dee dee dee*. Bill came up with that when they were missing a third verse, and Tarzan, who could ape anything, just got it. He sings this nonsense like it's, oh, something so jaunty. There's no insistence in the song, no need to prove anything. No, Tarzan just gives it over to us as though every care in the world can be nothing if you are only big enough.

I could go on. The way he caresses *all right*, this has every hope and need and hunger in it, and yet it's filled with pleasure, just the extraordinary pleasure of being. Ah, go play the record.

"Okay, I have that," said Sam over the speakers. It was deep in the middle of the night now, they were all flaming out. Floyd especially was bright-eyed, like he might drop and never rise. Had there ever been such a moment? When Floyd hit his strings he was looking into Tarzan's eyes and seeing the whole power of what it was to be a man – that this was going to be his. And Tarzan, looking back, what did he see? Inside Floyd, the pure believer that is alive in every child. A beautiful moment, full of both the Devil and all the angels. "It's there, boys," said Sam. "I think it's really there."

Mrs Presley had a stern eye fixed on Tarzan and she was just bristling. She pulled his plate of flapjacks away and had him attend to her. The little kitchen was a box of electric light – no shadows. With a rigid finger she was poking holes in the air. "As soon as you hear his name, you must be on guard. People think they can say it and it's just a word. It's not a word! It's his name, Tarzan. You say it and he comes. He has other names too, I'm going to say them now so you'll know, but I ain't callin' him – understand?" This last word was not said to him, it was said up into the air. "All right: Satan. All right: Lucifer. Old Nick. Beelzebub. The Fallen One. Let me see – the Demon Master. The Whoremaster. Old Scratch. The

Evil One. The Prince of Darkness. Oh, oh – now help me, Lord, I ain't callin' him."

Tarzan wondering if they had called him on that magic night – was that why the music had worked?

Every night now the music was working.

"But, *see*, he *was* an angel. Imagine that, Tarzan. He was an angel of the Lord, with every virtue that an angel can have" – her face, shining at this thought, it lit up the whole kitchen – "and it wasn't enough for him!" Her hand slammed the table. "All the knowledge of the universe, all the beauty and history, all of eternity – imagine having that inside you! That's what an angel has. And he lost that. And now he roams the earth, trying to find others who will join him. Join him in the fires. Because we all have it in us, you know." Now her finger was pointing again – was it pointing at him? "The potential. To burn everything down and then dance in the flames. To spend our souls. That's it. Our soul is like a huge sum of money in the bank which we just cannot spend."

It was as though, Tarzan thought, a whole world of hidden knowledge had been brought by her words into the kitchen – powers and shapes, and a new light, which was shifting on the plates and glasses and in the air.

Now Tarzan asked her, "And what does evil mean?"

In the closet in Elvis Presley's bedroom he found an old guitar, a dinky little one, not unlike the guitar Floyd had played. Tarzan held the instrument, touched it. The plink of the string was nothing that had any music in it. He sat on the bed, gazed around at Elvis's things – the pennants from Humes High, the ball glove smelling of a human hand. There were pictures pinned to the walls, glassy black-and-white photographs – of movie stars, Mrs Presley had said. She'd said the names: Tony Curtis, Marlon Bando, Dean Martin, James Dean. Tarzan studied the pictures and wondered, how did they all manage to get their hair to stand up like that?

Whole days spent wondering on such things.

He could smell Elvis Presley everywhere in the house. The smell was so strong – in fact it wasn't really a smell, it was like a feeling but a feeling made solid – every time he touched something it got itself on him.

Mrs Presley had said that Laura, Elvis's girlfriend from Humes High, would be calling around tomorrow, and would like to meet him. She didn't mention that Jane had called again.

Days hanging heavy, like wet sheets on the line. Tarzan carrying every one of those days as though it was a decade. People always ask, especially of this transitional time: What was he feeling? The truth is, under all that weight, he had no true feelings. He had only one idea, one faint understanding, which was, he had to hold still and be carried away.

Alone in America, with no brother to lend a hand.

So when Jane's call came through to the Sun studio, everyone was surprised – it was a surprise that someone knew him, that he had a past. Sam's voice, irritated, fell from the speakers. "Long distance for you, Tarzan. Take a break, guys."

They were really pushing now. They had Side One of a record, Sam said. He wouldn't let them hear it. He was working on it, he said, he had some technical things to do. But they could rest assured – it was something. He didn't know what, but. Well, no buts. It was there. But now they had to have a Flip Side. And so they were pushing. There were no leads. No one knew how, a second time, to get to the place that Tarzan and Floyd had found. Plus there was pressure – Floyd was due to go home in two days, and he seemed to be necessary.

By the cold-smelling glass window of the control room, Tarzan held the receiver near his ear. Jane has written about this call. *He was in the studio.* I cannot tell how those three words came to have such a doomed sound for me. *In the studio* – that's where I lost him. He was never a master of the telephone, he tended to hold it and let whole minutes go by, and this was long distance. I told him that I loved him. In fact I told him twice. And I did. Every bone in me ached to be in his arms. But he could only tell me that they had made a record. And I could hear from his voice that these two things were equal, for him. The record for him and love for me – that balanced. And the aching in me swelled and got more painful. I put down that phone and right then I resolved to go to Memphis.

I feel for Jane. This is now, what, nearly seventy years ago, you look back through thousands of days, like the branches of a thicket you're trying to push your way through, and try to get back to old feelings. When they come, suddenly it's with such force – old regret, old guilt, old happiness. Chemicals shifting inside you, internal electricity, and always the sense that somehow you have to see what happened then and pay for seeing by learning better how to live now. I'm eighty-one years old. I'm in a wheelchair. I'm so deaf, if a bomb went off in the room I'd be in bits without hearing a thing. I don't see myself going to any new places. There's the boy – I've never had a boy before. Of course I'm too old to think I'll hang around long enough to play ball with him – some ball, with brittle old dad in a wheelchair. But, Theo, I watch him struggle across the carpet on his belly, I see him pick up things and try the world out for taste. This is something new under my sun. And there's Loretta. What can a curvy twenty-two-year-old see in a wrinkly like me? I am amazed she said yes – obviously the money is the main attraction. That's okay, if it makes it okay for her. She is the one I am to give my human feelings to, she and Theo, and so I try and remember to have feelings, and to remember how they grew. What they're built on – old pictures. You go on looking back and put your foot in the dog shit again. Weeks spent in the company of the stink.

Are these pictures feelings?

I see now a picture of the studio – of Tarzan saying goodbye to Jane and then just putting the phone down. Tarzan rejoining the boys as they head out on the trail after the Flip Side. Those good old boys. In the picture, they are a unit now, I see them as a group. They understand that they have a chemistry. If I say volatile, I don't mean that they were fighting in there, but they did throw things at each other – they tried things.

In the end it was a country tune, but jumped up, that connected for Sam. This time Tarzan sounds more settled, his voice doesn't search so keenly for a home. Now, playing the flip side, the record sounds just natural, like a fast-beat sing-along that could have been a hit for anyone. But that's time, that's the distortion of so many days. Now, you can mix 'n' match music, you can sample, it's like any old style can go spinning into the blender. But, when it appeared in 1954, *Blue Moon of Kentucky* was strange. It was country with a city bump, it was fried eggs with peanut-butter dressing – as one deejay said, it was nothin' so much as a damned hermaphrodite.

19

Laura Mint, when she appeared, was a wide-eyed girl in a full white dress. Seventeen years old, she'd been Elvis Presley's girlfriend at the time of his death and even now, months later, had a pale, soulful look about her. Her dark eyes, framed by her full, dark head of hair, seemed serious. But Laura had always been a girl with an appetite for life – otherwise why in the first place was she seeing a truck driver from the wrong side of town? Having come once, she couldn't stay away. I'm not talking here about some fatal attraction for sideburns – given time, Laura found a nice lawyer and they raised four kids in Port Arthur, Texas. But in 1954 that was still to come. Elvis was gone, but Laura had hit it off with Mrs Presley, who had treated her from the first like a daughter-in-law, and so she came to call.

Tarzan looked at her – he was interested in girls with black hair – and smiled. He'd been learning how to smile a better smile, had had his cheek muscles stretched into shape by spending time with Bill Black, who could get a grin out of a puddle. This was before Tarzan had grasped the effect he had on women – the effect he could have if he wanted. He just gave her the full-on million-dollar grin, and Laura grinned back. "I like to see you happy," crowed Mrs Presley. "Now why don't you two just set out on the porch and I'll bring you out a nice drink – go on, Laura."

What did Laura think? That here was Elvis come back only bigger? They didn't look so much alike, Tarzan's face was longer, with that frown line – at this time he calls to mind the toothy, high-browed look I have seen on photos of the New Zealand mountaineer Edmund Hillary who, just one year earlier, had become world-famous for being the first to climb Mount Everest. Both men were big in the frame, though Tarzan was broader through the shoulders, and had a darker cast to his hair and eyebrows. But Laura had probably never seen Sir Ed, as he came to be known. So what was she seeing, now?

On the porch was an old swing seat and there they sat. Tarzan told her, slowly, carefully, why he was in Memphis. He sang *Cool Water* for her. "Elvis used to sing that one," she said.

Twelve hundred miles due west, Jane Porter was in a white Buick that Eve Kersting had borrowed from a friend. Eve was driving. Jane, in the passenger seat, had her bare feet up on the dash, elbow out the window. They were coming south, down through Southern California, changing stations, singing along as the wheels turned the miles under. It was stinking hot.

Tarzan had learned the walk over to Scotty's house – a specific route, do not deviate, through the smells and sounds of the city. People waved at him and he waved back. He wasn't famous in Memphis, just new. He did attract eyes, it was plain that he didn't fit. However, at Scotty's, this dropped away. The boys were busy. They had something in the bank, now they had to polish it.

By this time Floyd had gone home. After some head-scratching, Scotty had brought Floyd a new guitar and persuaded him to leave his little old one behind. Now Tarzan had that and, under Scotty's tutelage, was patiently applying his big fingers to the skinny neck. The instrument was obviously too small for him but Bill and Scotty were terrified to lose it. It was part of the new sound, that plunk, plunk, right there in the middle of the beat, and there could be no substitute. Tarzan had music in him, he was learning fast.

The wives brought Cokes and sat around. There was an event taking place in the parlour, a sensation. When they played *Blue Moon of Kentucky* Scotty's wife got up and shook her leg. She couldn't help it, she said, the music made her want to dance.

"Me too," said Tarzan.

The sight of that big man shaking his big leg was a thing you just had to watch.

In Elvis Presley's closet Tarzan found a pink shirt with black collars and cuffs. "Those were his favourite colours," said Mrs Presley. The shirt was too small, it just couldn't be made to fit.

Sam Phillips placed a microphone along at the far end of a corridor, played a tape of *That's All Right* – and what the mike picked up along there had an extra bump in it. This was a poor man's echo chamber. But Sam's ears were rich, he got a lovely sound, which in the history of rock 'n' roll came to be called "slap-back".

On Beale Street, Earl "Fatha" Hines plonked those keys and made the night a river you could drift away on.

*

Put that ear to the ground. Hear those hoofbeats.

Now here comes Laura, in white again, and Tarzan is in black – the suit, it has been decided by Mrs Presley, even if it does make him look a bit like he's fresh off the boat. He's all dolled up, he's got gunk in his hair, he looks like he could melt and leave a dark pool on the walk. Laura is somewhat reserved, not sure what's going on here. But beneath her quiet manner her face is flushed. It's as though for her there is a subterranean connection between the truck driver she lost and this jungle-land singer.

They climb into Vernon's long black Lincoln and slide off into the night – just a little smoke coming from the tailpipe. Laura is driving. Maybe that's a good thing. Elvis always drove, they dated in this very car, if she'd been across in the shotgun seat looking at Tarzan, who knows what she might have seen? She got them to their regular place at the drive-in, ordered for them. Shirley-Ann, who took the order, ducked her head, looked in across the vehicle and said, "Hmm, nice, Laura." But this wasn't meant unkindly, Shirley-Ann had been at Humes High with Elvis, everyone who knew was glad to see Laura out in the world again. Pity though that it had to be with a retard who couldn't drive.

They watched the show, *Frankenstein Meets the Wolfman*, and during the second scary part Laura as usual scooted over and sat close. He didn't attempt to hold her hand, just continued to sit quite still and upright, his eyes steady on the screen, as though this too was something he had to watch carefully and learn from. Would he ever make a joke, she wondered. Then it just got too scary altogether, the monster, great hands twitching, was about to squeeze a pale neck, and she absolutely had to seize his arm. He didn't react – he allowed this. As usual she thought the monster though scary was also sad. Tarzan thought so too. Maybe he saw himself in the part? Their stories have echoes. Laura sneaked a glance at his profile. He was so still – then she realised that he knew she was observing him.

Tarzan holding still while America passes before his eyes.

Afterwards she drove them, as Elvis had always done, up through the dark backstreets to a turning area where you could park up and see the river. There were other couples there, she was pleased to see that, but no one close alongside, she also noted, with a tiny thrill. But why? Beneath her white shirt-waist, her heart was beating fast. Why, why? But of course. She watched the river and her thoughts moved like the city lights on its dark surface, she thought she would just have to speak them out. Instead, finally she turned to him and moved close.

Tarzan had often parked up with Jane and he wasn't shy, he knew what to do, and so he took her in his arms and, eyes closed, placed his lips on hers, which were waiting. Kissing, this was called. It was a soft kiss, and after a moment Laura broke it. But she felt all right, safe, and so her eyes stayed closed and she waited, her face close to his, signalling that another kiss was possible. Thus she didn't see his hands come up to her throat and begin to unbutton her garment.

Coming to herself in a hurry, she grabbed his great wrists, as thick and hairy as the monster's, and tore them away. He was very strong, she could feel that, but he didn't resist, not in the slightest. His eyes were surprised, innocent, but she knew that was just an act and she slapped him anyway. He blinked and looked confused – *very* convincing, she thought. When he put a hand up to his burning cheek it was as though he wanted to feel what was there so that he might understand it.

Without a word she got herself back behind the wheel, got herself out of there. As they roared away, smoke pouring from the tailpipe of the swaying old Lincoln, they heard catcalls and laughter.

Vernon, at the sound of his car, came out onto the porch, but the vehicle drove off, leaving Tarzan on the walk, alone beneath the street lamp.

What followed, in short order, were the questions, the explanation, the outrage, then the forced march through the dark of the town. Standing, the three of them, on the doorstep of the Mint house, Mrs Presley puffed up and red and able only to splutter. Vernon shifted uneasily in the background. Tarzan was to hang his head, she ordered him, and so he did it. But he didn't understand. "Oh, Mrs Mint! Oh . . ." That was Mrs Presley. Tarzan was told to get down on his knees. So he did.

This made everyone embarrassed.

"Say you're sorry, Tarzan!"

"I am sorry."

"Say it to Laura. Look her in the face."

"I am sorry, Laura."

Everyone in the picture knew that this wasn't right, that he shouldn't be down there, but no one knew how to stop it.

In a roadside motel in Tucumcari, New Mexico, Jane Porter lay in the dark, listening to Eve's breathing, and wondered where he was right now and if he was thinking of her. She ran her own fingers through her own hair, touched her own throat. Eight hundred miles to go, it wasn't so far, maybe they should simply have kept driving. But Eve's breathing was low and even and also there was something nice about waiting, like the feeling on the night before Christmas, when all that you had to do was lie there in the dark, knowing that every minute the good thing came closer.

Sam Phillips held the acetate in his hands, read for the thousandth time the black words Marion had typed on the yellow Sun label: *That's All Right* and *Tarzan, with Scotty and Bill*. He couldn't wait, somebody had to hear this and hear it right now. So he called mad-dog deejay Dewey Phillips. Dewey, naturally, was awake, and he came right on down, it was only one thirty-five in the a.m. Memphis wasn't sleeping, it growled and hummed. A blue moon hung, Sam swears, full face, like an omen in the night. In the studio, the two men settled in the control booth and Sam put the thing over the speakers. Dewey trying to see the label but Sam wouldn't let him. Ears pricked. Then—

"What is *that*?" The deejay exploded off his stool, he snatched the disk off the turntable before it was finished and held it up to his face as though it was a mirror. "Play it again, Sam! Hot dawg! That is a white man, ain't it! Oh mutha, I believe you done it now!"

Before she would allow him to eat any breakfast Mrs Presley had Tarzan get down on his knees again, she got down there with him, and in the morning light of her kitchen had him pray with her. She read from her Bible, Tarzan listening hard. He acted ashamed, hung his head, as she had told him he must do. He must repent. From his knees he could see a spider moving back in under the icebox, he would get it later. And, okay, he would ask someone what repent meant and he would do it. Anything to make these people happy. But in his heart he felt no shame – he could not remember feeling the Devil made of fire come into him. However, he did think that he needed Jane, now, he wanted her to explain. Meanwhile Mrs Presley was telling him that evil was a little flame inside you that waited all the time to get big. He could see she was disturbed, upset, and the things she had said to him were bad things, angry. He would never see Laura again – that had been made clear. Maybe he couldn't even stay in this house. "Why, that poor girl practically lives here! And now she's afraid to come!" Words, torrents of them, falling like the waterfall on his head and shoulders. But he was listening to something else. *That's all right, mama*, at that point these were the only words he really cared about.

That afternoon he went to the movies again, the regular cinema this time, on his own. He knew how to do this and he had to get out of the house – Mrs Presley, puffed up with feelings, which she was always speaking out, that was one thing, but Vernon, prowling, silent, well, that was quite another. Tarzan asked for some money and Vernon gave him a dime, it almost seemed he had taken pity on him. So Tarzan was sitting there in row seventeen in the dark, watching the first feature, alone, when Mrs Presley came groping among the seats.

Mr Phillips had called. Dewey the deejay was foaming at the mouth, on any radio in Memphis he could be heard, he was playing the thing, the disk, that damned disk of Sam's, he was playing it over and over and his phones were running hot and so he wanted to interview this guy – this sensation! – right now, on the radio. Mrs Presley went to the cinema and, searching the profiles, picked him out and gripped his shoulder.

Jane, hunched over the radio of the Buick, heard his name and scrambled to turn up the volume. "Pull over! Pull over!" she shouted at Eve.

They got off the hardtop and came to rest beside a cornfield, on either side of the road the stalks were as high as an elephant's eye. There, in a kind of parting in the green sea of corn, they heard his voice coming out of the little speaker on the dash: ". . . and so I sang along."

"You sang for all the little critters, the birdies and them gorillas and all down in the jungle down there?"

"No, sir. I sang for myself."

"Kind of lonesome?"

"I was the only human being person there."

"An' now you're livin' right here in Memphis, over there on Alabama – who you livin' with, Tarzan?"

"I am living with Mrs Presley, sir. And Mr Presley."

"Whose boy died, whose boy Elvis sadly died, and they put you up, right there in their house, like kindly folks, an' you recorded this – tell the people how this perticler slice a vinyl came into the world, Tarzan."

Long pause. "I am sorry, sir. I do not understand."

With Dewey's fatherly assistance, Tarzan made his way through the interview and then, parked there in the opening in the corn, cars going past on the Interstate, the dash melting in the sun, Jane and Eve heard him for the first time go into the actual singing of *That's All Right*.

They stared at each other. It was like seeing your brother playing at being the president – and pulling it off! His singing had such style, such appeal. It sounded so utterly fresh, sweet, like a new variety of fruit.

While they listened, Dewey raved about the disk, about Sam Phillips, about the song, about the sound, and all the time the phone kept ringing, kids calling in, just begging him to play it again. "An' okay, this is for lemme see the seventh time this hour, you heard it right here, live from the centre of the universe, this is the sound of the day – man, this is the sound of the century! It was recorded right here in Memphis, this is Tarzan, on your mark, ready, get set, and – go, baby, go!" From the speakers came the slap-back sound of Floyd's plunky little guitar, and then, like a river of feeling, here came his vocal.

"Jane," said Eve in a voice faint with wonder, "Tarzan is going to be a big star."

Do you remember hula-hoops? How everybody just had to have one. Rubik's cube, there's another example. Yo-yos, knucklebones, the Twist. Frisbees, *the incredible flying disk*, suddenly everywhere you looked bits of plastic were sliding through the air. Skateboards. Super Balls. Fondue. Davy Crockett hats. *Trivial Pursuit.*

Another category is for instance that year when everyone put plastic bottles of water on the lawn to keep dogs from crapping.

Television was maybe the biggest, it arrived in the early 1950s and has stuck around the house ever since, suddenly you weren't alive unless you were watching it. It's kind of worn off now, unless there's a new war, but remember when. Television is I think more relevant here than the earlier examples, because in its own strange way television has a life. It changes with the times, it has an active presence in the room. This is closer to what I'm talking about.

Of course there'd been fad people before. Movie stars, sporting heroes, singers – Chaplin, to pick a name. Hemingway. Sinatra. Eva Peron. Adolf Hitler should get a nod here. Moving on – the Beatles (but not the Rolling Stones, and not Madonna, she turned every trick in the book but failed to get anyone interested in the drama of what she might be, she was just popular). Muhammad Ali. Maybe Michael Jackson – that freak was global. Princess Diana, definitely.

But Tarzan was bigger than them all. He was the most photographed person of the twentieth century. He is estimated to have sold over one billion records. In tiny atolls in the blue depths of the Pacific the guys climbing for coconuts copied his hairstyle – probably aliens on distant planets also. Kids screamed at him, they tore his clothes. Girls scraped the dust off his car and kept it in their hankies. They licked his car – and this is back in the 1950s when there was still some restraint. At his height he was so big, you couldn't actually do anything with him. He couldn't play concert halls, the kids just ripped up the carpet. He couldn't go out for blocking the traffic. He could literally wiggle his little finger and drive people into a frenzy – this actually happened.

Even now, it makes me proud.

All of which quickly had the effect of masking the music. People began to review the phenomenon, and they saw just the teen hysteria, a commodity being sold, and the commodity was a person. Well, to be frank, in time it did become that – but later. First, it really *was* about the music. If you want to say the rest was bubblegum with sex appeal, I don't mind. I think you miss Tarzan's charm, his unique qualities. He spoke to something inside people. They saw in him something they thought they wanted to lose – their place in the scheme of things. Right at the time when America was going modern with a vengeance, here was something so completely up to date, completely fresh and new – and yet embodying the primitive. But that is all so much sociology. Music was what it was all about. Tarzan was a great stylist, a great, great singer. He still is. And don't you forget it.

Meanwhile, he was learning how to correctly dry and put away Mrs Presley's dishes.

Meanwhile, he walked alone in Memphis. After the interview with Dewey Phillips, Tarzan found himself on the walk outside the studio, people going past, bumping his shoulder – suddenly Dewey's voice wasn't there running things. He first went back to the movie house. He was in a kind of daze. But the movie was over.

He wandered downtown, past the bars and steakhouses, went among the long, shiny vehicles, the shiny-faced people. A person could just wander, apparently, you didn't have to have an idea. The streets had music in them, he could hear snatches of it, fragments, from doorways, car windows. People shouted out words, steam hissed from pipes, engines throbbed. The ringing of a cash register, a telephone, the city produced sound after sound, it was over here – now it was over there.

And among the sounds was the one he had made. He understood that. Somewhere, people were listening to him singing on the radio.

He walked and walked, half-aware of his reflection accompanying him in the dark glass of the shop windows. In America you always knew you were there, you saw your own shape all the time. You were the thing you saw most, you and you, repeated. But no one knew your name. Even if you were on the radio, even if you spoke in an interview, America was busy with the mirror and no one knew you.

A car pulled up alongside and someone said his name. It was Jane Porter.

"Jane, Jane . . ." Tarzan embraced Jane and right there on the walk in downtown Memphis he undid her top button. To pull her hard against him, this was what he wanted, and she was kissing him back, not like angry Laura – so was this evil?

Jane was laughing, excited. "We went to Sun Studios, Sam Phillips sent us to the Presleys – and they said you was lost. Was you lost, darling? Probably you just wanted to get lost from that *woman*!" Holding Jane, he loved the way she made him feel he was really there. "The whole world is looking for you – we heard your record! Eve says you're going to be a star!" Jane ran her fingers though his hair – her expression said there was something she didn't like, but she went on. "Mr Presley says he's thinkin' on goin' out in the Lincoln, look fo' you, if only he could find some coal, I guess, to put in the engine of that thing. Sam Phillips said most likely you was captured by the Mafia, as a ransomable commodity – did you know there's a Mafia in Memphis, baby?"

Tarzan held her hard against him and he was just glad all over. He caught sight of their reflection, the two of them. This was different, to see them instead of just him, it was somehow exciting. "Baby," he said, trying out the word.

Eve drove them to a hotel, the Laverne, and they spent the night. Tarzan could feel that, over at 462 Alabama, Mrs Presley was searching for him, going from room to room, and coming out onto the sunporch to speak sharply to Vernon. It was, he knew it now, evil to hide from her. Now he had it. Evil was when you knew what people wanted you to do and you didn't do it. All right. All night he stayed in the hotel and was just evil with Jane.

The two of them ate a late breakfast, fried things, animals and their eggs, cooked Southern good, he liked the taste but then couldn't get rid of it, and after they walked by the river. Tarzan could feel that strong pull from Mrs Presley and he worked at ignoring it. He could also feel the laughing girl beside him, his armful, her hip pressed against his thigh, and he wanted to keep feeling that. Suddenly he felt completely solid inside himself. They kissed on a park bench, then crept off into the bushes. Just like in the bed of grasses, Jane thought, except for the smell of that old river. Then, at two after noon, they headed back to the hotel, to meet Eve Kersting.

Eve was standing on the walk, alongside the brass-and-drape of the Laverne entrance, arms folded, behind her dark lenses, pretending not to watch the people who went up and down the street. "Where's the car?" said Jane. Eve pointed to the ground – it was in the parking lot, below them. "So you gonna get it?"

"Where are we going?" said Tarzan. The pull of Mrs Presley was quite strong inside him now.

"We're going home, honey."

When Jane said this, it was a simple statement of fact, no great feeling in it, and at first Tarzan just nodded. Jane looked around as though the car might be appearing at any moment. It was Eve who made Tarzan think. She was watching, he realised, to see what would happen. In the same voice as Jane had used, just easy, he said, "I will go to Scotty Moore's house tonight, to get wild." And at the thought a big grin spread across his face.

"No, baby," said Jane, "tonight we're going to be in, oh, Kansas City, miles away."

"Kansas City," said Tarzan. Half a smile came to his lips. "They've got some crazy little women there," he said, "an' I'm gonna get me one."

Jane stared at him. Eve said quickly, "It's a song – it's a song, Jane!"

There are a number of accounts of this sidewalk moment. Eve wrote it up but didn't include it in her *New Yorker* piece. Her early draft has been used by some of the later biographers; here's the actual extract: . . . *and the gap between California sunshine, so clean, and good ol' Southern sweat was revealed right there. Tarzan had come home to the sound he could hear inside him, and Jane was always going to be a campus girl, a beach and country club girl, who read scientific journals and listened to Bartók. Inevitably she would soon be wearing eyeglasses and pinning her hair into a chignon. Whereas Tarzan . . . He was real estate of a completely different location. How he would wear his hair was not yet clear. When Jane met him it was full of oil – greasy kids' stuff, she said, and she had him wash it out in the hotel shower. But he ran his fingers back through it, as though he was missing something . . .*

The description Jane wrote in *her* book went to the heart of the matter. *To whom did he belong? I knew that he was mine. I found him, I taught him. His great big beautiful self, standing there on the walk outside the Laverne Hotel, completely relaxed in his bones, and listening all the time, watching. I was so proud of the way he had coped. He'd been away from me and he'd managed. He'd learned. I was so utterly proud of him.*

And, amazingly, he'd engaged with the machines and the processes of the industrialised world and he had made something – a record, that was good enough to be played on the radio. This was an astounding achievement.

But then I began to understand that he had an idea of himself that might be stronger than the idea of him and me together. This was the most painful knowledge of my life. It was such a lesson to me, and I have tried to take what I can from it. Everything has its essence, and what we are here for is to express that. To be truly ourselves. And he had a vision of himself and he was going to pursue it. If I was there with him, well, that would be nice. If not – well, that would be sad, but he could live with it.

I looked at him and grasped that he knew all this. Maybe not to put into words, but he had the emotional truths. He'd figured it all out, and I had not.

Now Jane and Tarzan went back to the river, back to the park bench. That old man river just kept rollin' along. But this was not the bed of grasses.

Sitting on the bench on the riverside, Jane had her head on his shoulder, was crying into it, when they were approached by a man in uniform – a policeman. He had a gun, it was right there on his hip, Tarzan wanted to hold it. Jane was rearranging her clothes. "Excuse me, suh, are you the one they call Tarzan?"

And so they were taken back, in a patrol car, to 462 Alabama, and the patrolman, whose name was George Sprule, delivered them up to Mrs Presley's care. He walked them up the path of her house – hand in hand they followed – the parties came together at the bottom of the steps. In that homely place there was the meeting of a number of strong forces, the glances ricocheted like a pinball. However, there was no visible disturbance. George Sprule merely said, "Well, here ya'll are then, Tarzan, son. Don't you go wandrin' off now. You shouldn't be makin' poor Mrs Presley worry." He ran his cop's rude stare slowly up and down Tarzan, then brought his eye up to hold the big man in judgement. "I have heard that record of yours. I'm not sure that ought to be allowed." *Ah'm. Orta.* "You keep decent, now, y'hear?" He gave a little huff of contempt, hitched his gun belt, and went away.

A long pause. A shifting of the forces, like something big rolling its shoulders.

Finally Mrs Presley, it was her house and so it was her right to do some eyeballing now, finally she said, "Well – I imagine you should better come inside. Lord knows where you've been, son. I was worried sick. Vernon, could you right now go upstairs and please ring poor Mr Phillips."

Jane came with him, defiantly. She was heartsick. But she wasn't letting go of his arm for that fat old cow. And, right there in Mrs Presley's kitchen, she kissed him on the cheek.

That night Jane Porter and Eve Kersting accompanied Tarzan to Scotty Moore's house and there they really saw something.

Tarzan had used the words *get wild* and both women had noted them as maybe the first informal expression he'd been heard to utter. Now, in the small crowded room at the front of Scotty's house, they were witness to a scene that was, well, a shock.

Scotty's house was everything that the California girls thought of as Southern. Heavy drapes, old dark furniture, dim rooms which made the blood run slow just to enter them. Here, in their pastel slacks, they felt utterly modern. But then something was happening in this house that was turning that feeling on its head.

Was it the music? True, it was too big for the room – everything, the curtains, the chairs, everything was too big for the room. But that wasn't it.

It was Tarzan. He shook when he sang, shook something

terrible. Was it nerves? Energy? Neither Jane nor Eve had ever seen him in anything that resembled a state, but plainly that's what he was in now. What was it? It was impossible to know why, but something had loosed a force inside him. Up close, it was terrifying. His chest shook, his fingers shivered. Most of all it was in his legs, especially the left leg. It was as though an earthquake was shaking his body from the inside, his left leg seemed to kick and break. In the sweaty, crowded room, the musicians urged him on, and suddenly there was Scotty's wife, Bobbie, who was dancing with him – well, not with him, but trying to copy him. Or was she coaching him? Jane and Eve had never seem anything like it. The music was fast, wild – simple, but somehow also wonderfully fresh. And pungent. Tarzan threw his head back, then forward, and his hair, heavy with sweat, fell down over his eyes. Oh, he was mesmerising. The fascination wasn't necessarily so much in what he was doing, which was often awkward, grotesque even, but in the search. He was on the trail of something, they all were. They were after a new thing under the sun. And they were finding it, too, right here in this room, you could see it – that's what they thought. They were all believers. There was a bond between them, they would grin at each other and whoop – Tarzan also.

One glance at this and Jane knew he would never leave Memphis.

All eyes were on him, he was the difference, a random thing, the nonce element. He could be led. Bobbie, who could really move, would from time to time suggest things to him. And there would be contributions from Bill's sisters Evelyn and Mary-Ann, who didn't dance but clapped, not in applause but rhythmically, clap-clap, ah-clap-clap. All suggestions were taken seriously. They tried new songs – a rocked-up version of *Over the Rainbow* just didn't work – and new tempos, new approaches. The music wasn't really loud, but it was just too big for the room. This thing was busting to get out. "Oh, that is so *gone*!" declared Bill. It was the highest praise.

They walked out in the Memphis night, Tarzan and Jane holding hands, Eve behind, hardly there. It was two a.m., Tarzan was sweaty, tired, but also exultant. The gladness in him seemed to glow in the murky street lighting, along with the sheen of sweat. Jane was sad, yes, but even she couldn't help but be thrilled by the sheer pleasure of being so close to that naked flame. That comet from outer darkness.

From her place in the observation lounge, Eve produced a question. She asked, "What are you going to wear, Tarzan? When you perform. You guys are going to perform these songs, aren't you."

It was a good point. Tonight he was in a white tee and chinos, this was fine for Scotty's front room, but when he was up and lots of people were looking at him? He had wondered about the suit. But it would be too hot, and you couldn't move inside it. "In Elvis Presley's room," he said, "there is a shirt. Could you look at it, please, Eve."

They walked on, getting used to the idea of Eve in the role of consultant. If Tarzan was aware of Jane's feelings, he didn't let on. But, oh, it was such a night, there was no room for feeling small. Jane tried to tell herself that.

What a way he'd come.

Then they were outside the gate at the Presleys'. Eve looked off into the shadows while Jane and Tarzan stood under the pale street light and kissed. They took their time. Suddenly everyone knew that if this wasn't actually the last dance then it wouldn't be long. Moths flew up into the cone of light. Tarzan and Jane cast long dark shapes on the pavement, which moved apart and then came together again. He was cooling now, less steam was rising. You could see that the evening had taken everything from him – so much concentration. To be learning all the time, it was like a child with growing pains. Jane had pains growing too. She held him but she was looking away into the night. Her heart was like a red, wet thing ragged inside her.

Over the next several days they had a wonderful time. Tarzan slept late in his single bed at the Presleys' house. Eve and Jane stayed at the hotel, and they all met in the park. They went shopping. Sam Phillips, on hearing of the get-him-dressed project, advanced some money, which they took to the shop that had made Elvis Presley's pink-and-black shirt, Lansky's on Beale Street, and had a copy made for him, only bigger. In the store there were other things, bright, vivid garments that were strange to see on a white man – maybe he even looked a little draggy. Seeing this, Jane showed him how to paint his eyes – might as well go the hog. Unselfconscious, he went with her to the druggist and bought cosmetics. Mrs Presley was scandalised when she saw, she told him to go wash his head, immediately, but he kept the things, the pencil and the black sticky stuff in the little bottle. Then, at night, they would all go to Scotty's for a session – with Tarzan now in what Bill called his cat clothes, the whole mood had changed.

Meanwhile Sam Phillips had had a pressing of the record made at Buster Williams' Plastic Products. Six thousand orders had come in from record stores within the catchment area of Dewey's radio show.

20

Sam Phillips loaded boxes of pressings into his station wagon and took them out on the road. He'd sold records before, even had a few hits – *That's All Right* was Sun Recording number 209. But some deejays wouldn't hardly let the thing finish. "That is so country, it's got 'pone up its nose!" "What the hang is that? Is that a mongrel or is that just a dog?" *Dawg*. Sam held his dignity. He was a believer, if people couldn't hear, well, give 'em time. They would find out. But there were questions other than those of a strictly musical nature. "Heck, if I played that they'd run me out of town!" said one jockey. "I'd like to help, Sam, but I don't want to get maself burned down."

Listening to the record, now, it's impossible that anyone thought Tarzan was a black man. Of course, our ears have come a long musical way since then, and some people back there had cloth and would always have cloth. But the main problem for those who *could* hear was not that he sounded like a Negro but that he was *trying* to. Why would a white man let the race down like that? It will have a bad influence on our children. The fact that he had been raised by monkeys just sealed it for some folk – the Negroes are fresh out of the trees and here is a jungle boy plain underscoring the fact. "Hell, no, I ain't playin' that!"

But, black or white, the kids didn't seem to care. The record store owners based their decisions not on racial politics but on demand. And, all over, the kids were demanding that record.

In Memphis, Tarzan was soon a highly recognisable figure. When he and Jane walked down the street, people shouted, "Hey, there's that guy!" Kids fell into step and strode a block, asking dumb questions just to hear him talk. Saying to each other, "He talks good!" Jane, by her own account, didn't handle this well. *I was snooty*, she says, *I had the idea that if you were a star you had to insist that you were above the common people, because that was what they wanted – something to worship. But these were other times.* Tarzan did better. He took everything straight, like a straight man, set himself instantly at the level of those he was with. On the street, he knew how to make them like him – well, they were predisposed, because in their minds he was a big swinger, for having cut that edge sound. But he could complete the circle, connect what they felt about his record with his in-person charm, and double his value.

Of course he wasn't straight. For a start there were the clothes. At this time there weren't too many white folk wearing anything that cut a hole in the day like that – shocking pink on a paleface man, it was unheard of. However, he was big enough to carry it, he was a one-man movement. Plus he was beautiful.

His hair had been restored by Eve to its truckdriver flop, full of stuff, Mr Worple's Tonsorial Enhancer, according to the legend on the tin, so that it stood up in front and then fell on his brow, dark and moody. Mrs Presley said it made her blood run thin to see it, but Tarzan persisted, and became an artist of the comb.

Tarzan and Jane, seen on the street, kissing. Laughing. Waving out to the kids. Hearing his record on the radios of cars that cruised slow.

So these were wonderful times, legendary days, and like all such days they were born to die.

The end began with a call from Carole, to Jane, taken upstairs on Mrs Fruchter's phone, asking where she was. Jane explaining politely in Mrs F's kosher kitchen – two of everything, it was like seeing double. "Okay, mom. Okay, I got it. Bye, mom."

Bring him home, he's ours, we have to own this, had been Carole's message. But Jane, now, had no intention of doing that.

She sat alone on the bench in the park by the river and watched the big old currents mixing there on the pockmarked surface of the brown-flowing water. She imagined herself hanging on his arm for, what would it take – a year? A crazy year. And then the year after, on his way down? And then another year of confusion and bitterness, of *I coulda been a contender*. And all that only if he was lucky – how many became a star, really? And what kind of star? No one knew where he fitted, he was kind of a freak, wouldn't he always be a bit of a freak-show? There was something ugly about that. This music that came from the negroes, was it really going to be popular? And what did she want with any of this?

The South – compared with California, it was so backward. But she wanted him.

She went down to the water's edge and threw a stick in, watched it float until it was out of sight, then threw another. The river had a sound, it was an under-gurgle, if you didn't listen for it it sank right into the grind of the city. A riverboat went past, splashing. People waved, rattled the ice in their juleps. Not backward, that was illiberal – but you had to be born to it.

With a bellyful of blues she went back to him. He was on Mrs Presley's porch, plunking on Floyd's guitar. She sat next to him, leaned her head on his shoulder. His chin rubbed on her scalp. For once the Presley woman showed some sensitivity, she gave them some room. Plunk, plunk went that kid's guitar. Was the world going to fall under the sway of that sound, really? But he had to find that out.

He had to see the shape of the thing that was in him. She knew what that meant. Oh, that bellyful. She put her arm through inside his and ran her forefinger on the soft skin on the underside there, that always got him going. She made him feel for her. Instantly, Mrs Presley or no, he wanted to find a bed of grasses. But she made him stay. She kept them there until she had transmitted her feeling. She felt it come over him. He rubbed his chin harder, rubbed his head against hers. He had stopped plunking now, and put his arm around her. "Darling," she said, "I'm going to go home soon."

It seemed as though he stayed on the porch for days, whenever anyone was looking for him, that's where he was, plunking. Singing quietly to himself, dressed in stage clothes, with eye make-up and a hank of hair that frequently had to be tossed off his forehead.

Jane drove the Buick home, alone. On the Interstate she leaned across and punched the dial, trying to find his voice. For a moment he would be there, coming to her straight out of the radio. The first time she heard it she pulled over to listen. She learned not to do that. You had to keep going. When that song came on, you sped up. It was exhilarating, that song. It made you drive faster. You couldn't be crying when you drove fast, it was too risky, you had to concentrate fiercely. Then gradually she drove herself out of the area where they were playing the thing.

Eve stayed. She rang home and finally quit her job. She was following a hunch, she told her boss. A oncer. She found work, waitressing in an outfit called *Slow Joe's*, and at nights she went to Scotty's to watch and listen.

Sam Phillips put miles on his stationwagon, visited every deejay, music retailer and jukebox man in every dead mule town, and all the live ones too, trying to place the record. Polite but firm, he would explain: "This is a new thing, understand." Many didn't. But Sam was a believer and he drove on, undaunted.

Dewey kept spinning the record and then having to spin it again.

Dewey went with *That's All Right*, he played and played it – wooh, there was nothing like it. But for most other stations that side was just too strange, it was just too much of an unaccountable thing. Too problematic. But then those stations found the flip, with *Blue Moon of Kentucky*, and while this was also, hold *on* there, oh so risky, there was no doubt that it cheered the feet. People liked it, they sang along with it. So the record was a one-two punch, an either-or-deal – if it didn't get you coming, said Sam, it got you going.

Hear those hoofbeats.

Sam had decided he needed one real big throw of the dice, a booster for his rocket, and, angling and wangling all the way, he managed to land a spot for Tarzan and the boys on the Grand Ole Opry.

In 1954 the Opry was a serious thing: the venerable home of country music, its church, its cathedral, with a weekly concert broadcast live and nationwide on WSM from Nashville, Tennessee – the biggest country music stage on the planet. *Country* music? I hear you spit out the poisoned words, and walk away – I see you reach for the dial. But there was at that time no name for what Tarzan was doing. Popular music consisted of, okay, country and western, and hillbilly, and gospel, and blues, and rhythm and blues, and these were all separate – they all had their own audiences and their own Hot One Hundred charts. The job of bringing those musics together, that was yet to be done. It was only later that people called Tarzan a rocker. Not much later. Everything happened kick-beat quick. Chuck Berry, Little Richard Penniman, Fats Domino, Carl Perkins, Jerry Lee – from all over guys started finding new shapes in their sound. Suddenly this all came together, like gasoline and a spark, to make a whole new thing – boom!

Though by 1954 this was yet to happen – rock didn't have a label round its neck and Tarzan had to take any context he could get. But, wah, the Grand Ole Opry – Scotty and Bill were just completely terrified. The Opry was the big time, and who were they, with their one little regional hit record, and never even played it anywhere? But Tarzan wasn't fazed. He hadn't heard of the Opry.

So, they went over to Nashville in Scotty's wagon, with Bill's bass strapped to the top, they went out on stage and did what they did – just as weird as hedgehog sox, Tarzan in eyeliner – and then they came on home. The Opry verdict was, he's trash – go back to the jungle, he'll never make it. Well, good to get that learned.

Sam massaged his chin, glowered into the mirror as he doctored his hair.

Then the second record appeared. *That's All Right* continued to ride high in the regional charts but Sam still had that urge to kick the whole thing up a level – to show that the lightning they'd caught that one night wasn't a oncer. This time it was a remake of an R&B classic, *Good Rockin' Tonight*. And this is a sweet item to listen to, even now. Tarzan growls. He sings all over the scale, his voice climbs and bumps, but not like it's chasing after something. No, it's more like something has been found, and now it has to be played with. Just so full of fun – that's what people forget. Well, let's not kid ourselves, music is a money industry, always has been. But today's sounds are so utterly calculated. So am I just talking about innocence? Well, they were different times, you can never step in the same river. You can never hear those early records for what they were. But you have to try, please try, or how will you ever understand him?

Meanwhile the boys had landed a gig, four nights a week at something called the Glory Hole, a bar attached to a roller rink. Scotty had fixed this. Hardly glamorous, but here, after the Opry fizzer, they started to work things out a little bit. They didn't play so much as rehearse in front of an audience – an audience on wheels. It was decided that it was better if Tarzan didn't shake his hands so much, it looked maybe spastic. Eve came up with a move where he tossed his head back then flung it forward so that his hair hung down. Bill got up on his bass fiddle, rode it like it was a Ferris wheel. There was no drummer – that made a big hole in the sound and, for me, hearing those first records now, it's this hole that is so beautiful. *That*'s a glory hole. Tarzan has to play guitar – he plunks away earnestly. It's a huge job of work for him, his big back bent over what is in fact not much more than a kid's toy. There's great drama in his concentration. But he always hits the beat.

Then in Shriveport they played something called the Louisiana Hayride, and the first set they did there, well, this was really the beginning. There were two records out now, and kids had heard about the Opry show, which, even if it had failed, had instantly made him legit, and they'd heard about this thing happening in the Hole down at the rink –

that jungle guy with the wild record. At the Hayride now, a crowd gathered. A country crowd, sure, but there were all kinds, guys in straw hats, guys in cheap suits, truck drivers, salesgirls, kids, heaps of kids, there was no shape to the thing. The stage boss looked out and scratched his head, so Scotty said later. Something was come over his show. Maybe he should get this out of the way – and suddenly he told Scotty, "You're next, son."

The first set was a miss. Tarzan came out from the wings at a run, came bursting out there like he was hitting the platform off a speeding train. He grabbed the mike (banged it with his guitar), flung himself at the audience. It was too much. In the old, bright-lit theatre, amid hay bales and pumpkins, the crowd sat stunned – you could see them actually leaning back, Scotty said, kind of trying to get away. There was maybe the fear that he couldn't control himself, that he might jump down and tangle with them personally. Afterwards there was sporadic clapping, and lots of confused, excited talk.

Sam Phillips had driven over for this show with his wagon full of product and was seated in the back row. In the break he spoke to Tarzan backstage, he said, "All right now. You've got 'em. Believe me on this. Just relax: this much," his finger quarter of an inch from his thumb, "and they'll swallow it whole."

It was maybe true.

For the second show the audience was bigger – lots of folk had bought another ticket, come back to get a second look. This time when he hit the stage there was a definite rush of excitement. He cut some figure. Shiny black pants with a thin red line of piping down the seams. Pink socks. Red belt. White shirt, pink jacket, with a black bow tie. And fabulous shoes. They were two-tone, black with white tongues, sometimes referred to as Co-respondent Shoes because, in divorce proceedings, they were what the well-dressed co-respondent would likely wear to court. They had slick leather soles, Tarzan sang up on his toes, way up, the stage was dark old boards shiny with age and so all his muscle and bulk was poised on just a couple of square inches of slick, slippery stuff – and did he fall? Hell, no. He was flying. The big man moved as though he was a juggler of worlds, he was tossing planets like they were bubbles. All of this to the beat. All of this with his little guitar hitting about all over the place. The rock 'n' roll devil, burning up, live – the place went *off*! Like a sudden change in the temperature – people up out their seats, pressing to get closer. Right along from Sam Phillips was a fat woman, let's not mince words, she was your proverbial jelly on a plate, she was deliciously fat, and she climbed up out of her seat, this was no small event, gripped the back of the row in front, and she began to sway. And the whole row moved. Sam reported later that she was talking while Tarzan was singing, just talking to the air, she said, "Did you ever see anything that good?" Kids running down the aisle to see better, up in the boxes people hollering, whooping.

And that was just the beginning.

Tarzan knew from that moment that he could get the crowd to go with him. He could take them. His shows began to get wilder. He studied, first with Eve, then after her departure with anyone who would discuss the subject, on focusing the energy, on drawing towards him all the light in the room. Soon it was a monstrous thing. Marion Keisker attended another show, soon after, also at the Hayride, where they'd scored a repeat booking, and she reported that there was screaming, "just this high, intense sound that was coming out of the throat of someone nearby. Then I realised that it was me! I was screaming along with everyone else. He was just completely something you wanted to scream at."

On the drive back to Memphis that first night Tarzan

suddenly announced that he wanted to take the wheel. This was unusual, he didn't make many direct requests. And everyone knew it was crazy. But this was a crazy night, they were exhilarated, and so Scotty pulled over. The car was a big long thing, a Studebaker wagon, made unsteady by Bill's bass strapped upstairs, and there was a tailwind. Tarzan gripped the wheel and they were away. He started carefully but soon they were going fast. Bill was whooping. Eve was trying not to look. Then Bill demanded the radio. It was a wild ride – fortunately they were on the Interstate, it was late, there were no other cars. The beat from the radio drove them forward. Then the inevitable happened – *Good Rockin' Tonight* came on and Tarzan really put his foot down. It had been that kind of a show at the Hayride, they had become legends, invincible, and now they could ride the winds. "Go! Go!" Bill was shouting. Tarzan had the wheel gripped like it was something he was wrestling to death, his fists were clenched – but he was grinning. The road was rushing towards them. Scotty, who would keep a straight head in a hurricane, leaned over, saw the needle swinging up towards 120, the vehicle was shuddering, and he said firmly, "Okay, Tarzan, lift your foot." When they were down to a crawl he told him, "Now pull over." Suddenly Scotty was white, drained. As they drifted to a halt, Eve opened a door, spilled out and, in the glare of the headlights, could be seen to go for a short walk.

The next day she caught a bus for home.

Now the shows at the Glory Hole became wild, uncontrollable. The records were hot, every radio station in the south was jumping on this thing. Tarzan was being interviewed, every next day there was something. Sam Phillips was working any angle he could figure, trying to think of new ways to get the boy exposed. The guys were exhausted. Scotty and Bill were still working each day at the tyre factory, and then playing nights – they *should* have been exhausted. But there was an excitement that was driving them. Hoofbeats, the chug of a locomotive. In the studio, hours went into each new song, as they searched for stuff which sounded like their feeling. It didn't come easy. But Sam Phillips was patient, very controlled. He kept them from ever settling for less than complete work. They got two more tunes in the bank, *Baby Let's Play House* and *Blue Moon*. The band were calling themselves the Blue Moon Boys now, they had little Western shirts that matched, shiny things with checked bibs, and dark ties. They didn't try to compete with Mr Flash out front.

It was like a rush on the stock market, the first days of a likely war – no one knew where this thing was going.

And in the eye of it all? Tarzan didn't work at the factory, he never had a day job at any point in his life. Nevertheless he continued to rise early. Even when he had come home at three in the morning he would be on the front porch at six in the a.m., usually in bare feet, sitting, thinking. He knew not to wake the neighbourhood with his guitar practice or singing so he would just sit and enjoy the cool of the dawn, study the sparkle of the dew.

In the afternoons girls would come, from the High School, and hang around the gate. Tarzan would go down to make talk and sign autograph books. They had a lot of fun out there on the walk. He was, he understood this, a figure they had dreams about. How much did he understand? The fact was, he never seemed to put a foot wrong. He would listen, consider their questions, though he never actually said too much. The girls fluttering, they would strut and preen. Teenage girls, American girls of the fifties, high-school queens, wearing eye make-up filched from mom and lots of spray in their hair. The cheeky ones would ask for a kiss and he would kiss them. But he never forgot his experience with Laura. He was always aware of Mrs Presley who would come out from time to time with trays of cookies and lemonade. She didn't disapprove, this was just good, clean fun. He was a lovely boy. Certainly, she could smell the whiff in the air, you couldn't miss it, definitely there was a risk. But she lectured Tarzan, in her kitchen she reminded him as he ate that God was always watching. So the scene at the gate was kind of blessed. Maybe it was like the old times in Greece, where the gods were around and you could encounter them, he was a guy who gave off such a glow, who should he choose to might change everything for you, if he would only connect with you, there was so much possibility around, and so you were happy to be near him, to be there in his presence.

It was the middle of the day when there was nothing to do.

Occasionally he went back to bed. But he couldn't sleep. His head was whirling, there were scenes inside it that he played over and over, and then he would force himself to open his eyes. He would lie in Elvis Presley's room and his gaze would wander. The faces on the photographs stuck to the walls seemed to watch him. Tony Curtis, Marlon Brando, they knew what was happening to him. Inside, he could feel the driveshaft, spinning.

What was he?

On the porch, he would keep company with Vernon. This never involved any talking. Vernon Presley wasn't a bad man. He'd been to prison, but only for a short stretch, and it was over a trifle, almost a misunderstanding, involving an altered check and a pig. No one thought he was bad. But he didn't have a great deal to do or say.

On the porch the minutes were like little holes, bubbles that slowly opened and absorbed a moment of your day, and then drifted away, you could see time passing as the shadow of the house crept across the dusty yard.

In his room he played records. He had asked Sam for money to buy a little record player and Sam took it from his royalties. Tarzan very rarely at any stage in his life had money in his pocket. If he wanted something he would just point, just ask for it. He didn't understand. He was on the verge of having more money than anyone in the known world. He knew what money did, that you could obtain things with it, but he was still thinking on what it was, really – what is money, really? Nevertheless, should he want a thing he got it. And so he would obtain records and play them in his room, and go inside them. If you talked to him at these times you weren't sure if he was there or back in the bush or somewhere out in space. He was gone. He wouldn't look up. He could really make you hear that music just by being in his presence.

But there was definitely time to kill.

Thus when Skippy Dent turned up at the Presleys' gate in the middle of one hot Wednesday morning and suggested a spot of fishing, nobody thought it was a bad idea. Skippy was almost famous. Not like Tarzan, not like Dewey. But he had been the star running back on a winning team at Humes High, people had talked about him for the big time until, in his last season, his knee got realigned by the vertical arrival of the butt of a large tackle. At twenty, he was a Memphis identity – men in bars knew his name. "School needs you, Skip," they would say, "maybe you should go back, explain the game to those creampuffs." This was a complicated remark, the part about going back, as Skip, since Humes, had never really found too much to do with himself. He'd dreamed of not working, of playing pro ball and then retiring to fish. Instead he'd gone straight to the fishing. Nobody knew what he did all day.

Vernon considered joining them then decided that maybe he had things to do on the Lincoln.

Since they had no car, Tarzan and Skip walked, which gave

them a chance for sizing up. Tarzan an inch taller, and definitely better-looking – Skip's face was lumpy, like golf balls in a plastic bag, and the pallor of his skin made Tarzan's tan seem even deeper. Tarzan felt Skip bump him, just casually, as they ambled. He knew this bump, Jimpi bumped you like this, it gave the other guy a chance to feel how hard you were, what you were made of – the right stuff, apparently. Skip moved along easy beside him, no limp these days, just a faint snag in what should have been an athlete's relaxed stride. Tarzan waited for the usual dopey questions – "So was your dad a monkey?" – but Skip never at any time asked about his past. Maybe he'd read the interviews? Tarzan's story was by now, especially in Memphis, a familiar thing. So, two well-known guys on the walk – people waved out to them.

They settled beside the river, not too far upcurrent from the park where Jane and Tarzan had reacquainted themselves, and Skip got the bobbers in the water. Two hours passed. So this is fishing, Tarzan thought. Watching the river flow. Then they went home.

It was a strange little encounter. Skip seemed to have no need to worship Tarzan – already Tarzan was tired of this, and it had yet to properly begin. Maybe that was it, that Skip knew what it was to have people think that just being around you would improve their day. Skip never once mentioned Tarzan's music or the prospects of his career, though it was impossible to be near him at that time and not feel he was about to be jetted away into the stars. But they just walked along easy, enjoying each other's presence. If they'd been in one of those countries where men hold hands they would have done so.

"No fish?" asked Vernon.

In fact Skip never caught any fish, as he never used any bait. No one knew this. But he liked to be by the river, and he liked to be left alone. He didn't want the bother of having to deal with anything he might catch. When Tarzan cottoned to this, the hunter-gatherer in him protested and after that they began bringing catfish home, which Mrs Presley would fry, and serve to the three men in her bright kitchen. As I said, Skip wasn't a great talker, neither was Vernon, and Tarzan only spoke when he had something to say, so the kitchen would be filled with the splattering sound of the frypan and an observant male silence. Mrs Presley paid no heed to that and kept up talk enough for them all. It was somehow for everybody a very satisfying thing. Yes, Skippy Dent was quickly established as welcome, and after that first time he was frequently there, until the time came when he was there all the time. He taught Tarzan how to go out wide for a long pass, how to sink a beer in a quiet bar at eleven in the morning. Skip tried to get him into clothes that attracted less attention but Tarzan took no notice of this and Skip quickly got the message. Such minor agenda items were efficiently sorted. Their association prospered.

Looking over this description I see I have made Skip sound like a loner. This wasn't so. He liked the river for being alone, but that was a particular time he needed – he had always gone there before big games. But Skip had buddies, he liked company. One guy, Frank Helbo, was from the ball team. Speed James had grown up with Skippy in Tupelo before their families had moved to Memphis at about the same time. There were others, another four or five of them. They weren't a gang, didn't get into fights or call attention to themselves, Skippy was too smart for that – though they did all wear the same brand of sunglasses. So what were they all about?

Some people called them the Memphis Mafia.

But fishing expeditions were only intermittently possible, as Tarzan was due to go on tour. Sam Phillips had raised a storm and now he had to drive it.

Sam was trying to shape the thing. He was right now seeing a pretty big picture. The reaction Tarzan was getting was exactly as he'd intuited it. Bewilderment from the slowcoaches, resentment from the entrenched minor talent, but beyond that a fervour of immeasurable proportions from a new audience – white *and* black – that seemed to have no boundaries. Sam knew, all he had to get was exposure. That meant television. But Tarzan wasn't ready for television, yet, he needed to learn just a little more stagecraft, and also to build a bigger base, a bigger platform. So Sam packed him up and sent him out on the road. Tennessee, Louisiana, Missouri, they drove for miles in Scotty's Studebaker with the double bass on top. So many remember these early tours – Buddy Holly for instance saw him performing in Lubbock, Texas, and this changed his life. Tarzan was a force of nature. It was of course obvious if you studied him that he was still learning. He did awkward things – he spat on stage, a big goober, he'd seen men in the street do it, so why not? He picked a girl out of the front row, hauled her up on stage and directed her to the wings. Everyone in town knew where she was going to spent the evening. Bill said to him, "Pick 'em later, it can be tricky in the stage lights, you want to be sure of what you're getting, jungle man."

But for the most it was rolling thunder, lightning on wheels. They stormed up little towns, left everyone drenched in feeling. So what was it at work here? Okay, the beat. Okay, he was good-looking. And he could dance. Plus there was the sense of being caught up in the fire that was consuming the nation – well, that's how it felt. Catching the new train. Yes, these were all elements. But the killer was how he could communicate. There are films of this. I saw one recently, I love to play the old films of him, where he's on a low stage, no more than apple-box high, and the front row girls are maybe six feet away. And they're in a fever. And they're still in their seats – passion and control right there inside every frenzied body.

This is nice to see, how they didn't break, they had their places and he had his, up on the little stage. And the thing is, those girls are just so happy about this! You never saw a group so in love with being where they are. They're laughing, all of them. Later it got to where people tore their hair and the photos from that time show audience faces that look like they're in pain. But early on, when it was all still being invented, this rock 'n' roll was such a sweet thing. Tarzan is laughing too, he's laughing with them, the girls and Tarzan, it's the mainline between them – they love each other. Yet he never misses the beat. The lights catch the sweat flying from his hair. He drops to one knee and everything is frozen. He holds a pose – then tears it open. Oh, he was hot! So what was it? Finally it was the sense of miraculous possibility, I think, seen up close. That you could swing in from the trees, unable to write your name even and some several months later be balancing civilisation on your fingertips. This was a story that was instinctively loved by every dreamer, since it promised them so much. It's the Superman promise, where we will all be seen for what we really are, heroic and fabulous, if only we can only find the right telephone box. It is I think the greatest, the most sustaining promise of modern times.

Scotty was married and so of course on tour he was strictly interested in where in the locality you might buy the best guitar strings. And Bill was married so Bill studied the regional variations in cooking. Hell, no, they never unzipped their trousers, not even to get them dry-cleaned.

Meanwhile, in hotel rooms, in cars, in corners backstage, behind curtains, behind trees, under tables, in elevators and in shower boxes, Tarzan turned out not to be married or even engaged. Girls arrived, some blushing, some with their panties in their hands – wherever he was, they came and found him. Tarzan was nineteen. And he welcomed them, them and their bodies – he was not fond of American interiors but there were exceptions. No one thought that on these occasions he should display any sentiment. He never performed, or worried. He never seduced. The show was the seduction. After, he simply fucked, and fucked, and fucked. He fucked more often than he ate. He fucked over and over. That word filled his head, he thought that the word was on him, on his skin, on his fingers – you could smell the word everywhere. On his face – "Hey, fuck-face," Scotty would call to him and Tarzan understood this.

Yes, that was what people saw, he understood, when they looked into his eyes, that he was the one who was fucking the most. This made sense to him. Kerchak had been the biggest fucker, and the world had been made to his order. It was what he was for, increasingly Tarzan saw this, it was the reason that people wanted him and why they admired him and wanted to touch him – men too. They applauded him. They urged him on. He was doing what everyone wanted to do and that made him the one.

Yes, this he understood.

When he was inside a girl he understood everything. It all made sense – the screaming, the sea voyage he had made with Jane, his boyhood with Kala – it had all been for this. He would lift his head back and say, suddenly, "Tell me your name." The quiff hanging ragged on his brow. Looking right at them, a dark eyebrow cocked – Cindy, Candy, Mandy – and then he would drive for home. Shirley, Betty, Natalie, Babs. Alice. Chicks. Suzette. Afterwards he would smile and this smile would make them so completely happy. Yes, in those moments, it all made perfect sense to him.

So he just went ahead and made as much sense as he could.

When he came home he was excited – and utterly exhausted. He crept into Elvis Presley's room, pulled the bedding up to his shoulder, slept around the clock.

Previously he'd never been late for breakfast. One morning Mrs Presley came in to look at him, he woke to hear her leaving, and he knew that she'd been over the bed, staring down at him. It was disturbing to realise that someone had been in the room with him and he hadn't been conscious. How much control was he losing?

Finally he appeared in her kitchen and took a place at her table. It was three in the afternoon. Perhaps it seemed as though he was demanding that the world now come serve him. But this wasn't so. She had been waiting for this moment. She cooked for him, in her apron with the thousand-flower pattern. She didn't ask him a single question, and in fact in this house his career was almost never discussed. Mrs Presley kept a scrapbook that, these days, is an invaluable archive document – it has pretty well everything published about him in the early years. The pieces are cut so carefully. *Tarzan leaves a Trail of Broken Hearts. Tarzan Teen Sensation! Was it an A-bomb? Yes, says Little Rock!* But in her kitchen he was just a big boy with bare feet and an appetite.

While she cooked she talked. She called him *Son* during these conversations and she told him all as though he was her son and knew all of her history. Black hair, particularly bright eyes, that's what you see in the photos of her, and her eyes are always on him. She strokes his hair as she tells him what Laura has been doing, she moves around him like a photographer, getting him from every angle.

Tarzan becoming used to being looked at.

Here they are, then, together in the kitchen – let's take a picture. Finally he's eaten all he can, a mountain of food. She clears away, but he's in no hurry to leave and so she sits at the table with him, talking, talking. Mid-sentence she takes his hand and he allows this. She strokes the hand slowly, absently, as she explains how Vernon has in recent days developed a fondness for late drives – they drive around Memphis, she says, going slow in the dark. It's clear that Tarzan will join them on their drive tonight.

And does she know what they got up to on tour? Yes, with every bone in her. She gets him down on his knees and has him join her in prayer. The light from the bulb above means they are kneeling in their own shadows. There's no discussion of what he's doing, no recrimination, but instead a pleading for something called his soul. Tarzan is curious but doesn't ask. She seems to need to do this and he doesn't mind. She explains that he's a good boy and is learning the paths of righteousness and can a special watch please be kept on him. Not much is required of him here, except that he be silent and maintain a special kind of look on his face. It comforts her, he can tell, to say it over and over again: "He's a good boy."

So what was in his head?

Whether he was down on his knees in her kitchen or lying in her son's bed, Tarzan at these times was always trying to see where he was going. Yes, how will events be sequenced, he asks, how does a human life go, so that he proceeds from being the loud and runaround thing that he is now to being as homely as Vernon, as solid as Gladys? They are what every human being turns into, increasingly he sees that, and so apparently one day he will be like them too. Which is somehow astonishing: the way they are so convinced of themselves. He has grasped it that people get married, that they have jobs. Personally he is right now in a special category that is called showbiz, he understands this, that is why he wears make-up and bright clothes, that is why every girl wants to fuck him, but surely that's a fault of his origins, yes, something unspoken makes it clear: this won't last.

But how will he arrive? It's as though he came to civilisation but didn't enter it. When will that start? On his knees, he tells himself again: he must have faith, and watch, and not make any mistakes, and wait.

*

During the drive that night no one speaks – has Mrs Presley ever been silent for so long? The old Lincoln is spotlessly clean, not like Scotty's Studebaker that they have been living out of, and Vernon's style at the wheel is everything that Scotty's is not. Going slow, Vernon brakes for shadows, he steers carefully over any irregularities in the blacktop surface, keeping them down to no more than walking pace. Tarzan is in back, his elbows along the tops of the seats, chin on his hands, eyes in the mirror. While the Lincoln glides through the night he examines himself. He has seen many of the ways of the world now but he simply has no clue what is happening to him. As he understands it, what is happening is not happening to anybody else. He stares into his own eyes and tries to catch a reason for this. Meanwhile Vernon drives like a funeral director, the long car scarcely disturbs the air. Out the windows, there's nothing special to look at, the pools of brightness cast by street lights, and fences, and the lit windows of houses. Tarzan is thinking all over again: So this is what it's like to be in an automobile – it's as though he's really here in this moment. It is pleasant. Mrs Presley's neck is not far from his nose and that nose, even some months out of the bush, is sharp – he smells her body and also the perfume and powder and lipstick she has applied to herself. Vernon's smell is in there too, along with the oil and metal smells of the automobile, but Tarzan isn't interested in these, he concentrates on Mrs Presley and it's as though he is drawing something out of her. This woman smell, he has collected it from Jane and from Laura and from the girls he fucked with on tour, but this is different, it's older, and very complicated – for instance, it also has Carole in it, and maybe even Kala, though the smells are of course entirely different. He decides that he likes it – because it is so utterly human. He lets it flow into him as they slide through the dark.

A mother. Maybe he could finally have one?

Then they're home and he's in bed and she brings him a glass of milk. She sits on his bed and he can smell another smell, the smell of tears on her powdered cheeks. But she's not actually crying now. As though they are still in the Lincoln, the room is quiet and nothing moves. She pats his big leg, there under the blankets, and she says, "Son." There's a moon, by its light the faces in the black-and-white photographs can be seen, watching, listening. She says, "Why don't you call me *Mom*, Son."

This isn't a question, he knows that, it's an invitation. He rolls this idea around and then says, without any strain, "Okay, Mom." She pats his leg again, nothing especially intimate, just like the bump that guys give you, just checking the substance of the world – takes his glass and leaves him alone in the dark with the photos.

The next day Mrs Presley produced a letter that had come, she said, a few days earlier, and left him alone with it. He studied the picture on the stamp, which was of the Statue of Liberty – a tall green woman holding a stick up into the air. He has previously asked to have these little pictures explained to him, but the descriptions of the postal service make his head dizzy. Out there it seems that thousands of people are in a big line, passing the thing called an envelope from hand to hand, across the country, and finally one of the people walks to your house with it, all because of this little picture. As he's travelled he's kept his eye out for this long line of people but has never spotted it. Fifty years later a stamp will appear with his face on, but by then he will be dead. But me, I was utterly proud. And then, in 2002, when he was number one again and thus had more number ones than even the Beatles, well, this was also a good day for me – yeah, baby. The letter of course was from Jane and of course he couldn't read it. But he knew it was from her. He held it close to his face and, just as he had done in the Lincoln the night before, drew out the essential information with his nose. Then he went through to the kitchen and asked Mrs Presley to read it for him.

For this task she took to her feet and began to declaim as though she was an orator. She was, he saw, going to mock this thing. But the letter was ready for this. *Dearest Tarzan,* it began, *please find someone kind and trustworthy to read this to you, as I need to tell you what is in my heart.* Tarzan, at the table, saw a picture of a heart from Jane's book, a red thing with tubes.

Do you know, Tarzan, that I can see you from here? I don't simply mean that I can see your picture, which was in the newspaper. And I can also hear your voice, but not only on the radio where your record is being played. You are not so far away. An airplane could take me to you in two hours. My skin thinks that at any moment you are going to touch it. When I'm walking, my legs wait for yours to walk beside them. Do you remember how we walked? All of my body is waiting, as though in just a moment you will be holding me. Isn't there a space inside your arms, my darling? Isn't there a shape you long to hold?

Now Mrs Presley sat down and read in less of a voice. *I'm not sending you a picture, my darling – only the picture that these words may make. I want you to want to see me. To miss me. I want you to feel the ache that I'm feeling. I won't seal this with a kiss. The girls you meet out there will do that. They will lipstick their lips and make a red outline on the page. Those girls are touching you – I know that. But they are not my real concern. You are my real concern. Not because you owe me something. You don't. I want you to feel free of all obligations to me. An obligation is like some money that you owe. If ever you did in any way owe me something, I now lift that from you. All I hope is that you will be free. But in fact that is not true – that is not all I hope. What I hope is that when you see you are free you will come to me. I feel as though I am not making perfect sense. I had thought I was going to write something else. But these words are full of sense – of my sense of you. Of all my senses. It is as though you made my senses grow up. I hadn't appreciated them before. But, then, they didn't make me ache. At nights I listen to the sound of the world, out there in the night. I know you are listening too. You always liked to listen. Under all those noises, which are just any old backyard noises, we are hearing the same things, darling, which is the sound of the blood moving inside us. Please listen for that, please listen for your heart, it's all that matters. Touch those girls – I know that this will happen. But do not let them touch you back.*

I can see you, darling. Can you see me? Do you know what love is, now? You are the one who might show everyone this. Everyone thinks they already know. But that is just a word. You might really learn. Keep trying to see what love is.

Yours with every sense I have in me – Jane.

In the little kitchen the dime-store clock up on the wall could be heard to tick. Mrs Presley folded the letter carefully, as though it was a live thing, and slid it across the table to him. "That poor girl is suffering," she said. Tarzan could feel the way that the letter had made the ache inside Mrs Presley grow strong again. "She should come here. Perhaps she could stay upstairs with Mrs Fruchter."

"No," said Tarzan.

Mrs Presley sighed. "Don't you love her, son?"

Tarzan took the letter and held it. He looked at the marks on its page. He could smell the ink. Jane seemed to be inside the marks, and she was also there in the smell that her fingers had put on the page. But now she was in him too, he could feel that – and he could also feel that that was what she had wanted. In a sudden movement he rose from the table, strode to the porch and, standing there in the noonday sun, let out a great yell as though he was in the valley. "Hey!" said Vernon, from his chair, but that was all he said.

Tarzan took no notice. He sat down on the top step and held his head in his hands.

In the tiny dressing room at the Glory Hole he said to Scotty and Bill, "Men, tell me – what is love?"

Bill was buttoning up his bibbed shirt. "Oh, baby!" he groaned. "If you gotta ask . . . What's her name, big guy?"

Scotty, who always kept at least one eye on Tarzan, said, "If you ain't sure then you don't have to worry. Forget it, Tarzan – we got a job to do."

On the banks of the Mississippi, Tarzan, sitting beside Skippy, said it again. "Tell me what love is."

"Well, I'll tell you," said Skippy. But then a large catfish caught ahold of the other end of his line and by the time they had the thing landed he had forgotten the question. So Tarzan asked again: "Love?" said Skip. "See that old catfish? See how he's gasping? He loves the water. He cain't breathe the air. He's in love with that water, he has to have it. That's what love is, when you just have to have it, to be alive. I'll put him back in, I think."

He let the wide-mouthed fish slip away into the swirling water. Tarzan asked, "Do you love somebody?"

"No," said Skip. His back was turned, he was squatting, looking across to the far bank. "Not some body. I'm in love with some thing." *Ahm.* "I'm in love with playin' ball. And I ain't never gonna play ball again. That's how it is with love, Tarzan – you've gotta have it, and you cain't have it. C'mon, we caught enough already. Let's go home."

21

The next phase kicked off with Tarzan flying to New York for a tryout for TV. Sam went with him, but not the boys – the TV show said it had a house band. Sam argued strongly agin this, but you don't really argue with TV, he'd pulled in nearabouts every favour he had owed to get the tryout. So off they flew.

But Tarzan needed the band. He needed his audience. He needed Memphis. This was for *The River of Diamonds*, a kind of talent show, where rising stars could rise further – or go back to the gutter. The house band played the notes of his new record, they even played them in the right order. But there was no music in it. They laughed at Tarzan, he heard them doing it. They said the noise he made wasn't singing. And as for his "dancing" – he saw them lift long arms to the sky and scratch their armpits, hoo-hoo. Where are those wise guys now? Delivering pizza.

Now this was a time when TV really mattered. It was the new medium, when it came in it hit bigger than Hiroshima. At the end of the Second World War there were less than seven thousand TV sets in America – by 1952 there were over twenty million. People walked all the way over to other people's houses just to see it. By 1955 television was rising to its heyday and its suction effect as it went up was overpowering. It pulled the nation with it. But not all were chosen. Tarzan was "not ready for television." That was the verdict. Might never be ready.

He did get to see the Empire State. A needle up there with clouds going past, a swaying point – down on the crowded walk, staring, he nearly broke his neck. They debated, he and Sam, whether to climb to the top, but decided: let's wait until he could sing there. But just to see it, to run an eye up its soaring, windowed walls, this made Tarzan remember the hours he had spent on the stoop of the cabin, gazing at the pages of the book with photographs and wondering inside himself: what am I? He had begun to dream of the bush more often now, flying high over the valley, not on the end of a vine but as the hawk, the hawk he had watched – somehow now he was that bird, he could see the whole thing from on high, he could balance above it. There were the gorillas. Down there were Kala's bones in the tree. Over there were the wetas. Waterfall, stream, cabin, he could see it all. But he couldn't descend. He was above it and could finally see the shape of it – how the valley was shaped, the map of it. But he couldn't be part of it any more.

Jane was down there.

And New York? There were duelling taxicabs, and a train that went under the ground, but Tarzan was not impressed. It was just more city, more of the noise, and he couldn't hear any music in it. He preferred 462 Alabama.

But: as Sam said, there for sure were a whole lot more people there to sell records to.

Home to 462 – not that this was any longer a quiet retreat. It seemed that every day now new strange things were happening outside the house. It was the girls. A good number of them were just plain slutty – this was Mrs Presley's opinion. To see some teen queen elbow her way through, palm off her milkshake, hoist her chest and then in front of everybody just thrust herself against him, this was disturbing. Leaning back in his arms, looking deep into his eyes, as though something serious was being exchanged, with a faint angelic smile playing at the corners of her mouth and all the while thrusting with her crutch – to do it and to pretend you weren't, this was the height of cool. Okay, they had their clothes on, but, right there on the walk – there orta be a law.

They toured again. They tore up little towns – I mean, *tore up*, clothes, theatre seats, a trail of destruction – and totally swept every other performer from any stage they appeared on. No one could follow him. It was a short set, twenty-five minutes at most, and to get to it the fans had to sit through dog acts, balloon benders, but no one seemed to mind. The news that he was in the building sent a quiver through every venue. He played his hits, honed at the Hole, but suddenly the music wasn't so important. That was on the records that you played at home. Instead it was him, now, the one, the guy who was worth putting a spotlight on. I have to say in all modesty that during this particular year he was very good to watch. He would sink to his knees – the crowd groaning – he would toss his head back so that the thick dark hair flew away from his brow, so nobly lined, and then toss it forward so that it hung down like something ragged with emotion. His shoulders slumped as though he had a blues that could not be carried, then he jackknifed open. He really cut the air.

Afterwards, they fornicated. In hotel corridors, in the wagon, in dressing rooms backstage, there were always girls.

All of this became routine, you will recall, as "rock 'n' roll" turned during the 1960s into "pop" and then "rock". The Rolling Stones, for instance, would arrive and everyone knew that this was a sex thing and that if you wandered backstage, what did you expect, discussion of Wittgenstein? But that was in the 1960s and by then sex was a thing that human beings were widely acknowledged to do. In Tarzan's day, babies were caused by marriage.

So maybe you can see the kind of trouble he brought to town. It was as though people thought, He's a wild thing and he doesn't know any better. They thought, He just does it. They thought, I could just do it too.

Listen to those pounding hooves, anyone could hear them. Mrs Presley – every morning she would have him on his knees praying with her. He learned the hypnotic words – *Our Father Who art in Heaven, hallowed be Thy name* – and, polite, would happily say them along with her.

The thing that came to interest him most from all that Mrs Presley told him was Judgement Day. This concept really appealed: a day in the future when it all came together. Everything was being recorded, she said, in a book, he liked that, and it would all be read out, each individual thing that you had done – so you didn't have to worry that you couldn't always remember. One day he would have a chance to look over all that was happening to him, to see it again, as he did when he dreamed he was the hawk. You would get a chance to see the shape of it all. And then you would go on to a new stage – to suddenly be the finished version of the thing you had been working towards. This he understood with utter clarity. It was going to be like the end of something that had started when he looked for the first time upon the cabin. Back then he had sensed he was as yet unmade. That ahead of him lay a state he couldn't imagine, when he would be one among his kind. He felt he was on a journey. At nights, now, as he lay frowning up into the dark of Elvis Presley's room, this was increasingly clear to him: far ahead, there would be a moment when someone else decided he had reached his final form.

Such frowning.

And then when the spotlight fell on him, suddenly he looked stylish and sharp, as though he already knew the lot.

One fine morning, when Tarzan and Skip were fishing from the banks of the Mississippi, they were joined by a couple of guys who, it was obvious, had arrived as part of some previous arrangement. Tarzan saw this. They acted natural, but they were way too studied. When Skip gestured, they sat down together, like twins. He didn't mind, it was always good to meet new people.

It was a pity to meet them here, though, by the river, in Skip's hideaway. These days, he and Skip had to climb over the back fence of the Presleys' house so as to get some time alone. Skip had suggested that Tarzan might buy a vehicle, now that he was earning, to make things easier. Tarzan was waiting to understand how a big thing like a car might be purchased. He could see himself at the wheel, but it was hard to know where it might be parked – wouldn't the girls just turn it to garbage?

Anyway, here they were, two new guys, Frank and Speed, a thinny and a fatty. Frank, having been on Skip's team, was the thin one. Like Skip, he didn't talk so much. But that apparently was what they had Speed for. Speed talked as though the world wasn't there unless you remarked upon it. "Lookit that river, where does it keep coming from? Do you guys always sit here? Good view of the ol' smokestacks, I guess. Lookit that smoke, willya. Don't they look like great big cigrettes sticking up there – like the building is having a cigrette. Smoke, Tarzan?" And he produced a packet of Luckies.

"Thank you, Speed."

"Anyway, as I was saying, my ol' man slept out in the rain last week, out in the yard, my mom put him out, yeah, an' now the guy's sick in bed and she has to bring him things, drives her crazy – say, Tarzan, talking of driving, d'you ever think of buying a car?"

This remark fell into a hole and reverberated, it lay on the riverbank like a fish gasping for air. The guys were glancing. Tarzan turned to study Speed's face and said, "Skip said I should do that too."

"Not *should*," said Skip quickly.

"Not *should*," repeated Tarzan. Not *should*. He felt he was really learning to speak better now, but then people would say things and he would lie at night in Elvis Presley's bed and try to understand what they might have meant. Plus there were *ways* of speaking, just as there were ways of behaving. Jane had taught him to speak carefully – "Use whole sentences." But it wasn't what Scotty did, or Bill. It was hard to talk like them, they only said little bits of things, but the things they said seemed to have a kind of bounce. For instance when Bill said, "That is real gone," it was as though something extra-special had occurred, something exciting. People liked the way Bill talked. Then when Tarzan said it, carefully, "That is real gone," well, it made everyone laugh too – but it wasn't the same laugh. So he listened when anyone said anything, and remembered, and tried it out later, just as he did when he made a move on stage that the audience liked. You had to be always learning. Scotty had said that once. Tarzan listened to Scotty, too, but that was different. Scotty was like Sam. They could see things.

Now Speed, unabashed, said, "Because if we had a vehicle we could go on over to Kansas City, I hear it's wild."

"They got some crazy little women there," said Tarzan.

Everyone looked to see how he might intend this. Tarzan wondered if he should sing the whole song for them. But Skip didn't know anything about music, that had been established. He thought that the music that Tarzan talked about was for niggers, he had told Tarzan so. Tarzan didn't sing when they were fishing.

"So I guess you want to," said Speed.

"Want to what?" said Skip.

"Go to Kansas City," said Speed.

The thing about words was, it mattered very much how you pronounced them. What kind of slope you put on them – was that it? For instance, you could say, "It's gone," and that meant there was none left – no sugar in the bowl. But if you said, "It's *gone*," well, that was completely different. That meant it belonged to a special category of things to get wild about, that it was certified good – which was another phrase that Bill made an event out of. Sometimes Tarzan wore a shirt that was gone, according to Bill, quite often, in fact. Tarzan kept a mental list of things that were gone and things that were not.

But what he wanted most was to talk gone. When he tried, oh dear, it made them laugh – it broke them up. Now, broke them up, that didn't mean that anything was broken – well, the laughter broke up the conversation, maybe that was it?

But he could sing gone. Oh yes. Tarzan singing gone was something that they had worked on and it was a skill he really enjoyed. It had lots of angles to it, and he wanted to master them all. Some words you gave a special shape to, some words you held back. One way to sing gone consisted of taking a little word and doing something with it. The first time he got this right was when they'd recorded *Good Rockin' Tonight*. The song had sounded okay, it was working, but then Bill suggested he might add one word to the lyrics and the word was *Well*. Bill suggested that they put this word right at the beginning of the song, and when Tarzan asked him what it meant, Bill said, "Let's see – *Well* is like a word you say before you're gonna say something – right, Scotty?"

They were in the pale green loomy old studio at Sun, which was becoming one of the few rooms that Tarzan liked – it wasn't the smells, it was the sounds that seemed to have lodged in the carpet and wall panels. Scotty, hunched over his guitar, said, "*Well now listen up, I got something I'm gonna say –* yeah, that's about it."

"Somethin' like, *Well, why don't you get on with it?*" This was Sam from the control booth.

"We jest be explorin' the motherin' ol' English tongue here, coach," said Bill. "The lingo, y'know. The lyrics. Tarzan, why don't you give us a kind of *people get ready* thing at the intro, there, kind of like you're gettin' ready to give it to us."

And that's how it occurred that *Good Rockin' Tonight* starts with the word *Well*. But it wasn't just any old *well*. This word is drawn out. The more Tarzan drew it out, the more gone it was, apparently. Just that one little word, once they got it right, then everything else in the song was sublime-time music right on down the line. Tarzan stretches the word out as though it's a limousine, it's something you can ride on, he sounds so expansive, it just opens you right up. *Wwweeeeellllll* . . . – from there it was good rockin' all the way to the mighty Pacific.

But that was just the start. A couple of months after they had spent half the night on *Well*, another little word got a working over. This time the word was *Baby. Babe-babe-b-b-b-b-babe-babe* – he said the word, the first letter of the word, over and over at the beginning of a new song, *Let's Play House*. It was like stutterin' they said, which wasn't a term he knew, he would ask later, but he could tell they liked it. They worked on this *Baby*, then they put it on the record. You can hear it today – he stutters the word seventeen times before the song starts.

And this meant it was *real* gone. *Let's Play House* was his biggest hit yet. It *broke out*, it went nationwide. It went and it went, that thing just kept on going. No one could hear it enough, when they played it live on stage they had to stand back, it made the audience press forward in a way that seemed dangerous. Wooh, how the girls laughed and screamed at the same time. Those shows were so good-humoured – yearning and craziness, it's a fireball mix. It got so that he would just utter that spluttering *B-B-Baby* and the venue would erupt as though the world was ending.

Let's Play House made the Top Ten on the Billboard Hot One Hundred. Which was the big time.

So was Jane his baby? Tarzan lay in Elvis Presley's bed and tried to figure it. Your baby was the one who haunted you, she was the one who had power over you – *that's* what the songs said. In Elvis Presley's room, night after night – he didn't think that word, *power*, but who thinks in actual words? Rather he had feelings, that were like shapes that moved close about him, shifting, grappling with each other. This was all chemicals, Jane had said, and electricity – inside his head. Was he in his head? Or in Elvis Presley's room? The room had a personality that was as strong as his own – was he being taken over by something in the room? He didn't understand electricity, no one could explain it. He would have to learn to read for that. This was one of the goals he had set for himself, that when he became the person who he could imagine up ahead, when he filled that shape, he would be able to read.

In the blotchy light the faces in Elvis Presley's photographs were like a circle of judges.

But he could not see that Jane would be coming close to him again. This thought became certain knowledge almost as soon as it first occurred to him. Then, as he lay there, the knowledge changed, it seemed, and became a feeling – a feeling of sadness. Do you know sad, Tarzan? Sadness had Kala in it, sadness was about his family who he would never know. The cross on the hill. His mother and father, these were shapes he didn't have and he knew it. So sadness was about what you didn't have, was that it? About something you didn't have any more. Every other human being had those shapes within them, it seemed. They had brothers, too, and buddies, and they had childhood friends, people they'd grown up with. Also they had old things. He could smell Elvis Presley's things, the old ball glove, the clothes still in the closet. Suddenly he was overcome by a desire to have things, things that were old and were his.

So was that what Jane was, a thing that contained good old feelings? This was kind of sad, too. This was the blues, maybe. The blues were another thing that the songs that said *baby* said. The blues he thought he understood. It was about a colour, something not unlike the light here in the night in Elvis Presley's room, a little bit purple, a little bit yellow, murky, shadowy, filled with shapes that you couldn't properly make out.

Mrs Presley in her kitchen, Tarzan at her table, barefoot – she's making him flapjacks. Her hands reach to open cupboards, they find ingredients, pour salt and flour. The hands move fast but they never make a mistake. Meanwhile she is talking. But it is her hands that Tarzan is watching as they move her around the kitchen.

Then everything is in the bowl and now she takes up the eggbeater. For a moment her voice disappears as she concentrates. Tarzan watches. He is remembering seeing an eggbeater for the first time. Jane had shown him how it was operated. But she did not use it. To see this thing now, being used according to design: this is a kind of miracle.

To see how Mrs Presley adds the ingredients. She knows exactly how much. Her hands know. They know when to turn the flapjacks. They drive the eggbeater. They put these things together and make a new thing. This, thinks, Tarzan, is what it is to be human.

On tour now, things were getting dangerously wild. There were people who drove miles to see them, fans, who had bought all his records and had brought his photograph, dark and glossy like the ones on the wall in Elvis Presley's room. They had waited in lines to have him make a mark on the photographs and record sleeves and on their clothes with a ballpoint – his signature. He made two marks, as Marion had taught him, these made a tee, and then three marks, these made a zee, she said, and next to that he put a squiggle – and this apparently was his name. Well, he'd done that thousands of times. Sometimes when he did it it was just good fun, everyone excited, the girls all working themselves up, he could feel it, to touch him, to maybe ask him for a kiss. But sometimes they didn't wait. Sometimes they just ran at him, and tore at his clothes. Should he just let them? Hell, no! said Bill, they'll kill us all. But Tarzan saw that it was a kind of game – that if he stayed and allowed himself to be fought over the excitement would die down. The idea was to run so that they had to chase him, and to get away so that they weren't satisfied. This is what Sam wanted, and what Bill and Scotty wanted, and he also understood that really it was what the fans wanted too, so he did it. For himself, he would have just stayed and let them have what they were after.

The fan-dom was taking a shape. It had a name, which was rock 'n' roll, and it had a sound, on the records, and it had a dance style which, increasingly, was inspired by Tarzan himself. Also there was a dress code which he had also been a leader in developing. Plus the hairstyle – already at his appearances there were guys who had gunked up their hair to make it look like his, standing up a little at the front and then falling to make a dark slashed line across the forehead. But most of all rock 'n' roll was a feeling – that this was a wild new thing, a whole new way of life. Sociologists have written that these were the years when teenagehood was invented, that in the centuries preceding you were just a kid until you grew up. Coincidentally the economy was booming. Coincidentally TV was looking for product, things they could put a frame around and sell. The stars of that day seemed to come closer – Marilyn Monroe, she was so infinitely remote that you could almost touch her.

Now rock 'n' roll just seemed perfectly designed to bring all of that together into, wah, a whole new thing. It was like an art movement, suddenly everyone finds a way of saying what has been locked up inside.

And the man who seemed destined to carry the movement, the cat who was the wildest, the strangest, yet the least threatening, the one with the most astonishing potential, was Tarzan the Ape Man, the swinger with the jungle beat, oh, here he comes now, ladies and gentlemen, you can hear screams from the audience, he's fumbling with the microphone right now, he's giving his cue to the boys, he's winding up his leg. And here he goes with . . . look out! He's snaking his hips! Oh, that shape in the air. That *feeling*. The girls are screaming right now, they're starting to weep and tear their clothes. He falls to the stage! Oh! Oh! To be here, ladies and gentlemen, in his actual presence, which is the presence of this whole new way of being, this rock 'n' roll, to be actually looking at him, watching him do the thing he does – this is *it!* He is the centre of the new world. Boys and girls, truly: he is the one who can never be repeated.

However such a thing is hard to manage and Sam Phillips was, financially speaking, struggling just a little to stay ahead of it. That seems crazy, when everything was selling so well.

But a tidal wave is hard to ride. The orders for Tarzan's records were pouring in, unprecedented, and Sam had to press copies to satisfy that demand. The pressings had to be paid for, cash, the distribution, the promotion, and if he didn't keep in good with the deejays and jukebox playlist men and the retailers and the boosters, well, the whole thing might fade. These guys were businessmen, they didn't care about rock 'n' roll – hell, lots of them hated this crossover stuff, this was Nigra music wasn't it? Okay, it's selling now, but this is just a fad. Naw, rock 'n' roll isn't going to last. And they'd always had sixty days to pay – so just send us over another ten thousand of that jungle disk, Sam, and we'll settle with you when the clock runs around.

Sam was all but broke.

Also, he had other things on his mind. Tarzan was the first, sure, he was Sam's personal discovery and would always hold a special place, but if it could happen once, Sam reckoned, it could happen again. No one else thought this, but Sam was always reaching. Suddenly there was all kinds of talent at his door. Sun had previously recorded Negro artists but now, because of Tarzan, every kind of wild white-boy singer came forth, and Sam was a man who understood where such talent might be taken. He already had Johnny Cash and Jerry Lee, who were showing promise – but this new signing, Carl Perkins, he could be even bigger than Tarzan. No, there was no need to limit your thinking. But you had to ride the wave, and that might require some pretty fancy footwork . . .

Increasingly Tarzan's fame – his notoriety – was an interference in any kind of life except being famous. Sure, it was a kick to do the shows, to feel that adoring blast from the open hearts, but then it couldn't be turned off. He had to be careful where he went – one night the audience learned he was in the movie theatre and they stopped the show. They made such a commotion that the lights came up and then everyone was screaming. And this was in Memphis, where he lived.

So it was that he liked going with Skip down to the riverbank. A car had been purchased, a Cadillac like Sam's, but pink. At times it was unclear who actually owned the car. Tarzan had definitely paid for it. When it came to money, he was like a tourist – point and then pass over a handful of notes, wait to see if that's enough. In the Caddy they'd been to Kansas City – it was true what the song said – and to other locations, many of them less illustrious, and had always managed to have some fun. There were times when Tarzan wondered if they really needed to go to another city just to throw a football, but he didn't mind being in the gang, at times it was just like roughhousing with the gorillas. The big car had room for six, easy, and so along with Skip, Speed and Frank, they began to be accompanied by two other guys, Delmo and Art. Art was another football player – ex-player, now a bellhop at the Laverne, except that he never seemed to be on duty – but it was Delmo that Tarzan came to spend most time with. In some ways Delmo seemed as much a newcomer as Tarzan himself. He was Skip's kin, Skip said, but not close kin, from the questions Skip would ask him – "So where are you livin', Del?" But the great thing about Delmo was, he liked nigger music. Not that he used that word, that was Skip, that was Speed, Delmo called it R&B, rhythm and blues, and he would sit alongside Tarzan in the front seat and operate the radio. He and Tarzan would talk music. Delmo was tremblingly excited by what Tarzan was doing, beat-wise, his large dark eyes would swell as he went into long rhapsodies, long raves about the history of the rhythm, all the time slapping his hand on his thigh in time with the radio. Delmo had dark hair slicked across and ears that stuck out so wide they seemed likely to impede his progress through the air, but you could see he was a straight man, all heart, and that heart was saved for the music.

They threw footballs in Texas, Kentucky and Kansas. They checked out every burger bar and shake palace for a radius of one hundred miles. Tarzan quite enjoyed some of it. But that was true of most of his life. Signing for the fans. Being interviewed. Driving somewhere – sure, why not? Riding merry-go-round horses, riding dodgems. Buying clothes. The movies – sure, let's go again.

A thing it was possible to like, he discovered, was being the boss. As for the rest of it . . .

There were three circumstances he really did like to be in: being on stage, being in the studio, or being with Mrs Presley in her kitchen. From time to time Mrs Presley forgot herself and called him Elvis. He didn't correct her. In her kitchen, she was like a person who had lost the love of her life and then rediscovered the lover inside someone else. In her kitchen, Tarzan always tried to be what Mrs Presley wanted him to be.

So – as she talks Tarzan stares up at the light bulb hanging on the end of its cord, burning away above them, tireless, and wonders if the thing that is in it is part of the majesty she is speaking about, the light which comes from God. He has climbed up there and looked, studied what Vernon called the filament up close, it looked like burning spiderweb, like something utterly implacable. Was this the thing which burned inside America? Now, his sentence composed beforehand, he asks her, "Mom, what is the conjunction between electricity and God?"

She rolls her eyes.

"Lordy, Tarzan, where did you learn conjunction? From that Speed, I guess." She pats his hand. "Well, let's see. Well, God gives us electricity, Tarzan, He sends it to us, to light our dark places and give us comfort. That's about it."

Tarzan nods. "Is that is what is lightning?"

"Oh, son, I don't rightly know about that. Vernon, what is lightning, can you explain it to this boy?"

Vernon stirs from his long diagonal in the doorway and looks up at the bulb as though he is reading a message. He sighs, and in the kitchen everything seems to be waiting. It's bright in there, Tarzan's clothes, Mrs Presley's apron, the yellow paper on the walls, Vernon squints, and they can hear the sound of thought, which is a strange sound, it always makes everyone nervous – have you ever noticed that? How hard it is to wait while someone thinks? Tarzan often made people wait, it drove them crazy. Now Vernon says carefully, "It comes from the clouds, I reckon."

A storm came and hammered on the roofs. Vernon and Tarzan stood on the porch, leaning, one either side of the door, and listened to the sound of the thing, a restless growling overhead – was this God? Lightning made its jagged marks on the dark sky. Tarzan thought of a time when he had been in the bush, when a storm like this had brought branches down, torn at the leaves. He was unclear – was it also stormy right now where the gorillas where? After the clouds had passed, they stayed there, listening on. The gurgling as the rain choked the gutters was a pleasant thing, like laughter. The wet smell of everything, and then the warm steaminess, yes, this was very pleasant.

With Vernon, you never felt, in his silence, that he was trying to say something. Nor was he observant. There's no denying it, Vernon didn't busy himself. It was as though the prison spell, followed by his son's death, had done for him. Any eloquence he had ever had was gone. He had nothing to tell the world. He was simply concentrated upon keeping himself decent.

So it was a surprise when Tarzan spoke up and asked him, in that quiet, clean-washed time after the storm, a serious question. He said, "Mr Presley, can you please tell me – do you think the music is evil?"

From his side of the door Vernon's face didn't shift but his eyes moved once, they slid over towards Tarzan. Was there something frightened in them? Large, round features, these eyes that had to speak for him – now they rested on Tarzan while the rest of the face was immobile. "I don't reckon you'll go to Parchman for it," he said finally.

"Pardon me."

"To jail. I don't reckon they'll jail you for it."

"But will they prevent me?"

Vernon's head lifted, just a little. "Heck, no, son, I don't reckon the US Army itself could prevent you."

His eyes went back to the straight and narrow, to the thing just beyond the middle distance which always seemed to elude him, and that was all that was said.

Nevertheless, this subject was on Tarzan's mind. He had spoken of it with Sam and been reassured. Sam had said, "There are forces in this heah country that you don't understand about, Tarzan. And you don't want to understand about 'em. Just listen to me: you are doing a fine thing, a decent thing, in making this music, an' one day the nation will be better because of you and this will be known." In later life people often likened Sam to a Southern preacher and, yes, there was some of that quality about him. He was definitely a thinking man. He knew what he was doing with Tarzan, where he was sending him.

But Sam didn't have to wear the heat. It was Tarzan, not Sam, who'd been denounced: ". . . this jungle bop boogaloo, its entire purpose is to bring the white man down to the level of the Nigra and when it chooses our children who are easily led to do its evil work, that makes it all the more sinister." *Thet*. This message was broadcast on the television by a man who wore a hat while he spoke and anyone could see he was an authority. "That music should be made illegal and all the radio stations that play it should orta be shut down." Mrs

Presley had raised herself from her chair and turned off the set but the words hung in the air. Another broadcast actually named him: "... the entertainer called Tarzan, doesn't even have a family name or know his parentage, this person was raised by monkeys and now here he comes selling this frenetic stuff with the purpose – I believe it is purposeful – of bringing our good white children down into the dirt and depravity, that he himself, pore creature, used to live in."

This was a storm too, a big one, it was a big stink. The Civil War was won but the South at the time was still segregated, you can see the signs which made it so in the museums today. *Coloured peoples water cooler*. The music industry wasn't immune. It did have the slight advantage that people couldn't see the singers on the radio and so they just enjoyed. But then at a live performance the moment of recognition would occur. Chuck Berry coming out to play his hits, and in the audience you could hear whispers. "I thought he was white." The Coasters regularly turned up to sold-right-out gigs only to have the promoter say, "You ain't The Coasters, The Coasters ain't niggers – we ain't lettin' you in!"

Such encouraging times.

Added to the mix, the swirl that was stirring the air around Tarzan was not just the race thing but also the race thing with sex in it. What does rock 'n' roll mean but fucking? In fact the actual etymology of the term is debated, go check a million websites, but you and I already know the truth and what's the point in spilling more beer over it? *Work With Me Annie* – is there anyone out there who thought this was a plea to a colleague? *Love Your Jelly Roll* is a cooking song? *My Boy Lollipop*, suck on that, of course it makes your heart go giddyup.

Not that you could hear the words at any performance that Tarzan gave. There was only noise, now, and most of that came from the audience. He wanted to sing – he loved to sing. But it was impossible for the musicians to hear each other. Scotty Moore has said, "We were the only band in history that was led by an ass," and while that makes a charming picture, it didn't do much for musical quality. But the kids didn't care. They didn't care about the music, they had the records for the music. What they wanted was him.

Increasingly, his moves were what it was all about. He bought himself a tall mirror and went to work, he got himself up on his toes and fell like he'd been shot. The legs of his trousers were full, in the fashion of the day, and when he shook his leg, well, it looked like every kind of action was taking place in there. Plus when he thrust with his pelvis, this movement was like an earthquake, the shock waves rippled and ran. No, I shouldn't say the music didn't matter – not when I believe that, in the end, it was really all that did. But you see the films of him performing and you think, to thrust like that, in the 1950s, when what they'd been getting was Patti Page, sweet as pie, eyes uplifted, moving serenely in a full white dress before a penguin-suit orchestra . . . Tarzan live, it was like the apocalypse.

On television they could only show him from the waist up.

So there was a great swirl around him – while he personally was calm, a hurricane was blowing. The performances were ridiculous, the car journeys endless, the food was Southern fried and heavy. The sex was endless, the interviews were endless, the photo sessions, the handshaking, the jive, the hicks and the hucksters. Sam couldn't pay his bills, everyone wanted a piece, Tarzan was trying to get a fix on evil, the race thing was a monster, swelling to a roar, plus charges of causing delinquency – it was all blowing up into a big ugly storm, it was all too much, and something had to give.

22

The arrival of Colonel Thomas A. Parker into this story is for many commentators the place where the end begins. But the end was always there in its beginnings. When Sam Phillips said that if he had a white boy who could sing like a black man he'd make a million dollars, right there you had it: no one had the slightest idea what to do once the million was made. Well, the prospect seemed so unlikely. And, as everyone knows, it's the making that's the fun.

For the making, now, Tom Parker was your man. From the start he took twenty-five percent of everything Tarzan earned. Later, it was fifty percent, except for items covered by "special considerations" clauses, where he took seventy-five. So he had a solid incentive to get in there and manage – to manage Tarzan right up to the stars. But Col. Tom was not so much a manager as a salesman. He sold a product brilliantly, and if he saw that a different product would sell better, why, simply change your product. Offer it then keep it back – regulate its availability to the market. Aim your product at the taste-free sector – as P.T. Barnum said, No one ever went broke underestimating the taste of the American public. Remember this brilliant maxim and, bingo! You have a golden goose.

Unfortunately for Tarzan, the goose was a human being.

So now I am going to try to tell you what the Colonel was like.

As common-or-garden as the Devil himself, he looked like a cross between Alfred Hitchcock and W.C. Fields. There was the Hitchcock waddle and the chins, there was the impressive waistline and the malevolent stare, but he like Fields also had a scornful mastery of all upon whom his gaze fell – when he looked at you you remembered every dumb thing you'd ever done. His origins were murky. Most probably he was Dutch and had entered the States as an illegal alien – his name had once been Andreas Cornelis van Kuijk – though I never knew this, any of this, until long after I was dead and started reading the biographies. During the 1930s he polished his scorn as a carny, selling sparrows dyed yellow as canaries to the small-town suckers, offering foot-long hotdogs where the sausage hung out the bun's ends but was missing from the middle. His dancing chickens danced because they were standing on a hot plate – classy stuff. He was said to have a way with elephants, ponies, geese and mice. He'd been a dog catcher, the founder of a pet cemetery. Through his talents as a booster he worked his way into the music business and became the brains behind rising country star Eddy Arnold. Together they rode the up-elevator until, suddenly, overnight, Arnold fired him. This gave the Colonel the final element he needed in life, a poisonous desire never to be bested.

After the break with Arnold, the Colonel nursed his grievance and, like a low dog moving cunningly on its belly, searched for a fresh opportunity. When his chance at Tarzan came, he was ready.

His sources had informed him of this hot new talent. The Colonel read the trades, asked around. It is said that before the signing he never condescended to attend a Tarzan performance, though, for a man of his caution, this is hard to imagine. Perhaps he sat in his car across the road from 462 Alabama and watched the after-school girls? Maybe he simply put his ear to the ground. Whatever: at some point he decided that Tarzan would be his master project and began developing a plan.

Over and over I ask myself: Could anyone have survived the Colonel's plan?

Sam instructed Tarzan to meet him, saying, "This is someone who might be interesting for you." Interesting how? But Tarzan always did as Sam asked and so when in the early afternoon the Colonel's car arrived at the Presleys', Tarzan was ready, in black shoes with green laces, black trousers, a lime green shirt with red buttons and a heavy black quiff. The driver, wearing full livery including cap, came to the gate. He looked over and called, without any apparent regard for Tarzan's fame, "The Colonel is waiting."

So Tarzan went to the Colonel.

The driver held the back door of the long dark limousine open and Tarzan got in. He was used to limousines but this one had a device on the door, like the device on the driver's cap, and then there was the occupant – usually Tarzan was the first to enter any given car. Between them, on the seat, was a black bowler hat. The occupant turned a large, fleshy head towards Tarzan and pale blue eyes looked at him as though mildly curious. There was no smile. The head spoke. Quietly it said, "Thank you, John." And the big car moved off.

Of course the car and driver were hired, and Col. Tom was never known, before or subsequently, to wear a bowler.

In silence they drove to a part of Memphis that Tarzan had not visited. Colonel Parker – if that's who he was, Tarzan wasn't sure and in times of doubt he had learned to look like a million bucks and keep his mouth shut – held his blue gaze on the road ahead. The heavy car angled towards the curb. "Now, Tarzan," said the Colonel, "I want to show you America," and John came round and opened Tarzan's door. Tarzan waited on the walk while John attended to the Colonel. Here, dark buildings rose narrowly. His nose wrinkled – there was a smell. America was full of smells, oily, metallic, chemical. But this was human.

Down between the buildings the Colonel led them, his stick tapping. Here were the humans. But Tarzan had never seen human beings like these, lying on the ground in their clothes. Were they sick? This was a bad place to lie, where rotting things and garbage was strewn. Some had red marks on their faces. No one had shaved. Some sat upright, leaning against the cold buildings between the garbage cans, not looking anywhere in particular. There were bottles, fiercely held. One man growled as they passed like a wounded animal from the bush but Tarzan couldn't understand his language.

From inside his suit the Colonel produced a wallet and passed a long, flat dollar bill to each man. Now the eyes of the men shrank, as though an anger had to be indrawn. Hands reached for the bills. The Colonel, coming to a poor fellow who was insensate, lifted the filthy head with his stick and, leaning down, tenderly slid a bill into the moist place where an ear had pressed to the ground.

As they departed, Tarzan looked back to see one of the other men removing this bill.

"Yes, John," said the Colonel and the limousine moved away. Now the Colonel had a small bottle and was tipping a sweet-smelling liquid onto his hands, wiping them with a large white handkerchief. He passed the bottle to Tarzan. But Tarzan had no handkerchief and so he simply held the bottle and waited.

Tarzan could feel the man beside him maintaining the silence.

They drove to the Memphis airport, boarded a small airplane and climbed into the sky. When the craft levelled out, the Colonel looked around at the blue outside the windows and nodded as though he was satisfied. Now he smiled, and turned his smile on Tarzan, who was beside him. Tarzan smiled back, of course. He had the sense that his smile went into the meaty head only three feet from his own and was held there, like something to be measured, later. He wanted to ask where they were going. Surely it was okay to ask? The question rose to his lips but exactly at that point the Colonel spoke. He said again, "I'm going to show you America."

They landed, entered another limousine, drove again. "Is this Memphis?" asked Tarzan.

"Is this Memphis, John?"

"No, sir," said the driver.

"Good," said the Colonel. "Drive on, John."

Sometimes the guys played games with him – once Bill had dressed himself as a woman and come thrusting at him; Tarzan said, "Hi, Bill," – and maybe this was a game? The Colonel and the driver seemed to know. Tarzan rested his hands on his thighs and waited.

It was as though the Colonel was careful to keep his eyes to himself.

The car pulled to a curb. They were beside a vacant lot, there was no one to be seen. John the driver went to the trunk and then brought something to Tarzan's door, a long dark coat. "Please," he said, in the same voice he'd used to call from the gate, no special respect. Tarzan got out, put on the coat. The driver helped him. Tarzan saw there was also a hat, but not a rounded one like the one on the seat. Both hats were black, but this one had a wide flat brim, it was maybe a preacher's hat. He'd never worn a hat before. It was like shoes, and rooms – it constricted you.

When the driver indicated he should return to the car, he had to duck his head to get the hat in. Now the Colonel handed him something hairy. "It's a beard," he said. "Where we're going, they don't usually allow people like you." He glanced once to see if Tarzan had understood *allow*. "Of course, you're also famous here. We don't want anyone to recognise you." And then he gave a smile that used the fatness of his face, a full smile that pulled at his chins, a wonderful smile that strongly made you so want to agree.

In the new city, they came to a nicer part of town, the buildings were further apart and the trees grew eagerly from bright green grass. They came to a grand white building, with pillars and, above it, in inscribed letters the colour of sand, the words *Dorothea Therkle Gallery of Modern Art*. Tarzan saw the letters, his eye traced their shapes, but he couldn't read them. They passed from the heat of the long-shadowed afternoon into a cool lobby where there was a guard. The Colonel held Tarzan with a gesture and went forward. His hands moved as though he was making a special sign. The guard nodded gravely. The Colonel motioned Tarzan forward – Tarzan hidden inside the dark coat and hat. But the guard noted his shoelaces.

They passed through long, high-ceilinged halls. The walls were red, a red that was dark and rich, and at the join with the ceiling a gold strip ran round, like braid. On the ceilings there were paintings, inside circles, of little naked boys and women whose clothes were being tugged away by a wind. Around the walls stood naked white men made of white stone, throwing things and looking angry. Tarzan noted their postures for his stage act. The Colonel moved slowly, as though there was something to look at – as though being in this place was something to be appreciated. He seemed to be inhaling the air, but to Tarzan it smelled dry, as though it never moved. The floors were of polished wood and in shoes it was almost impossible to walk without making loud footsteps. Guards stood in every room, eyes cut for anyone who wasn't allowed here. In fact there was almost no one else about. Every guard noted the shoelaces.

The beard itched.

The colour of the walls changed. They turned a corner and now the walls were white and the ceilings were bare. Now the gold braid was on the walls, in rectangular frames. Inside the frames were shapes and colours. Sometimes they looked like something Tarzan could recognise, a city or a meal. Sometimes there were faces of men and women that made him remember Kerchak and Kala. It was a place that made you remember things, despite the dead air Tarzan was pleased to be here. It was as though he had finally been brought to a room that it was good to be in.

There were no doors. Each room connected to another, there was always somewhere to go.

The Colonel found a low wooden bench and sat on one end so that there was room for Tarzan. He was gazing at the picture in front of them as though it was special so Tarzan gazed at it too. It was good to look at – Tarzan stored the colours and shapes in his memory and, years later, put a name to them: Matisse. Now, in a low voice that you might use to tell a secret, the Colonel spoke. "Everything in America is for sale." Tarzan looked at the picture – were they going to buy it? In the background a guard coughed warningly and the Colonel moved his head closer, lowered his voice. "You know that Sam Phillips has put you up for sale, don't you." Tarzan didn't know this. And he wasn't sure exactly what it meant, but, from the Colonel's tone, it didn't sound good. "Everyone wants to buy you but none of them know what to do with you. You haven't seen all of America yet, Tarzan. Have you." The Colonel said this kindly. "All the time you've been in this country you've had good friends and they've shown you nice places. They've looked after you. But out there in America," and here the Colonel moved away a little so that his hand might swing in a great, slow arc, "there are so many places where a man might fall." He paused and Tarzan understood that he was supposed to remember the men lying on the ground. "There are holes in America, Tarzan, which open in front of you and just go down and down and when you hit the bottom you just lie there and never look up again, because the sky is so far away." Tarzan thought. He'd never seen any holes like that.

Now the Colonel continued speaking but his voice had changed. "And there are other places that you haven't been to either. Elegant places, where there are people of distinction. You don't know the word elegant, do you. There are many, many words that you don't know, Tarzan, and many places, and remarkable people, and things to see that your eyes never get tired of looking at." The Colonel's eyes went up to the painting and he and Tarzan gazed at it together. Then, moving in the same slow arc that his hand had made, the Colonel's eyes came sweeping back. Tarzan felt them coming, he lifted his own gaze, and there was the Colonel, smiling at him again. The light inside the Colonel's eyes was pale blue, as though they were holes into a set of rooms which went on and on, rooms where you could wander, filled with lovely things, and the endless blue of wide open skies. Something was out of sight, though. Now the Colonel blinked and then his head lifted and his eyes went away. But there was a smile on his face and, behind the beard, Tarzan realised that his face was smiling back.

He could see that the Colonel was a clever man, who could make the world do what he wanted.

"I will arrange everything," said the Colonel. "You are still a minor, so you can't sign a contract – do you know what a contract is?" Tarzan heard a different sound and he knew that if he could see into the Colonel's head he would see the thing that had been out of sight. "So I have arranged for Mr and Mrs Presley to adopt you and they will sign on your behalf. Legally, they will be your mother and father, and you will have their second name. Everyone has a mother and a father, Tarzan, and everyone has a second name – for the first time in your life you'll really be legitimate. They will be paid from the contract to look after you and keep you. I will manage you. That is my job. You will be my only client and all my skills will be devoted to you."

Tarzan stood up. He wanted to walk. The Colonel was surprised, Tarzan understood that, but he didn't care. The Colonel rose and accompanied him. Tarzan walked fast through the rooms, it made him feel better to walk. He wasn't looking at anything. Then he stopped and looked sideways at the Colonel. He said, "Could Sam Phillips be my father?"

"No," said the Colonel. "This is the end of Sam Phillips. Sam Phillips is putting you up for sale." The Colonel looked to see if Tarzan had understood. "Sam Phillips is telling you to go away."

Tarzan went on walking. Then he said, "I want Scotty and Bill Black."

"Okay," said the Colonel. Walking fast had made the Colonel breathless, sweat ran down his face, which he mopped with a huge white handkerchief, Tarzan had never seen one so big. "Those guys can be on the payroll, just like Mrs and Mrs Presley."

There were rooms that lay ahead but Tarzan stopped. There were pictures on every wall, pictures so strange that you wanted to look at them for as long as you were allowed. Yes, he liked being here, but there was a pressure. A steady pressure was coming from the Colonel.

23

And then, as though all that had preceded it had been mere prelude, a warm-up act, Tarzan commenced to provoke a reaction that was unprecedented, and utterly wild – a contagious mania that spread like ink poured on a map of the American continent.

It was true, as the Colonel said, that Sam Phillips had put Tarzan up for sale. But Tarzan wasn't sold to the Colonel – oh, no. The Colonel didn't pay a cent. It was RCA who paid, $35,000, plus $5,000 to Tarzan to cover royalties that Sam owed him but had been unable to pay. RCA was a major label and Tarzan now had, according to everyone, the machine to launch him nationwide. This was the deal that the Colonel, with great skill, had brokered.

$40,000 doesn't seem like much in today's money, but at the time it was an unheard of amount, a fortune, especially to pay for a singer who didn't seem to belong to a known category and who had never had a hit outside the South. It was a mad gamble, and was regarded within the industry as a joke.

At RCA there was a fat man named Steve Sholes and he was sweating. (Steve, Speed, the Colonel – increasingly Tarzan noticed he was surrounded by fat men. So was he going to be fat himself one day?) Steve Sholes had paid a record amount, a fool's number, according to the trades, for a freak show, a flash in the pan – a fad that surely had peaked. True, Tarzan had five singles out, all selling huge numbers, all charting *at the same time* – the latest, *Mystery Train*, was as wonderfully compelling as anything he'd done – but these were Sun records, recorded and produced by the legendary Sam Phillips. Where was the million-selling RCA product? Meanwhile the man Steve could have signed instead, Carl Perkins, was number one everywhere you looked.

And the first RCA session had been a fiasco.

Instead of Sun's intimate faded old green music room, he was shown into a huge Nashville recording studio where your voice never seemed to reach the walls. Bill and Scotty were there, sure, but there were other musicians too, strangers, session men, names like Chet Atkins who Scotty had worshipped for years, old pros, and the idea was to throw all this together, just play through one of these songs with the tape running, wasn't it, and it would automatically sell a million copies – isn't that how you did it, guys? But nothing happened. The songs seemed wrong, tired oldies, or bad imitations of things he'd already done, or else this strange new item, a morbid number based on a true story about a lonely guy in a hotel who shot himself. Bill and Scotty felt they were there on sufferance, and surely someone was missing – where was Sam, who had always found a direction? It was as though they were trying to imitate something, trying to remember something – a good feeling once had. When Steve Sholes took the tapes back to New York, the RCA executives said to him, "You got nothin' here." They wanted him to turn around, go back to Nashville, bring in Sam Phillips. Start again.

Of course it was Steve Sholes who had the last laugh.

I have to say that when it comes on the radio I fight with

Heartbreak Hotel. Tarzan chose it – "that one will be the hit" – and Steve Sholes, desperate, pushed it out into the world, to see what it looked like in the light. I like the words of the song, they're melodramatic but they do make pictures. I can really see that desk clerk dressed in black. During the early eighties I spent a lot of time in down hotels and those words bring back their every cockroach. The song was based on something that really happened, a story in the newspapers about a guy whose wife left him – he killed himself in a hotel room and left a note, "I walk a lonely street." And Tarzan sings it out with everything he's got. But the beat... where is it? The record is stuck in the mud, it just won't get going. And the sound is also mud. They wanted pistol shots from the drums, the boom of death, and all they got was a dull thud, and Tarzan's voice fighting for some traction. No, you can keep *Heartbreak Hotel*.

In fact, phew, the stink, you can keep the rest of the RCA catalogue. Yes, let's do it – let's burn down the cornfield. Let's dump twenty years of dreck into the ocean. Okay, at last I'm really going to do this – go down to the end of the wharf at midnight and send everything he recorded at RCA spinning out over the water. The moon will be up there, half-clouded, the sound of the waves slapping against the piles will be the backslap that RCA could never get. The surge, the undersuck. The light will be lemon-black and patchy. There's no one around. I back my wagon up and open the trunk. And out into the night they fly. They're all gold disks, of course, every one of these beauties sold by the wagon-train load. But you can't listen to them. Here we go – stop me if there's one you'd like to hear. Okay, *Jailhouse Rock*, a lunker that never did rock – see how those thick old sides of vinyl just frisbee out over the waves. *Hound Dog* – get serious, it was a joke lyric that Tarzan read straight, it's embarrassing. *Teddy Bear. Devil in Disguise. Your Cheatin' Heart. Wooden Heart. Return to*

Sender – hey, shout out if there's ever one you'd like to keep, but, me, I hear any of this stuff I change the station. *GI Blues. Good Luck Charm. Can't Help Falling in Love. Wear My Ring Around Your Neck. All Shook Up. King Creole. If I Can Dream. Moody Blue.* It's schlock – bloated, slow, overheated – honest, it's just plain awful. And the music from the movies: *He's Your Uncle Not Your Dad. Yoga is as Yoga Does* – remember those beauties? Try listening for example to the *Roustabout* soundtrack. No serious artist should have this stuff in his oeuvre – and there's truckloads of it. *Love Me Tender* – okay, I do have a soft spot for that one, let's keep it for old times' sake. The rest: everything must go. Those old disks really fly, they skim and plane in the shifting light. Flecks of foam in my face, it's cold, and there's so many of these old things, my throwing arm gets tired. But, oh the relief. To be rid of that. Tarzan's post-Sun music, it's just product. It sleeps with the fishes.

Heartbreak Hotel was Tarzan's first million-seller. The feeling that the record inspired, of that wild jungle man singing his blues in civilisation's lonely hotel room, well, this was just perfect. This was *art* – this validated the whole thing. Everyone had to have a copy, they had to be hearing it right now, they had to be having their friends hear it. *Billboard* shouted out the news: *Tarzan Hot As $1 Pistol!* He was on top of every chart that they made.

After that he was just a product that had to be managed. And for million-dollar management, Colonel Tom Parker was your man.

It was the Colonel who manoeuvred Tarzan into the movies. He saw quickly that you couldn't have your product so visible, seen in the uncontrolled conditions of a live show. Sure, it was wild and you could sell glossy pix to the fans as though they were drops of his blood, but every reporter in the country was in attendance now, and the headlines dripped poison. *Tarzan Sells Sex to Phoenix. Is it All Right, Mama? He Wants to Rock Your Daughter.* No, this was bad for business. Even TV wasn't the answer. Tarzan went out live from the Ed Sullivan Show, it broke every audience record, the fee was astronomical – but what did people see? An organ. A bulge. Man, it seemed like all anyone could think about was his trousers – a whole lotta shakin' going on. No, that wasn't going to work either. For his next appearance on the little screen they cleaned him up, put him in a tux, showed him strictly from the waist up, singing *Hound Dog* to an actual basset hound. But this was just sad and everyone knew it. This would lower the temperature, the thing would fizzle. No, no, get him out of there. He's only a fad anyway, it's only a blip in time, this music. Get him into a real industry, where thousands pay to see him, millions, but where what he does is controlled. This was the Colonel's thinking. Get him singing some nice songs to the camera, put them on a soundtrack – now there's your modern product.

Shortly he was, according to a press release of the Colonel's, *the highest paid actor working in motion pictures today.*

Okay, and now for the movies themselves. They run them for laughs on the late show – these hint at how an era can outstay its welcome. Get set there on the couch next to Loretta and we'll watch them through together. Here we go: *Love Me Tender, Loving You, Jailhouse Rock, King Creole, GI Blues, Flaming Star, Wild in the Country, Blue Hawaii, Follow That Dream, Kid Galahad, Girls! Girls! Girls!, It Happened At the World's Fair, Fun in Acapulco, Kissin' Cousins, Viva Las Vegas, Roustabout, Girl Happy, Tickle Me, Harum Scarum, Frankie and Johnny, Paradise Hawaiian Style, Spinout, Double Trouble, Easy Come Easy Go, Clambake, Stay Away Joe, Wild Jungle Girls, Speedway, Charro!, The Trouble With Girls,* and *Change of Habit.* He made thirty-one movies in thirteen years and not one of them can be sat through without the aid of a tankerload of beer.

Deep-six them entire.

Well, with the movies in the tide, along with the music he made at RCA, that about knocks off twenty years of work. And when you think that Tarzan died when he was forty-two, and only came to our notice aged eighteen, well, it means that his period of beauty, of sublime expression, was very short. Maybe two years. Maybe only eighteen months.

Now that I've got myself worked up nor do I want to pause for Priscilla. Sure, she's a person, she is the woman he married. Her black hair was an aspect of her appeal, I have no doubt of that, but she also had something of the angel about her. Oh, she was precious enough, I admit it, but, now I've got started on this, she was just his wife. I am not going to be held up by a wife. In the end she was just another girl, and there were more girls in Tarzan's life than anyone can imagine. The guys would go downstairs wherever they were hotelled and review the occupants of the lobby. In the lobby – they called it the Mink Farm – several would be selected, the good-looking ones, according to the judgement of Skippy or Speed or whoever was on duty, and they would come up and sit in the suite, arrange themselves among the couches, and eventually he would appear. He would talk nice to them all, he was always polite, and then drift out again, having given Skippy or Speed the high sign. The guys could have whatever was left over.

Think what you like – it happened.

The lucky girl would be given clean pyjamas, a toothbrush still in its wrapping, told to shower – "Tarzan likes you to be really clean" – and then sent through to his room to wait. He would turn up eventually, and then the fun would begin.

And then what should he do all day, between girls?

How many motorbikes can one man ride? Cadillacs? Colt .45s? How many cuddly toys is too many? What does it avail a man should he gain his fortune but lose his soul? Airplanes, horses, personal soda fountains with your name worked on them in diamonds. Custom-made guitars, solid gold taps, a black Rolls Royce with purple leather seats and pink trim – that monster was so big that somehow even Tarzan looked diminished beside it, one hand resting possessively on the hood as he gazes manfully at the camera. Movies, oh – night after night at the movies. Tarzan was now so big he could not see a movie like anyone else, the screaming would stop the show, so he took to renting movie houses after-hours and going in for all-night five-movie sessions with the guys and whichever girl. This could also be done at the roller rink, the local Lunar Park, any given playground. Ride'em all night, boys, we got the run of the place. Darlin', another fluffy toy? It's yours, baby. Sincerely. Now where's my waterpistol? I need burgers. Yeah, bring on the burgers.

Such fun. In fact the girls were sometimes surprised, when finally they were alone with him in his room, at exactly what took place. He was always nice. They would be, wah, excited, and fluttery, not sure how to act. Some of them would make like they knew what this was about and start to strip – he would hold up a hand. Others sat, adoring, and waited patiently to be told. Some were completely overcome and hysterical. All of them he treated with respect. He put them at their ease – "Hey, lookit you!" And sometimes, sure, they would make out right way. But more often, if there was the faintest hint of a possible distraction from the inevitable, he would take it. So they would find themselves sitting on his lap as he peered intently into, say, a display of tropical fish. He would stare into the warped world inside the lighted tanks as though he had gone into a dream. And then, slowly, turn to look at them, from up close, his famous face so nearby, and it was as though he was now looking into your head and seeing the fish swimming in there too. Seeing your dream. Okay, then the sex – Tarzan always took care of business. He would get to know you really quickly, sometimes after twenty minutes with him you'd be in a pillow fight, laughing, screaming, tearing round the room like kids. More sex. All the time you'd be thinking, It's him. It's really him. And then he would say it. "Now, could you please look at this with me, please."

From his bag, from under his pillow, would come something you'd seen in grade school, a reader, he'd bought a box of them at a fair, they were old and faded and you couldn't believe a rich man like him had such things, tired by the use of the world. Dog-eared, limp. And you would sit beside him, often on the bed, it would be three, four in the morning, you'd had your fun, now what was this? *Mrs Clancy Rides the Railroad – number four in the You Can Read series.* He would put his finger under the words as he formed them, one by one, his lips carefully shaping the words. "And. She. Paid. The. Man. In. The. Ticket. Office."

Now could you help me with my reading, please – it really shook some of them, it reminded them who they were sexing with. A man out of the trees. He couldn't even do the everyday thing that they could all do, which was simply to read the words in these dumb kids' books and effortlessly know what they meant. For some this was the time to retreat to the bathroom and think. But they always came back. He was too big, now, for anyone to leave. So they would read with him, slowly, word by word, side by side, often naked, his large brown thigh alongside your sleek one, the curtained room full of intimate scents, with sweat and internal moistures at hand, and you listening, tenderly now, as he worked his way through the pages. From the other side of the door music, shouting, the party could be heard, though that door never opened, ever. And in fact it was rather nice to be here with him, this large, frowning man holding the battered old book so seriously.

Later, sleep in his arms. Well, he would sleep. You might pretend, but after such excitement, no, it was better to lie there and look at him, to feel his hands on you and know that for the rest of your life you would have this, this, that no one could take away from you, ever.

You could if you wished keep the pyjamas.

How many mansions? He bought lots of houses but in fact there was only really ever one that mattered. Mrs Presley found it. Tarzan had asked her to look, after sitting with her in the kitchen at 462 Alabama and hearing her sigh that she loved these old boards, this was fine for her, but he, surely he would soon be moving on – this was no place for a man of his stature, son, needing as he did all the guys around him all the time now . . . So he bought Graceland, he could see it was the right thing to do, it cost $102,500, but money was no problem, Vernon was making sure of that, and it did look grand, there on its little hill, with the tall white pillars, and the driveway which curved to its portico, and ornate windows symmetrically distributed across its façade. A hired designer did a great job in there, splashing Tarzan's favourite colours around, hanging waterfalls and televisions, making each room like a little theme park, and he also managed to recreate Elvis Presley's room, upstairs, in a back corner, where Tarzan often visited and sat with Mrs Presley. But Tarzan didn't sleep there any more. He had his own room now, larger, the biggest, done in pink and black leather. Graceland, it was a kind of icon, even its name seemed designed to inspire wonder, it became the most famous house in the country. Gladys and Vernon moved into this slice of heaven with him, after all they were his parents, plus they were on the payroll – as were the guys. This was the point that everyone moved in, and stayed.

He said to the designer, "I want elegance, a place for people with distinction." He had an idea in his head, the cool of white walls. But the designer knew better. He knew what the Tarzan style was.

Only one Graceland. And in it, only one room. There he closed the door. In there, with the door shut, he would take his book and work away at the words. *In the beginning God created the Heavens and the Earth.*

Graceland had all the mirrors a man might require, and a showroom for the cars, and a milkbar, where Tarzan could hold court, directing which flavour each guy was to suck on. It was strange how, when you were bored, making them do things was almost interesting. You could make one of them, Speed for instance, go with the cutest girl – Speed never minded. In fact a special light came into Speed's eyes, he looked at you as though you were the life-giver, the reason.

Tarzan remembered how Kerchak had sometimes made them do things.

But the best thing about Graceland, he discovered, was that it had an estate. There were grounds that flowed around it – a part that was outside. A football field was laid down, and a speedway track. And, in a far corner, Tarzan found a little hollow that no one was interested in and it was here that he began on something that in time the guys referred to as his hobby.

When they first came to look he made them stand in a group just outside the hollow's edge. He took a stick and dragged it behind him as he walked, making a line in the dirt. When he'd completely encircled the hollow he stood inside the line and looked pointedly at where the toes of their shoes

– blue suede, patent leather – came close to touching. Everyone moved back. From ten metres away, he waved at them. They all waved back. He was the boss and if he waved, everyone waved. Tarzan nodded. Then he flicked the air away with his hand and they understood that they were all to go disappear.

He sat in the middle of the hollow – it had patchy grass, mowed once a month – and listened. Nothing.

Perfect.

Returning to the house, he found the little room that Vernon called his office and stood in front of Vernon's desk – there was no client chair; Vernon didn't encourage visitors – with his arms folded and his frown prominent. This way, he had understood, he could make everyone understand that he meant business – it also helped to have your lower lip a little prominent. "Mr Vernon, please," he said, "I want to talk with the man who had the hammer and all the other tools." Vernon's eyes searched up inside his memory. "He had a pencil on top of his ear."

"Ah know the guy," said Vernon, "who did the renovations. Shorty, Shorty, lemme see . . . Shorty Pink. Is there a problem with the work he done?"

Eventually Tarzan was able to have a meeting at the hollow with Shorty Pink, though it started badly. Skip, knowing that Shorty would come, had arranged for two chairs and a table to be placed at the centre of circle that Tarzan had drawn, with beer and glasses. These items were thrown so violently in the direction of the guys that a leg of the table broke off. The guys retreated, and stayed retreated. Tarzan never even had to glance balefully.

He stood in the middle of the circle with Shorty Pink, who was, ha ha, as tall as he was, and looked for a moment at the pencil behind Shorty Pink's ear. He liked the way it stayed there, a little log, somehow suspended in the air. Some men kept cigarettes, he had noticed, and once a woman had worn a flower. Both men had their arms folded. "I want you to go on a ship," he said to Shorty Pink, "on the ocean."

Something about being inside the line made you cranky, he thought. It made you want to throw things. Then once you understood how to be cranky, you could be like that in other places. And once everyone understood just how cranky you could get, why, there was no need ever to be cranky ever again.

Not that that meant you never were.

Another possibility was to be demanding. "I would like a green shirt now," he would say and even if they were on an airplane somehow a green shirt would appear. "I would like all the cars parked out front of the house. No, wait up – all the cars facing *towards* the house." Thus it was eventually made clear to Shorty Pink that it was in his interest to go on a ship to New Zealand and to find the cabin that had been where Tarzan once lived and to come back with all its measurements and details.

Shorty Pink was given a camera and instructed in its use, and the photographs he took are today an important part of the Archive.

He came onto the payroll, which by this time was a significant item. Once a month the Colonel's limousine would pull up to the pillars of Graceland, to deliver the small envelopes with the pay in them – the emphasis here was on small – along with an envelope for Tarzan, stuffed with cash. Otherwise Coltom, as the guys liked to call him, stayed away, he was too busy working to make Tarzan rich, he said, for three-day parties. He had an office in Palm Springs, where he kept one of his wives, and a team of operators who made certain that Tarzan was always number one. The guys liked to figure, who had the bigger team, the boss or Coltom – it depended on how you counted the hangers-on. During the parties they threw fat water-filled balloons into the guitar-shaped pool and shouted, Thar he blows! They imitated his waddle and the way he tapped with his stick to emphasise a point. Cheap laughs. But no one ever wanted to go one-to-one with the Colonel, it was hard on your dignity.

The Colonel liked to go out into America with Tarzan, on tour or to sit in on recording sessions, in fact he insisted on it. He was always in visible attendance at any press conference or interview. On every occasion he seemed to make a point of wearing the wrong clothes – a dark suit for the studio, bulging out of loud Hawaiian shirts on any formal occasion. Once he arrived at a movie première sporting shorts, grinning and back-slapping as he turned up his nose. But he was scrupulous about never upstaging his star. The Colonel knew where the gold mine was.

From time to time Tarzan would describe for the guys the place where the Colonel had once taken him, with the rooms and the white walls. Despite their desperate desire to please, when they said, "There's nothing like that round here, boss," this was only the truth.

Tarzan studied; he was always studying – television for instance, or the movies: So this is what men do? But he never once believed. In him there was always the feeling that had grown in the gorilla valley, that out there somewhere there was something else.

When he asked the guys about this they would say, "Hey, no, boss, this is the life, boss, we're at the centre of the world right here. Hey, let's go down the Mardy Grass, whaddyasay?"

At the back of the Graceland mansion he had had a porch built, for Gladys, and he would sit with her on this porch in bare feet and try to remember. Try to understand. He had been to a few places now, had seen things – but America was full of things, and where did they all come from? A factory, the guys said. He had, he remembered, once been in a factory

– in the early days with Sam there had been a visit to the plant where they were pressing his records. There he had seen the dark presses coming down, like jaws clamping, with a hiss, and then opening to reveal how the grains of vinyl had been transformed into a shiny black disk that nimble fingers snatched from the hub, just in time before the machine closed its mouth again. The smells there had been extraordinary, human sweat, tired-faced human people, who gave him broad, grim smiles, sweat rags round their heads, faces streaked, and close by them, as though in kinship, the great machines, so pungent smelling that they seemed also to be alive. He tried to take this in, to see how it worked. And the machines, how did they come into being? What about the people – where did they live? Did they like being in the factory all day? Their faces said both no and yes. They liked him, he could feel that, they liked him coming to see them – he was special in their eyes, which said that they themselves were not special. But they could understand these machines and he couldn't. He had looked hard at everything and tried to see.

Judgement Day was like a voice inside him – Welcome, Tarzan, and what did you find out on the afternoon of June 6th, 1962? It was all known, how he spent his time, what he learned – he had always to be getting ready for that.

All the guys seemed to have completed the learning part of their lives.

So could he work in a factory? Frowning, struggling, in the shade of the porch, trying to find a way. It never seemed, these days, that there was any new thing he should be going to. There was just more.

Shorty Pink was, it transpired, a doer, not a talker. Sure, he could build a cabin like the one down there in Noo Zealan, in his sleep, but then he had this guy, who you had to take serious, in his loud shirt and bare feet, this guy on his shoulder like some big dumb kid, wanting to know everything. Shorty got riled and walked off the job. But his wife, Bitsy, spoke to him, explained what building the cabin might mean to a person like Tarzan, from the jungle and all, and so Shorty came back, with his pencil behind his ear and tried to give satisfaction. Especially since, which Bitsy also explained, Mr Tarzan was paying triple.

So here they are at the cabin, mid-morning, beneath a wide, sun-pummelled Tennessee sky: the foundations have been whumped into the ground and now Shorty is hefting a hammer with which he is proposing to drive the first nail of the floorboards. In it goes, tap, tap, bang – Shorty hits that thing smack on the head. Tarzan's nose close to the action and then he asks.

"Why is it called a nail?"

"Well," says Shorty, "I don't rightly know that, son." He takes a shiny four-incher, looks at it contemplatively, then deals to it with the hammer. "I guess I don't know about the names of things. For that you need a professor."

Tarzan remembers Prof Hingle who he met with Jane. Should he have paid him more attention? But Prof Hingle, a dried-up man, only knew about dried-up things.

"Where do the nails come from?" he asks.

"Hardware store." Then Shorty stops, remembers what Bitsy told him, wipes his brow, sighs. "Hardware store gottem from the mongery dealer. Mongery dealer got 'em from the factory."

"A factory," says Tarzan. "I have seen a factory."

"Good," says Shorty Pink, and whacks another nail home. Now one length of floorboard was anchored at one end – at this pace the cabin should be up by, oh, turn of the century, easy.

"Everything is made in a factory," says Tarzan.

"Yes sir."

Tarzan squats, feet in the dirt, and remembers. Was there

a factory near his cabin in the bush? He doesn't imagine. But somehow the nails and tools necessary had come to that place and been wielded, by someone, had been used correctly by someone who knew how. That's it: he looks at Shorty hammering and thinks, Yes, in the gorilla valley, someone did what he is doing.

"The nail is made of iron."

"Right again," says Shorty.

There is a pause and then Shorty says, "And where does the iron come from? Okay, lemme see: the iron comes from the ground, it's like a rock that they dig outa the ground an' they dig it up and melt it – in a factory – and they make, it's called pig iron, out of it, and the pig iron comes on a train to another factory and they melt it again into these nails. I guess that's how they do it. Son, you orta hire yourself a school teacher."

"No, this is the right way," says Tarzan, and he motions for the work to recommence.

It feels strange to sit here doing nothing while the other man sweats, but Tarzan has become used to this particular strangeness. It is a thing he dislikes, to always be the one, but he knows now that this is his situation and he tries to accept it – because he can sing, and because of his body, and because of his history, which he can't understand but which according to the eyes of everyone he meets he always has with him. Now his gaze runs slowly round the perimeter of the hollow, seeing where he will command for trees to be placed and where the windmill should go. Will he come and live here? That is unclear; everything that will happen next is unclear to him. What he has to do, he has discovered, is try to stay inside whatever moment he happens to be in, and not worry. It can be done. But what is strange about that is that is the way he was when he lived in the valley. He considers this: you have come all the way here to learn to be how you were there.

When he looks at Shorty Pink's sweaty face – rubbery,

deep-cut by lines – he tries to imagine if the same thoughts are occurring to him. Shorty Pink works hard, with never a break, and Tarzan sits and watches – and yet Tarzan is the one who has more money than Shorty Pink.

This will be why, Tarzan thinks, Shorty Pink has a bad feeling in him towards Tarzan. Many men have this bad feeling towards him.

"I would like to hit a nail."

"I was afraid of that," says Shorty Pink.

Tarzan was not good at driving nails. Well, he had an eye, and he had good muscles, but he was no carpenter.

Nor could he write a letter, nor tell you if Abraham Lincoln was a man, a car, or a highway. He couldn't do most of the things that every human being can do. Any kid could teach him a thing or two.

Of course, he could sing. In a jam, he could always sing.

But quite suddenly, without him really grasping that it was happening, Tarzan found that he was not singing in public any more. His last concert was in 1957 and then, apart from two charity concerts in Hawaii, he didn't sing before a real audience until the live sequences of his 1968 Comeback Special. He couldn't even sing on TV, the Colonel had banned that, just as he had banned the concerts – all too risky. Too many random elements. No, movies were his thing now, just look at the money he was making.

"Hollywood is the biggest stage in the world, Tarzan – you're the biggest star on the biggest stage in the world." This was the Colonel talking. "When you sing into that movie camera, that's when you're connecting. Go visit any movie house, all over the world, people are singing along with you." It was a tough logic and Tarzan couldn't crack it. He retreated to his room to study his lines.

Of course, he kept making music.

24

Okay, maybe I was hasty there at the end of the wharf. The moonlight gets to you. You get carried away. Once that feeling of disgust about the past comes, the desire to be free of it is too powerful.

America too was pleased to be rid of Tarzan. Not just his music. His ever having existed appeared to be an embarrassment to the nation. After his death in 1977 the official recorders of significant American events threw Tarzan Presley away entire. He was tipped into the garbage by post-hip critics wearing face masks and disinfectant. Holding their noses, they buried him in the mass grave which contains Lawrence Welk, Liberace, Grand Funk Railroad, all the millionaire talent that always played to packed houses. A millionaire in that great nation was, fortunately, only a millionaire, the continent was knee-deep in them – making a million was nothing special. Forget him. He's a part of the country we should strive to forget.

Like poverty.

Meanwhile in little America, in the shabby houses and the trailer parks, in the laundromats, in the lonesome rooms, the diners and the dim-lit bars, in these lowly places the common people mourned. They came in their thousands, when he died, to file into his home, and left a mountain of flowers. They rent their clothes. Several of them died outside the Graceland gates, in the heat and hysteria. Even though he hadn't had a hit for years they bought his old records all over again, to be intimate with him through the thrill of purchase. They couldn't live without him and so they declared he was living still – that he would never die. He wasn't a millionaire to them. He wasn't an entertainer. He was the one who had come up from under to speak their language back to them. He brought their lives out into the sun. For them, he connected back, to every dream they'd ever been sold: that in America everything was possible. To every dream that had failed them. To every dream that was, as he proved, nevertheless true. They kept playing his records. In little America he was no entertainer. He offered deliverance. In little America they kept his music alive.

The music Tarzan made after he no longer had Sam Phillips to guide him is strange, strange. For a start, there's so much of it – and it's so varied. Tarzan would sing anything. If you gave him the back of the cereal box and a microphone he wouldn't hesitate. *So chock full of goodness, yet the taste is mighty fine* – and here's the thing, this would be given the full thunder of emotion that its copywriter hoped a breakfast eater might find in it. That is what's so hard to take about his RCA catalogue – the big emotion of it. You want so often to say to him, "Guy, I'm more sophisticated, I can't be that big-hearted." Pumped up, muscle-bound, told he has to perform, Tarzan belts out the emotions that we are now too worldly to admit to having.

I guess it's the gospel music you have to start with. This he sang for Mrs Presley. She led him to it – played him the Statesmen and the Blackwoods and all the great gospel artists that he came so to respect. She explained what a lyric like *His Hand in Mine* might mean. And so at Graceland he would sit at the gold piano, playing thirds by ear, primitive, but with that music the more primitive the better, it's the churches that like heavy drapes and lots of flowers, in case someone doesn't take it all seriously enough. No, the real religion comes naked. And in the middle of the Graceland party he would be sitting alone, singing tenderly to himself. People would gather – gradually this would be everybody. The girls who had come for the glamour would sit, legs tucked under, looking carefully to check that this was what you were supposed to do, and the guys would be nodding, saying, yes, this is the way it is. He sings and we all get lucky. This is the real Tarzan. This is why we hang around him. See, it's not just a money thing.

In My Father's House. Peace in the Valley. Run On. I'm Gonna Walk Dem Golden Stairs. So High. I Believe in the Man in the Sky. Whatever your religious persuasion, go get the CDs and listen to him make it real. So was he a believer? No, not ever. But he liked to please Mrs Presley, her heart ached so.

Then when you've done the religious music, just settle back and open your ears. At the piano he would shift effortlessly into *Love Me Tender* – who can say no to that? Then before you knew it the guitars were out and it was *One Night With You*. Now that is a song. That is a performance. *A Mess of Blues. Like a Baby. Reconsider, Baby. Baby What Do You Want Me to Do. Don't Be Cruel. Paralysed. Don't.* Here we go now, this is all gold. *Love Me. Long Black Limousine. Any Day Now. Any Way You Want Me. I'll Hold You in My Heart. How's the World Treating You. Anything That's Part of You. I'm Counting on You. After Loving You. I'm Gonna Sit Right Down and Cry Over You. When My Blue Moon Turns to Gold Again. I'll Never Let You Go (Little Darlin').* Hell, let's drag *Heartbreak Hotel* back to the surface, I never quite managed to hate it enough. *Guitar Man*, why not. Even on the movie soundtracks, if you listen out carefully enough

– for instance, from *Viva Las Vegas* there's *I Need Somebody to Lean On*, he sings that with real feeling. The title track is also acceptable. I admit it, I got carried away there at the end of the wharf. There's some music there that should be saved – that anyone with ears will respond to.

Anyone who has a heart.

He tries everything he's ever heard, sometimes in the same song. He will try anything with a tune, sometimes you want to say, Why, Tarzan? Don't. Don't sing *In the Ghetto*, that pious crud, people are smarter than that, if you play that schmaltz it will be used against you forever. And then he makes it over, and the strangest feeling comes upon you. As though for a number of years now you haven't really been listening.

But, without him really grasping that it was happening, Tarzan was not singing in public any more. Instead – surprise! – he was a movie star. Hollywood, they told him, you're going to Hollywood, Tarzan! Always with an exclamation mark. So off he went.

When the movie phase of his life started, the Colonel took him aside. He said, "Son, you are the quickest learner anyone has ever seen, and you can learn this too. Just use your brain and do what they tell you. And don't get caught with your pants down."

Okay: being an actor. Not a real actor, of course, who understood what they were doing. No, this was trying to look the way they wanted you to look, and saying what they wanted you to say. Which was just more of the same.

Of course the guys went with him. Of course the Colonel was there. These were the things you needed to make a movie. All day on the set, waving at people, grinning – listening, then doing what you were told. Everything was very important. Then, at night, Skip would assign someone to go over his lines with him.

Tarzan would carefully memorise his part and, incidentally, the entire script. So, instead of the collected works of William Shakespeare in your head you have *Girls! Girls! Girls!*, every deathless word of it. Oh but I am still angry about what they did to him in Hollywood.

So, the movies. No, Hollywood wasn't what he was looking for. Of course, the guys loved it out there, and he liked them to be happy, it was easier when they were happy, he could find time to think. But there was nothing to see in Hollywood.
He had thought he might see elegance, people of distinction. Their big car rolled through the wide streets past the big houses with the high fences. "Hey, Tarzan," they said, "that's her house, man – Natalie Wood! Remember we saw her in a bikini in *Crazy For You* – let's go and meet her, man, she's hot. Hey guys, be cool, Tarzan wants to meet Natalie, we're stopping." But Natalie, Marlon, Kirk – he could see the movie stars were maybe curious to get a look at him, the biggest thing in show business, and with that freak-show childhood too. But the stars were bored. Everyone in Hollywood was bored – they were all waiting all the time, that's what making movies was, waiting. They were quickly bored with him, he could see that, he didn't have whatever it was they wanted, and his guys they didn't want at all, lousing up the place. No, but he was honoured, honoured – that's what you had to say – and then they were back in the car.
"Man, that Natalie, she's . . ."
"Stacked!"
"Man, she's stacked, Tarzan!"
"Reckon you could get her, Tarzan?"

On location he would try and find things to understand. One time, in Florida, filming *Wild Jungle Girls*, he saw something that stayed in his mind. A girl, just some bikini girl, adding tit to the set, that's what everyone said later, got attacked by a crocodile. They had been filming the scene where he fought it, a struggle, since his muscles were so gone to sausage these days, and the director had shouted, "Cut!" He was back in his robe and heading towards the trailers, when there was a cry. The girl, stupid they said, had gone to feed the thing a bit of chicken and got bit. A real crocodile, suddenly a real bite – Fontella, Fontella Queens, apparently that was her name, made a cry, apparently it wasn't tethered properly and then it had her by the wrist and it was dragging her into the pool. "Get a gun!" someone shouted, and then they all shouted it, "Get a gun!" But then they looked at him. And he saw what they were thinking – that he would know how to kill this thing.

The knife he'd used for the scene was very blunt but it had a long blade. He took it in his hand, shook off his robe. In the water they could see a terrible splashing and blood. Standing now in his loincloth and the tan they had painted on him – *Wild Jungle Girls* is the one, remember, where, in the face of plummeting box offices, the Colonel had relented and finally allowed them to make a movie which exploited his apeman origins – Tarzan could feel how his muscles were weak, he had wrestled with a crocodile but it had been made of rubber, the real wrestling had been done by a stunt man who had gone home. Tarzan knew he had to go fight but he was afraid. He took the first step – then the Colonel arrived to stand in front of him. The Colonel in a safari suit, arms spread wide and laying down the law. "The contracts say no."

The contracts were the Colonel's most urgent point. The marks you made on pieces of paper, these were bigger than any machine, these were the rules, he said, which were the real laws of the world, the rules which could never be broken. Tarzan saw the contracts as something like the guys, things which surrounded him, a thing like a house, with walls in every direction. He stopped, held by the Colonel's eyes. The Colonel let him look in . . . blue, an endless soft blue, through which you fell but never landed . . . While he was held there the splashing died away and further worries about what the contracts said were unnecessary.

The Colonel took it upon himself to tidy the matter. Sally Jennings, which was the girl's real name, was from Twisted Fork, Montana and the Colonel said he would travel there and speak to her parents and provide them with what he called comfort and amelioration. Skip said this meant that the Colonel would take her hand, which had been found floating in the pool, home to them and also a handbag made out of crocodile skin. Speed said, Yeah, that's what you need for a hand, you need a handbag. Delmo said that they were jerking and that what the Colonel would do was give them money.

And so what Tarzan saw now, alone in his trailer, was how you could have money instead of a person. How Gladys and Vernon could have him instead of Elvis, as long as they were paid for it. How Scotty and Bill could be paid to go away. He stared out the window at the pool, quiet now, and saw how Sam Phillips could have $35,000 instead of him. There were pictures of people on the money, faces of men, and instead you had them. He saw how those faces, if you stared at them long enough, would become like the black-and-white pictures on the walls in Elvis Presley's room, faces which watched you and kept you company.

His body was . . . evolving. Well, this was only natural, all the guys said so, it was bound to happen, wasn't it, with the change of diet he had undergone, and the change of habitat, your body had to adjust to that. He wasn't killing for food anymore. And so it was decided that he should continue to take the pills, the ones he had been introduced to in the Army – I will come to the Army – they gave them to you when there was a long patrol to do, and, man, those little pills really helped you think when you had to keep thinking, had to concentrate, after eleven hours on patrol. He had, on his return to Graceland in 1960, told Skip about the pills and Skip instantly arranged for a supply, to keep him healthy, because the life he was living was of course very demanding. Everyone took them, Skip said, absolutely everyone these days, and so it was a regular thing to make sure that Tarzan got his health pills at some point during the morning, so he'd be ready for shooting, for the recording session or the appearance or the interview or the photo call, whatever was scheduled. Little white pills, like pearls, no taste really, smaller than a button, they really got you ready, and in every jar there were thousands of them.

Ready for America.

Okay, let's say it: these are the years when America failed Tarzan. They had his beauty – he'd danced for them, sung for them, they had put him in their gone-ape clothes and turned him into his picture. They'd had the glory of his innocent beauty and in return had given him things, cars, a house, all the girls that money could buy. Well, and it wasn't nothing. But I've been hinting at it, suggesting around it, and now it's time to say it plainly: What do you really offer, America, to your favoured sons? Houses, cars and girls – is that it? Okay, adoration. Okay, a sense of power, and sometimes wellbeing. Any amount of television. A better diet, of course – a Happy Meal. Yes, a generous waistline, along with naturally a generous line of credit. Yes, but what do you *offer*? If you don't mind me saying, from the safety of distance and a decade: in the terrible years that followed the destruction of the Twin Towers, this was the question that no one wished to give voice to.

To be fair, in truth such questions are asked inside. In the quiet of the dark, then, lying on top of the bedclothes while waiting for the children to drop off, lying silent with our wives, our husbands, we ask this of ourselves. Tarzan did. Over and over through these years, in such language as he had, with such cognition as he could muster, he put it to himself: Is there something?

Anything?

I have tried with the aid of textbooks and video to reconstruct these glory days, these lost years, when he was informed at every hand that he had conquered – when being the conqueror of America was said to be the state he was in. But the life he lived was so cut off from the actual world that all I get is scenes. Scenes full of colour, full of feeling and import – but no sequence. Sure, the products have a sequence. I can for example tell you that the classic *From Tarzan In Memphis* was cut in 1969, because I have checked that date in a book. If I look at documentaries covering those years I can see him in the Memphis studio – that year he was wearing neck-scarves and shirts with big collars. I watch as his throat brings forth the golden sounds and my own throat aches. But I can't remember myself being there, being inside that moment. Those years are a soup – a millionaire's soup, granted – and all I can offer is scenes.

And the scenes which really matter are recorded precisely nowhere.

This, for example: when might this have been? It's at Graceland, the centre of the world, the fabulous party that ran no clock; in Tarzan's room, upstairs, along at the end of the corridor of mirrors. Through the studded door – I can camera around the room but of course that room I can construct from pictures in any Tarzan book. There's a girl, but I can't see her face. I can't even really see her body, though I can sense it. It would be a good body, the guys always made sure of that, young and tan, and I can sense enough to know that it had no clothes on. Of course, I can't see Tarzan either but that's no surprise. I would say he was also naked. I would say that they had sexed.

Yes, Tarzan pilled and ready. Tarzan back from Hollywood, which always made Graceland seem better, there was no home in Hollywood. Tarzan at home, with a girl, and naked, that sounds about right. He'd performed. And now he turns to her and asks will she do something for him?

Well, anything . . .

Hey, baby. Whoa! Whoa. Baby.

Is she out there somewhere, this girl, who would also I guess be in a wheelchair, now, and does she remember? Could she be found? None of the biographies mention anyone like her and so probably she is gone, or else she understood, maybe from this encounter, that there's more to living, and got married, got herself a life. But that night she was there.

Tarzan tries again, asks her: Could you help me?

And so they sat, hip to hip, on a black leather couch, this I can see, moist skin coming away with a tearing sound every time they moved, and bent over an exercise book. With her help Tarzan made marks on pieces of paper.

Tarzan learning how to write.

Somehow this is mixed up in my head with earlier scenes, with girls and words and trying to learn – them concentrating there together as though they were school buddies working on a tricky piece of homework. Darkness at the windows. Tarzan grasping the pencil and working – at some point she got cold and he put a blanket over her, but he wouldn't stop. Copying the letters that she drew. His tongue between his teeth, brow furrowed, and she, I think she must have been a good girl, kind, I imagine she became someone else, slowly, someone who had a glimpse of the creature behind the glossy photographs, and perhaps gained also a glimpse to the creature-nature inside herself – this is always what Tarzan offered, to those interested in such things – she quietened down, this I can also bring back, she became serious, and she helped him. A lovely girl, the best there is, and together they wrote a message, which consisted of single letters of the alphabet added stroke by stroke, like carving in marble, to a good copy.

It was Tarzan who decided what the words would say. Well, maybe she helped a little with the grammar? But it was his message.

Dear Jane
I would so like to talk to you.
Yours sincerely
Tarzan

His handwriting never really became anything very confident. And then of course there's the mystery of trying to figure what it was that you intended to say. I sit here at this keyboard and these words run out the ends of my fingers as though my thoughts have found a way to have concrete form in the world, and it's a kind of miracle.

So what happened next? I can only guess. Did they go back to bed? Did they sex again? I like to think not. I like to think they lay together with some faint sense of who they were, under the stars. The thing after sex, that is what living in the world has to offer; when the urge is gone, it could come back, but for now is gone. And there's time. If you smoke cigarettes, well, this is the moment. But I have never smoked and I like it better without. As the silence gathers. As the stars come back and again make their presence felt. Personally I don't try to sleep, with a strange body beside you it's unlikely. Sometimes, as the dawn first shows, I need to plunge again. Well, it's a common impulse. But it's not what matters. What matters is that time there silent under the stars, and the feeling that perhaps you aren't completely alone.

To be in America, and to be alone . . .

In the morning, or more likely it was some time during the

next day, he called Skip and instructed him to find an address for Jane Porter.

Sealing the message inside. Going with Skip in the Caddy or maybe the T-Bird, who knows, none of that I can bring back. All I can see is the hand. I see Tarzan's hand posting the envelope into the slot of the postbox. The white rectangle thrust into the dark. Staring into that dark, trying to imagine what will happen next: this I can remember. The words he had written going off like a message in a bottle.

Then home to Graceland, foot flat to the floor, and the grin fixed on his face like a photograph.

When, two years ago, I made a return to Graceland, I looked for that letterbox, but how when your memory is so full of hunger do you know? It'd been the best part of four decades. I arrived in the middle of the afternoon at a postbox on Tarzan Presley Boulevard and stared at it. Manoeuvring my chair close, I peered into the slot. Same darkness inside? Who knows. Darkness is darkness.

I had finally figured there was no risk. If in age I was exposed, what would I lose? Well, something. I would lose the satisfaction that I had got away and stayed away. That I had fooled them all. Also – and this, I think, is more significant – that I had genuinely managed to give it all up. Who retires willingly? Especially from the big jobs, where you have the daily satisfaction of turning down interviewers and photographers by the thousand? Look at all those ex-presidents who wander the globe, trying to attract the spotlight again. No, I had the imagination to see that there was life beyond, and the strength to hold out, and this was a personal possession that I had no intention of giving up.

So I didn't want to be exposed. But what was the risk? At Graceland not a lot of people were looking too hard at a wheelchair driven by an old dude in a towelling hat.

I joined the cluster at the musical gates, got my ticket punched. Crowds were down, I was sad to see. But it was the off-season; they still get half a million a year. His records still sell. He was last at number one in 2002 and don't you forget it. Then we were shepherded up the curving driveway, the main cluster in golf carts and me like a duckling in my chair behind. If I'm honest I wasn't overcome. My return to the gorilla valley, some years earlier, that had been a choke-fest, but here I felt old and dried out and suddenly I couldn't go through with it. The chair has a German motor, it can hit a good clip on open stretches and I veered off to the left and took a path round to the side. I had a little map – did I really need a map? Lots of people do this, I was told, the emotion of going inside is too much for them and they just sit in the Meditation Garden and, you know, meditate. So I headed that way, except that I didn't want to meditate either. Actually, I was starting to wish I hadn't come. Graceland had never at any time been what Tarzan was after. It was the home of the Tarzan industry, its factory, and in it he had been the number one product. But I'd been touring the South and thought, You should.

Then I spotted the Automobile Museum. And I have always had a soft spot for class wheels.

Okay, starting with, up on a concrete plinth, a pink Cadillac Fleetwood 250 convertible with white-walls and looking here like an absolute dreamboat. A Cadillac Eldorado '56, the purple of squashed grapes, with chrome enough to pipe a city. Ah, but he had good cars. Drooling over them, I felt my age and my immobility. But I didn't like the smell of those monsters, all polish and no oil, they hadn't any of them been out for an age and I rolled away, into the shade of the milkbar, which was where I found her.

The place was deserted, and silent, which is unusual for Graceland, usually his greatest hits are pounding out on high-

rotate. But she didn't have her apron on yet – she came bustling out of the back room in a 1950s summer dress, green and white stripes like a St Patrick's Day peppermint, saying, "Excuse me sir, you're early, you've caught me, I'm so sorry." *Ahm.* "I'll just turn ever'thin' on."

"Please don't."

Tumbling black hair, dark eyes, and curves – a goddess in a milkbar, it's kind of a classic scene. If I had been fifty years younger . . . Now, because I was in a chair, she sat down on the seat of a booth to take my order. The booths were red leatherette, with pale yellow Formica tabletops. She smiled at me, sweetly, and waited.

Maybe the old stamping ground had got the sap rising? Whatever, I refused to give an order. I held her there, used her politeness against her. I acted like I was someone. She accepted it, sweetly. But I didn't want sweetly. "My name is Marshall Sturt," I said, and I took off my shades as though this was an action of great significance.

Maybe, across the years, she connected with something? She says, now, that she did. But that might just be kindness to a vain old man.

"Loretta Russett," she said, and I made her shake. Her lovely hand in my crabbed old claw.

There have been girls in my life. Hell, there's even been women. For many years I travelled and had, as they say, one in every port. But nothing ever stuck.

I hung onto her hand, tightly. I figured I had about ten minutes, soon they would all arrive. What followed was, I guess, like that moment when the wanna-be writer finds he's sharing the elevator with the hot director: pitch your script but quick. "Now, listen to me," I started. I guess I sounded a little like the Colonel. "You are maybe twenty-two years old and you're here in the milkbar and minute by minute your life is going past. Tomorrow I will leave $20,000 in an envelope at Passenger Services at Memphis Airport with your name on it. You could collect it and come back here and go on pulling shakes, and nothing I can do would ever change that. I'll be gone. In the envelope will be directions to my home in Australia: if you arrive there I will pass you another twenty thousand at the gate."

The intoxication it gave me to say this!

She pulled her hand out of mine now, sat back and gave me an entirely different look. This was calculation. Her head on one side, she was trying to read me. Intense, her gaze swept over my shoes, my hands, my pouchy, saggy old face. I took off my hat and laid it on the table so she could get a better look. Her nostrils were pinched. There was a little stitch in her brow, she was trying by extending her senses to go into me, to get a reading on my stuff. Again, like the Colonel, I held myself open, I let her go in through my eyes and poke around. But I had nothing held out of sight.

"And then?"

I didn't try to win her. She would, I knew, have to win herself. I said plainly, "I'm an old guy and I would like to have a pretty girl to dust my parlour. A pretty girl with her life in front of her and thinking at every moment: soon I'll be out of here and getting on with the adventure of my life – I'll enjoy that. I'll pay a thousand US a week, in cash, to get my housekeeping done, no more, you'll have cash money and I'm a slow coach in a wheelchair, you can run out on me any time you feel like it."

Yes, she was astonished. But she was fighting that. She looked away now so as to not be under any spell I might be casting and I let her. Then, without warning, her hand came out and she took a piece of my cheek between her finger and thumb. She squeezed. This was no love-nip, she squeezed hard. She hurt me. I took it. She held me and her dark eyes, full of feeling, looked hard into mine. Her hands were strong from a life of work and with each moment now she was working harder.

When I resumed my tour of Graceland – I had missed the main event, but had had, you know, a main event all of my own – my old heart was soaring in my chest like a bird freed of the cage. My, how big the sky is! I was lucky I didn't die right there of excitement. Now I could no longer hear the prattle of his fans. I shouldn't say that, I love his fans, not when I am in fact his biggest fan, but prattle is prattle and there were people here who could only talk of how they just knew he was still alive, still around someplace. How they could just feel him, here. Well, maybe they had a point, except that I knew they said this stuff whether I was there or not.

I had thought I would roll around the grounds and that memories would come back. But who cares about memories if you've got some livin' to do? When, over the loudspeakers, they played *Tiger Man*, well, right then I knew: they were playing my song.

So I never did get the memory fix I had planned on.

I had for some years been reconstructing the arc of his understanding, trying to enter and be inside the arrow of it as it flew through his life . . .

His health was suffering. I see pictures of him from the Graceland years and I know what was happening inside. By this point his body was all around him, on him, he could feel it there, something attached to him, something that, on the worst days, hung from him. He wasn't fat like Speed – but no one was fat like Speed. But he wasn't the gorgeous hunk from the jungle anymore.

When he noticed that he was fat he complained to Skip and Skip would give him different pills, sweat him down so that he was fit to be seen in public.

But it wasn't just his body. His mind wasn't always inside his head, sometimes he looked around and saw that his mind had gone off somewhere, he wasn't sure of what he was doing. When he saw this he was afraid. Afraid of himself, afraid of the life he was living. He was becoming something, he could tell that, but he couldn't tell what. He would talk to Skip and Skip would look at him in amazement. "Boss, you're the biggest thing in America! Take it easy. You're a big winner, Tarzan – not everyone is a winner. Hey, let's go up the back and shoot somethin'."

The guns . . . The guns were a definite phase – this I can remember. Tarzan had learned to shoot in the Army and at that time it had been a new skill, which was something he always wanted to acquire. But the guns – every now and then he would look at them and wonder at the intensity squeezed within.

First it had just been shooting at targets. Then they shot at a bird in a tree. Then they hit a bird on the wing – that was Skip, who could really shoot straight – and it fell from the skies and went thud at their feet. A dead duck, well, look at that. This was up the back of the Graceland property, west of the cabin, where there was some rough ground that had been kept for development, a movie house, maybe, or a fairground, they were always changing the plans. And then it came into its own as a shooting range, where they could hunt around and find things that needed shooting, a centipede or maybe a gopher – you had to sit and wait until they came up out of their holes. Then, blam! They got such a surprise when you blew their heads off.

Guns were a new thing to buy. There were gun dealers who would make house calls – soon, everyone had at least two. Guns with pearl handles, guns with your name done in diamonds on the butt. Cute guns, unusual guns, household and table guns, guns for every occasion.

Tarzan shot one of the hens – Gladys had been dead for some years now and there was no one to growl at him about this. He shot snakes, frogs and lizards. Down at the river they tried to shoot a fish but, underwater, bullets just didn't seem to work. Tarzan wanted to go below, hold his breath, see what the bullets looked like as they broke the surface, see what happened down there, but Skip talked him out of it.

Then one morning they were up the back, just Skip and Tarzan, they had a tommy gun and had been blasting away at an old tree – making patterns with the bullet holes, a heart, Tarzan's initials. When the ammo ran out they sat together on a log and looked up at the Tennessee skies.

"Phew," said Skip. "Man."

"No shit, man," said Tarzan.

"That tommy is no shit, man," said Skip. They were both full of pills, Skip had pills in his pocket, mixed with bullets of various sizes for the assortment of weapons. Tarzan had three different guns in his belt, a Luger, a Colt .45 and a little Derringer. Then without really planning anything he had this little gun in his hand, lying on his hand, warm from his skin, dark metal, and he imagined the bullets waiting there inside it. He looked at Skip.

"You know what I've been thinkin', man," he said. "I've been wanting to know what a bullet does to a person. What does it do, Skip? Does it like really hurt, or does it hit you so fast that it's happened and then you try to understand it but your mind can't go so fast and you feel it later?"

"To waste somebody," said Skip.

"Yeah," said Tarzan, "exactly, man. To waste somebody, that would be interesting. To shoot a person – what would that be like?" He had the gun in his hand and was looking at Skip.

"Hey, man!" said Skip. But he wasn't really worried.

Now they looked around – stumps, old gopher holes, but

nothing moving. Up here everything was already dead.

Then Tarzan took the gun and, looking down, carefully shot a bullet through his left foot. His foot was bare and the bullet passed right through, leaving a puckered pink puncture mark on the top and something similar on the bottom – like a little arsehole, as Speed remarked later. It turned out that the pain was immediate.

Several appearances had to be cancelled and this brought the Colonel on a mission of investigation. Contracts were brandished, harsh words were spoken. Vernon took the opportunity to gripe about money that lately had been just thrown away. Tarzan limped about, chastened. For a few days everyone kept quiet, it was as though there was an older person in the house who was sick.

Then one night he saw something on the television which displeased him and, drawing a Colt from under a cushion, blew the screen out. After that things quickly returned to normal.

Meanwhile, in the sanctuary of the hollow, Shorty Pink doggedly proceeded with his carpentry. The trees that Tarzan had commanded stood now in a protective semicircle, screening the construction from the eyes of the world. Little animals, woodchucks and snakes, had to Tarzan's great satisfaction taken up residence among them, along with spiders, worms and flies. The cabin had a ceiling and windows – Tarzan struggling with Shorty to understand how glass might be produced from sand. By heat, Shorty said, through melting – the same as the nails. Hearing this, Tarzan remembered how Jane had once told him that at the centre of the earth there was a great fire, and how all of life on the surface of the earth was made possible by the blaze of the sun. He stood in the dirt of the hollow in his bare feet and felt warmth coming from below; took off his shirt and felt his skin being charged.

Was this, he wondered for the thousandth time, the force that made everything go? That had made him the one?

He was the one but he still couldn't see why.

Everything in the cabin was of course brand new and Tarzan didn't know how to solve this problem. But he told himself that the original cabin must have once been new and that the people who had lived there – he didn't know how to think of them as his mother and father – must have once lived in it when it was fresh-made and strong-smelling.

He had talked to Shorty about the smell. "I want it to smell like the cabin I lived in, how can you do that?"

Shorty and Tarzan squatting on their heels on the stoop. Shorty drew a figure in the dust with his finger. Tarzan looked hard but it was only a squiggle. Then he said, "Son, the situation is: this here is no real cabin. And down there in Noo Zealan, that ain't no longer your cabin either. The real cabin . . . I reckon that's in your mind. That's what we're doin' here, we're making a cabin in your mind. Ain't it so?" Then he stayed there, squatting beside Tarzan while this idea was allowed to settle. Tarzan liked this about Shorty Pink, the way he knew when to delay a piece of work because he knew that Tarzan would want to be there to see how it was done – the construction of the chimney. That he knew about the right order of things.

Tarzan went through the guys' quarters until he found two old toothbrushes – it was hard to find old things at Graceland – which he sprinkled with salt before hanging them in the toothbrush stand that Shorty mounted above the basin.

Shorty cheated on the radio, and on electricity. Electricity was not his skill, he said, and he had the cabin wired so that it was connected to a cable that ran juice out from the big house. No, he said, the radio could not be made to play the songs that Tarzan used to hear. If Tarzan was able to arrange that, well, good.

But he threw himself wholeheartedly into the construction of the windmill.

It stood in the corner of the hollow that was most distant from the house, where the estate ended. If you climbed it, you could see back country, running for miles, open Tennessee, its wooded hills and valleys, and Tarzan liked to be up there. The feeling he got had nothing to do with the valley of the gorillas. Instead he saw a land where roads ran and trees grew. Where a single man might be a small thing and not be remarked upon.

On the day when Shorty was finally ready to connect the turning vanes to the gear-works, they climbed up; Shorty gave Tarzan an oilcan and had him liberally spread its contents on the ridged teeth of the cogs. "I don't reckon I have told you enough about oil," he said. They were up high, the roof of the cabin could be seen and, as though they were in an airplane, the pattern of the land around them. Immediately at hand the great vanes were turning and this was somehow maddening, this and the gear-works, which, when Shorty eased the clutch lever finally to Engage, made the driveshaft turn. Together Shorty and Tarzan leaned in to look down into the long, strut-encased interior of the windmill where the length of the driveshaft rotated. There was a faint vibration.

They stared and stared, and got dizzy. "That's it, I reckon," said Shorty Pink, lifting his gaze. "That is what is taking place inside your head, son. Somethin' like that. You are spinnin' in there. That shaft is churnin' out power, ah niver bin close to a body like you for power an' ah reckon that somewhere in there is the best answer to ever' question you ever have asked yourself."

Tarzan up in the windmill, Tarzan sitting, dreamy, in the cabin – these are scenes I can see. Sitting on the Graceland porch with Mrs P, which must have been when she was still alive,

Tarzan barefoot and being given the good word. The driveshaft in his head and listening to how she talked. Mrs P didn't talk gone, she was just a normal person, there was no showbiz in her, none of that desire to speak impressively so that your words stood in the air. Tarzan could speak okay, now, because most of the time you didn't have to say that much, not if you put enough gone into it. You could if you put enough into it say *Hey, baby!* in reply to just about everything.

Minutes, hours, with no particular place to go.

Days coming and then going. Nights that were days, no one had any sense of the clock, impulses were followed until they ran dry. Hey, now everybody should be wearing fringed trousers, Indian-style.

Outside in the world – beyond the musical gates of Graceland, beyond Memphis, north of the Mason-Dixon and especially out in California – America was changing. Tarzan, who had never really been clear what America was like in the first place, only noticed this change in the way that it changed the way he looked. Now he wore his hair longer at the back. He had thicker sideburns – so did all the guys. And there were different things on TV, the Beatles and, later, bombs, raining down on villages in somewhere called Vietnam. Skip had explained that the skinny people with their hands tied were Communists, who wanted to take everyone's money away. There was some cool action on those TV shows from Vietnam, villages of sticks definitively blown to splinters – and the guns! Far-out guns. Tarzan also liked the Beatles, he played their records every day.

But Bob Dylan was not a singer he cared to listen to.

That sound of protest, the music where there was no funk, no blues, this he ignored. And why would you listen to someone called Lothar And The Hand People? When you could listen to Bobby Bland? No, they didn't care for the love generation at Graceland. They had their guns, and their TV, and their fun. Tarzan wasn't making movies anymore, and the only records he'd cut for years now were movie soundtracks so there was no music that had to be made. Of course they still sang round the piano. Play that blues chord, Delmo. In Graceland, Tarzan was still and always would be The King – Amen and pass the burgers.

But out in America the nation was changing. Love was the thing. Peace. Acid. Acid rock – *Anthem of the Sun* by the Grateful Dead. The walls were falling, that's what everyone thought, America was on the move, hear the hoofbeats, there was a frontier again, a wave, a new generation, led by barefoot kids and a notion so vague – "something more honest" – that it was bound to be dissipated, and corrupted.

San Francisco wear some flowers in your hair – far out!

And yet walls did fall. Here for example is an issue of *Time* magazine, the organ of official America in those days, dated June 28th, 1968. On the cover of that issue is a woman, and she's black – huh. And the woman is Aretha Franklin, Lady Soul herself, making timeless music during that period. Inside the magazine you find official America questioning itself on every score. Is it okay to hold "girlie galas"? asks a piece on beauty contests. Should the FBI enter churches that have given sanctuary to those who will not soldier for their country? And in the heart of the issue, the long, desperate-to-be-hip piece on Aretha and recent black music, there is a chart: Have You Got Soul? This is a thoughtful list, divided into columns, the Have Souls and the Have Nots. Soul brother Holden Caulfield yes but sappy old Superman no. Sitting Bull okay but not Custer. Tonto but not the Lone Ranger. Yes for Robert E Lee but forget about it, Ulysses S. Grant. The Mona Lisa but not Nude Descending a Staircase – really?

And down at the foot of the column: Bo Diddley but not Tarzan.

25

Jane Porter's book, when it appeared in 1965, landed in Graceland like a bomb – blew the musical gates right open. Everything Tarzan had grown beyond, here it was again, dragged back onto the stage, in the intimate detail that the tabloid heart of the nation had always hankered for. What was it like to live naked out in the rain? To eat leaves? To talk to the animals? Oh, the savage killer that you have made your pin-up! . . . *and when I saw his great jaws sink those strong teeth into the raw meat of the wild pig he had speared – when I saw the blood running down his chin, I remembered that I had loved with this creature and I looked inside myself and was afraid. Now I ask: afraid of what? That I wasn't really civilised? That I had been civilised but was now regressing? That what I wanted was to regress? Yes, as I looked at him crouched there in the broken light of the bush, that is what I wanted. Oh, yes. To feel the rain on my back, to run clad only in my skin through the wet grasses. To clasp him to me and hold him as fiercely, as closely as I could. To go down into the dirt with him, to throw away my upbringing, to forget all books, all manners, all learning . . .*

Such sequences were invariably the ones chosen by interviewers for discussion, by chat show hosts and reporters, as Jane promoted her way across the country. Tarzan was, all over again, confirmed as a sex god, a bulge in the nation's pants. Following the Colonel's clean-him-up campaign, featuring Tarzan in good-timey movie roles, singing sentimental schlock, the jungle man had become as wholesome and American as Betty Crocker. Now the master salesman was outraged and schemed to get the book banned. This failed, and added to its cachet. But Coltom's rage was so great that Skippy began to talk openly of a hit, to shut her up – not that Skippy minded the book, in itself, in fact he had found it fascinating, they all had, but he could hear what the Colonel was saying: "This threatens us all." But then Tarzan got word, and said, There will be no hit.

His reading, which had seen him slowly working his way through the Bible, was coming along, but it was still slow. His finger moved across the page beneath the words, his lips moved. A dictionary lay as he read on the bed beside him but a dictionary is only useful if you already know most of the words it uses. He struggled. But this kind of reading, though slow, goes deep. When Jane's book appeared he asked Speed to buy him a copy and then laid the Bible aside, never to be returned to. In fact, *My Wild Heart* was the first book he read from beginning to end.

. . . I climbed the hill behind him, aware always of the play of light upon his skin, the way his muscles moved. I was always aware of him as a physical being. This was only partly because of his remarkable physique, the way his body was so completely inhabited by him. That emphasis was also produced by his silence. I had to look for ways of knowing what he was thinking that did not involve words. He was an expressive man, he could communicate what was in his head – this was one of the marvels of him, and those of you who

have seen him performing will know what I mean. Something inside the man comes out and touches you.

Now the land was falling away and you could see down the bush-covered slope to the valley where his gorilla family were presently encamped, and, looking across, pick out the bright vertical line of the waterfall. We headed along the back of a spur and came at its end to a point which hung in the air. This was a place of winds, the broad-winged hawks circled, rising slowly on the updrafts, tilting, sliding, passing close. My skin was cold, I wrapped my arms around myself. Glancing across to the south I saw the cabin in its clearing, tiny, and, to the east, the dip between the seaward hills through which I had come. The ridgeline was above and behind us, but this spur was like a seat in the circle – you could look down on everything in the valley. We were standing amid scrubby bush and bracken and now Tarzan was indicating that I should look into a long opening which had been made there in the ground cover. And I saw what he had brought me to.

There was a rounded stake, perhaps a branch of the tree called manuka, that had been driven into the ground. The manuka has stout, unbending limbs, ideal for walking sticks, and this stake, though it had clearly been here for many years, stood as firm as a rock. Attached to it by means of a bolt was a short crosspiece. Both these wooden parts were covered in lichen. I knelt down and, with a glance at him to ensure that it was okay, began to scrape the lichen away. But there were no letters, no marks, no dates. I said this to him but at that point he was, I think, unable to understand enough of what I meant. Then I said, "Your mother."

This he seemed to grasp. Perhaps not the actual words so much as the idea. He had been here before, and thought. I do not think he had known the meaning of those two crossed sticks – this was a recognition that was awakened in him when, a day before, I had made a similar cross to mark the place where we buried the bones of the creature I was sure had been his father. The father, I was sure now, had killed himself. The nearly empty bottle of whiskey, the rat poison I found nearby, the smell of vomit which, even after many years, could still faintly be detected in the cabin – it was speculation, but these elements did seem to make a coherent picture. His wife had succumbed, victim perhaps to the isolated life they had chosen – perhaps it was he who chose? – and had been unable to endure. Was that it? But would a man kill himself, leaving his son to survive, to die alone? Tarzan will tell you that he has no memory of anyone before the gorillas. He thinks of the gorilla called Kala, whose bones lie high in a tree, as his mother, though he understands that in fact she cannot have been. So his parents were gone from him by the time he was one year old at the latest. Who would leave a baby of one to fend for itself in the wild? The kind of man, perhaps, who had brought his wife out to the dark edge of the world, armed only with his wits and something to prove.

These thoughts went through my mind as I knelt there by the cross. I found it hard to look at him. He was so healthy, so vigorous, and yet anyone could sense the yearning inside him, feel the tug born of so many years of living without kin, without like kind. Should I comfort him? But I have never been a mother, and never wanted to be. I want a man I can stand beside, who has his own comfort inside, who can be my mate. I didn't want to pick hairs from his collar, darn his socks in the night when there's nobody there.

But Tarzan was long used to his condition. Yes, it was true he was thoughtful as we descended from that place, and for several days I noticed that there was an even greater silence around him than usual. But he had grown up hard in this hard country, had fended for himself and survived. He had grown into this thing that, though only about seventeen years *old, was as fierce-spirited and capable as any city-bred "man" I had encountered at any time in my life* . . .

Alone in his room, or in the company of a wide-eyed girl, Tarzan read this stuff to himself. He was used to mirrors, now – he saw images of himself everywhere he looked, in the photographs that the Colonel sold, on the sleeves of records, on movie posters, in the movies themselves. Has anyone ever been so reflected? The pharaohs, maybe. But this book contained something different. This was an informed account of who and what he was, what he had been, lovingly made, full of feelings and impressions recorded at first hand by a trained observer. This was, he understood, all the bible he was ever really going to have. He read certain passages over and over, trying to be sure of their meaning.

He understood that she had loved him.

In fact the whole book was a kind of love letter. Perhaps not to him. Perhaps to the thing he had been. Perhaps to the life that he and Jane might have had. He also felt the sadness in the book, because it was also plainly stated. If Jane had not spared him neither had she spared herself. You could feel the way he had opened her up, brought her into her womanhood, her selfhood, and then decided that the inclination of his heart led him elsewhere. This troubled him the most. Feelings he had successfully managed for years began to bubble up in him. He became visibly moody, withdrawn. And it was then, or soon after, that he finally made a commitment, of sorts, to Priscilla, who for some time had been floating ambiguously within his circle.

I can see now that I will have to deal with Priscilla.

Jane's promotional tour carried her across the states and grew, expanded in scale as her publishers increasingly saw the possibility of turning a bestseller into a monster. Within Graceland a kind of "Jane-watch" developed – at one point Speed had a map stuck to the wall of the Ocean Room with coloured pins to indicate her progress, but Skip, sensing Tarzan's irritation, had him relocate it to the hut out the back that the mafia used as a hangout. There it joined the girlie pictures and trophy photographs (Speed with Tuesday Weld!) that covered every surface. But Jane was still a presence – her face talked on one or other of the televisions which ran continuously in every corner of that many-roomed house. Closer and closer to Memphis Jane came. Anyone could know what inevitably would occur.

And so it was that when finally Jane appeared in person Graceland had steeled itself to welcome her. After all, there were going to be cameras. The gates were thrown open. The Colonel, who made an art of exploiting the inevitable, had shifted ground – had worked his contacts, and so his cameras were there too. Behind the cameras were the fans. They formed a huge semicircle bounded by the lines which the police had established under the direction of George Sprule, who was, by that time, more or less the personal policeman of the Tarzan clan. The fans had flowers, which they threw. There was confetti – as though she'd come to marry him. Some of them, the women mostly, cried, from happiness, and also from jealousy. Emotion was in the air, the lines surged, invisible forces were at work. Through all this Jane walked, head held high, chin perhaps a little to the fore, her eyes flashing dark. Tarzan, who had dressed for the cameras, looked spiffing, his wave of black hair offset by a red neckerchief and a lime-coloured jacket. When Jane extended her hand there was cheering, but Tarzan, used to girls and cameras, drew her close and kissed her, and then turned, his arm around her shoulders, to wave for the crowd – a victory wave. Jane had no choice but to wave too. As the clips from that time show, she was fighting tears – so many years' hard work upon her heart undone in just a few moments.

Then the big musical gates of Graceland were wheeled back

into place and the couple, hand in hand, began slowly to make their way up to the house. They were trailed by just a couple of photographers, the Colonel's favoured few, and by the guys, again culled especially for the day, and by Jane's offsider, whom at first Tarzan didn't notice, in headscarf and darkened glasses. This was Eve Kersting.

This is where Eve reenters his story.

Graceland had been cleared of hangers-on and was looking its best, white and rather grand in the mild, warm sunlight. Tarzan chatted casually, as he had done with the starlets out in Hollywood. He was used to adulation, it made things easy. But this was all a pose, and anyone who knew him could see it. He was struggling. It wasn't that Jane was so pretty. Well – pretty enough, but he had for many years now been exclusively in the company of women who made their lives with their faces. Jane had, he was shocked to notice, something of a moustache on her upper lip, quite a growth for a female. And while her profile was noble, classical even, face-to-face suddenly it seemed that her eyes were perhaps slightly too close together – was that it? There was something crossed in her gaze which was nevertheless compelling, as though you should go in there and find the focus she herself was searching for.

At the grand doorway they posed one last time, between the pillars, then turned, and went in, leaving the rest of the party outside. Eve didn't complain – when had she ever? She took a seat on the steps and began waiting, put her head in a book, but the guys took it hard. They raced around to the back of the house, and commenced to make a noisy party in their outbuilding.

The Colonel and the publisher's flack shook hands.

From the entrance area Grandma, Vernon's mother, could be heard scolding one of the maids in the kitchen, and Vernon, never to be turned out, was most probably in there too. Tarzan wished the scolding would stop. Not showing the house, simply steering her through it, he got them into the Music Room, always the place he sought under pressure, and got the big doors closed. He guided her to a seat, a huge soft thing that threatened to enclose her in mush. He drew up a low wooden stool that Delmo liked to sit on when he picked guitar. Then, across the heavy oak coffee table, he settled to look at her.

The room had half-columns set into the walls, standing vertically like sentries. There was a fireplace but never a fire – Tarzan liked the house to be chilly-cool. A grand piano, gold, and an assortment of guitars which stood on stands in a semicircle, waiting like courtiers. Seven flower arrangements. Twenty-eight ashtrays. Forty-five ivory drink coasters – all freshly cleaned and waiting. Tarzan's chitchat had stopped. Now it was his turn to have tears in his eyes. He looked at her and wasn't able to speak. She had a little confetti in her hair, he wanted to pick it out, but wasn't close enough. After a moment, when hard things settled into a final shape inside his chest, he got onto his knees and came to drop his head in her lap. It was a big head. She stroked his neck, ran fingers through the black hair at the nape. "So this is where you live now," she said.

They had very little to say. In the distant rooms, footsteps could be heard, agitated voices, dying away – this was the Presley relatives, who, at times, seemed to outnumber even the guys. Tarzan rose, put a gospel record onto the spindle, then returned to where he had been, crouched awkwardly, his arms around her now, though, in the mush of the seat, she was hard to find. Gradually the use of his senses was returning to him. He could smell her – this was the smell he had always known, the smell of the first human he had ever been close to. The womanly smell of her. It was all so familiar, so historic – very powerful for a man with no history. In his head words were forming but he was not able to find a way to say them. He wanted to see the three moles on the underside of her arm but her sleeve was buttoned at the cuff. He felt unsettled. Tarzan was not used to sexual tension. There was never anything tense about sex for him, he always just had any sex he felt like having.

Eventually he gathered himself and offered to take her on a tour. Well, this at least was something to do. The Jungle Room, the Trophy Room, the Waterfall In The Bush. They climbed the mirrored stairs, made their way along past the Elvis Presley Room, past the Grand Wardrobe, through the Little Lobby, to the chamber, three rooms made into one, at the end of the hall which was the area Tarzan kept for himself. Here the ceiling was naugahyde, studded with televisions. Most of the room was empty – there was a table with a record player and records, all in their sleeves, leaned against the walls. The walls were powder blue, Tarzan's favourite colour, as was the coverlet of the great bed, at the head of the room, where they sat. Overhead a cluster of three televisions, set at an angle so that he could study up at them without straining his neck, cast a jittery light. They emitted a faint hum but no voices. Outside, the guys could be heard, Tarzan was tempted to shout down but instead he closed the smoked-glass windows.

Across a corner of the bed they sat and held hands. She said, "Are you happy?" and he sighed. He didn't ask her this question in return. Instead he showed her his copy of her book and told her that he had read it. This information was redundant, the book was dog-eared, passages were marked in pencil. It lay between them, with his picture on the cover, one she had taken in the bush, with a blur where his groin should be, and then a jagged-edged photo of Jane, torn down the middle, looking at him. "Did it upset you?" she said.

"No." He shook his head. "It made me remember. It made

me think. I can't stop thinking, Jane. They give me pills and the pills make you think you're thinking and inside your head everything comes running, you know, all the ideas come at once but they all just go round in there, you can't get anything out so you can look at it."

Outside, now, firecrackers could be heard. A skyrocket buzzed the window.

"I wish I could talk," he said. "I can only sing, Jane. Someone else writes the words. Sometimes the words are too much for me, I feel like if I sing them I'll die. I can't stop myself going into them. It's wonderful, to sing like that, it's everything I ever hoped for. And then when you get to the end of the song you just have to start singing again or else you have got nothing to say and nothing to do."

Jane wasn't going to tell him anything.

She looked hard at him. He saw this hard look and it was a jolt to him. No one ever looked hard at him. The Colonel, true, but the Colonel had nothing to do with him, really. He saw that she was not going to take him out of this particular piece of bush – that maybe he'd been hoping for that. He saw that a wonderful softness, an open warmth that had been in her when they had met in the country of the gorillas, this was now gone. She was older, grown up, she knew the price of everything and felt that she had paid, and now was going to reap the rewards. He'd never felt so strongly before that he was a small man who wasn't made of anything very important.

Now, wanting to know about her, he did turn her question back – was she happy? She steadied her head, full-face, and lowered her brow towards him, so that her gaze was tilted up – this was somehow comical. Yes, there was a smile on her lips, down there. She donked her head on his chest, twice, and then smiled right at him. "Don't be a dope," she said.

"I want to ask you things," he said.

"What things?"

"I wrote to you."

"Yes, you did." She pulled his letter from an inside pocket and held it out to him.

What should he do? How did this work? If he took it, well, it seemed he had taken his message back, it was as though she wouldn't receive it. But he couldn't make her take it. This was typical. He could sing in the spotlight, but when it came to the little exchanges he struggled to grasp the rules.

It seemed he was taking the letter back.

Holding it, he said, "There is something about words that I cannot understand. Some people can say words that come out and they stand there and never go away. And other people can say them and there's nothing! The same words!" From the distance, sounds could now be heard, hooters, frightened animals, shouting, perhaps a pistol shot. "The guys," he said despairingly.

"But they're on your side," Jane told him. "They're your mafia, the Memphis Mafia, everyone says so. They famously keep everyone away."

"I can't seem to tell them not to."

Her gaze drifted upwards, away. Did she have something for him? She said, "When I wrote my book . . ." She smiled at him, and then commenced upon a long explanation.

Now a mood settled into the room, it was made of the blue of the walls, and the farawayness of the sounds, maybe the gospel record could be heard in there, or just the knowledge that it was playing downstairs, and the television hum, and on the walls the shifting tones which the television pictures threw. Into this mood Tarzan sank, he went swimming. He felt his body go far away and himself become just a small thing, a quiet thing that had an immense world around it, that he could watch and listen to. His place in the bush and Jane explaining, the mood contained both of these and it was more pleasing than anything he could remember. He reached out a finger and touched, very lightly, her moustache.

"When I wrote my book I was able to see what had happened and why. How one thing led to another. Someone said to me, So now you know, and they meant that I now had everything written down in the book and could look it up. But it wasn't that. I never look at the book. To write a book, what you have to do is . . ."

Tarzan heard these words and a new idea began to form inside him.

"You seem to be making yourself," she said.

She picked up the book, read to him. *"And so I saw that he would be my project, my life's work and that through him I would . . ."* Tarzan there being filled by words, they were coming into him in great shoals, they were myriad like stars, he was getting what every day he longed for – but all at once Jane was jumping up and she led them out of there. Tarzan in a daze, something was becoming clear to him, if she would only . . . But down the hall they went, she leading him by the hand. Suddenly Jane was firmly in command, she knew that she had to be. He had nothing to do, nowhere to go – he was falling into her. She had to get a grip on herself, emerge from this with herself intact. Yes, she had a tour to do, a book to sell, she had a life she was going to go back to. This was madness. He was like a king without kingly duties, it was terrifying. It was like the mushy chair which had threatened to engulf her. All she had to do was get out of here with dignity – honour was satisfied, she could cry in her hotel room.

Tarzan was distraught.

But they stepped out into the afternoon sun, waved and smiled again for the photographers. It'd been three hours, everyone looked for signs that her clothing was disarranged, and found them – *Three Hours of Passion,* one headline read. Eve was there, waiting quietly. From behind the house now a crackling sound could be heard, a tree had been set alight and smoke was rising into the sky. Jane saw Tarzan's face as he looked at the twisting, circling column – it was not a good face, that.

Coolly, she introduced Eve to Tarzan – of course, Tarzan knew her at once. Little Eve, grown dumpy now, grey eyes hidden behind dark lenses, took his hand, laughed, told him how suave he looked, stood back and spread her hands at the house, the cars. All this! But her every word, every gesture was a question and Tarzan's manner, always open and communicative, like a visitor's book, acknowledged the trappings and also the trap. Several of the sharper reporters caught this exchange and above their pieces there were headlines like *Jungle Man With Juju Blues?* Eve's own piece, commissioned by the *New Yorker* as a follow-up to the profile she had published in 1957, she held back, declined to publish. Of course the researchers have it now, it's been in twenty biographies . . . *Watching his face as he poses out front of his many-roomed house you know that rooms are not where he wants to be. That he would rather be somewhere else, but he doesn't know where, now. To go back is unthinkable. To stand still is to acknowledge that this is what he came to America for – fairground rides, the movies, TV with the guys. So he has to go on. But where to? Naturally, everyone that surrounds him can supply an expert opinion on this subject. But where are they going? When you hear them at his house, grown men, chasing each other with water pistols, you hear the terror in the word "fun". That is why Luna Park wears such a huge grin, so that you don't notice what big teeth she has. Half-naked girls running up the stairs. In fact the "mafia" are all ordinary, reasonable, patriotic Americans and I believe they are doing what they think is right for him. All of them good-looking, more or less, all endlessly enthusiastic – they're living a teenage dream. But he is a unique individual and has other* needs. *This is what you feel every moment that you are with him. He could, he could – well, the temptation is overwhelming. For example, he could, I suspect, become the President with ease. But that would be terrible, for America, and for him.*

Hand in hand, both of them back at work now, Jane and Tarzan moved slowly down the curved driveway, waving, smiling. Tarzan blew kisses to the girls, grinned. Jane looked up at him as though, oh, he was her hero. This seemed to work for everybody, and so Jane found a way to get into the waiting car, to wind down the window and wave, to look like who she was supposed to be, until they were well out of sight, just another diminishing speck on the long strip of blacktop which would one day be renamed the Tarzan Highway.

He stayed at the gates, signing, grinning. In fact he liked the fans, they weren't tiresome to him. He had something to give to them, they needed what he had. It was so easy to give the fans what they wanted.

In the months that followed Tarzan tried without success to ring Jane. He chased her all over the country, running up the kind of bills that had Vernon knitting his brows to the point of rupture. One of these where-can-she-be calls went to Eve: did she know how Jane might be contacted?

Eve got him talking.

And so it began that Tarzan would put a call through to Eve Kersting two or three times a week. No one knew about this – after all, who was she? It was as though he had a secret, a secret life. Eve listened to him read, long-distance, from whatever book he was labouring over – *The Status Seekers, The Old Man and the Sea* – and helped him to find things worth thinking about. But she would not tell him what to be. He had to find his own way. Maybe there was something parental in this? Watching your children grow, trying to stay out of the way so that they don't turn into you. Worrying, trying to listen without steering. Eve, just a voice on the other end of a phone, did however prompt him. Even after Jane's death in 1967 she continued to hear him, every week, and the path he eventually walked was, I believe, one that she helped him find.

It was Eve, for example, who had casually remarked that maybe the way to escape the movie-making he had so come to loathe was to gradually withdraw his talent. Whatever the reason, this is what happened, and whether it was a conscious policy or not, it worked. His on-screen presence, which had at first been intense, if uncertain, gradually became tired, mild, weak. He stood where he was required to stand, said the lines he had been taught. But you dial up *Clambake* and tell me what you see. A clam.

Thus the movie work gradually dwindled. He was not singing in public. He didn't do TV. He hadn't cut a record in anger for years. Mostly he stayed in his room, reading, or trying to find someone to talk to. He'd seen every movie that Hollywood released, twice, five times, followed every twist of every TV show from *The Munsters* to *The Beverly Hillbillies*. He did things, sure – "Let's go fishing!" was often followed by, "Let's go bowling!" He ate any hamburger that was passing. Sure, the world was full of things to do. In this spirit he married Priscilla.

Some of the biographies argue that Priscilla starts with the Army, that he got stuck on her when he was out of his home waters, swimming through the unknown over there in Germany, but I think, looking back, that it really begins with the death of Mrs Presley, just before he went in, in 1958.

That was back in the crazy years, when his future was getting bigger by the minute, and Mrs Presley had been a still point, a point of reference. The one who sat at his kitchen table and talked like family to him. And then, quite suddenly, Gladys Presley was gone. He'd felt the weakness inside her but, like everyone, had assumed it was grief.

He stood beside the pool at Graceland with Vernon – Vernon who had his arm reached up so that it would go around Tarzan's shoulder – and watched the wobbling shapes down in the water. Vernon was sobbing, long wailing cries were coming out of him. They walked. Do you know sad, Tarzan? He didn't know this sad. The death of Kala came to his mind. Now Vernon, hand extended, was sobbing. "Lookit them chickens!" They were up at the chicken run, the pecking heads were busy. "Mama ain't gonna see them chickens no more, Tarzan." Tarzan thought of Jane, of the sadness inside her. The wailing that came from Vernon touched him, he found a sadness in himself and he sobbed too. He remembered Mrs Presley coming into Elvis Presley's room, talking to him in the night. He remembered the smell of her neck in the old Lincoln. Together they sank to their knees in the dirt, and howled.

But later when he reflected upon this moment he found that he had been sad for himself. Whereas Vernon ... Vernon had had something torn from him.

Vernon never really recovered. In time he found other women and, eventually, a new wife. But this was all just something to do. Elvis gone and then Gladys, and that was the end of life. Tarzan saw that the humans allowed things to grow in them until it was pain to the point of death when they were lost. He had allowed nothing like that.

However, Mrs Presley had been the woman in his life. The rest were all girls, all floaters who thought they might get close, touch him, become special. And of course, they all were, they all did – the Kathys and Barbs and Suzies and Anitas, little Nancy, and Patsy, and cute Stacey – but they were all cute. It's a strange word, that, it used to have an "a" at the beginning, and be *acute*, and it meant sharp. That quality is still buried in the word – these cute girls were sharp, they had sliced their way through the crowds, through the barriers, now they were here, in the same room as him, close, getting really close now. There was excitement, hope, determination. You might say it was tawdry and who would argue? But all that energy in one place, and somehow available, somehow unprotected – it was a clear temptation. Not that he liked worldly women. No, the diggers all found themselves on the outer, contemplating a night with Speed, who was a degenerate, or maybe a late-night taxi. Tarzan seemed to go for those who most closely ran his own path – who were somehow surprised by the world, still finding it.

This was a quality most readily found in the young and in the late 1950s Tarzan sometimes dated girls that needed chaperones – actual girls, not much more than children, who were simply thrilled to be in his company. He loved giving that thrill. You could see them shiver with delight – actually shiver. In their little frilly party frocks, their best patent leather flats, they would sit beside him in his latest vehicular acquisition and, rather than thinking about getting naked with him, they were storing away things to tell their classmates. Often, as he drove, he would sing to them – like a scene from one of his movies. He bought them soft toys. The guys hated these "kiddy-dates", they had to mind their language, and the sex went out of the atmosphere, but Tarzan always went his own way where women were concerned.

In this way he picked out the daughter of an American airforce captain stationed in Germany, who came to the barracks where Tarzan was encamped, at Bad Nauheim, near Frankfurt, in the company of her older sister, Sylvia. Sylvia had wangled an introduction through a guy from his company that she'd dated, and now they were in the mess hall – the radio up loud, Tarzan's stuff but also the latest from Stateside,

Miss Peggy Lee swingin' in with *Golden Earrings*. Tarzan lounging, trim in his fatigues, Sylvia just goggle-eyed that she had managed to pull off this thing, being cool, but highly flushed, her face blotchy with excitement, sat up on a bar stool, sipping a long Coke. And beside her, aged fourteen, was an angel.

It was Mrs Presley who had introduced Tarzan to the existence of angels. She introduced him to evil, she used to say that to her kitchen cronies: "I introduced that boy to evil, ha ha ha," and then catch herself, and frown. Tarzan's soul was something she had felt it her duty to tend. So, in her kitchens, first at 462 Alabama and then in the larger, brighter kitchen at Graceland, she would also explain to him about angels. This topic, like Judgement Day, caught his imagination, and he would often work her around to it. Mrs Presley explained that the best place to look for an angel was at the end of your bed. Just at that time, she said, when sleep is coming, when finally you're about to go under, right then you are at your most open, and vulnerable. And if you happen to be at risk, if your life is in the balance and you could go either way, up or down, why, then the good Lord might send a messenger and as you faded you would know as you slept that you were accompanied. If you woke refreshed, if you had no recall but were strangely lifted free of your troubles and felt able to do those right things which had, the night before, seemed too hard, why then you had enjoyed an angel-sleep, and were blessed.

    Tarzan, sitting at the table, quite upright above his bacon and five eggs, would ask, "So what does an angel look like?"

    Mrs Presley rarely sat down, she liked to work while she talked, it drove the help crazy – what were *they* supposed to do? "You never see an angel, Tarzan," she would say. "You only remember. You don't see her clearly, but she's inside you, like just the hugest light that you must have seen or else how would you have the memory?"

"So you don't see her?"

"Of course you see her – how could she do you any good otherwise?"

And Tarzan would nod, and go back to his eggs.

But, to a hungerer like Tarzan, this description was not satisfying and so, when the chance presented itself, he would introduce the subject into a conversation and then ask what an angel might look like. Now this was the late 1950s, in the South, and while people might makes jokes about evil, they were uneasy jokes. And angels – no one made jokes about angels. He got all kinds of answers. He began to expect wings, lots of white light, a beautiful face that shone, shimmering robes. Big chords on an organ, maybe, with a choir. But nobody really seemed to have any details. Then he fell one day into a conversation with Delmo McMullins on this subject and Delmo proved to have superior information.

Usually they discussed music. Delmo, with his big ears, for listenin' good, he always said, and his slicked-across hair, was not a leader among the guys, but he had always earned his place by providing Tarzan with his musical bumps. The angel conversation took place in a car, they were going to Nashville to buy a new guitar pick, Tarzan was at the wheel of course, and the topic came up out of the landscape, like a billboard which slowly comes into view, during a conversation where Delmo was describing his musical roots. His father was, at the piano, a three-note plonker, he said, but his mother, well, she had the touch of an angel. Tarzan saw the billboard. He asked, "What is the touch of an angel like, Delmo?"

Dear Delmo, not always given to seeing all sides of a question, began talking about his mother's playing. But Tarzan persisted. Ah . . . Now Delmo replied, in high seriousness, "I never felt that. But you know my brother did."

"He felt the touch of an angel?"

They were driving through deserted country, the long dividing line of blacktop shimmering in the sun. Tarzan reached across and snapped the radio off, right in the middle of a song. Delmo was still nodding to the beat. "We used to go bird nesting – we'd blow the eggs, we had a collection in our tree house. This one time Eddie went out by himself, cain't remember why, and he got himself out on a branch which broke, and had to hang on, you know, just dangling there by his hands, he was way up high, and out over a drop, the nest he was after was bouncin' around out there on the end of the branch and in fact it bounced so much that one of those eggs bounced right out and fell down and smashed, he could see it, way down in the ground, all smashed and yellow and he said to himself, hangin' there, I am going to be just like that egg. Anyways, there was this one branch which was over to the side, he had to let go a hand to reach it, he'd tried, he just couldn't reach that thing, and was just hanging there, he was just waiting to get tired and drop – an' there's this voice in the air. Not in his head, he said. The voice was all around him. It was an everythin' voice, that's what he said – it had everythin' in it, anger and promises and his mama and the whole history of the whole world – an' it said, Will you always look for me? Well, Eddie said, Yes. I mean, he would have said yes if it had been, Would you pick your ass and wipe it on the dean, but this voice, it was the kind of voice you would always be looking out to hear again."

Tarzan slowed the car, pulled over. Beside them was broken country, with gopher mounds and weed, stirred by a dirty wind. A hand-painted sign said *Eddie & Annie's Good Eats, 4 miles.*

Delmo, flushed, went on. "So then once he's said yes he knows that everythin' is changed now, he doesn't need to be told, whatever happens to him now he will always have the knowledge of her with him. So he tries again for that branch and you have to know that that thing was definitely out of reach. I went back up there with him the next day, I climbed that tree, I looked and measured. There was no way he could have got it. But he did. He turned and extended his hand and it seemed like his hand just went on extending, it grew, you know, and he got his fingers around it, he got a hold, and was able to swing over, and get his legs set, and, well, then he came down."

In the driver's seat, Tarzan was sitting very still.

"And then he commenced to look for her. Because he hadn't seen her, he just had the memory of her voice in his head."

Tarzan found a connection here with what Mrs Presley had told him, which was that you didn't *see* an angel. He found this frustrating. He started the car, got them out of there.

But after a silent mile Delmo continued. "And he said, Eddie said, that once he started to look, he became aware that there were angel places."

"Angel places."

"Yeah." Delmo took out a white handkerchief and mopped his sweaty face. "Now these were places where an angel had been. Or would be," he said. "Eddie began to notice them. Angels like to have a kind of frame around them, he said. They like to have a setting. People think they just are there in the empty air, but it ain't so. That's what he said. An' he took me to see this place, it was under a bridge. You should always look under bridges, he said. There's like the arch of the bridge over, and the banks on the sides," Delmo's hands moving to make these parts, "and there's the water to stand on, and the light is just right there. Just right. Anyways, we went in under this bridge, and when you stood on one side and looked across, on the other side there was a space between where the two big bearers, maybe they're called trusses, anyway these two big arches that held up this bridge, they were there, and between them, up and under, it was, how can I say that? – it was like a little theatre. And Eddie said this was an angel place."

Tarzan staring at him. "Why did he say that?"

"He said that it was a feeling. You looked at a place an' it occurred to you. It occurred to you to think of an angel and then the more you looked the more you realised that an angel had been there. You could see the light she had left."

"Did *you* see the light?"

Delmo looked away into the distance. There were mountains, puffy clouds. "He was my brother," he said.

Tarzan thought about this. He recognised a sensitive subject. He decided to wait.

Delmo said, "Sometimes he showed you places where angels would appear, in the future." This was said in a faraway voice, as though Delmo had gone somewhere else. "He said you could see the light gatherin'. He used to show me places – there was this one place, it was up under the eaves of an old barn. This barn was nearabouts falling down, it wasn't good for anything, no one would glance at it twice but ol' Eddie looked it over. He took me round the back, and there was this place, where the roof came to a point, up in under there, I could see up there that if you did want to make an appearance, that would be a good place."

In his mind's eye Tarzan saw the car they were in from high above, alone on the highway, and nothing else moving for miles. "So you would just have to stay there and wait," he said, "and the angel would appear?"

Delmo heard something in Tarzan's voice and he said quickly, "You might have to wait years, Tarzan."

Tarzan revved the engine and they burned rubber. "Okay, Delmo," he said, "Take me to Eddie. I want to meet him."

*

It is satisfying to me to finally get this long conversation fixed and written down. Over the years since I have replayed it in my head so often, I have tried to remember each piece of it, and the effect it had. Every time I write a word it is as though I am closing a door, fixing something forever. But this is now the time for that. I have wanted to get my own version straight, before the Day.

I have tried to shape this account so that it is true. I know I have gone round in circles, but that was always part of my design; because that is how he lived, then. I wanted to have a design. This was always the accusation against Tarzan, that he never shaped anything. And I accept this. He was never a songwriter. He never wrote anything, and this is why writing was invented, I think, to fix things, in a shape, so they can be looked at and understood. But Tarzan tried to remember without writing.

Over time it came to him that if he wanted to understand one day he would have to stop and write everything down.

So now I go back to that vehicle, with those two young men in it, I see them in there, its wheels sticking to the sweaty blacktop, and as it speeds down the road that is one vehicle full of feelings.

But Tarzan never did meet Eddie McMullins, because Eddie was dead, had died, to Tarzan's frustration, some years earlier. But the feelings his story engendered just would not go away. And maybe this is his legacy.

I have recounted all of this so as to take the scenic route to come around to the subject of Priscilla.

Because that subject is a mystery. Why did Tarzan choose her? I have developed my ideas on this matter over many years, long hours staring out the window at whiskey time, and I have come to believe that the angel factor was relevant here. Priscilla was good-looking, sure, in fact she was gorgeous. She had wonderful bones – softened by puppy fat – and a cute little nose, and translucent skin; the skin of her cheeks seemed to shine. She had black hair. Tarzan always went for black hair. She had great big dark eyes – fine. But Tarzan, let me tell you, when it came to attractive women, Tarzan was pretty much surrounded on a daily basis by the cream. So was she maybe the best of them all? Who can say. Everyone says she was gorgeous, no one ever contested that. But she was fourteen. For serious, Tarzan liked older women. He didn't even sleep with her, not at first. He kept her pure, much to her frustration. In the end the girl was begging him.

After he had seen her there in the mess in the company of her sister, Tarzan waited. He was always good at waiting, and at that time, while he was in the Army, he was being especially watchful and cautious. It was a time, he knew, when he had many new things to learn, he needed lots of help, and so he was being extra-careful about doing the right thing. The grunts had their eyes on him, checking to be sure that he didn't get star treatment, or else go ape on them – people were always on the lookout for him to return to the trees. But he arranged to meet her on a furlough and there they kissed. As I say, she was fourteen.

When his tour of duty was over, Skip organised it with her family for her to come to the States – he presented Vernon's second wife Dee as a chaperone, and showed photographs of what was said to be Dee and Vernon's house, where Priscilla would stay – oh, that sounds loopy! Doesn't it? What respectable family would let their fourteen-year-old darling go off overseas to, what, "spend time with" the sexiest singer in the world? But it happened!

In short order Priscilla was installed in Graceland. Her status there was ambiguous, Tarzan continued to see other women, especially when he was away – this was smack in the middle of the period when he was making three, four movies a year, and the starlets were just yummy yummy yummy. Ann-Margret! Ursula Andress! Priscilla waited at home, like a teddy bear, like a doll. He would ring her, hold the phone and listen to her breathing.

He kept her there and slept with her most nights, which is to say, she slept in his bed beside him. They would kiss – but the pyjamas stayed on. He had promised her father. Also I think the Colonel played a part here. He had explained to Tarzan in graphic terms – showed him the instruments – what would happen if it was known that he had broken the law in this particular way. The fall of Jerry Lee Lewis, who had married his thirteen-year-old cousin Myra, was instructive here. Also the fate of Chuck Berry, imprisoned for "transporting a minor across state lines." Plus there was the memory of Laura, an experience which continued to haunt Tarzan.

Oh, but let's say it openly: I'm fishing. His marriage to Priscilla was as big a mystery as anything in his life.

But it did take place, the records show that, in Las Vegas. There was a last-minute aspect to the whole thing, and the selection of guests and witnesses was given as much thought as a shopping list. Then he was man and wife – but what did this mean to Tarzan? None of the other guys were married. Jane Porter had no husband, neither did her mother, nor Eve, nor Marion Keisker nor any of the women in his circle. What was a husband? What was a marriage? For models there were only the Colonel and his invisible wives, and the silent Vernon – plus Mr and Mrs Herman Munster, of course. He learned a lot from TV.

Then finally they did have sex and more or less immediately Tarzan had a daughter, Lisa-Marie, and he was a dad. He had a wife, a child – he had these things in the same way he had Graceland, or a career in the movies. Other people thought he should have them. He was only trying to do what he was told.

But you have to come back to it: he did choose her. He started it with Priscilla – I stare at this fact and try to figure. And it comes to my mind: there were forces working. He wasn't singing, he wasn't making movies. For the first time, he wasn't special – he was, for god's sakes, just another Joe in the Army. He was in a foreign land. Mrs Presley was dead. Maybe he wanted somehow to replace her at the heart of Graceland? During her pre-death convalescence in hospital, the atmosphere in the big house changed. Things got disordered, there was a hint of violence. Skip, sensing a weakness in Vernon, took to directing every aspect of life, including the finances, and for some time no one countermanded him.

So I can see the thought in Tarzan's head that he would, over time, build something that might give him some influence over his own home.

But he built so carelessly, he failed to make her into the wife he needed. This wasn't like him, Tarzan was a good and thoughtful builder – think of his better humpy. His lifelong interest in shaping, design. No, his entire behaviour towards his chosen one was so strange that I have to look elsewhere for a rationale.

It's true he was taking pills. Speed put them in his food.

But in my thoughts on these matters I always come round to those talks he had, first with Mrs Presley, and then with Delmo. I have to ask: was he looking for another angel? Jane had come to him like a miracle in the bush and now he needed another deliverer. He was deep in a hole – there was a world out there but he couldn't get to it. In the privacy of his room he would, as I have said, refuse to have sex with her. But he did remove her blouse. Well, you're saying, and maybe you're right – definitely, a glimpse of her breasts there. But what he liked was to have her lie on her stomach. He would stroke her back. Priscilla has written of this in her autobiography* – *Tarzan loved my back. I used to spend hours, when he was away, trying to see it in a mirror – what was so special back there? Nothing. But he would stroke me, stroke me and sing to me. I loved it. There was an atmosphere of enchantment. These were our happiest times.* Now I think he was looking for wings. Glistening feathers coming through the skin – he was trying to prompt them. Priscilla says that he smothered her shoulder blades with kisses.

He searched everywhere for information on the subject of angels. But facts were hard to come by.

So I see Tarzan in his one big room in his great mansion of a house, listening to the guys outside, stroking Priscilla, crooning over her. I see the light in the halls, which was dim, and the chill air-conditioned air, through which he would ramble, prowl, looking for something. I see Priscilla there, face down on the bed, her lovely back exposed to the night. The atmosphere of expectation was overwhelming. Through the haze of pills, the strange hours, the travelling, the lost days on the movie sets . . . The interviews, the musical interludes, the photo sessions. The starlets, the fans, the purchases. The fun, fun, fun.

Through all this I see him waiting, waiting. Everyone knew that his life was going somewhere. They were all looking to see, to make sure they were going with him.

---

* *Tarzan's Woman*, with Sandra Harmon, Putnam, 1985

26

And now we come at last to the final phase of his life.

As we know, Tarzan died in 1977. He was, by common consent, forty-two years old. He was in decline, and those around him had seen this event coming for a number of years and prepared themselves. The Colonel moved to secure the post-Tarzan merchandising rights, a number of the guys cashed in, selling tell-all memoirs, claimed a car or a house as their own. They'd had twenty-odd wild years, but you can't retire on it.

More has been written about his death than perhaps any other aspect of his life. Along with the uncertainty about who killed JKF, this remains a prime subject for late-night exposés, reconstructions, docudramas. The Internet has maybe 120,000 Tarzan-AND-death sites. There is very little that's new to know about what happened, so they all concentrate on why. Why did the most successful entertainer of his century kill himself? And where should the blame lie?

For some the end begins with the signing to RCA. These people point to his catalogue of dreck and say, He threw himself away on *Can't Help Falling in Love*. Others blame the Colonel. Or the movies. The pills, the girls, the burgers. But I think it began in Germany in 1958.

John Lennon once remarked that "Tarzan was dead the day he went into the Army."

Of course it was astonishing that he went in. Name me another public figure of his stature who laid down his celebrity, changed into fatigues, said, Where do I stow my kitbag? Of course, there *is* no other public figure of his stature – Michael Jordan at the height of his career, maybe. Can you hear Big Michael saying, "Sorry, people, no more hoops – I gotta serve." Get serious. No one could believe it was really happening, that Tarzan would really go. The Colonel pulled all known strings. But the enrolment date came closer every day.

Tarzan had had Skip explain it to him. "Tarzan, you'll be in there with every other guy, man – they'll make you be nobody!"

"Just like everybody else?"

"Exactly so! Wear the same boots, get the same haircut, eat the same food – boss, Army food is just shit!"

"Huh."

Skip could not follow it. Somehow what he'd said seemed to have pleased the big man. Next time Tarzan spoke to a reporter he informed him that he had signed his draft papers and was keenly awaiting his call-up. He talked about how it was going to be his next big challenge, how he hoped the men he met would accept him. By six that night the entire nation had heard the news.

The Colonel counterpunched by announcing that Tarzan would not serve as a regular soldier, rather was going to spearhead what he termed a "Special Entertainment Force" which would "happy up the troops" – for a record fee, of course. The Army announced that it was paying no fees, that Tarzan would receive the regular soldier's wage, which was $78 a month (down from $100,000). The final word on the matter was given by the man himself. Tarzan went down to the Graceland gates, searched among the fans until he found a guy with a flashbulb and a notepad, motioned him over. "I want you to tell all the people," he said – and immediately the fans were quiet, waiting to hear – "I want you to say it that I will not be singing any rock 'n' roll while I am in the Army." A wail went up from the fans, but the flashbulb man was listening closely. "I am going be a regular human man, just like everyone else." Never! cried the fans. "Then I will come back," he said, and grinned his famous grin, and waved. The girls screamed. Flash went the flashbulb. *Biggest Star "Just Like Everyone Else"* said the headline. It was the first positive press he'd had for over a year.

The Colonel bowed to the inevitable, and set about making this into good news. "My boy is a real American," he growled to anyone who would listen. There was no way to sell tickets but this could be, he saw, the final stage in his "clean him up" strategy. Plus, if handled right, there could be truckloads of free publicity . . .

And so it was that, before the cameras, Tarzan's guitar was sealed in its velvet-lined case and his pretty clothes folded lovingly and packed into drawers strewn thickly with mothballs. His co-respondent shoes were wrapped in tissue and put away. Photos of him at the Fort Hood weigh-in, his magnificent chest bared for the nation, went out across television screens. It was plain that he was going to star in this new role too: Tarzan gets his Army haircut, live. Dockside, reporters spoke urgently into microphones. "He's going up the gangplank now. He's waving. The girls are screaming, you can probably hear them. He's waving – he's waving goodbye. There he goes – see you in eighteen months, Private Tarzan."

The mafia fell into depression.

But Tarzan was elated. Somehow, at last, he had entered

America. Now, at last, he looked the same as everyone else. He ate the same food, sat at the same tables. The grunts watched him, sure, but he was watching back, as an equal. They laughed at him when he didn't understand, but he accepted this, it was human. That was all he had ever wanted to be. Only human.

In Germany he confined himself to barracks – refused to be a public figure at all. Repeatedly he stood guard duty or kitchen patrol for other soldiers. In time they figured how humble he was, how prepared to be regular. He often had to ask for help, and, once they'd seen he was no bumbler but simply didn't understand, they helped him. He was, physically, the biggest guy in their unit and this did him no harm. In fact Tarzan revelled in the chance to be outdoors again, to run and climb and dodge. At these activities he could not be beaten.

He learned to shoot and, in time, to drive a tank. Out on manoeuvres he was issued with pills that would keep him awake during the long night hours. Wonderful pills, so tiny and yet there was a galaxy of thoughts inside each one – like exploding stars. Looking out the slot window of the tank he could see a slice of the country called Germany. Its orderly, wooded pastures stretched away in the moonlight and out there he sensed another world. It was the same when he looked out the windows at Graceland – he knew there were people with lives out there. But he never left the barracks. The guys urged him but while he was in the Army he liked the closed world that it provided. He liked the routines. He knew that out there he would have to grin and be Tarzan. He stayed in the bunkhouse and polished everyone's boots. The other guys would sit around and tell him their life stories. Truck drivers, machine hands, the sons of farmers, they explained the everyday to him. He was a great listener. To him, everything sounded utterly fantastic.

He was watching them so closely, trying to learn their secret.

When his tour was over, he inquired as to the possibility of signing up, long-term, full-time. The brass weren't sure. Despite his humbleness and restraint, his celebrity had been a problem – the German fans had mobbed the gate of the barracks just as their Graceland counterparts had done. Girls tried to sneak in, the thing was hell to control – and did he have the makings of a regular soldier, really? The dude couldn't read. But this was never a serious discussion. Here came the Colonel, brandishing his contracts. Tarzan was committed.

But he never forgot. In the Army he had been a regular guy.

On Tarzan's last day his sergeant came and, in a little ceremony, told him in front of the other guys how well he'd done, considering. This was no flashbulb occasion; they were in the bunkhouse, surrounded by the smells of bedding and boot-polish. The guys clapped. Then they all looked at him.

For Tarzan it was like the moment he'd had on stage at the bowling alley, with everyone expectant. But at that time a script had been provided. Now he looked round at the faces – no cameras here. He wanted to say something. He wanted to know what to say – "Hey, baby!", if he said that, they would all break up. But it wasn't what he was after.

They waited.

Under pressure, he finally got something out. "I do not know how to do it," he said. "But I am trying to be like you." To speak for himself, without gone, without resort to the million-dollar Tarzan Presley sound, this was almost beyond him. But he resolved that he would learn.

Yes, it was in the Army that he got the idea: if he could learn to read, if he could escape the spotlight, there was, he realised, another life possible, for him, a place out there, somewhere.

*

Starting in 1968 he made a series of comebacks. There was a TV special, followed by a triumphant return to the stage. This was greeted by the Colonel with relief. Tarzan movies had become yawn-fests, with their star just smiling passively – in time the box office was also passive. His records had stopped selling, mainly because the songs he was given to record were such stinkers – then suddenly he was earning again. In triumph he took to the stage at Las Vegas and proved himself all over again to be the biggest attraction on the planet. People who witnessed those early shows still talk about his astonishing charisma, his ability to bring even a crowd of media hacks and professional cynics to its feet. It was as though he sang to you – to the private person inside, lonely, maybe afraid, peering out, hopeful of a better world. This was his talent. He knew you and could speak to you. Speak for you. Plus he was a mover.

He cut a classic record, *From Tarzan in Memphis*.

But it didn't last. Returning each year to the Las Vegas stage, he seemed reduced – why? He wasn't old. He still had all his hair. But his body had begun to change. Everyone noticed this. His waistline was something that constantly required new costumes. He had begun to eat – no one had seen anything like it. He'd always had an appetite, but this was different, as though the food was something he had to get through. They gave him pills to keep him going. Sometimes his body shook, as though chemical reactions were taking place inside it. Sweat poured from him – performing, he would go through a stack of towels. Then, when he came off stage, shaken, soaked, they would pill him down. It was like seeing a great ship shuddering to a halt – they had to make sure that when he fell he was near a bed.

That was what he looked like, from the outside.

Inside, he could see it all. It had worked with the movies and now it could work with this too – he could withdraw his talent.

This sounds strange, I know. For a man who lived to sing, who came alive when his chest was open, to be closing that chest, that mighty throat, to constrict it, this seems perverse. But maybe it was the only logic available? To get the music he craved he had to live in Graceland and be a star. Gradually it occurred to him that he had to stop being a star.

He spent hours mooning around up at his cabin – trying to think. Trying to remember. But the cabin had become like an old photograph looked at too many times, its power wore thin and in time he just sat on its stoop like a tired drunk and let his eyelids fall. Since the cabin was off-limits to the guys it became an impediment to managing him, and when Skip judged that he could get away with it he blew it up – "We was just playing with explosives, Boss, and it went. Want me get another built?" Tarzan saw through this – as much as he saw anything – and shook his weary head. At one point he instructed that they were now to build there a full-scale replica of the Empire State Building, and foundations were laid. But he had lost the habit of visiting the hollow and Skip quietly gave the order for work to cease. On occasions Tarzan would return to that place, its bowl deepened by the explosion, the lumps of foundation concrete standing like stelae, like gravestones, and rest there, letting the wind of waste blow through his bones. But any memories that came belonged to another man, another time.

He retired to his room and wouldn't come out. They sent his meals up, each meal freighted with chemicals. To lie on his bed after ingesting a truckload of amphetamine, this took willpower – and lots of television. To eat when he wasn't hungry. To stay in out of the sun so that his skin turned pale and doughy, this was a man's work.

They would crank him up – "Showtime, Tarzan!" – and send him out there. On stage he would sway, gaze about as though bemused. The fans continued to love him. Their affection for him never waned. But the critics had sharper eyes. *Tarzan Sleepwalks Vegas.*

Priscilla was long gone. Apparently he had bought her a house of her own in California, where she lived now with Lisa-Marie – this was his understanding – until he recovered.

He saw from the gossip columns that she had another man and now it was his turn to order that a hit be made. But this was, like so many at this time, an order that Skip allowed to drift into the Pending file, and then into No Action.

Tarzan held his anger inside.

Inside, inside: could he hold his path steady in there? It was a terrible struggle. His head didn't seem to belong to him, it floated above his body as he lay on the bed, with the latest girl, the latest book. What was it again he was trying to achieve? That's right, he was going to fail.

But he couldn't fail. No matter how bad he was, no matter how brokenly he stumbled through each song, the people came. They flocked to see him, the object they loved. Plus, he was so famous, you came simply to see the thing that had been talked about for so many years. The rawness of it – the hard lights, the exposed stage, the heavy white costumes that they draped on him, this was worth seeing, if you had the stomach for it. The greatness and the ghost of greatness. His arms spread, the wings of an eagle, with flapping fringes of suede, as he roared his way to the top of *An American Trilogy* – and his soul goes marching on. Stumbling on, but somehow we love our heroes better when they stumble. We like to know they are human. Yes, Tarzan is really just like us. See, he's forgotten the words again. Hell, it's just like me, singing through a hangover in the shower.

Through the haze, he studied and researched. The Internet would have been helpful to him, but at that time it was not yet invented.

Finally he saw that failure wasn't working. He was going to have to die.

His near-death experiences were legendary. Pilled to the eyeballs, he fell forward into a bowl of soup and came close to drowning. He fell down the Mirror Stairs and broke a collarbone. The guys watched him in shifts. Every girl that was sent up was schooled in watching him, in making sure that he didn't choke on his own vomit. In fact, he was getting older, these days the girls were women. They would see his dead eye fall on them and wonder, What am I doing here?

He saw that he could work the guys with gifts. No one would bring him the books he was after. He would phone out to bookstores and tie the clerks up for hours, reviewing the stock of the shop by phone, ordering entire sections. Of course the guys routinely opened his mail and made sure that the bulk of his purchases never made it up to his room. But he discovered that he could take them shopping. None of them was getting any younger and, while a lifetime of being kept had been fun, acquiring actual money for themselves was a long-term problem. So they encouraged him to take them out, late at night, to car dealers. The proprietor would be found, at two a.m., and would hurry down to open his showroom. Eight Cadillacs, in an hour, no problem – Vernon, pay the man. Then on the way home, with the pink slips in his hand, he would initiate a stop at an all-night bookstore. And on these occasions they would humour him. They got the cars, he brought home a trunkful of reading.

His plan was like a big old sleepy catfish lying at the bottom of the river. Sometimes he would peer down in there and wonder if it was still alive. Yes, there, it was just stirring, there, there, sluggish, heavy, as though drugged, hidden in the mud. Waiting, like Judgement Day, for its moment.

*

The Colonel called him to a summit meeting. This was in Palm Springs, Skip drove him over – Skip was, like everyone, keen after all these years finally to get a look at the Colonel's setup. Tarzan, typical for that year, was resplendent in blue velvet cape, pink cravat, and wraparound aviator shades with significant holes in the frame.

But the Colonel turned Skip away at the door, growling, "You sit in the car."

On the way home, Skip asked, "So what was it like in there?" Skip himself paunchy these days, well on his way to becoming a major showbiz bureaucrat. "Just looks like any ol' house, boss."

Tarzan had thought so too, when they arrived. He saw the green square of lawn, the little white fence, and thought, the Colonel lives like an American. The thought angered him. The pills made anger a thing that rose inside you like a wind, sometimes you had to fire off a gun to get rid of it.

The Colonel led him down the hall. It was just an ordinary house, it seemed, from what Tarzan could see, modest, everyday – patterned carpet, dark wooden walls. Sounds of housework could be heard, vacuum cleaning and the song of a kitchen radio. But there was something Hollywood at work here, Tarzan thought, if you went through a door you would come to where the scenery ran out. Now the Colonel was hurrying him – the hall turned out to be a corridor that, despite several twists and turns, was just a path that ran right through the house and out the back door – took them along something like an airbridge, with no windows, then delivered them into what seemed to be house number two. Back here there was a lobby, with a receptionist, male, one of the Colonel's assistants, maybe his name was Arthur, Tarzan couldn't recall, but he'd been seen before. Tarzan managed a grin, shook hands while he was looking around. Just a lobby, with grey carpet and polished wood. Was this it? Didn't the Colonel have any flash at all?

But through the next door was a room big enough to house a mighty machine.

It was all but empty. Polished boards running in parallel, white walls, windows high so that all you could see was sky – the Colonel walked out into the middle of the floor and turned. On his feet he was light, nimble, but there was no hiding the fact that these days he was immensely fat. His brown suit bulged at the buttons, his stick, tapping the floor, tapped a long way from his feet. "This is where I come," he said, "when I'm building new dreams." He was gazing around fondly and so Tarzan gazed too, but he was searching for something to look at. Now he saw that in the polished floor there were small holes and, in places, scrape marks. But the Colonel was leading him on.

From the gloom in the distance an island of furniture appeared: couch, coffee-table, a desk. The desk was small, especially once the Colonel was behind it. There was nothing on it except a toy telephone made of bright plastic. Tarzan strolled around, gazing. There was no exit to the place, nothing further to see. Finally, not knowing what else to do, he accepted a seat on the couch, put his feet on the coffee table – the black hand-tooled boots caught the polish.

Immediately the Colonel began speaking. "I said I would open every door in America for you, Tarzan. And I have done it." His voice faded quickly in the vast space, he left pauses so that his words might gather weight. "You have everything an American can dream of – in the future, every American boy is going to dream of being you. And every American girl will dream that you might want to marry them." The pause was longer this time. The Colonel was not looking at Tarzan, his eyes were lifted, towards the sky-filled windows, but Tarzan could see nothing of significance there, only blue, so he continued to look at the Colonel. The Colonel didn't look good. His face was the colour of meat. Yes, there was a weakness in him, in his breathing, that Tarzan had never detected before, it reminded him of Gladys, how she had been before she died.

Nevertheless the Colonel's voice was still strong. "But you don't want what I've given you. That's what you're telling yourself." Now the pale blue gaze came down so that Tarzan could look in. Yes, there were the rooms he had once glimpsed. Something, something . . . something was definitely hidden there. Tarzan resolved to look away, and as he looked around the great empty room he understood that something was hidden here too. "The guys tell me that you're dying. Are you going to die on me, son? You've stopped caring for yourself. You don't care about being Tarzan Presley any more, do you."

Tarzan remembered his plan, lying deep, but he was afraid now to think of it – the Colonel seemed in danger of reading his intentions. Tarzan could feel the anger in his body, it was rising, and, beneath his cloak, his hand went to the butt of his Colt .45. Did the Colonel know about the gun? It was the pills, Tarzan knew, that made everything he looked at seem as though something was about to be revealed. This room, for example: something was about to appear here.

"Just look at the state of you," said the Colonel. "You're so fat I can't sell you."

"You can sell me," said Tarzan.

"Not when you're dead."

"You'll sell me when I'm dead, Colonel Tom. Anyways, baby, I ain't dead yet."

Now the Colonel's meaty head rolled on its soft neck and Tarzan had the thought that the head was going to detach itself and float away. But the voice kept coming out of it. The voice was softer, more attractive, and Tarzan thought he should be afraid. "I've opened every door for you, Tarzan, I've given America to you. But you – you just can't see how it is with America."

"I know it!" Tarzan was on his feet now. "America is all around me and I can't get to it! I live inside fuckin' Graceland – everywhere I go it's still fuckin' Graceland!" And he drew the Colt and fired a shot into the floor.

This produced a small, dark hole. From the barrel a curl of smoke emerged, which Tarzan, lifting the gun to his lips, dismissed with a contemptuous puff. Immediately the door to the lobby was flung open by Arthur, whose running feet slapped out an echo. "It's okay," the Colonel growled, "Tarzan is just emptying his weapon – aren't you, son." So Tarzan fired off the rest of his bullets, bang, bang, bang, while the old man nodded approvingly. "Thank you, Arthur."

Back on the couch, Tarzan sank deep into himself. The Colonel continued to talk but the words, small sounds after the gunshots, seemed like the same talk that the Colonel always gave. The responsibilities, the fans, the honour. The contracts. Tarzan recalled suddenly that at their first meeting, long ago, the Colonel had spoken of how there were holes in America – he felt he had fallen into one. The pills stirred inside him but they seemed to be the only life in his heavy body. His body was an immense weight the couch had to carry – he could sense it sagging beneath him.

His gaze drifted across the floor and now he saw again that there were holes – where the bullets had entered, yes, but the other holes, what were they?

". . . and I am working on a stage for you that will place you where every single person in the world can see you at the same time . . ."

Now he saw that the Colonel had a plan too. These holes, this room . . . all at once he saw that something had been removed from this place. Definitely, he was sure of it – something big was being built here.

". . . and so I will send my special assistant to Graceland . . ."

"No way," said Tarzan. "None of your people at Graceland."

". . . for meetings . . ."

"Not at Graceland."

"D'you want to go back to the jungle, son? It could be arranged."

And now there was a silence.

The Colonel's eyes had gone to the high windows again and as Tarzan looked up he understood that here a lofty machine was being built that would take the Colonel on to some kind of final immortality. Yes, he sensed it now. It was a pity that the pills prevented final clarity but now that he had made these connections Tarzan had a great sense of wellbeing. He gazed around and realised that he was finished here.

"You want to see everything," said the Colonel softly. "And you pretend you don't care about it, but I know better: you also want to be seen. You want fame, Tarzan. To be known by men, that is what you came here for. So: I am building you a stage as high as the Empire State and from up there you'll become a legend that is never forgotten as long as there are men on the planet."

Tarzan's eyes toured the room. Now there was a familiar smell – he thought that if he shut his eyes he would remember something. He tried it, but the pills got in the way. But it was there, something big and old, he was certain of it now – when he slept a picture of it would come.

He gave a heartfelt sigh, which made the couch groan.

The Colonel, urgent now, as keen as Tarzan had ever seen him, leaned in and said, "I am building you a cage in the sky, Tarzan. And in the cage there will be a weta."

"All the wetas are dead."

"Not all. Not every single one. And before the eyes of the world I will put you in that cage. Tarzan versus the Weta, it will be like the Colosseum, like something from the Bible – like a movie but it's real, and televised live right round the world. It will be your greatest performance. You're going to have to go into training, son." He eyed Tarzan, then said harshly, "You need something to fight for. Something to give you a reason. I'm having songs written for the soundtrack, I am putting together the kind of deal that means that history will never forget our names. It's a new vision. And then you will see: we'll all be happy again." He gave his widest smile, and said softly, in the clear blue light of that great room, "You know that I love you, Tarzan."

"Hey, baby," was all that Tarzan said.

When the Colonel offered him a dotted line, Tarzan didn't hesitate. Signing, he knew that this was the final thing that was needed.

The bait for the catfish.

Together Tarzan and the Colonel passed back through the scenery house and the Colonel warmly bid him goodbye. Tarzan told the guys, told Skip, that in back of his house the Colonel had a palace, just like Graceland – a replica in every detail. And for many years this was what everyone understood to be the truth.

According to Vernon Presley's calculations, during the year of 1975 Tarzan Presley purchased eighty-three automobiles. Tarzan bought guns, jewelry, horses, at least six houses. There was only one rule about these gifts – he insisted on leaving Graceland to make the purchase. The guys would say, "Boss, we'll bring it up – the jewelry guy does house calls." But when the mood to spend came upon him, nobody wanted to interfere. This was payday, the guy was on the way out, it was time to be thinking about the future.

Finally he bought an aircraft. It was the era of the Learjet, all the stars had one, and he had decided. He found a dealer, tracked down a Lockheed JetStar that was in hock through a credit default, and ordered that it be made over in the Tarzan style, pink and black, and solid gold. "Where does he think he's going?" the guys asked. But he was into cash at this time, he kept demanding it from Vernon, and when the mood took him, handing out fistfuls of the stuff – it kept everyone quiet.

Then one night he disappeared.

This was in 1976, a year before his death. The Colonel ordered an investigation, the guys were spoken to personally: "How did this happen?" Well, he said he wanted to be alone with – what was her name this month? Kathy? – and had ordered them not to follow. A car had been parked across the drive, with its rotor arm removed. How the fuck did he know about rotor arms? Oh, yeah, the Army – and by the time they got after him he had escaped. This Kathy drove him to the plane, he dumped her and had himself flown to Denver. He used the plane phone to order thirty-six Famous Old Pigs and have them delivered. An hour later they arrived, wrapped in foil. A Pig was a long sandwich, filled with strips of fried bacon and slabs of barbecue pork and dripping – the kind of thing a death row killer from the black swamps might order for his last meal. Tarzan ate three, right there on the tarmac. He settled back in his Commander's Chair and watched the Denver channels on one of his TVs. The picture was somewhat on the fritz, due to signal crush at the airport, but this wasn't the point. He read a little, slept. His pilot kept coming back to see if he was okay but Tarzan only insisted that he join him in a Pig – and that there be no radio communication with Graceland. His stewardess, Nancy-Ann, watched from the servants' quarters, somewhat alarmed, but Tarzan was entirely at ease and in the end she accepted that he didn't want anything, that he wasn't suffering, and that they should all just await his pleasure.

In all he was away nine hours.

Afterwards he was conspicuously well-behaved and the incident was forgotten. His Vegas show that season was laughable, but the returns were astronomical and everyone was relieved that, for another year, they could keep the lumbering, monstrous Tarzan contraption on the road. He even made a little tour, of the cities that were close enough for him to fly home from each night. Good grosses, said the Colonel – not even hotels to pay for. But the catfish was lying deep. Without warning he was gone again and this time it was for five days.

It's now known that he flew to Switzerland. And, since he knew that the Colonel would eventually screw it out of the pilot, Tarzan told them as much. He was consulting a specialist, he said, about his weight. Which specialist? That's my business. But we have to check this guy out, said Skip, he might be dangerous, he might be a crank – he might be after your money. Why go to Switzerland, boss, we have doctors right here? That's my business.

He was at this point a frustrating man to discipline, as there didn't seem to be anything he wanted – nothing you could take away. The Colonel ordered that the jet be sold but found that he couldn't swing this – and when he fired the pilot Tarzan just doubled his salary and reinstated him. Vernon tried to pretend that money was short but discovered that Tarzan had learned the words *fraud* and *lawyer* and this angle too was soon dropped. The Colonel spoke harshly to Tarzan about the upcoming bout with the weta – but in fact no date had been set. The truth was, Tarzan was simply too blubbery and to stage that battle now would be to promote a murder. The Colonel fumed – an uncommon thing.

Now Tarzan put in a call to Eve Kersting and shortly afterwards she arrived at Graceland to interview him. Again the Colonel tried to intervene but again he was frustrated. Tarzan said firmly that she had never published a bad word about him, that he trusted her, that she had enough material for the quality book on him that would counter this rubbish that recently was being published. Negotiations on these matters took place in the kitchen at Graceland, where the Colonel would pace, just as Mrs Presley had once done, his hard-edged voice bouncing off the gleaming whiteware. The cooks and assembled Presley relatives would hang, well within earshot, and make noises, oooh, aaah, when a particularly heavy blow was struck. "Get them out of here!" the Colonel would thunder.

"Colonel," said Tarzan, "it's my house, they live here. Mary, I would like more cheeseburgers, please." And so the cook would tell the Colonel to move over, and the heat would rise. Skip would catch the Colonel's eye and take him into the lobby for a whispered conference. Tarzan would go on eating. He was a real heavyweight now, puffy and pale. It seemed that he had no control over his appetite. But the catfish was lying deep. He heard out warnings from the Colonel that any activity which prevented the fulfilment of contracts would produce legal action, and simply nodded. He called for another round of fried banana and peanut butter sandwiches.

So Eve came and was alone with him for three days in his room.

Eve Kersting has been dead now for a good twenty years. She left no papers, no journals or records that indicate in any way her role in Tarzan's life during the 1970s. Neither of her novels*, even read in hindsight, hint at the efforts she made on his behalf. She cleaned up as scrupulously as a spy. Her seventies passport is missing. So are any minor papers – phone bills, parking tickets – from that time, anything that might record her connection to him. In fact there was no need for

---

* *The Conductor of Lightning*, Random House, 1983, and *King Tide*, Random House, 1987

her to go to these lengths, because in fact suspicion never fell on her. Eve was the kind of person skilled at making herself seem insignificant. She was one of those who wanted most to understand – and she knew the best place to watch from was in the background. She never sold Tarzan out. From the first, she looked and saw clearly. By the time of his death she was more or less the only person of his acquaintance that he trusted.

Monstrously overweight, green of skin, lumbering, bloated, he shambled his way through what was to be his last engagement at Las Vegas in January of 1977. The reviews were better, strangely. Even the reporters saw that they were witnessing something terrible, something tragic and also maybe heroic. They had had their fun with him; now at last the sight of him on his knees seemed to bring out human feeling. *Terrifying Performance From Entertainment Colossus. The most honest sweat money ever bought . . . If He Falls, Look Out Below.* The Colonel, never slow to see an angle, understood that he was now selling a life-and-death scene. He talked frankly of "the end" and how this might be the last chance to see him. The fans willed Tarzan to carry on. Up on the stage he grinned, gave his fat ass a wiggle – they cheered – then stood, gripping the mike stand, swaying, openly figuring what he should do next. Sometimes he would talk, rambling over the hillsides of his youth, evoking the gorillas, painting pictures – this seemed easier for him now than singing, which plainly produced emotions he found hard to manage. Something like *Bridge Over Troubled Water* became a kind of psychodrama, with Tarzan insisting he would be your guide at the same time as he made it clear he had no idea of where to go.

But he did have an idea. On August 16th, 1977 he again flew the coop. Once again his pilot was instructed not to make a call home – not to call anybody except air traffic control, and then only when it was strictly necessary.

They flew to Zurich. This was established within two days, as Tarzan and Eve had figured it would be. Not that Eve was with him, or anyone. Tarzan spoke kindly to his stewardess Nancy-Ann, listened to her account of her sister's recent wedding, as she was soon telling reporters, with real interest. Upon landing he told the pilot to be on stand-by, he would only be a few hours. He left the plane with no luggage, nothing except a large coat, which Nancy-Ann saw him pulling over his shoulders as he descended to the tarmac. As he went in to the terminal she saw that he had put on a dark felt hat and sunglasses.

Investigation proved that he didn't avail himself of the VIP facilities. It seemed that he had queued quietly and passed, unremarked, through passport control and customs. Then he vanished from the radar screen.

The last photographs of Tarzan Presley are the ones so beloved by the tabloids, from his final stage appearance, where his sideburns cannot cover his chipmunk cheeks, where his towel can hardly find a neck to go round. Sweat-streaked, white-faced, puffy, shuddering, immense and dazed in the spotlight. A monument to brainless excess: this we are told is how we must see him.

Every life must yield its tabloid of message.

But I can't leave it at that – we are near the end now, and I can't let him leave that way. I am going to give you another picture and in it if you must have one is the message that his life delivers. This photograph is from 1971 and at first glance it's just one among millions.

But I want to go inside it.

It's a black-and-white, glossy. In the photograph you can see that his hair is a bit longer at the back. He's wearing a dark suit in which he looks restrained, even if a golden scarf is bursting out at his throat. Yes, somehow he's brushed and combed, not just his hair but his limbs. Somehow he's stiff. That's it: finally he has acquired the stiffness that we humans have to fight in the moments before we are to perform. There's something in his hand.

This as I said is in 1971 and Tarzan is about to go on stage. He's about to perform. He's in Memphis, at the Tulane Memorial Centre, and there's an adoring hometown crowd. But he's not going to sing.

In 1971 Tarzan was included by the President in his list of The Ten Most Outstanding Young Men of the Year – the mayor of Memphis is about to award him the key to the city. The order of the day says, first the mayor speaks, then the key is given. Handshake, photographs. Then Tarzan speaks.

In his hand is a piece of paper with words on it. But that is just a prop. He's not going to read. By now he can read, and, after a fashion, he can also write. He can make the marks. But writing isn't only the making of the marks. It's not about knowing enough words. What is it about? It's about having a sense of culture – the human culture. It's about knowing what has previously been said, and done, and been – about what humans have been – and what they are being. That's it: it's about knowing what humans have been and are being, knowing that and what you are to that.

And so I want now to go inside his head.

He's in his room at Graceland. There's a mirror, a dressing table. He's alone. On and off he's in there – his head's in there – for six weeks. Writing. They bring him meals, and sometimes he goes out to play. No one really knows what he's doing. They bring him girls.

But this time he doesn't get the girls to help. He doesn't talk to Eve about this, either, although he sometimes asks her strange questions.

Inside his head he is trying to do what Jane said, to put his life down in a sequence that makes sense. But you should never have a mirror before you when you write. It took him weeks to understand this.

And then the photograph starts to move. He steps up on stage, waves to everyone. Flashes the famous grin. The mayor speaks. Well, I won't bore you, the mayor's speech has been the same for the last hundred years. Tarzan accepts the key, which is as long as his forearm – a cubit for a king. Then he turns and there's the microphone. So what should he do with the key? He fumbles, nobody likes a fumbler, then finally, rather awkwardly, puts it on the floor. That's not a good place for such an important, such a symbolic thing, he can feel this, but what should he do, give it back to the mayor? So he leaves it. Straightens up. Has he ever been so stiff? Now he realises that he has also left his bit of paper on the floor. But he knows what he's going to say.

I want to go inside his head.

The years are not crossable. But I am what he became, I am the son of him, of the impulse that was him. And yet I'm so much older than he was then, than he ever was, I look back and when I go inside him I am feeling fatherly, as though I am proud of him and anxious and fascinated all at the same time. We study our children for the ways of us that to our astonishment are becoming new ways inside them.

"Hello," he says, and they all roar. He looks down and sees their faces. He doesn't try to smile – he's nervous. He was never nervous. But they are with him. "Hello," he says again, and this time no one shouts, *You already said that*, though he waits as though expecting it. "I am Tarzan. I am from New Zealand. I was raised in the wild by the gorillas. I never had met another human being until the year 1954." As he speaks he is looking down at all the humans. They are looking into him, into the feelings inside him. They are reaching – they want what he is feeling. "I came to America to learn the ways of the world."

Now everyone roars, they drum their feet and he knows he should grin. But then he would say, *Hey, baby!* and the moment would be gone. So, although it is painful, he stands with his head bowed, and waits. There is something disappointing in the way he makes the roar die away, and he feels that, he hates to disappoint them. How has it turned out that everyone is dependent on him? Maybe the yell? But to give the yell, now, would only be a version of *Hey, baby*.

On the floor is his bit of paper and he could reach down for it. But he knows what it says. But what it says isn't right, now. So he looks up, until he is looking just above their faces. What's back there? Nothing that he is looking at.

It's as though he's underwater – as though he's trying to go upstream against a current, by pulling himself forward. It's as though there are stones, the words are stones, and he has to gasp each stone and, against a strong current, pull himself forward to the next one. Yes, his lungs are bursting but he must keep control. "I came here," he says carefully, "to see. To see what I would be. Everybody was kind," he said, and now he did smile, but it wasn't the grin. They were with him, urging him on. "Everyone I met showed me one little thing. So I am saying thank you for that." He sensed that he had gone through a passage of easy words and that if he kept going easy he would lose the way. Frowning down, he made himself wait. Everyone waited. "And I have learned."

Now he did lift his head and grin, and took their applause. Why not? But he held his hand up. "But what I have learned is that I still want to know: what will I be? And that is what everybody wants." His lungs were bursting but he could see the surface now. Yes, he was going to make it. "It is what my body wants. It wants it all the time. If it stops wanting it then my body will die. I thought I would come to America and then I would be here. And I am here. But always in my body there will be: what am I becoming?" He frowned down harder, then looked up and included them in. "What are everybody becoming?"

"Is," he said sheepishly, and this brought the house to its feet.

So that is the picture of him I want you to have.

Now, get on his plane with him, fly with me to Switzerland.

Two days after his disappearance a pile of clothing was found on a deserted stretch of shoreline bounding a Swiss lake, Lac Gorte. A long coat, wraparound sunglasses, a dark hat. Black trousers, a pink shirt. Co-respondent shoes. In the shoes was eighty-two thousand American dollars in cash and a pendant made of a hard green jade-like stone.

Parked in a layby just along the road was a pale blue Volkswagen with Swiss plates. It transpired that this vehicle had been purchased, for cash, from a used-car dealer, three weeks before, in Zurich, by an American woman about whom very little could be discovered. Her signature proved indecipherable, a squiggle. Her address had been given as the Hotel Regent in Geneva, but there *was* no Hotel Regent. She was a little overweight, a bit dumpy, was all the car dealer, a Mr Kung, could tell the police, and then later the world's media. She smoked, he said, smoked incessantly – Marlboros. A quiet person. Dark glasses. Grey hair. She said she owned a Volks back in the States and wanted one for touring in Europe. This woman was never identified.

However, the presence of her vehicle in the story made everyone understand that this might be a complicated matter. It was true, everyone agreed, that if Tarzan could pass through passport control and customs, then it was also possible that he could have moved about Switzerland without being noticed.

Switzerland was not a rock 'n' roll country, and letting people get on with their business was a source of national pride.

The car had no fingerprints. In fact, the police announced, it had been wiped clean. Only 700 kilometres had been put on its clock since its purchase – which 700 kilometres were those? For some months these questions were asked over and over but nothing of consequence was ever discovered.

Was the car even connected to him?

And in the end the focus always came back to the lake, Lac Gorte. Its blue shape on the map became familiar – not unlike the shape of an eye. Camera crews traversed the road between Zurich and Berne, saying that Tarzan must have come this way on his final drive. They trod the shoreline and turned their lenses on its cold waters.

Lac Gorte is not famous – perhaps that is partly why Tarzan and Eve chose it. There are the usual shorefront cottages, the private jetties and haul-out places for boats, but nothing special, nothing to mark it out from any other lake in Europe. People sail yachts. Four big marinas. Water skiing, fishing. Switzerland has many such lakes. Its only distinguishing feature is that it is said by the locals to be bottomless. Indeed, local legend has it that if you drown there, your body will not rise to the surface. Rather it will go down, pulled by strong currents. No one of significance had until that point died there to put this legend to the test. But now teams of police divers descended into the cold blue waters and searched. The images of them – the rubber-sheathed bodies fossicking among gently waving weeds, their weak torch beams picking out refuse thrown from yachts – went around the world.

Fans began to gather on the shore. German fans, who had his signature from his time at Bad Nauheim. Greasy French rockers. Tearful Greeks. Kiwis who claimed him as a homeboy. Then an American contingent arrived – America had the greatest claim, they felt – and stood out in the cold, looking across the waters, measuring the icy peaks of the nearby mountains. This had been his last view of the world, they told themselves.

Increasingly, now, this was accepted: Tarzan is dead. The lack of a body gave hope to the most needy but the signs were bad. In particular the piece of greenstone, famous as perhaps the single material thing that he really cared about, this was cited as something he would not have left behind if he had wanted to go on living. Yes, he always wore it when he swam, Skip said to the cameras, he never took it off. So why did he take it off now? This question was asked. He could have swum out into the lake and held it while he went down.

People didn't like to think of that large, pale body, out in the middle of this foreign lake, its lungs filling with water, fighting, as he'd fought on at the end on stage. Slowly sinking.

The Colonel announced that a funeral would be held. This was to be, he said, a chance for the fans to come and say goodbye. He commissioned a wax replica of Tarzan and this was placed in a coffin and exhibited at Graceland. Around the neck of the model the greenstone pendant was placed, as a link between the model and the real man. For seven hours the fans filed past the coffin, weeping. It was a hot day, steamy, many fainted. There was hysteria. Someone sighted his face in a cloud – there were screams. Ambulances carried the distraught away. A mountain of flowers. The cameras caught it all, sent pictures round the world. Tarzan dead, at presumed forty-two. In death he had become slim again, tanned and beautiful. The Colonel had imported experts from Madame Tussauds – it was an excellent model, very lifelike, everyone said. It really looked like him, dead.

They buried the model (Priscilla removed the pendant) in the Peace Garden at Graceland. Today, tour parties stand at the grave and read the inscription. *He rocked the world.*

The occasional wreath is still cast upon the waters of Lac Gorte. Investigative reporters continue to sniff around, hoping to crack the story. There is a plaque. But it is not a happy place. No one likes to think of him, dulled and pale, and going down. It is generally thought, however, to be a good thing that he died away from Graceland, away from home. At Graceland, he never died. People would rather see him there in his prime, athletic and confident and full of that eager yearning which just drew you to him.

PART THREE

Marshall Sturt

27

I found it hard to give up being Tarzan. I had never realised how many doors he opened for me. The world stands in your way and says, "Yeah, what do you want? Who are you?" Suddenly I had no choice but to answer, I'm just anyone. "Yeah, so why don't you fuck off."

But then, on the other hand, you could – fuck off. You were free to go. No one cared. The freedom, to explore whatever took your fancy, this was simply extraordinary. In a way it was bewildering, and there were days when every circumstance appeared to be a crossroads, where I was required to make a life-determining choice. To choose, and then have to choose again, and again – this is tiring. It's why so many people live lives so strongly governed by pattern.

But the sense that the world is open, that you can go out into it and find something to bring home, something to think about, this was extraordinary. Not, of course, that it was true, at first. For one thing I had no home. And, first, I had to make good with my escape and this required that no hint be given that I might still be alive.

*

August 16th, 1977. After exiting customs in Zurich, I kept my head down. The feeling that I was out in the world was dizzying, but I did not want to pause so that people might get a look at me – a big guy staring around the arrivals lounge as though he's just dropped off Mars. I didn't buy so much as a stick of gum, but put my head down and made for the exit. As planned, Zurich was formal enough that men still wore coats and hats, no matter what the weather. I didn't stand out.

Plus Eve had coached me, her voice on the phone, about looking small. "People notice you," she said, "because you're so open, so confident and relaxed. This is unusual, Tarzan. You need to move as though you're smaller. Take shorter strides, be prepared to follow a path that goes around people rather than straight ahead. Be just a little more stiff, as though only being correct will keep you safe." Well, I tried to do all that – who knows how successfully? I have no picture of myself taking the fifty paces needed to traverse the lobby and yet, like someone crossing from East Berlin, this was the over-the-wall zone where I might have been arrested. Late afternoon – through the lobby, through the swinging doors, out into the Swiss sunlight, both thin and sharp, perhaps not quite bright enough to justify sunglasses, but I kept them on – kept my head down and kept going. Through the ranks of taxis and into the carpark. Row W, space number 87, I had it written on my hand. It was okay to search here, Eve said, because everyone searches in carparks. I had her instructions running in my head. So much advice, such detailed rehearsals, rung through long distance, on one occasion, from this carpark itself. Ah, there was the car, squat and lumpy – Eve had made sure I knew what a Volkswagen looked like. Then I had to wander off, as, three along, a guy was filling his trunk with luggage. Finally he drove away and I was able to feel around down inside the left rear tyre for the keys.

Inside the car the temptation to sit and breathe was overwhelming. But I wasn't away yet. I had to concentrate, to remember – to do everything in the right order. I had Eve's voice in my head. "Now, you're sitting in the car: don't go checking that everything is in place. Just reach across to the glove compartment and open it. There you'll find the parking ticket and the correct Swiss coins. Drive slowly to the exit, it's at the back on the left. It's okay to drive slowly, people have crashes in carparks. Keep your hat on. This will seem strange, especially with you being so big inside the Volks, but you need it, I think, at least until you're through the cashier."

Out onto the open road.

It was then that my first taste of real life began. The Volks was a hopeless trundler compared to the big-engined Caddys that I was used to, I had to go slow and wait for long gaps in the traffic, but this didn't worry me. To be alone. To be unknown. Eve had chosen this particular vehicle because it had an anti-glare frosting of blue across the top of its windscreen and so I felt safe in there, private. I kept the windows wound up. I was still inside a bubble. For so many years, I had realised, I'd been inside a bubble. But now the bubble was free. I did as I'd been told, got onto the highway which, according to the big signs, would lead me to Berne, and just moved along with the rest of the traffic. To be out in the world and to be managing – I was so proud.

"Don't you start noticing things," said Eve. "Don't get interested. You have the rest of your life for that." And she was right. But I couldn't help noticing the mountains. I'd never seen anything like them, such bright, jagged things hanging in the air. People climbed those – I found this unimaginable. I vowed, right then, that I was going to get to the top of a mountain. I was thrilled by this thought – that you could see something and just decide to go and be part of it.

To be on another continent.

But at the same time the mountains were producing other feelings in me. I had a sense of them watching. Eve had told me that they would surround the lake where I was to swim. They will shine in the night, she said. When she told me this I had a nice picture of something friendly, like a kind of fire glowing warmly in the sky. But these mountains were nothing like that. They were hard, cold. They were going to watch me die.

Gradually, as the day passed, this thought took hold of me. This was the place I was going to die. This was the end of my name, the end of the Tarzan story. I was going to die, live – just as I'd entered the Army live, these mountains were going to watch it happen. A voice – not Eve's voice – began to say to me, Do you want this, really? Why don't you just keep driving? You've got a fistful of dollars, you could just have a bit of a ramble, and then go home . . . The more I listened to this voice the better I knew to whom it belonged. Skip was talking to me. For so many years now he'd been there at my side, fixing things, pointing me. He would be frantic, right now – on the phone to the Colonel, who would be sending out every kind of APB. "Find him!"

But Eve had anticipated this, too. "All kind of thoughts will occur to you. Unimaginable thoughts." This is what she told me, over and over. "You will think things no one can anticipate. You have had such a life, Tarzan. You will have to be careful. The time to decide is not on that day. You have to decide now. Once you start on that day, you have to believe that everything is already decided, and stick to the plan. And you will have to keep doing that, more or less, for a number of years." Oh. She was right, of course, and I had listened to her, and thought, and agreed. But now, on the road, in the little European car, with a tank of gas, and new countries in every direction that you looked, this was different. Beneath those mountains, to be choosing to die – this was hard.

"You can't buy food," she had told me. "You have maybe eight hours to kill. You can't buy anything. Drive along the lakeside, find a parking lot, and gaze at the view. Listen to the radio if you want. If anyone even glances your way, just start the car and move on. There's no reason why you shouldn't drive for the entire time, if you have to. But don't turn up early at the place you'll swim from."

Dear Eve, those steady grey eyes, watching over me.

So I drove. Many thoughts now began to come into my head. Partly it was the pills, I had become so used to functioning behind them, but that was my usual functions – order a burger, change channels. Now the world was coming at me, in something like a stream, the world was flowing towards me, and the flow just set me off. Soon my head was full of voices and faces and pictures. Meanwhile I had to avoid causing a wreck.

After an hour or so on the motorway I saw the sign, Lac Gorte, and took the exit. The slip road took me down a long slope, through slim trees – to either side I glimpsed delicate, slender trunks. Couldn't I just hide in there? Then the lake itself. Theoretically its colour was blue but this was only the colour a child would have chosen from a box of paints. In fact it was black, anyone could see that. And above it the mountains were black too, irregardless of their shining white – it was a black white. I found the layby that Eve had described, ten minutes short of the village, and parked. When I got out I was shivering, despite the coat and the hat. Around the parking lot was a low stone fence, with a gap in it, and a gravel path. When I took the path the gravel crunched.

The sense that I was being looked for was overwhelming.

The mountains, the water, the water's edge – as Eve had said, along to the left stood a large spreading tree and, close by, an attendant group of smaller trees. Their leaves were beginning to turn, to dry out. Soon they would fall. It didn't pay for me to be looking at those leaves. It didn't pay for me to look at anything – everything had a sign of life in it, or death. I just scanned the area, placed things. The trees, then a slope of dirty gravel, then the water's edge, where the lake wash slopped. I glanced along to the right. In fact, according to the plan, I was not to use that particular layby, there was another, further along, a ten minute walk away. Eve's idea was that this little gap between parked car and pile of clothes would confuse any early investigators, give me more time. But, now, in my daylight reckoning, I was starting to have thoughts of my own. Wouldn't they find my footprints in the gravel along the lake shore? So shouldn't I walk up and down as though I was trying to decide? Or would it be more natural if I just parked close by here, walked straight into the water? Acted on some impulse long harboured? Now I remembered Speed in Hollywood, talking me through my lines – try to figure your motivation, Tarzan.

Across the water, somewhere, was my destination – would the plan work? Did I want it to, really? My head was beginning to spin and I knew at once that all I had was that plan, that it might not be perfect, but if I started trying to think I would end up rocking back and forth on the shoreline as though I had slipped a cog. So I did as I had been told – drove the Volks along, found the next layby, parked alongside the cars that were there. I saw that in the next-door car a couple were drinking coffee from a thermos, that they would have nothing to look at but me, and I backed out again. But, no problems there, it was just a layby, I could find it again, and I turned back, took the slip road, and got back onto the motorway. The autobahn.

More driving. I couldn't think of anything else to do. The sun sank, the daylight crept away. The air turned chill, I was forced to turn on the heater, and became drowsy. A sleep would be nice. I had reached Berne by now, made a circuit of a roundabout, and started back. Just driving. Trying not to think. No one was looking for me, no one cared. I told myself this. But, after the life I had led, it was difficult to believe that you weren't turning heads.

Skip, the Colonel, everyone at home, searching, searching.

I found another layby – these nowhere places were where I spent my last hours – tipped my hat down over my eyes, and tilted the seat back. I still had my shades on.

When I surfaced it was dark. I felt terrible – my mouth was thick, cracked. I remembered Eve had told me that I would need water, when the pills started to wear off, and I felt under the seat. There was the canteen. As I drew it out the back of my hand touched something clammy. The neoprene.

Now all sense of freedom was gone. Now I had to stick to the plan. I strongly resented this, I could feel myself fighting it. But Eve had been stern on this point. "You won't escape all at once. It'll take work to get free. You will really have to work hard – as hard as you've ever worked, Tarzan." And so, grimly, I put in the hours. All the time the fear was rising inside me. I've always been a good swimmer, and for weeks now I had at Graceland been getting myself into the pool each day and floating, imagining myself in the lake. Plus I would have the wetsuit. But my body was fat, bloated, my arms hung like sausages. I had no power inside me, only pills, which were giving me the shakes.

I forced myself to remove my shades. I felt naked without them – it's your eyes you have to hide, isn't it. I stared about, straining at the dark. My watch was still on Memphis time. Maybe I'd overslept? My heart was pounding as I started the engine and headed back to the autobahn.

A clock on a gas station said it was 11:22. Three hours.

I drove to Zurich, turned again, and started back. Killing time. In yet another layby, my fourth of the day, I sat, rocking slightly, my fat body full of worry, full of pills. I had finished the water and my tongue was swollen again. There would be nothing to drink now until I crossed the lake. I couldn't wait, and yet I was shivering, afraid of what was to come.

These events, of forty years ago, are perfectly preserved, like a movie, in my mind.

Now my watch, which I had adjusted, told me it was 1:03. Eve had said the best time was between one and two. Closer to two. What I had to watch for was people out giving their dog a late walk. Europe is full of dogs, and insomniacs – there's plenty that prevents them from sleeping over there.

As I had done earlier, I drove to the appointed spot, which was empty of cars, took the heavy plastic bag from under the driver's seat, wiped the interior down with the chamois cloth in the bag, wiped the canteen – reached down into the darkness under the dash and wiped the brake and transmission pedals. Locked the vehicle. Started walking. I looked back, once. The homely Volkswagen, sitting in the dark of the parking lot, looked like some familiar and intensely personal object that I was leaving forever. No looking back, Tarzan. I walked at first on the gravel but it crunched loudly so I took to walking on the grass. What had Eve said about this? Nothing. I looked both ahead and behind. No one. The lake slopped noisily, there was a kind of under-suck. I came to the trees. No one. I wished now that I would see another human being. I wanted to say something to someone – last words. No, that's not true. I wanted a justification for delay.

I stood in the shelter of the tree and looked across the water. This was my last hope. If the light wasn't there – but no. There she was, the Angel, high on the mountain slopes across on the distant shore. She was another reason why Eve had chosen this lake. The Angel was what I was to swim for. I looked at her, shining so pale there against the black snow, and I hated her.

I waited ten, twenty minutes, for someone to rescue me. This plan, that damned plan that kept on working.

It is shameful to tell this, how I trembled on the brink. How I procrastinated. But such a situation was extraordinary, even in a life like mine. Some people took terrible risks to save themselves, fugitives, desperate refugees, but did I have to save myself? Couldn't I just hang on, inside my bubble, continue being Tarzan? Beside any large body of water that you are going to swim in there is always a chill wind, which makes you ask, Do I really want to? This wind was in my face now, my ears were full of the slopping, sucking sound – was it getting louder? Finally, in anger that for once there was no one there when I wanted them, I threw down my bundle and began undressing. And now Eve's voice was there to help me. Wonderful Eve, who had a real brain and went over this thing inch by inch ahead of me and figured what I would be feeling, and spoke words into the phone, that now came into my head, as though the phone was implanted there, they played like a recording and helped me. She said, "At the edge of the water, make yourself go slow. Be methodical. It's actually the last thing you have to do right. Be brave. It won't be easy to get undressed there in the dark. Try to imagine you're in your bedroom, leave everything neat. Don't think too much. Just keep working at it."

So that is what I tried to do. If someone had come along at that moment I would have embraced them, shoved my famous face into theirs, crooned *Love Me Tender* – but no one came. I had begun to shiver. Partly it was the cold. But the pills were wearing off now and I had a hole opening inside me. Naked, I unfolded the neoprene wetsuit from the bag. It was the best model American money could buy, equipped with zips for ease of entry, but it seemed to be an age before I was inside it. Then I felt sick, it was so hot and clammy, and at my joints it bunched horribly.

But finally I was in. Now there were only the final tasks to get right.

"Put the keys around your wrist." I did so. "Zip the plastic bag into the front of the wetsuit." Check. "Put some nice fresh fingerprints on the canteen and place it so it won't roll into the water." Check. "Don't – don't! – absolutely make sure you do *not* put on the flippers while you're on shore, or even in the shallows. They will search the mud for footprints. If they find the slightest hint that you had swimming gear they will search for you forever. Then, go."

The hardest thing was the greenstone. That beautifully slim thing, cool, with the deep-water colours inside it, I broke Eve's sequence for that stone. I should have removed it before I began putting on the suit. Out of one skin and into another. To the last, I wasn't sure I would leave it. As I held it in my hand, warm from my body, I remembered finding it, in the dirt, upslope from the valley where I'd lived with the gorillas. I spoke to that stone as though it were human. Doesn't that sound dumb. It sounds wet. But it's what happened. I said to it, "You will go home. Someone will take you back to where you came from. And I am going home too. I am going back. I will meet you there." This terrible stuff, coming out of my mouth, there on the edge of a lake in the middle of the night in Switzerland. Carefully I placed it inside the shoes, its treasure box. What the Maori people who made it would call a waka huia. Not that I knew what a waka huia was, then.

I must have shifted from foot to foot on that lake shore for at least twenty minutes. Then all in a rush I was making my way out into the water. My feet were bare and the lake's bottom was alternately sharp and slimy. I was so fat, I had lost so much of my grace – I felt I was inside two skins, the wetsuit, and then the layer of fat that, somehow, wasn't actually me. I was a little thing, deep inside, twisted by pills. But the cold brought me out of that. It made me know that this was really happening. Suddenly I saw clearly what I had to do – I had to make all this suffering worth it. The plan was going to work. In that instant I knew I had been splashing loudly and I calmed myself, sank into the water and, letting the wetsuit take my weight, began to paddle slowly out into the darkness. The flippers under my arm hampered me, but I just took my time. The cold water splashed on my face, came round my wrists and ankles. Quite soon however the suit began to warm my body.

Putting on flippers, strange flippers, in water that is over your head, in strange water, in the dark, without losing one, it's difficult. Fortunately they floated – I got one on then started on the other. Then I looked up, found the Angel on the hillside, and began to swim.

28

The Angel of Gorte was built by the villagers of that place at the end of the nineteenth century after a baby boy, who had been missing for two days, was found in the shallows of the lake, not drowned, but splashing happily. She was placed on the slopes of the alps directly across from the village so that the villagers could see her, hovering there. Originally she was made of wood and painted white, and the custom was to light fires at her feet late on Saturday night so that she might be visible through the dark hours of the Sunday, but in 1927 a fire was built too big and she burned to ash. Then, after the Second World War, in which the village lost not a house nor a son, it was decided that she should be rebuilt. This time she was made of concrete and steel and coated with white plaster. This time the lights were electric and, since that day, they have shone, so that you can see her, above the lake, wings spread, long drapes of white, head bowed. I have been back to have another look at that angel.

I've been back to have another look at just about everything.

I've stood on the shoreline at Lac Gorte, with the plaque that bears Tarzan's name at the base of the trees behind me, and looked out, and remembered. In fact the swim was no big deal. I had the wetsuit, I had the flippers, I had Eve. "Every five minutes or so, stop and have a good look, right around the clock, for local boats out night fishing. You mustn't be seen or even heard. Just keep swimming directly towards the Angel. There's no hurry." The big deal was inside me. I was afraid I would have a heart attack, it was so long since I'd done any sustained exercise. Even in the cold water I could feel myself sweating, a horrible feeling. The water kept slapping me in the face. But that was good for me. I tried to think about the gorillas. Now I could go and see them all again. Kerchak would probably be dead now but Bo and Jimpi might still be around. I'd seen a documentary called *Tarzan's Ape Years* and there were some gorilla faces I thought I recognised, though television distorts everything. I would see Kala's tree again. I would see the cabin. These were the pictures I made myself concentrate on as I swam. My arms flopped, my kick was feeble. But it was only two and a half miles. But I wouldn't see Jane again. This was a source of real sadness to me and as I was out in the middle of the lake, where the pull down into the deeps was supposed to be the greatest, this is where I thought of her. I could feel a great weight of loss down under my belly and I wallowed. The girls – there would be no more girls. No more fans. No more music. So what would there be? No more Eve. Nothing. Jane was gone. It was all gone.

There were no fishing boats.

Mrs Presley was gone too. But now I heard her voice, she came through for me. "That angel is liftin' you, Tarzan, feel her liftin' you. You're just floatin' in her light." It was a comfort to remember her, she had always been so kind. And it was true that I felt buoyant. That was the wetsuit. Also, there was the story of that baby boy, who hadn't drowned here. And then on the other hand there was the pull of the deeps, that never gave up their dead, and the mountains, shining in their own way as brightly as the Angel, but black-faced, stern. The greenstone was calling me back, Skip and the Colonel were calling to me, the fans were calling, "Come back!" Between these things I passed, in the twist of their forces, going on, swimming on, through the dark water, to arrive, beneath the Angel, at the farther shore. The first thing I heard was slapping – water on wood. It was the marina.

I lay in the water, panting. There were pains in my arms, my thighs, but not large pains. This swim had been no epic. And yet I was marvellously pleased with myself. It was all working out. Shading my eyes against the upper brightness of the night, I studied the layout of the place. Yes, there in the gloom were the numbered piles which marked the various entrances. There was the pile with the figure 3 in white upon it. The boats were tight-packed, their bows jostled. Moving quietly now, like a log low in the water, I flippered my way down that row, in the same way I had searched the Zurich parking lot. Row three, left hand side, third craft in. The *Yilmaz* – a touring yacht of the type you see in the eastern Mediterranean, wooden, faded, but with a long, easy sweep to her lines, riding shoulder to shoulder with white-gleaming neighbours. At her stern there was, as advertised, a wooden ladder which dipped and then rose above the now oily surface of the water – I was holding my mouth clear. As silently as possible I approached. Above, masts and lines of rigging swayed, an uneasy motion, and the water slapped like a circle of idiots. But everything here was touched by the faint light of the Angel.

"The ladder is slippery," said Eve, "and don't lose your flippers. And don't throw them ahead of you." The angel is inside you – that was Mrs Presley again. Up I went, awkward, slow, suddenly the tiredness hitting me as the support of the water fell away and I had to carry my weight. At the top of the ladder I lost my footing and fell into the boat with a loud thump.

No one came.

I lay on the deck for as long as I could bear it, listening to the terrible sound of my breathing. What had I done to my body? Once it had been such a pleasure to me. Now it was like an outer person, a stranger, who I lived inside. Ah, the temptation to just lie there, to just give up.

But finally I collected the flippers, crawled across the decking, fitted the key that was on the chain round my wrist to the lock of the deck-house door, and crawled inside.

For three months, an entire lifetime, I lived below, in the belly of the *Yilmaz*. The curtains were always drawn. The air was always stale.

And I became even weaker. I could not move – I was not allowed to make any sound. My body hung from me. Mostly I slept. This was no huge problem. It was as though I had ten, twenty years of rest to catch up on. I ate dried fruit, raw vegetables, food from tins, drank water from bottles. To a degree I starved myself. I wasn't interested in food – suddenly, food disgusted me. My body didn't get any stronger but, after a while, there seemed to be less of it. The pills signalled that they were passing from my system by causing me to shake – it was as though they were forcing me to wave them goodbye. I would wake, gasping, and drink gouts of water.

The hardest thing was not to talk loudly to yourself.

The *Yilmaz* belonged to Dr Ünlü, who was Turkish, a plastic surgeon who I had contacted on my first visit to Zurich. He had agreed to help me change my face. Discretion, he said, was his business. For a price, he could be very discreet. From there it was only a matter of money and arrangements. He seemed a good bet, Eve and I agreed on this. He was already somewhat removed from the world, in that he was blind.

Every few days he would arrive at the boat and would work upon my face. These were difficult periods – Ünlü's fingers tugging at my cheeks, pinching my jaw. He injected me against the pain, and I kept my eyes firmly closed, but nothing could prevent the images that formed in my head. I could feel his breath on my cheek as he worked. *Now the blade is cutting to your jaw – it wasn't your flesh that winced but your chemicals.*

That was during the night. During the day he would sit in a chair up on the deck, listening to music – I would listen too. Sometimes he would try to find a radio station in English so that I could hear the news. Through the painkillers, through the deck, over the sound of the water lapping against the hull, I strained to catch a word.

After he had handed over fresh supplies of water and food he would lock up and leave. But in a certain way he was never gone from me. Like the Angel, he hovered. As I lay on my bunk the image of his face was above me – a face alert to the messages of his fingers. He was the only human being I saw and so I relished the sight of him. His skin was tan, like that of his Turkish countrymen, with a greying frame of hair, and a stern jaw that, on the weekends, was heavy with bristle. An expressive mouth, though it was usually closed. Thick eyebrows over milky eyes. The eyes were closed also – you could see them, but nothing could be read. But above them the brow was wide and open. Here everything he was seeing was visible to you too. What was it, an inch, maybe two, of skin, and yet his brow seemed like a countryside on which shadows moved, seasons. I would study this face, collect it – blind, it nevertheless seemed perfectly aware of my scrutiny.

And then I would be alone, again, with my own face stretched and aching, bandaged, my body again filled with drugs.

My only diversion was a biography, written by Eve, typed

out by her on four pages of white paper, of a man who had been born in 1935 in Little Rock, Arkansas. *My name is Marshall Sturt. A year ago, skiing in Squaw Valley, I went out of control and sustained a bang to my head, here, above my right ear.*

Eve had said to me, "Sorry about the bang on the head thing, it's a cliché. But I think you need it. You do kind of pause to think before you speak, which is only a sign that you have a brain. But until you get used to being Marshall I think your pauses might for a while get even longer, and you need some cover for that."

My father, Clifford Sturt, according to the biography, was an apiarist – a bee keeper. We called him Cliff. It was all there: my marriage to Jean, who died of cancer in 1972. My work as a helicopter pilot, a vocation I was no longer able to pursue because of the head-bang, my hobbies – harmonising barbershop, dog training – my friends Wojak and Jim, my mother Carla. My dog Bo, a Labrador-cross. I intended to find work as a driver, maybe a truck driver, or maybe just local deliveries, I wasn't sure, and I was trying to move on, to find a new place to settle, but for now, as long as I was careful, thanks to the insurance, money wasn't a problem . . . My only problem was the sadness about Jean, which meant I had to keep moving on . . . "Of course these are just the bones," said Eve. "You have to put in the rest. Make it true. You should imagine every scene. Imagine yourself playing in your yard with Bo while your wife Jean smokes a cigarette and reads a magazine on the lounger – which magazine? Look out for details that will make your story seem true. Probably no one will question you, really – people just aren't that interested, not if you seem ordinary. It's only if something doesn't fit that they start asking."

So I did as she suggested. In the rocking, dim belly of the *Yilmaz* I would see myself walking up the aisle with Jean, see myself kissing her. I liked the name Jean, I liked the way Eve had done that, married me to Jane, made Kala my mother, connected my old life to my new one. Jean and me in our happy home, left to me by my father, I decided, after he died in the car crash, there were still hives on the property. Of course I had never really learned how to look after them, Dad always said honey was for the birds, a fool's way to make a living, but it was nice to go down into the orchard with a book, read down there while the bees buzzed away in the background. Yes, we always wanted to have children – slapping sounds as the little waves of the marina came against the side of the boat. Foreign voices, engines. And then when Jean died of cancer, well, it was hard to care, really – I just rented the property, took off. Actually, I've never been much of a skier.

Dr Ünlü didn't ever shift the *Yilmaz* from its mooring. He simply used it as a holiday home, a place to come. It reminded him of his boyhood, apparently, in a fishing village in Southern Turkey, called Bozburun, where such boats had always been moored, he said. Bozburun was where I was headed, next.

Finally the day came.

Ünlü took me up on deck. It was early evening, a weekday, dusky, late enough for most people to have left the marina but not so late as to seem suspicious. I stood, swaying somewhat, in my coat and hat, no shades, but I did have a pair of glasses with clear lenses which changed the shape of my face and obscured my eyes. Plus there were the bandages, of course. However, no one was watching. I took in huge lungfuls, looked cautiously around. There were the mountains, quite beautiful now, and there was the lake, with its dank smell that I knew too well, and there was the Angel, who had guided me. But Ünlü wanted to get going.

We took a taxi back to Gorte and then a late train to Zurich.

I kept my head down, a bandaged man leading a blind man, except that it was the blind man who knew where to go. People looked at us, sure, but they didn't look at me, not me by myself. That was my impression. I kept the brim of my hat low. The desire to stare around was intense, but I kept it buried – I was too busy coping.

And it had to be tried. All the preparations had been made. Now I had to go out into the world and see if I could pass.

I slept a night at Ünlü's house, then, at noon the next day, caught a flight from Zurich to Istanbul. This was tricky, I had to manage the passage through Passport Control with my new name and documentation, wearing the brown-tinted contact lenses that made me blink. I had always to remember not to speak out – "It's your voice which, finally, will snag in someone's memory," Eve had said. This was on the phone from California, from Ünlü's study. It was so good to hear her, I almost wept.

The passengers clapped as the pilot touched the plane down on the runway.

Then I was there – walking, alone, through Immigration and Customs, and then out into the concourse. People sitting on rugs, drinking tea from glasses, people with dark eyes in dark faces. Istanbul.

A taksi carried me to a hotel that took American dollars, sure thing Chief, I had a sweaty night and was woken at five a.m. by the call to prayer – was served olives and watermelon and cold boiled eggs for breakfast. Istanbul when I went out into it was impossible, terrifyingly crowded and busy, an anthill, but I had a mission, it was all written in my instructions, the plan worked out by Ünlü and Eve. A bus, overnight, to Marmaris, way in the south somewhere, more or less a straight line down the map, then ask for a dolmush, which apparently was some kind of a shared taxi, to Bozburun.

Find a pension, which was some kind of a hotel.

Turkey unseen, huge out the dark windows of the bus. Horns honking. Trying to sleep in the narrow seat.

Everything rushing at me.

And then I was in the dolmush, which was an old white Commer van, dusty, with nine other men, all completely uninterested in strangers. Polite men, a little bit formal after Americans, I liked them, with their heavy stubble and sweaty faces. They wore hats too. They didn't stare at me and I tried not to stare back. The air was full of brown dust. For an hour we swayed along dirt roads, I had to duck to see out the windows – glimpses of a burned, stony land. Then when we came down a steep hill, slowly, the brakes straining, there was the sea, radiantly blue. Round a corner and, dodging a running rooster, into the village – and I knew that Ünlü had sent me to a paradise.

I stayed in Bozburun for eight months

I walked in the hills, went swimming, ate carefully. My body began to change. Each morning in my room I did exercises. During the day I set myself challenges – run to the top of the stubby hill in eighteen minutes – and regained my agility, my sense of smell. I was proud of myself. But Eve's voice was always in my ear. "Move as though you're smaller. Shorter strides, be prepared to take the path that goes around people rather than straight ahead. Be just a little more stiff." This was difficult, when what I wanted to do was to make every step a huge one, to push myself – to run as though I was running myself into being someone else. The people who lived here strode out also. They moved as I did, easily, relaxed, and so I didn't worry too hard. Sure, I kept to myself, and I was always on the lookout for foreigners. Boats came to Bozburun, suddenly you heard English voices. But it seemed I had escaped.

It did feel like that – an escape from prison.

In my pension, two rooms at the top of a large white house called *Welcome*, I used the instructions Eve had given me to improve my writing. "Find a passage in a book, copy it out." Even today, my writing looks strange, like a handwritten imitation of type. "You have to be able to read and write if you're going to survive. And practice your *Marshall* signature." Sometimes the boats played music – *Me And You And A Dog Named Boo* – and I would sit upright at my table in the cafe and hold still, listening.

But mostly it was a world of roosters crowing, tractor sounds, the blue of the harbour, grey grizzled hills, dusty streets, fish making ripples, lizards, the call to prayer, a tortoise under a sharp-prickled bush, women in headscarves, warm loaves with a pale crack down the back. I loved to watch the people going about their lives. In America this had been hard to do, there was always a crowd looking back at me. Here I could walk slowly among the backyards, see the meals being cooked out among the animals. The lives of humans, I always want to see that. I have never really had my fill of that.

Gradually my bandages came off. I would spend hours at the mirror, trying to judge whether the broader nose, the cheekbones, the thicker jaw were enough. Outside I always wore sunglasses and a hat, plus a full beard – surely?

Enough for what, exactly? I now had a good version of my past worked up, names, pictures I could call on – but what pictures could I see that constituted a future? Eve had never said anything about that. I saw myself sitting in my room with a girl and her slowly peeling the hat away from my head. The shades. "Why don't you shave? There's something about you . . ." Would I run? Or would I trust her? Or would I have to keep playing a game?

Bozburun was cheap, cheap, I could have lived there forever. But I wanted to see things. That was it. I wanted to see the world – to see what the world was. One morning when the call to prayer came I was already up, at the balcony rail, watching the fishing boats putter out through the entrance to the harbour and I thought, I'll go too. By midday I was packed, paid up, hat on, shades, and was waiting for the midday dolmush with four of the villagers. No one waved me goodbye. But as the van groaned up out of the town I felt a new sensation – the goodbye blues. I'd been at peace there. I had a life, of sorts, but I was leaving. I remembered leaving the gorilla valley and, later, leaving Jane. It was as though, then, I didn't know what I was being parted from. I had never really had a home, not a place I had chosen, or even a place that had chosen me. Those two rooms in Bozburun, with the view of the harbour, how peacefully they had contained me, and yet they were guest rooms. As the engine of the van roared I saw that I was a kind of guest, a visitor to the lives of other people. I did want to see the world. But also I was looking, for a place I would not have to leave.

For a month I took local buses and was in that countryside, looking, looking. At Olympos there were ruins, cold stones that had once been warmed by people, and, high on a mountainside, in the night, blue flames which sprang from bare rock and had burned there for two thousand years – a mystery. At Üçagiz the ruins were under water, you saw steps going down a cliff-face to wobbling blue rooms that fish swam through. Every village, every bus stop had something to see from a world of human lives that had, so long ago, made a mark before leaving. The Turkish people would show you and explain, knowing that you would be interested, but they themselves simply lived among these things. I saw that just to look, to have what your eyes could give you, a piece of the world, this was a big part of what the people who came to stare at Tarzan had been after. Another world that was your world.

But I wasn't only seeing. There were so many little ways to learn. Waiting, for instance. In America, Tarzan had never waited for anything. Whatever you asked for arrived, right now. He had never queued. The way the body must go into a float at these times, the way that you must observe the turning of the shadows, must simply hang in the air while, tick, tick, drip by drip, the minutes pass. I tried to think but the sun beat down, you can't always be thinking.

And so I began, quite casually at first, to look for those spaces that had been described to me by Delmo McMullins. In courtyards, bus stations, seated in a rectangle of shade and waiting for a connection, I would gaze about from under my hat, searching for angel places.

I returned to Istanbul and made myself endure the crush of that anthill city. Wah – this was humankind. The way the faces streamed at you, when you walked down through the covered bazaar, it was clear that they were endless, would always keep coming, and that the singleness that you felt inside was something replicated every fifteen inches by the next man and the next and the next. As Tarzan I had been tight-pressed by crowds, but beyond them I could see the car, the hotel, a walled and private space of some sort. Here, your flesh was always going to be pressed, you were always going to be reminded of how you were replicated. How common you were.

I crossed the Bosporus, took local trains down through Greece, alert always for those who spoke English. There were more of them here. I avoided anyone who would speak to me – inside my head I was always practising what I might say. From Athens I flew to Cairo and rode a swaying camel out across the rippling sands to see the pyramids. The Sphinx gazed above my head. So was this an angel's face? Had the Sphinx actually been an angel? No. This face was pitiless, a quality which might be part of what was in an angel's face, but surely an angel was also devoted to recognition?

Yes, I realised there in the landscape of sand: the quality of an angel was intimate. She was the one who had read the book of your life. The more I thought about this, the more I was sure of it. The spaces I stared into had the faintest glow, I noticed, as though a residue had been left there. Sometimes you had to look away to catch this, or wait for the right time of day. Which corresponded with what Mrs Presley had told me, that a visit from an angel would leave a trace inside you.

The Sphinx simply absorbed whatever you gave it.

Working it all out in my head while beneath me the camel trod and trod. The angel spaces were areas for which there was no other purpose. The world used everything that it could, anyone could see that. But there were vacant corners, eddies, sites that had no worldly purpose. Here the memories collected, the abandoned feelings, the lost impulses. This is what attracted the angels, I decided, whose task it was to record all – especially what you had forgotten – and give it back to you for your use on Judgement Day.

In Cairo I bought a camera and began to take photographs of those angel places. And I now began to direct my travels towards seeing faces. Not an angel's face, you can't pursue that directly, but on the one hand the faces in my old book from the cabin, my first bible – all the tribes of the world. In Ghana, in Chile, among the Inuit I travelled, and ate their food, and walked beside them. Slept in their dwellings. And on the other hand I looked at the faces they had made to watch over themselves. Some of these were painted, some were carved in wood. But the faces I stared into longest were carved in stone. In the museums was where you saw most of these, now, so old that many of their features were gone. A shaped stone, two metres high, in a sunny room at the rear of the Museum For Ancient Man in the district of Mitte, in Berlin, in West Germany . . . outside in the garden a busker is playing *Für Elise* on an electric piano and it comes faintly into the high-civilised, temperature-controlled room, where there are amber beads and hammered bronze hairpins and skinny daggers, all laid out inside glass cases, numbered and dated, with a history of how in the nineteenth century these things were scratched from the dirt and brought here to rest – here he stands. The little white card which is all he has now for a name is on the floor beside his feet, it's in German and I can't learn much from it, only that he's from the sixth century BC and is maybe from Syria – there's a question mark. As tall as I am, chunky, this standing stone, his colour is dark, a black-grey that has some red in it. He has stumpy little legs, stumpy arms, a square chest, a big block of a head. Time has knocked most of the chips from the block. Almost all his features are now gone, in the cold stone now there are just faint hollows for eyes, the ghost of a line where his nose descended, white, and then, as you stare, his mouth can be made out. It's down-turned. And in the museum light of the room you stare into his face and because it's expressive it's the mouth that finally your gaze falls on. Why so grim? Did the people wish to say to the world, If you fuck with us you'll be sorry? It's possible, but I don't think so. No, he seems to me to be something they made for themselves. Okay, but to say what? To remind themselves to do right, because they will never be forgiven? To say that nothing stands in the face of time? His eyes don't follow you. He doesn't see you. None of these figures see you. They gaze, like the Sphinx, like the Colonel, out towards something that is so remote that you can't imagine what it might be. Some people say they were built by spacemen and I can understand the idea, that they have their eyes on the distant home. But this is not what I think. To me these faces, which now stand mostly in museums, they were the stone end of a scale – the terrible silence which is moved by nothing, which sees starving children with swollen bellies, the terrible waters which rise, the absences of water, the way that blood is let out of bodies to run into the soil, on and on through every moment of the world's existence, and is not moved. Won't speak. And along at the other end? Well, this is why you can only laugh at the stone angels that you see, tragic-faced, in graveyards. Stone wings with stone feathers – these never flew. At the other end of that scale there is only light, and faint light at that, almost nothing. But at the angel end every tiny tremor within you is known.

I had never seen an Aboriginal of Australia and so I worked my way down through Indonesia, catching local boats, hopping from island to island, until I came to the biggest island of them all, hanging there on the underside of the globe, baked hard by the sun, where the shadows seem so long and the dust has been stirred and stirred. I had been Marshall Sturt now for four years, and now I was coming home, it seemed like that, partly because the gorilla valley was just across the water now, in New Zealand, but also because of the explorer, Captain Charles Sturt, from whom I had borrowed my aftername. In Australia, everyone remarked on that Sturt and I would nod and say, no, I'm not related, but I know about him. That was okay – as long as you knew. But also home because I saw at once that never had I been in a place where the traces of the angels were so thick on the ground. Every tree had an angel face. Such a dried-out land. At dusk I would walk through the city parks and my scalp would rise. You could hear the birds calling, strange sounds from a singular continent, but under that was a tone that was so loud, so deep that it was astonishing that everything didn't fall flat before it. And everywhere I looked the faded yellow light, loaded with dust, would gather in, say, the space between two trunks – under a bench, in a gateway – and you would be aware of a shape forming, a pattern of light that all but had features.

For several years I had been using coloured film to capture these places, and having my photographs developed by any old chemist. Finally one man, this was back in Cape Town, said to me, "Son, what are your pictures of?" *Pictures orv.* "There is nothing in them." He wore a white lab coat, and had a round brown head like a beaten copper balloon, a little dented, with just some strings of hair glued across the top of it. I told him, angel places, and he stared at me and then asked if he could look at the pictures again. He was standing close to me and I could feel the beefy weakness of him, he was blown up too big and was going to die soon – he knew this too and he was afraid, you could feel that fear in him, that his life of eating up large now had to be paid for. He gave the pictures back to me and he said, "You won't get what you want, that way. Are these what you want?" and his thick finger flicked the packet that held the photographs. Well, he was right, I was always disappointed in the photographs, but that hadn't bothered me, I had got what I was after when I pressed the shutter. He said, "You will need black-and-white film, and you should learn to develop your own pictures. If you would like I will teach you."

So I stayed in a hostel and each night I went to the darkroom at the side of his big, gated house (black-and-white, darkroom, these at that time were loaded words in South Africa) and he showed me how to make the images come floating out of the liquid. The chemicals there made you dizzy. In the plastic tray the pictures came swimming up. Each time I was almost afraid. These were his pictures, of course, he took snaps of his family, of his home and garden and shop. I didn't understand what his pictures were for. It seemed that he just liked the idea that you stood dizzy in this dark room and something came towards you, proof of what you had acquired, maybe. If you could prove you had managed to surround yourself with the things of life then you could say you were alive – was that it?

I could have talked to him about that.

Anyway – after that I used black-and-white film and carried it with me, in a black-lined bag, waiting until the day I found a place to stop, where I could set up a room to do my own developing. By the time I reached Australia that bag was getting pretty full.

Up north, I visited the Aboriginals but I left my camera behind. I knew they wanted to keep their souls. This idea had begun to worry me, that having so many pictures taken of myself had taken something away. Did I have a soul left? The Aboriginals liked me, so maybe that was a good sign – that's what I thought, then. But I was only a guest, only a visitor to their lives. I climbed their rock and all the time I was trying to look at them – I thought they were maybe like the me I had been when I lived among the gorillas. But they know what you're doing. They don't like you being on their rock, you can tell it, and they don't like themselves for allowing you to come, and the whole thing is bad. The Aboriginals don't look good, you see them drunk or just sitting and you think about what Australia should do. Now that I live here I have come to care about that.

But at that time I had had other business. I said, well, that's Aboriginals crossed off your list – that's what I told myself, and I started to look around at other things. There really is no place like Australia for things – everywhere you look there is another thing that is Australian. Everything here has got total Australia in it. It occurs to me, has occurred to me now for some years, that Australia is the next America. Increasingly, I see the world looking this way and I ask myself: is that why the angels are here?

These thoughts were just beginning, I think, to form in

me, when, back then, I started in earnest upon a new phase, which was the local, down-this-road-or-that search for somewhere that I might stop and sink my feet into the mud. I was starting to tire. For four years, I'd kept moving, if anyone gave me so much as a second glance I'd up sticks and be out of town in five minutes, but in fact the glances they gave me were probably no more than the kind of flicker you give everything that crosses your path. I had managed, by working on it, not to stand out. This I regarded as the final proof that I had joined the world of men – that they no longer needed to notice me. You could get bored of that. There were times when, in some endless queue or just hanging at a counter in a big store, waiting for service, there was the temptation to straighten up, shake my hips, and let rip with, "Hey, fellas, this don't move me! Let's get real, real gone for a change!" It was a strain at times, in the nothing moments, not being Tarzan any more. Sometimes I would look at a girl and think – then when she looked back I would shrink away as though I didn't mean it. I bought myself sex at different times, in Asia and in France – in Paris, stepping down the Rue St Martin, early evening, I saw a blonde cutie in a doorway and realised that she wasn't waiting for a bus, not in her underwear, and that I wasn't getting any younger. She dusted the cobwebs, but it gave me the blues. I wanted to lie back, to be with her. I wanted to have her round the place. Yes, that was it – I wanted to have a place. Tarzan didn't have a place. I never forgot that. So I wasn't tempted to go back to him, never – not really. But when it was raining, when I had the lonesome blues, definitely, the thought of singing my way back to Graceland, it did occur.

I took trains and buses. No hitchhiking, people do actually look at you then, I found, expect to be told a bit about you. I avoided the cities. Any place where there was a scene. I knew what I wanted, somewhere small, a cottage, an orchard. Beehives . . . An address. And a job – I had gradually come to this. To work is the most human thing and I had never done any. Big boss man – I'd had to get Speed to explain what the words meant.

Not that Speed was an item I thought a great deal on.

The plan I had was to circle the island, do the outline of Australia and see what I bumped into. I had this idea that if you went around the edge you would kind of lasso everything that was in the middle, really get hold of it, and maybe it would have worked, too, but then maybe not, because Australia is so, deep breath, big. The atlases fool you, you see it all by itself on a page and think, yeah, I can contain that shape. But on an atlas page it's not alongside anything, you can't compare. Man, this place really is the great southern land, it's miles. And I was tired when I began.

So I was drifting up the Gold Coast, I'd been beaching it, eating pineapples, getting sand in my hair, and then one day a wind got up and I had an idle thought – a sheltered valley, some green. And so I turned inland.

The names of the little places on the road out here are now like beads on a string, like crumbs on a trail, I have sat by the window with my map at dusk and said them over to myself – birds calling outside, the baked air just starting to cool. Kempsey, Coffs Harbour, Grafton, Lismore, these are the names. Nimbin. Then Longster. That's how I came here.

I guess there were maybe four hundred people in the town itself in those days. A main street, where the buildings all had high façades, like the set for a Western, except that behind the façades there were lives being lived. Hardware stores, you could buy hardware for Africa, and a bakery, three pubs, a bank – this was back in the days when every small town still had a bank and a post office. A little supermarket, a stock agent, a gas station – petrol, they called it. And in the back streets there were great, light-shafted sheds, where men hammered and drilled and welded and screwed. I guess you'd call it a rural service town. But it wasn't anything so definite. It was just a town. Longster. I couldn't say I even liked it, especially, not at first. It was just a quiet little place that couldn't give a damn about you.

I stayed in the hotel – the Golden Days – and wandered the back streets. The houses began to run out, I liked this, the road went quiet, you began to hear the sound of the land and the sound of the heat – it sang in your ears. Yes, this was the kind of place, where everyone was a survivor – but how do you find a house?

I saw the perfect place, a verandah-house among lofty trees. There was a garden, a display of flowers, a thick hedge, a gate – every colour softened by dust. You could go, I thought, through the gate in that hedge and just never come back. Of course someone had thought of this ahead of me. Nevertheless I approached. There was a dog, naturally, and he snapped at me, but I don't mind dogs and I stood holding him off until someone came, and looked around at the way you could make a garden be just like a room – so lived in, so everyday and personalised, but open-air. Dog, pond, umbrella, weathered furniture, all of it perfect. Also I could see the angel places, in the corners, the dark angles of the hedge. And now here was the genius who had created all this fabulous ordinariness, a woman, solid, grey hair pulled back, hard face, hard like a resinous wood, and eyes bright like something a magpie might steal. She wiped her hands on her apron, glanced about to see that nothing had been stolen, then said up at me, "Whaddya want?"

Not necessarily unfriendly. I produced a piece of dialogue, the first time for years that I hadn't been intent on turning someone away. "Hello, I'm an American. I'm looking for a place in this area. Marshall Sturt is my name."

"A place?"

"A house."

She priced my sneakers, my jeans, my baggy tee. I could see she wanted to know what was in the backpack. So that she would trust me I took off my sunglasses and hat – people like to see the whites. "Somewhere to sleep?" she asked.

My heart was starting to pound. "Somewhere to stop for a bit."

How do you say to someone, I want to live here among you? No one would say that, I knew it, it's like saying, I want us to get married. No, you have to make it that you have a definite reason, nothing to do with them, some driving and personal need, that forces you to be here, in this place which they already know is not paradise, some reason that means we didn't choose each other, we are just forced to be together, so we have to get on with it – this can work.

Now she was really having a look at me. Quickly I started in. "I'm a photographer. I want to do some work on my pictures." She was really staring now, I realised that I didn't have my coloured lenses in.

"You look like someone," she said – slow and considering. "That singer." She insisted that I hold her eye while she riffled through the faces in her index. How can you hide your face when someone is looking right at it? Then she clicked. "Barry Manilow."

"I'm not Barry Manilow," I said, with a big grin.

I saw that the grin had opened another part of her memory, and wiped it from my face. She was still struggling to drag something to the surface. But suddenly the hard work was done – suddenly she liked me – maybe she'd been a Tarzan fan? Anyway, she said, "Well, look – I know a place that might suit you. Go down the main road, there's a big gum fallen along there, it's buggered the fence – just past that, on the same side, knock at the pink house there and ask old

Dusty if he'd let you have a dink at his cottage. Where you from?"

"Arkansas. Little Rock, Arkansas. In America." I was tempted to sing her the Little Rock song but I knew for certain that that would be the last piece of her jigsaw.

She stood in her gateway, watching me go. I could see that her memory was still working, and in some ways I felt I owed her – definitely, I knew it inside, she had been a fan, in a cardboard box inside the big house she had all his records, and when her husband was out of town she would commune with him in the dark. As soon as I was out of sight, I sat down by the side of the road, put in my lenses, got my hat on. Then I set off to find Dusty.

And so it was that I managed to rent something. No cottage, it was more of a shed, that had been converted at one time for the use of cowhands. It was stuck away at the end of a long double-rutted driveway that ran past Dusty Hammond's place. I could see that, there, I would always be under his eye and so I didn't plan to stay forever, but it was a start. It was a place.

To sit on a kitchen chair outside your own back door, with your shirt off, with a beer. To doze. The whole of Australia is out there, endless miles of it. To listen to the sounds of nature. The shed was on a rough piece of land, there were stumps and scrub and powdery, dusty paths that wound between the eucalypts, every now and then there would be a noise that I rose to investigate – a lizard, mosaic-patterned along its breathing underbelly. A brown snake. A blue bird. I needed a book, I saw, with the names of everything. What, for instance, were those wonderful high puffy white clouds called? What did they mean? I needed thousands of books. Meanwhile I sat. I worked my feet into the dirt and let the sun give me a copper plating.

This lasted, oh, four days. A week.

Then I began to get itchy, energetic. I walked back into town, bought a bicycle, and really began to explore.

And now I am going to describe this place where I am sitting as I write this, because this is where this book is going to end.

It's so very strange to be coming to the end of this.

I can see now that I have come to the end of the story I wanted to tell – nearly to the end. I have a little list on my pad here at my elbow, there's things I still need to cover, but the list is getting short now. Yes, I'm going to finish. And so what I'm trying to be sure of is that I did what I intended. It's hard to know. I mean, I wanted to tell my story, but everybody wants to do that. But I also want this to be proof, which means that Loretta and little Theo will be beneficiaries of the Tarzan estate. I have, in my bank in Zurich, a book-length account of his part in Tarzan's death by Dr Ünlü, which he asked that I have published after my own death, that his grandchildren might benefit, and this will back up my story. I know that Lisa-Marie and the Tarzan Estate will contest Loretta's claim and that Lisa-Marie's sense of bewilderment, which I have read about and suffered over, her loss, will be enlarged. If there's a single thing on the planet which has ever really tempted me to return to being Tarzan it's Lisa-Marie. But the truth is, I never really knew her. I never really knew you, darling. I was never your daddy, was I; only your father. I play your CD, darling. I listen to you. Sorry to you, baby.

This I think will count against me on Judgement Day.

And the other thing I wanted to do in writing this book, and this is the thing which vexes me most, it has kept me awake nights all through these last seven months as I have spent each day trying to write this story down – the thing I want this to do is to make the world understand the intelligence that was inside Tarzan. Since his death the world has not thought well of him. It has shown him wobbling, gross, fat around the neck, bloated and pale. It has nutshelled him by saying twenty-eight hamburgers a day. By saying multiple Cadillacs and mountains of cuddly toys, showrooms of guitars and streets of houses – by saying girls and his Mafia and pink-and-black leather ceilings. It has said he was a victim of all that. And it's true that this was gross, and also that it's horribly dated now. But partly that is only because, since he was so utterly famous, we know about it – we still know what Tarzan-style was. Once it was the high style and everyone copied it. Please keep that in mind. And everyone has now told on the guy, everyone sold a piece of him and cashed in. Insult sells and they thought he was dead and wouldn't mind. So for many years he was a joke and I couldn't bear to think about him.

But gradually he came back. A man called Greil Marcus started it, I believe, he wrote an honest piece in a book called *Mystery Train*, and from that time people started again to listen. Then the giant biography written by Peter Guralnick – I wept over every page. It was like having life breathed into you again.

And so what I wanted to offer here was the fact that Tarzan was conscious in there. Alone on the inside, he taught himself to read and, as you can see, to write. How well he can write, this you will judge for yourself. That will happen when I am no longer around to argue for him.

But there is something I want you to understand, and if you don't then this book has failed. Something I want you to recognise when you next hear Tarzan's voice on your radio – because you don't have a CD of his, do you. Check your collection – no, I thought not. But, despite you, they are still selling. Hear me on this: the Tarzan estate is no small potatoes. People are still listening to him, and not all of them are eighty-year-olds. Check his listing on Amazon.com – over 5,000 items, every one of them for sale. So next time you hear him, don't think he was a commodity. It's true he was sold. But everything gets sold, on this planet. In the end, buying and selling, it's just how things move around the place. There's no shame in money, it's just a different kind of breathing, a different kind of air.

What I want is for you to listen for him in there. He didn't just open his mouth and make a noise. The guy was talking to you, in the only language he had at the time. He was giving himself to you and he wasn't saving any for later.

Make sure now that you don't listen to the dross. Dig out the good stuff. The Sun years, sure, but everywhere else there are moments where he really speaks. I'll give you one for starters. It's easiest to get on a recent compilation, *Tarzan Country*. He sings to the piano, just Floyd Cramer's quiet little chords, and his voice coming across the years, play it on the headphones, let the guy in – *Anything That's Part of You*.

This house wasn't much when I found it, rather ugly in fact, just a square old place, built Australian-style, up on legs so that the air can pass through beneath and cool it – I used to like to crawl in under there, though you had to mind the critters – and verandas and doors on every side. But what made the place, and continues to make it, is its setting. We're standing here on the edge of a drop. You didn't know that, as you read, but all the time we've been on the edge of a cliff. Out the front windows there's a lip, tufted with grass, and beyond it: nothing. When Theo grows, that lip will have to be fenced off. But the lip is not what you look at. If you want to you can go out and poke your nose over, look down, see the river, the old Mungeree lying looped and sluggish, way down below. But I never do that, these days – I know what's down there. Why should I look down? No, the place to look is out. Way out. There's Australia, brother, there's the MBA, as the locals say – Miles of Bloody Australia. There's nothing to see, particularly. Haze, and brown-grey plains, and drifting formations of dust. Green verticals, away to the left, that's gums, and there's patches of scrub. Patterns – it's all patterns. With the binoculars you can make out homesteads, follow vehicles along the roads, but why should you do that? What I like is the clouds, the way they roll across, draw shadows across the great stretch of land that lies out there. I have no desire to go there, any more. What I'd like is to *be* a cloud, something immense, soft and white, spread over the land – I'd like to feel it warm under my belly.

Okay, so I found the house and I began to dig in. I ordered books, I bought a vehicle, I had a skylight installed.

The first job I had was as a driver. It was a strange circumstance: a flu bug hit the town, everyone was sick or tending to the sick, it missed me because I kept to myself, and a man came to my door and asked me, could I drive? It was necessary that someone went to Lismore to pick up supplies of vaccine.

From this errand there grew, over time, the need for me to get a driver's license – Tarzan had never had one – a ute, a second ute, a small office with a Marlene to wrangle the phone and, eventually, a place to park and service half a dozen of the large, slat-sided vehicles that Australians use to transport livestock from farm to killing-place. This enterprise came to be known as Sturt's Movement, a name which pleased the locals and which got me out of town from time to time. Well, this is not the place to tell the story of my modest little success in business, it was straightforward enough, it simply served a need, which was not so much to give me an income as to provide me, finally, with the cover I needed to settle down properly in one location and become part of the known world.

For a time, in fact for a number of years, one of the Marlenes came here and was also wrangler of shopping, vacuuming and intercourse in this house, but eventually she accused me of watching her, of weighing and measuring her, she said, and there was I am afraid an element of truth in this. She found it spooky. I can only apologise. She was a species that was exotic to me, an ordinary person, seen up close and acting natural. I had been used to girls, pretty girls. This was a woman, she was so interesting – I used to follow her about, just observing. "And you don't love me," she said, bitterly, and unfortunately this also was true.

Ah, love. Now we're coming to it.

After I had driven every road in the district, had got out and examined everything worth a second glance, I began to travel again. This wasn't a return to the backpacking days, this was more fly-in-fly-out, visiting places or things I had read about. Now this I loved. To discover something in my books, the Komodo Dragon for example, and fly off to see one. And there he is now, the Dragon, all upright head and shoulders, up on his stumpy legs, rocking slightly in the Sri Lankan heat, a lizard big enough to tear half your thigh away. When I put him in my head next to the articulated skeleton of the Brachiosaurus that I had seen in a museum in Spain, its skull bumping the roof of the atrium, two stories high, I had a vision of a dinosaur planet where little men on two legs had better be good at running. These visions I did love – the dioramas I constructed in my mind. I visited the Nuba, drank cows' blood and milk – joined the hippies and watched the solstice sun rise at Stonehenge. Worked a season as a driver at McMurdo in the Antarctic. And, eventually, got to the top of the Empire State. This was a sentimental journey, and a risky one – the cult of Tarzan was alive and well at that time, the late 1980s in America, and people were sighting him in laundromats and checkout lines. There were, I read, a number of churches dedicated to worship of him and, when the Internet eventually came in, more Tarzan-Lives sites than you can shake a stick at (I have never found the origin of that expression). Even today the Internet has more on him that you could read in a lifetime.

I love the Internet. But for some things you actually have to go there.

So I had to go to the Empire State, in full disguise, and when finally I got to the top I couldn't sing. I kept my head down, chin tucked in, and then, on the viewing platform, while everybody else was looking out, I took my chance and looked up. I had been in airplanes, of course, which go miles higher, but to we humans impression is everything, and the impression here was that you could kiss the sky. Inside my head I sang to the clouds, which were moving above in stately formation. Inside that tumbling noggin of mine, that poor old swede, in there I sang my little heart out.

On a green hill
On a blue day
Your brown eyes
Looked my way
And told me,
With a smile,
That you were gone . . .

The tears poured down my face, the voice in me rose and the temptation to say, To hell with it, I'm really gonna sing was overwhelming – almost overwhelming. I remembered coming here with Sam Phillips and looking up. I remembered looking down from so many stages and seeing the tear-streaked faces of the fans. I remembered being on my rock, back in the gorilla valley, with the radio giving me the tune and the hawks flying, the looping fantails, the circle of trees – everything listening. I felt every impulse in me had finally arrived at a moment, at a spot of glory. There was no clapping, no audience. It was just a private thing.

Crossing things off my list now.

And then in the mid-1990s I finally gathered my courage and took a flight across the Tasman Sea and joined a package tour in Wellington, New Zealand, that was headed for the Tarzan Valley Experience.

I had just turned sixty but was still pretty vigorous – when finally you get there, sixty is nothing (hope I die before I get old). I figured that in a busload of Tarzan enthusiasts I might just bump into someone who would give me a hard second look and so I had to prepare extra-carefully. I bought a walking stick and practised walking with a stoop, so that my face might face the ground. I decided I would have a skin condition that was highly sensitive to the sun – unfortunate if you lived in Australia, but never mind – so that I could wear kinky zinky, a bright yellow daub on my lips and cheeks, and those huge wraparound sunglasses that old people wore over their spectacles at that time. In this get-up I was nearly rejected for the tour – "There's a fair bit of uphill walking, you know, Pops," said the booking clerk in the Wellington office. I waved my stick at him and growled.

By bus we did a return version of the trip that Jane and I had made, from Wellington to the Wairarapa – now the countryside looked ordinary to me, but, gazing out the window at the farms and fences, I could still recall what it had felt like to encounter civilisation for the first time, and the chemicals and electricity in me really started to brew. Then, by four-wheel-drive, we proceeded up the coast – of course there was now a sealed road, the Tarzan Valley was attracting about sixty thousand visits a year at that time; it's more these days. But the horizon hadn't changed and I stared at it, remembering the first time I had seen the ocean. Then finally, in wire cages on the back of four-wheeled motorbikes, we wound through the hills, to a point where they cut the engines and coasted down, through the bush, quiet please, so that we wouldn't scare the gorillas.

There was rubbish along the path. Coke cans and food packaging.

At the bottom of the hill we had to climb. Their helicopter had overflown earlier in the day and found where the main group were feeding. They were hard up against the wire fence, and it was a stiff ascent, especially if you had a stoop to maintain. But I had no shortage of energy. With every step the smells of that place were coming back to me. Oh, it was too much, way too much, and I was pleased I had thought to hide my face.

We got to within maybe sixty metres and then were asked to sign a second no-claims-for-damages form. "They *are* wild, you know," we were told, before the hardy few – in the end there were only twenty of us – climbed the last slope. And there they were, a stone's toss away. We were tucked in among the grasses and ferns, but they knew we were there. Ah, they looked sad. It was the fence, I think – there had never been a fence. They looked bored.

Nevertheless the temptation to go and join them was running in me. "The big one, he's called Taniwha," whispered the guide, "he's the boss, and that one there, he's Stallone, and that one, with the white spot, she's the one they're all after, she's called Babe." I could see that Babe was in fact male. "They've eaten now," he whispered, "and they're digesting all those leaves – they have an extra stomach." Actually what they were doing was simply waiting for us to go away – it was plain, they were pissed off. I couldn't look any more and I started back down the hill. "Pops!" hissed the guide but I kept on going. I wanted to take my shoes off, feel the dirt, and, sitting on a log, did just that. My paleface feet were too tender to do anything but tiptoe, but I didn't care. My head was just open, I was receiving all kinds of stuff, I could smell the bush, the flowers of the manuka, the flowers of the kowhai, the smell of the dirt and the damp, woody smell of the tree bark. I could smell the waterfall, I could hear the water splashing, feel its weight breaking on my back. Oh, I could see Jane, her body dashed with water, spray in the air and the sun shining on everything. My head was open but my heart was clenched inside me like a fist. You should never go back.

I went down the hill, carrying my shoes, stoop forgotten now, oblivious to the low, urgent calls of the guides – "Hey, Pops! Hey, fella!" – crossed the path, and headed upslope to the grove where – but it wasn't there. Everything had been changed. There was a picnic table, and beside it an arrow, *To Kala's Tree*, and so I followed the arrow – how the hell could I be needing directions here? – and came into a clearing that shouldn't have been there. At the foot of the biggest manuka they could find was a sign, *This is Kala's tree*. "No, it's not!" I shouted. The sign had Tarzan's photograph on it and he was cradling some gorilla, *Kala*, it said, Tarzan looked grief-stricken, but this had been done with Photoshop or one of those programs, there never *was* a photo of Tarzan and Kala together. When I looked up, sure, there were bones, but who had put them there? This was not Kala's tree, this wasn't where Tarzan sat on a branch and decided to leave the valley with Jane. None of that had happened here – and suddenly I was glad. This wasn't where I had lived. This was the Tarzan Valley Experience and it had nothing whatsoever to do with me.

Two guides approached. I was sitting quietly at the foot of the wrong tree now, my head full of pictures – I let them help me up, and agreed to put my shoes back on. I had to get back into my stooped old man role. It was completely ridiculous, one minute I could sprint up a slope and the next had to struggle along with the aid of a stick, but people don't care about such contradictions, especially if they're working – they just want to get on with their shift. The group had rejoined us now, but I had to lag behind so I would not have to listen to the commentary, which was spreading lies about Tarzan.

I saw a hawk, it caught my eye and I stayed with it, saw the valley spread below me, made a tour of *my* Tarzan valley. A young guide, concerned that I was missing out, fell back to give me his personal impression, actually he wasn't too bad: ". . . you've got to imagine how quiet it was here in those days, no fences, the guy lived out here under the sky. I can understand why you took your shoes off, that's how he lived, it must have been kind of raw, you know, with everything scratching your skin all the time, and no house with central heating to go and take a break in . . ." I let him maunder on. "Of course the old people knew the gorillas were here, it was like a secret from the Pakeha, there was a lot of secrets in those days. That's what I reckon he lived like, you know, like the old people – and then he went from that rock to America, it must have been some kind of a head trip, to plunge, you know, right into the heart of Western civilisation."

"D'you like his music?"

"Personally?" The guide looked at me for the first time. I stood, leaning on my stick, face tilted towards the ground, waiting for the verdict. "He's kind of a classic, you've gotta respect that. Personally, I go for opera."

"I think he could have sung opera if he'd wanted to."

"You have to read music for that," he said.

We came now to yet another clearing and got onto the tramway which would carry us up to the cabin. Tinny little speakers played *Are You Lonesome Tonight*, and this made the party happy. I listened carefully. A number of them were Americans, his following was still strongest in America, and most were old, but there were enough kids, I saw, to carry his legend into the future. Everyone sang along. This I liked. Low, I sang along with them.

Up through the bush, its green heads bowed. But the smell of the oil on the tramway cable was overpowering. Ah, the cabin. It had been bright-painted, and there was a lawn. I didn't go near any of that.

Set to one side there was a long, low building, themed as a giant humpy, somewhat incongruous, and in there was the Tarzan Archive. I went in to see what they had made of him.

I drifted among the museum cases that contained all that had been captured of his past. A Cutty Sark bottle, and a label with a quote from Jane's book which told how she had swigged from it before they first had sex. The original radio receiver, with headphones that you could put on and hear the NZBS program that Tarzan would have listened to in the postwar years. The spade from the cabin, the tins and jars with their faded labels – somehow this was like visiting Scott's hut in the Antarctic, where everything has been preserved by the ice, except that this had been preserved by money. Oh, and by love – I mustn't be so sore. Also there was a waterfall recreation scene, where a plastic Tarzan washed a plastic Jane to the strains of *Love Me Tender*. This was all very bemusing, somehow I was pleased. People make of things what they must, they talk about you in the only language they can find. The pictures had stopped coming into my head now, I had regained my equilibrium, and was enjoying myself – I stood in the dim museum light and turned slowly, a grin spreading. People still cared. Then my eye fell on a single case, long and slim, surrounded by the pink-and-black leather which had graced Tarzan's room in Graceland, lifted by a dais, and lit for maximum drama. A photograph showed Lac Gorte. And there, behind glass, was my piece of greenstone.

It pained me to see that. I wanted to smash the glass – that thing is mine! I stared at it and felt as though I had been pierced by it. I remembered finding it in the dirt, I remembered how it had felt, hard but warm, as it bumped on its thong against the drum of my chest. How can a thing that belongs to someone who is alive be in a museum?

I had to go outside, I had to get away. The guides had finished the tour of the hut and were bringing the group over to do the Archive. I found a seat and turned my head away. The friendly young guide sought me out, made sure I was okay – "Lots of people get overcome," he said, "it's very emotional." I nodded slowly.

I had to get this over with.

I waited until no one was looking then took the uphill path through the bush that was signposted as *Jane's Last Walk*. Once out of sight I ran, ran hard. I was sweaty inside my disguising clothes, I wanted to strip and feel the air of that place, surely that hadn't changed, to feel it on my skin. I wanted to climb a tree and give a yell that would still the whole valley. Instead I hurried up the path. This was the way she had come.

It was not exactly clear how it had happened. Jane had returned to the valley three times as a consultant and knew exactly where the wetas were likely to be found – knew better than anyone: by that time she was probably the world's leading expert on the subject. It had been she who suggested that they should not have a fence – that an electric pulse would do, if it was strong enough. She had left the working party she was with, early one evening, no one had seen her go, and headed off, up through the trees. This way. Of course it would all have been so much more thickly bush-covered then. The tours in those days were apparently amazingly authentic – it was less than fifteen years since Tarzan had left the valley, and seeing the wetas was part of what must have been a pretty exciting trip. Of course they were extinct by the time I was back there.

There's nothing in her notebooks to indicate what she was thinking. A half-empty bottle of Cutty Sark was later found beside the path.

I don't believe she meant to die. She came up here thinking

of him, remembering herself, and the air was the same and the sounds were the same and she became intoxicated. She had everything to live for, she had popular success and also scientific respectability. She was in love with a guy she'd met on one of her tours, David Kingston, a tough guy, from the way he came across in the media, no bullshit – he wouldn't try, he said to the cameras, and explain what she'd done, because he didn't understand. A tough guy crying, everyone respects that.

She unlaced her shoes – they were found further up the trail. She kept her clothes on, as one reporter remarked. The world never got tired of enjoying the thought of Tarzan and Jane humping in that humpy.

Then she walked through the barrier and seems to have simply advanced on the wetas' caves. Her party heard terrible sounds in the distance – no screams. The wetas often did raise the dust in the evening, it was normal, like lions in the distance, if you live near a zoo they drive you crazy.

In the morning they searched and, eventually, from the observation platform, her remains were spotted.

I think of her walking in there, famous Jane Porter, as upright as a new thought, her lovely face just a mask for what was happening behind it. She didn't see the wetas coming, her thoughts were for herself, of herself and of all the wonderful things she had felt and been and seen in her life. She wasn't sad. I can't bear the thought that she was sad.

The younger members of our tour took the Vine Highway back downslope, giving Tarzan yells (puny ones), whooping as they swung on the end of the long ropes, out into the air, which hadn't changed.

29

I flew home full of rage, and somehow chastened. I had to get that piece of greenstone back. I had to save the gorillas. I began working on a plan to buy the whole valley. I would clear everything out, close down the tours, build a real fence and live in a humpy.

Well, that passed.

It took a lot of Cutty Sark, and single malt also, you might as well have quality hangovers, but eventually I did find my equilibrium again. Partly this was through music. I had started going in, cautiously at first, to the Golden Days hotel on Friday nights, sipping a beer, studying the faded pictures of Australia's sporting heroes – Don Bradman, Phar Lap – who witnessed the rowdy happiness which as the evening progressed rose in that room like water filling a tank. I liked that happiness, I wanted to be part of it. Wasn't this just like the fun of my Mafia guys that I had given up everything to escape? No. These people were earning their beer. Sometimes they would drag me into their talk, they knew my face – everybody's stock had been in my trucks. They would push me round a bit, they sort of nudge you, and say, "Well, what do you know,

Marshall?" You could, I discovered, say anything you liked in reply to this question – there's enough concrete in the Grand Coulee Dam to pave a highway from LA to New York. But this wasn't really what I was after – that warm-bodied pushing, that intimacy that wasn't intimate.

Then one evening I took a chance, and went over to the old piano, which had never, in my experience, been used. Lifting the lid that covered the keys, I saw a row of yellowing teeth. I gave one a plonk – surprisingly, it produced a nice, round sound. I played a chord. Suddenly a wave of feeling fell through me and I seized a chair, sat down and began to pick out a tune. Now this was happiness.

I had denied myself music for so many years. Even at home I had been scared to sing. Now I started in and, on that first night, played for three hours. I played every song that Tarzan never recorded – this took some effort. The desire to suddenly swing into *One Night With You* was strong. Instead I played *How Much Is That Doggie in the Window*.

This was accepted: old Marsh can play the piano. Give us a tune, Marshall. No one acclaimed me. No one said, "This guy is amazing." Well, I was hurt by that. Of course, I was holding back, and trying hard not to sound like him – and he is my natural voice. Without your natural voice you're nothing. But they did like me.

And it grew from there. I played once or twice a week. The bar began to change – the men's wives began to appear. Hello, Mavis, oh, hello Dawn. I bought myself a piano for home, improved my playing, learned some Australian songs. You can really jump up *Waltzing Matilda* if you want to.

At home, when no one was around, then I would really let go.

I studied up on all kinds of things, tried hard to fill in the gaps in my understanding. Electrical theory – the positive and the negative, the waves and the electrons and the currents – the thing that spun at the heart of the driveshaft. I have to say that I still don't understand, not so that it really makes sense to me. But I continue to use electricity, no problem. It's like life. I don't really understand. But understanding doesn't, in the end, seem to be the crucial part. It seems to be use that matters.

But that is somehow frustrating. To be so busy and never know why.

It was strange, playing like that for yourself. Alone in a big house at the top of a cliff, belting out *An American Trilogy* – who is it for? This thought was always in my head. Who is this life all for? Of course I knew. That angel, listening in so that she could write everything down.

Now that I was settled, I had a confidence that my angel was settled too. As I explored the district I found many, many places where she had been, or would be. A light which gathered in corners, under bridges. The photographs I took of these places were not always successful. It took me quite some time to learn how the best could be obtained from the black-and-white film, and how to get my darkroom ordered right; how to choose the right print, how to crop. But then an image would come up, one from hundreds, and it would all but have her face. She was in the district, all right. She was close.

I have made a selection of the best pictures and left money in my will for a book of these to be published after I am dead.

I would try and move that angel, with my singing. I would try and woo her. I tried to show her how much I had learned in my life, and that I was conscious of what I learned, and could express it. I tried to win her over. It's true that, alone in the big house, thinking back on all I had done, I was often full of doubt about my character. Not that I thought I was going to Hell, or even Heaven for that matter. Mrs Presley had talked about these places – just as she had talked a lot about God. But that was her religion. Religion never gained a purchase on me. No, what I wanted was for her to love me.

It's an ordinary desire. But this was typical, I think, of me – that I had come so far, and, I think, put such a lot of work into achieving my goal, which was to become human. This, finally, seemed to be it – I wanted to be a human being. To be human through and through. It's actually not a modest goal. Most of the people you are presented with are more than human. It's true. You stare at them and they have taken great strides. They have spent their lives making damned sure they aren't ordinary. Or else – I hate to say it – they are less than human. They are just dull. It can't entirely be their fault, this. Life must do it to them – perhaps dulled is a better word. They just operate their bodies, occupy their days. Well, perhaps it's best to shift the light from them.

But the human beings, who remember at every moment that human and mortal and free to be kind is what they are, these are the ones which amaze me. Eve who saw what I needed. Marion Keisker, Sam Phillips, Scotty Moore, Delmo McMullins, Mrs Presley – and so many whose names I never learned, who wanted to know me. Who wanted the best for me. There are thousands of them out there, the human beings. Millions.

All I ever wanted was to be one of that number.

It was Theo who discovered where she was. Maybe there is something instructive in this, for me – if I had raised a child earlier would I have learned faster? If I had attended, perhaps, to Lisa-Marie – where is she now? On the cover of magazines at my super. I will never see Lisa-Marie now, and I don't deserve to.

But little Theo, there he is, a leading ankle-biter, and on his belly he goes – you have to keep things up off the carpet, he's got an eagle eye for a crumb. So filthy – I started to wonder if he was hungry. Well, he would keep going to the refrigerator. He would wriggle himself into the kitchen, and this was hard to understand, as the carpet ends where the kitchen starts, and to me it seemed that the kitchen floor, which is slate, would have been hard and cold. But Theo kept squirming his way in there and then he would go up close to the fridge and laugh. It was the most wonderful thing. I swear he was laughing. Loretta thought so too. The noises that came out of him, you just wanted to hear more of them. I have them on tape. Now that is happiness. That is delight.

Loretta would open the door of the fridge and show him the contents, and Theo would reach out with his pudgy fingers. But the open fridge gave off a chilly blast and so these naming sessions – "Milk. Juice. Egg, Theo. Say, egg. Egg, egg, egg." – would never last for long.

Was he hungry? Loretta seemed to satisfy him with her breast. I got some in my mouth once – so sweet! No wonder kids long for candy. And yet he would always be back there, at the fridge, laughing.

Not that I really spent much thought on this. At the time, as I recall, a new double CD set had just been issued, *Tarzan in Conversation*, and I was busy with that, listening to catch him. I now have a copy of pretty much everything that exists in any recorded form. This will all go to the Archive.

Then one night I was down here, looking out into the dark, I had the lights off, I recall, because there had been an electrical storm playing out over the land. Now that's electricity! And I needed an OJ – there was a taste of dust in the air. And I went to the fridge.

There was just the faintest light coming from under the fridge door.

I thought there must be a perished spot in the seal and got down to investigate – quite a task at my age. But it looked okay. Then when I shut the door again, there was that low light, faint in the darkness of the kitchen.

Finally I got right down on my belly and applied my eye to the gap under the fridge. And there I saw what had been making Theo laugh.

At first she didn't seem very brightly lit. And she seemed small – tiny, in fact. It wasn't a big space under there, but I could see how, as Delmo had told me, so many years ago, there was a frame for her, with the stubby back legs of the fridge standing on either side of her, like pillars. She was white of course – not a dazzling white, not burning, more a faded, soft colour, the colour of soap. There was light around her and where the light ran out she appeared to be standing on a field of deep blue. Blue velvet. Her hair was black. Despite her size, every detail of her was astonishingly clear – it was as though she was one of those tiny ivory sculptures carved by hunched Oriental men with eyepieces, except that she was alive. Then you saw that she wasn't tiny. She wasn't small at all. She was incredibly far away. The more you took this in the more you grasped that she was simply immense. I don't mean tall like the Empire State. I mean that she stretched right up into the stratosphere – those puffy things playing around her calves were clouds. Her head was set against the stars. And then, this was strange, you realised that she wasn't in fact far away – not when you felt the presence of her. She was as close as she could be, being so big. Somehow, she was no further from you than the back of the fridge, and you forced your head against the fridge door, and twisted your eye up, trying to see her face. There were, from time to time, steady blasts of chill air, which ran over your cheeks and these you realised were from the long, slow beats of her wings.

Great wings, sweeping against the stars. I guess it was laughter that I felt. Laughter, and happiness, and a bit of fear.

It wasn't that she bent, but maybe my desperate efforts to see her face finally won through, maybe I tried hard enough: whatever, I could now see that she was looking interestedly at me. Of course she was lovely. Of course. But this was not your nicely arranged features as seen on fashionable models. Her loveliness was that her face was so complicated. In that face, as she allowed me to look, I saw all the faces I had ever seen. Ah, even then I knew – this was the book, here in her eyes was the record of my life. All the eyes that had ever looked into mine, and as she gazed at me memories came streaming back.

I was humbled by the love that had come my way. Adoration, this I knew about, enthusiasm, wonder, hunger, frantic happiness – but now I saw how the fans had loved me and I was utterly humbled by that, that I had been, however unwittingly, responsible for the creation of all that emotion in the world. And I thought: surely that will count in my favour?

Loretta found me in the morning and she thought I was dead. I responded to her touch, I looked up, saw her face, signalled that I was all right. Dear Loretta. I tried to hold her. I was shaking. Also my neck was stiff – it is still stiff, months later.

How could I drag myself away? Because she was gone. When Loretta spoke I realised that I had been lying there for hours and that she was gone.

Sitting around the house became my major occupation. Of course it has been this way for some years, there's only so much you can do from a wheelchair. But I forgot about Tarzan for a bit. Now I had something new to recapture. Her face –

was it the face of my mother? There had been a face in hers that I was left with. I was reminded of Elizabeth Taylor and I spent a lot of time trying to shift that famous face aside so I could see something that lay behind it. An angel with black hair? Angels don't have black hair – what was she trying to tell me?

I tried oh how I tried to see that face. I stared at my own face, bristly and pouched, sagging in the mirror, and tried to see how it had been once, before the plastic surgery, before a million flashbulbs had blurred its lines.

One day it snowed. This was a once-in-forty-years event in sun-warmed Longster and I rolled to the window and watched the way it accumulated out there on the ledges and planes. I imagined myself lying out there, on my back, on the ground, and looking up – the snowflakes coming down out of an infinite sky, and I wondered: where are the ridges and planes of my face? Where would the snow accumulate?

It's going to be cold in the ground.

I saw that once I had seen her the end would not be long in coming. I can't complain. I've seen it all now.

Soon after, I began writing.

So how will I go, on Judgement Day?

I think upon this and I make my assessment. Okay, deep breath, and here we go.

I think I will be forgiven my life among the gorillas – there's nothing to linger on there. I didn't stove Jimpi's head in. Then you come to the decision to leave the valley, followed by the decision to leave Jane. These I think can be forgiven. The movies will not be forgiven and this is rightly so. There's a lot of bloated music – that should all be deleted from the catalogue. I mean it. Someone should forget about the fans, the Tarzan believers. Someone with real ears, someone with a strong heart, someone who wants to do me a kindness, should put together, oh, three CDs with no dreck – it could be done. I need this to happen to swing things my way.

There's the Sun recordings which, excuse me, but these are peerless and I think they will count in my favour.

The cultural judgement on my music is that I worked in an artistic field but was not an artist. Because I didn't write songs. I didn't express myself. Sinatra expressed himself. He didn't write songs either, but he made the songs into his autobiography as he sang them. I didn't do that. I simply gave the public a noise to go with an image that it liked. I let the buyers read whatever they wanted into what I sang. They imagined me in there, behind the songs. But I just sang them.

And yet I sounded so moved. I loved singing, I loved making that sound – surely that counts for something?

But I never loved another and I never raised a child.

After Jane was gone I began to understand what I felt for her. Isn't this the way in life. Your feelings only start to make sense to you years later, and then everything has changed and you've got new feelings – you catch yourself in the mirror and suddenly realise your hair is falling out and your life is over. And this is the trick of it, I think, to make sense of your feelings as you have them. I know, that sounds like the title for a pop-psych bestseller, but, sorry, I have to stick with it. This has been a big deal for me – catching up with myself.

I'm nearly there.

I never loved Priscilla, that was just something to do with the combination of black hair and white underwear. I was in no condition to love her, or anything. My daughter Lisa-Marie, I swam away from her.

All of this will go against me.

I won't say I loved Eve, this would be dumb, she would be embarrassed, but I do love what she did for me.

Mrs Presley I was tender towards. She had such bruises inside, that woman, I think she died of lost love. She loved Elvis Presley more than herself. No, I think I was okay towards Mrs Presley.

The fans – I did love the fans. Not the girls, that was just sex, it wasn't bad but it wasn't good either, it was just there like the weather (lovely weather). But the fans meant everything to me and I kept the faith with them, I think.

But that isn't real love – is it?

So it all comes down to Jane, really. I think I let myself off too easy on her, before.

What will I say on Jane when the angel's eyes are on me for the last time? That I was true day by day? That every day the idea of her unfolded inside me and I was true to what I understood? That this is what I have learned, maybe.

Okay, I admit it: I am worried about how I'll be questioned on Jane.

The music – that also I can't leave alone. Okay, I have listened to Schubert – I listen to that day by day. I listen to Brahms, Bach, Debussy. Fine. But this is music for life as it is thought; for life as it is reflected upon. My music, the rock 'n' roll, this is music for life as it is lived. Buses, bosses, meals, meal breaks, crap TV fuzzy at the laundromat, back roads, a flat tyre in the rain when you're miles from home – the people you live with though you don't know them from Adam. Cars, tired furniture, the rent. Cigarettes after sex. Work. My music is the music of a life with hours of earning-your-paycheck work in it and this nobody can deny.

It was good that I was such a mover. You can't capture that, what it feels like to be in the room when someone is really cutting up. That's the biggest thing, if you ask me – that thing that I released. The records try their best to get it – some of them come close. The movies thought they wanted it then found they didn't need it and that it was too hard. So it just exists finally as a spirit. What I brought into the room. What I released – a thing that has no substance but is powerful.

This book will eventually be published and what it earns will go to Lisa-Marie and Priscilla and also to Loretta and Theo. They will find out about each other for the first time – I hope that goes okay. Yes, to those of you who I should have loved better: please read this and forgive. And everyone – the critics, the historians, the fans – will find out about me, all over again. This pleases me. To set the record straight. And maybe to surprise everyone all over again. That is fun to think about.

But that isn't what I wrote this down for.

Acknowledgements

Let me begin by deploying a phrase that Maurice Gee uses in the Notes to his most recent novel, *The Scornful Moon*: "Several small changes in historical fact have been made to help the story along."

My thanks must start with Edgar Rice Burroughs and Elvis Presley, without whom, etc. Peter Guralnick's two-volume biography of Elvis (*Last Train to Memphis* and *Careless Love*) was an inspiration, as were various writings by Greil Marcus. Inspiration of another kind was provided through the years I spent at the baches my family owns at Mataikona, north of Castlepoint, where, thanks to those "small changes", the landscape of "Tarzan's valley" can be found.

I would also like to acknowledge Martina Lüdicke, Bill Manhire, Michelle Tayler, Natasha Fairweather of A.P. Watt and Emma Parry of Fletcher & Parry, all of whom offered editorial assistance and encouragement. Trevor Crosby of Landcare Research described my emailed query as "one of the more unusual requests I've received!" but nevertheless managed to guide me to what I hope is the correct species of dragonfly for Jane to see in the Wairarapa, and David Prout, Department of Biological Sciences, University of Waikato, helped me establish a scientific name for the wetas. My mother Delphine Cox, the indefatigable, undertook many research tasks. Rodney Smith (www.infernalbbq.com) came up with the perfect trash-i-delic cover; Gelia Eisert suffered my camera-phobia to provide the author photo; Rachel Barrowman applied a zealous eye to the copy-editing. Thanks must also go to my wife Susanna and our kids, who through the up and downs of the production of this book reminded me always of what really matters; and to all of the team at VUP. But the biggest thank-you should go to my publisher and friend Fergus Barrowman who was the first to read and like the novel, who always made me feel he really did want to read it one more time, who had a thousand additions, deletions, corrections and improvements to offer, and who shared with me the idea that this possibly daft object was something that really did deserve to exist in the world.